CARAD THORN CLUTCHED THE GREEN JEWEL . . .

At once the peridot began to glow with a nauseous light. The knuckles and bones of his finger showed darkly through the skin as the light grew stronger. Then the light encompassed his fist.

"Stupid Domain fools!" Carad Thorn cried triumphantly. "I'll shred your souls as easily as you did my bed!"

The weird greenish light surged outward. Robert felt its icy force sapping his strength and will. He tried to shut his eyes, hoping to shut out that evil glow, but couldn't. A frigid veil settled over his mind, enveloped his body.

The peridot blazed with its cold fire. Robert felt his blood turning to ice. He screamed inside, desperately trying to summon some iota of his own willpower to resist. . . .

TRIUMPH OF THE DRAGON

TRIUMPH
OF THE
DRAGON

by

Robin Wayne Bailey

A ROC BOOK

ROC
Published by the Penguin Group
Penguin Books USA Inc., 375 Hudson Street,
New York, New York 10014, U.S.A.
Penguin Books Ltd, 27 Wrights Lane,
London W8 5TZ, England
Penguin Books Australia Ltd, Ringwood,
Victoria, Australia
Penguin Books Canada Ltd, 10 Alcorn Avenue,
Toronto, Ontario, Canada M4V 3B2
Penguin Books (N.Z.) Ltd, 182–190 Wairau Road,
Auckland 10, New Zealand

Penguin Books Ltd, Registered Offices:
Harmondsworth, Middlesex, England

First published by Roc, an imprint of Dutton Signet,
a division of Penguin Books USA Inc.

First Printing, February, 1995
10   9   8   7   6   5   4   3   2   1

 REGISTERED TRADEMARK—MARCA REGISTRADA

Printed in the United States of America

For David Govaker, who's never far from my thoughts;

For Jim DeGarmo, with apologies for all the B movies I drag him to see;

For Monte Scarborough, friend and computer surgeon, without whom this book, literally, would not have been possible;

For Diana, my favorite stargazer, to remember all the eclipses and meteor showers we've shared;

But most of all, this one's for me.

Chapter One

THE Heart of Darkness leaned forward on her onyx throne and frowned. She sat alone in her vast columned chamber. Not a shadow stirred. The blackness of night filled her abode, unrelieved by lamp or candle flame or brazier. She sighed, a vaguely troubled sound that sliced through the tomblike silence like a knife through crisp silk.

At the smallest gesture of her hand the eastern wall vanished. Stars glittered in the black heavens, white and sharp as ice. The Heart of Darkness rose with regal grace and descended the three steps from her throne to the floor. Where the wall had been there was now a splendid balcony. Soundlessly, She moved to the cold, marble edge and set her delicate hands upon the rail.

Her frown deepened. Beneath her palms a long crack shivered through the stone. A piece of the railing fell away into the long, deep echoless darkness. She stared at the broken marble, not with fear, but with a feeling of strangeness and a growing unease. Unconcerned for her safety, She leaned on the rail again.

Night lay heavily over Boraga, her keep, and over the canyon on whose southern rim the great structure soared. Its five towers stretched up like slender fingers to grasp the sky and everything beyond. The smooth black stone of which they were made gleamed and glistened in the starlight, in the moonlight, in the pale illumination of the blue ring that floated across the zenith.

The Heart of Darkness regarded the blue ring, and her eyes narrowed to catlike slits. Mianur was its name, called by some the Bridge to Paradise. Once it had been a moon, a second moon, far more beautiful than its companion, Thanador. A taste of bitterness filled her mouth. Once, She had coveted Mianur, but its people had dared to deny her need.

The pale blue ring was all that remained of Mianur's arrogance.

Why did She think of that now? She remembered Mianur's beauty and tried to brush the memories aside. Her lush mouth curled into a sneer. She had destroyed beauty before. Tonight, though, the memories were not so easily dismissed. They seemed to possess a haunting power.

The night was too still. She craved a wind to enliven the darkness, and a wind came. It caressed the silken strands of raven hair that floated about her shoulders, rustled the stygian folds of her satin gown, played over her face, and teased the tender globes of her exposed breasts. She touched a nipple, and it hardened in response.

Her pleasure was short-lived. Again She felt the strangeness in the air. The Heart of Darkness bit her lip and tasted her own blood. That, at least, was something to savor.

She sent her gaze out across the vast canyon, out across the deserts and shadow-haunted mountains of Srimourna, seeking the source of the strangeness. A sensation worried at Her like a half-perceived irritation, a vague discomfort, and it tried to hide from Her, to mask itself.

She saw nothing, heard nothing. Srimourna was still as death. The land was silent, perfect in its emptiness.

A door opened on the far side of her Royal Chamber. A tiny man, his legs shorter than the rest of his torso and bent outward at the knees, waddled through the darkness, bearing a wicker basket. Small silver bells jingled on his cloth slippers and on the hems of his sleeves. A tiny oil lamp lit his way around the many columns until he reached the balcony. Its weak, amber light made his face and his polished bald head glow.

"You dare to disturb me, Gaultnimble?" The Heart of Darkness raised one eyebrow and turned a menacing expression on her fool.

"Divinity," Gaultnimble cooed, his black eyes glimmering with evil mischief as he bowed awkwardly and looked up at his dreaded mistress. "You know I love you even more than I love your sweet punishments. In my insignificant quarters in the bowels of Boraga I sensed your mood. It sweeps through the corridors like a flood." He held up the wicker basket. "So, because I love you more than pain itself, I bring my goddess a gift for cheer."

"What have you there?" She demanded, unmoved.

Gaultnimble looked coy as he set his oil lamp on the balcony rail. "If Divinity doth ask it, I will tell about the basket. . . ."

"Come, fool!" She snapped, sparks of fire leaping into her stern gaze. "None of your songs or tales. You walk a narrow ledge tonight." She pointed a cold finger straight at his heart.

The little dwarf paled and tried to hide a small

shiver. He lifted the lid on the basket ever so slightly. A timorous *meow* issued from within.

"Ah, a kitten." The Heart of Darkness sighed. The anger left her face as she put her hand inside and drew the tiny, furry creature out in her palm. Its eyes were barely open. A little fanged mouth gaped and emitted another pitiful, plaintive sound.

The Heart of Darkness drew the kitten to her breast and stroked its soft yellow fur until the mewls gave way to a warm, gentle purring. A small, slender tail lashed back and forth over her flesh. The sensation was almost erotic.

When the kitten was at last content, the Heart of Darkness drew a razor-sharp thumbnail down its soft belly. Tiny claws tore at her skin. The kitten cried in panic and sudden pain. The Heart of Darkness squeezed the poor animal to her breast and let its innocent blood flow over her skin, into the folds of her gown.

When the kitten was dead, she dropped it back into the basket. "You are a sometimes considerate fool, Gaultnimble," she whispered. "That was a pleasant diversion."

"Diversion, Queen of Souls?" Gaultnimble grinned. He inclined his head toward the chamber's dark interior. "Quite a show, if I may stoop to theatrical criticism. We all enjoyed it."

The Heart of Darkness frowned again as she stared back into her Royal Chamber.

The chamber was no longer empty. The shadows stirred with shades and apparitions. Spectral forms floated in the air or wafted among the many columns. The souls of her enemies. One or two She recognized, but for the most part She no longer knew their names, if she had ever known them at all. They watched her coldly, those spirits, and She could taste their hunger, their thirst for vengeance.

She gave a little gasp. The sound was mostly surprise, but there was a note of fear in it. "How did they get in here?" She murmured in wonderment. "Into my most private sanctum? It's not possible that mere ghosts could breach my wards."

Gaultnimble waddled to the marble banister and heaved the wicker basket with its contents over the side. He brushed his hands together noisily and wiped them on his tunic. "Some of them have been waiting at the door for generations," he reminded her with an inappropriate joviality. "Perhaps, Divinity, you let the door crack a bit."

The Heart of Darkness whipped her hand across Gaultnimble's face in a loud slap. The fool sprawled upon the floor, then rose up on one elbow, a hand rubbing at his cheek as he looked back at his mistress.

"Thank you, my Lady," he said with a twisted grin. "You so rarely play with me like that anymore." His grin turned to a pout. "Sometimes I think I am not your favorite fool."

The Heart of Darkness turned away from her fool and the staring ghosts. Let the specters glower; they were nothing to Her.

Yet, that they were here at all in her private chambers, was one more element in a night that seemed made of strangeness. Troubled, She leaned again on the marble railing. For all Gaultnimble's impertinence, there had been something in his words.

A crack in the door.

She paled at a sudden thought. Could it be? She put her hand upon the jagged spot in the marble railing where a piece had cracked and fallen into the abyss. The kitten's blood, still warm on her fingers, made a wet, black smear on the stone.

The Heart of Darkness threw back her head and screamed, her eyes alight with dreadful understanding. The strangeness. She knew at last what it was. Her fool had put her on to it. She felt it now like a tingle in the air, like the faintest vibration in the stone beneath her touch—a barely perceptible weakening of her power.

Gaultnimble sprang to her side. "My Queen!" he said.

In a black rage, the Heart of Darkness spun on her fool and beat him with her fists until he fell senseless at her feet. She continued to kick him until the worst of her anger had spent itself. Then, batting at the intangible spirits that sought to block her way, She strode to her onyx throne, climbed the steps of the dais, and sat down.

Gaultnimble rolled over on his back. "Oh, Divinity!" he croaked through breathless gasps. "That was the best ever." He struggled to rise, but could get no further than his hands and knees. "We must have another bout. Just give me a few minutes and I'll be up again."

The Heart of Darkness no longer listened. With the smallest part of her power She pushed the ghosts away from her. The gloom at the foot of her throne parted. Three crystal caldrons appeared, gleaming with sourceless light. The water they contained was pure and perfectly still.

"Gaultnimble!" Her voice shivered through the chamber, calm once more, icy in its power. "Blood."

The fool scrambled to his feet. As fast as his dwarf's legs would carry him, he hurried to her side and thrust out his bare arm. "Open a vein, Lady!" he told her, the words hissing ecstatically through his teeth. "Open it deep!"

"Only a few droplets," she answered, raking his offered flesh with her thumbnail. A crimson line welled up on the soft underside of his arm.

Gaultnimble descended the dais steps and went to the crystal caldrons. Their glow uplit his face, masking him with eerie shadows as he extended his arm and spilled three drops of blood into each one.

The droplets struck the still water and spread, opening like small, delicate roses at the first touch of morning. Tiny ripples danced through the caldrons. In moments the pure water turned a rosy pink.

Gaultnimble stood back, blood dripping from his arm onto the floor. Throughout the sanctum, the ghosts dared to steal closer, drawn by a fearful curiosity to this magic working.

The Heart of Darkness waited silently for the ripples to stop, for the water in the caldrons to become still. There could be only one reason for even the slightest weakening of her power. *The Child.* Her bitterest foe was in the world once more. She glanced toward the open veranda. Somewhere out there, moving through her own Dark Lands, perhaps even through Srimourna, itself, he lived again.

She gazed down at her hand and curled her fingers into a fist. The wheel was turning again. This time She had almost won. The world was almost Hers. Only a few nations, the cursed Domains of Light, still stood against her, and in a matter of months, they too would have fallen to her sway.

She opened her hand again and smiled darkly. Well, the game was not over yet. She still had trumps to play. She looked around for her fool. "Gaultnimble," she ordered. "Send a *chimorg* to Carad Thorn in Shadark. Tell him to unleash Cha Mak Nul."

The little dwarf turned toward her and cocked an eyebrow. "If I hesitate, will you beat me. Queen of Souls?" he asked.

There was no humor in her response. "If you hesitate, I will kill you quickly."

Gaultnimble frowned in displeasure as he stalked off. "Well, there would be no fun at all in that."

The Heart of Darkness returned to brooding as the moments ticked by. The caldrons were growing still at last.

The ghosts wafted through the vast chamber like currents of wind. Their footfalls made no sound on the cold marble tiles, yet echoes seemed to cry down through the ages, echoes of the snuffing out of voices and lives, as a candle sometimes hisses when suddenly extinguished.

She allowed them closer, those ghosts of her enemies, as she rose from her throne and descended toward the crystal caldrons. Let them look, she thought. Let them watch her schemes unfold. And let the despair they felt in death be ever greater for the watching.

As the specters and apparitions pressed around Her, the Heart of Darkness stretched her hand over the caldrons. An image took shape in the first: a dark-haired man whose straight locks blew in the wind as he soared above the world on a great, winged *sekoye*. His green eyes flashed in the sunlight as he played upon an unfamiliar silver instrument, which he cupped in his hands and pressed to his lips.

Upon the water of the second caldron another image began to form. The ghosts recoiled in wonderment, and the Heart of Darkness laughed at them.

"No, my old foes," She whispered teasingly, "It is not the Son of the Morning you see."

And yet, the second image was a man with the golden hair and emerald-sharp eyes that only the *Child* should have. There was a hardness to his face that belied his youth and marked him as dangerous. As the Heart of Darkness studied the image, it seemed almost to turn toward her, to return her gaze, and She felt a wave of hatred emanating from it that made her step back.

She bent over the third caldron. The blood-pink color had faded, leaving the water crystal pure once again.

The Heart of Darkness frowned as She leaned closer. "The woman," she hissed. "Where is the woman?" She passed her hand over the caldron, pouring her power into it, but it resisted her. The surface remained still and clear.

A strand of her own black hair slipped forward and fell into the water. The Heart of Darkness studied her reflection. She loved her own beauty, her soft ruby lips and pale cheeks, the black depths of her perfectly formed eyes, the shining strands of her hair. And most of all, She loved the smooth slender horn that sprouted upward from her brow, loved how it gleamed when it caught the light, loved its sharpness, loved how it felt cool as stone to her touch.

She drew her hair out of the water and stepped back from the third caldron, remembering her purpose. The woman was a mystery to be solved, and any mystery right now posed a possible problem. If she were dead, the caldron would crack and the water seep away. Yet the caldron was intact. Katherine Dowd was not dead.

She turned back to the first and second caldrons and regarded the two men whose images floated on the waters. How easy it was to see that they were brothers. Despite the colors of their hair, the resemblances were strong.

A little laugh rolled through the chamber, a sound full of both anticipation and nervousness. Indeed, the game was far from over. She placed one hand on the first caldron. "Eric," she murmured. Then she touched the second. "Robert." Her whisper was sensuous and deadly, like a knife sliding over captive flesh, promising a cut, but not cutting.

"Come to me, my Brothers of the Dragon. Come to me."

And how, She wondered, could She hurry them along? So many ways, so many means, and all of them wonderfully cruel and devious. She climbed the three steps with infinite grace and sank languidly onto her throne again.

A darkly delicate smile turned up the corners of her lips. She pressed a fingernail against her right palm until a tiny crimson bud welled up. For a long moment She stared at the droplet and wet her lips until they gleamed. Then She pressed her palms together.

After a few moments She opened a small space between her thumbs and peered inside. A diminutive light winked in the black chamber formed by her clasped hands. She smiled again as She felt the flutter of small wings.

"My sweet pet," she whispered as She opened her hands. The blood droplet was gone. A lonely firefly sprang from her palm and wandered about in the darkness that filled the chamber until it found the balcony and the broad, waiting night beyond.

The Heart of Darkness laughed. She went once more to study the faces floating on the waters in her caldrons. "My pretty boys," she murmured in a tone that was both seductive and mocking. "Come play with me."

But the images melted away. Inexplicably, the water turned clear in all the caldrons. The Heart of Darkness caught her breath. She whirled about, climbed to her throne again, and leaned one hand on the back of it as She stared at the crystal vessels.

A rare sensation shivered through Her. It took a full instant to identify it.

Fear.

The Heart of Darkness sat down upon the glittering onyx seat and folded her arms about Herself.

Even fear was a sensation to be savored.

Chapter Two

CARAD Thorn paced in thoughtful deliberation
before the fireplace in his laboratory. The crackling flames gave a red sheen to his thin, finely boned
face and dark mustache, and his deeply set eyes glittered under a pinched and narrowed brow. Idly, he
rubbed one finger over his lips. His shadow stretched
across the floor, over a worktable, and dominated the
opposite wall.

Just tonight he had received an order from the
Heart of Darkness.

The fire popped suddenly, and a small knot of wood
exploded in a shower of sparks that swirled up the
chimney. Tonight the hearth was empty of all the caldrons and kettles and bottles and vials that so often
cluttered it. Only the shimmering flames lit the chamber. Carad Thorn stared into them, unblinking, and
loosened his lavishly embroidered robe to feel the
heat upon his bare, hairless chest.

A figure moved in the entrance.

Carad Thorn spoke in a deep whisper as if he re-
vered the silence and hesitated to break it. "You have
it, Magul?"

The figure glided forward. He said nothing, but held
out his two hands. On his palms sat a beautiful rectangular box of elaborately worked gold. The box rested

on four tiny clawed feet; its lid was inset with rose rubies and amber tourmalines. The fire's glow caressed it like a too-eager lover, drawing passionate sparks of color from the precious stones.

Carad Thorn laid one ring-covered hand gently upon the lid. Then he took his hand away and peered into the darkly hooded eyes and the fine-boned face of his loyal assistant. "You have done well to keep it safe for me," Thorn said with muted solemnity. "This night we will complete the formula."

Magul only nodded. He turned away from the fire and carried the box to the long worktable in the center of the room. He placed the box on the table, then backed away to the comfort and concealment of the room's shadows.

The ruler of Shadark resumed his pacing, folding his loosely sleeved arms across his chest. His slippered feet made no noise on the stone tiles. Except for the crackle of the fireplace, no sound at all disturbed his thoughts. Not even his garments dared rustle.

Then a clatter and a bumping came from the corridor outside the laboratory. A few moments later, four men squeezed through the entrance, bearing among themselves an old, worm-eaten wooden coffin.

"On the floor, gentlemen," Carad Thorn ordered as he turned a watchful eye from the hearth.

The four weary-looking workmen set the coffin down. Thick, freshly turned earth covered their clothes. Dirt and damp mud clung to their sandals. One, a fat, bearded man, pulled a filthy rag from out of his belt and wiped his face with it. The rest merely looked down at their feet.

Carad Thorn brought four newly minted pieces of silver from his robe's pocket. "You have not only my pay," he murmured as he pressed a coin into each of their seemingly reluctant hands, "but my appreciation. Yet, know you this. It is Her work you are about this night."

The man with the filthy rag hesitated, then began to tremble as he stared at the bit of silver he held in his hand.

One of the others spoke up weakly. "What more do you require of us, Lord?"

Carad Thorn allowed himself a faint smile, and he shook his head. "Only your love, citizen, and your loyalty."

"Which is to say," came a sibilant whisper from the shadows behind the workers, an evil sound sufficient to make them jump, "your hearts and your souls."

"Hush, Magul," Carad Thorn chided. "You'll frighten these poor men. They have worked hard on our behalf this evening. Disinterment at midnight under a new moon is no pleasant task."

Another of the four spoke in a quavering voice. "May we go, then, Lord? My woman's heavy with a comin' child, an' her time's close near."

Carad Thorn pursed his lips as he regarded the speaker. Then he slipped off one of his many rings. "You may go, then, citizen," he answered. "Give your woman this gift to ease her labors, and say it is with my gratitude for enriching my lands with one more life." He glanced at the other workmen. "Two more of you may go also, but one must stay." His gaze fell on the man with the filthy rag still in his hands. "You will stay."

"Me, Lord?" the man squeaked nervously as he watched his comrades desert him and vanish into the dark corridor beyond the laboratory.

Shadark's ruler laid a hand gently on the workman's shoulder. "What is your name, citizen?"

The poor workman's voice failed him. He stammered helplessly.

"Krackit," Magul supplied without emerging from his hiding place.

Carad Thorn patted Krackit on the arm, then returned to his place before the hearth. A red corona seemed to surround him.

"Well, Krackit, open the coffin." He clasped his hands together patiently.

Krackit's lower lip trembled and sweat began to run down his face. He stared wide-eyed at his lord, wringing and twisting the strip of cloth he held. At last he swallowed and moved toward the coffin. It obviously belonged to a poor man, for there were no nails, not even wooden pegs, to seal it shut. Probably it had been bound shut with ropes, but those had long since rotted away.

Swallowing again, the fearful workman bent and pushed off the lid. It fell with a loud crash onto the floor, and the workman jumped back.

The firelight was barely adequate to show the shriveled remains within. Hard to tell if the corpse was male or female. Skin dry as parchment still stretched over the bones, but the scalp had slipped sideways, spilling dark strands of hair over the left ear only. The fingernails were almost clawlike, the hands folded neatly just above the top of a loincloth that once had been white, but now was caked with dirt and yellowed with age.

"Eat," Carad Thorn instructed.

The workman's mouth fell open. His single word was a barely audible croak. "What?"

Carad Thorn regarded him dispassionately. "It's a simple enough word, only three letters." He wagged a ringed finger toward the coffin. "Eat some part of the citizen down there. You may choose the part you like best."

"Like best?" Krackit echoed in disbelief. He risked a glance toward the entrance, his body tensed as if to make a dash. But Magul had come out of the shadows to block the way, and he slapped a long, double-edged dagger menacingly against one palm.

Krackit fell weakly to his knees and folded his hands in supplication. "Please, Lord!" he whimpered as tears began leaking from his eyes. "Don't make me do this!"

"You're a fat fellow," Magul sneered from the doorway. The dagger's blade continued to slap softly as it lightly struck flesh. "You obviously know how to enjoy a good meal."

Krackit raised his hands higher and interlaced his fingers. "Please!" he begged, weeping. "How have I offended you, Lord? What did I do?"

Carad Thorn stood stiffly before the fireplace and waited for the sobbing to cease. He was not a cruel or impatient man. He knew that such emotions had to run their course. Finally, Krackit dared to turn a reddened eye his way. The workman wiped a hand at his nose.

"Tell me, Citizen Krackit," Carad Thorn said evenly when he had the workman's attention. "Which do you fear most? The taste of a corpse's flesh?" He took a single step forward, and his shadow fell directly across Krackit's puffy face. "Or me?"

Krackit began to sob again, softly at first, then with volume. Tears ran down his cheeks, down his neck, and spilled on the stone floor as he dragged himself toward the dirty coffin and bent over the side. The wooden boards of the box cracked and splintered under his weight, but Krackit barely seemed to notice as he righted himself.

One of the corpse's arms slipped out of its pose and sank upon the broken siding. A fleshless finger bone uncurled and seemed to point at Krackit. The workman blubbered hysterically, his gaze darting from the finger to Carad Thorn and back.

"Eat!" Magul shouted from the doorway.

Carad Thorn said, "Hush, Magul."

Every breath from the terrified workman was a choked, gasping scream. Whimpering, he bent over the corpse again. He reached out a hand, then hesitated. His fingers touched the chest and swiftly withdrew, afraid of the contact. He shot another glance at Carad Thorn and tore his gaze away. His fingers ripped savagely at a piece of leathery skin on the corpse's chest. With a cry of horror he stuffed it into his mouth, squeezed his eyes shut, and chewed.

The sound of chewing filled the otherwise quiet laboratory.

When Krackit had swallowed, Carad Thorn gave a subtle nod. Magul strode up behind the workman, caught him by the hair, and jerked his head back. The blade slid smoothly over a quivering throat.

"Quickly now," Carad Thorn said, going to the silver box on the table. He eased back the hinged lid to reveal a brown powder within. Heedless of the blood staining his robes, he bent close to catch the crimson flow in the box, to watch it mingle with the finely textured powder into a thick, muddy-colored liquid.

A high-pitched shriek suddenly ripped through the chamber. Magul jumped, bumping the table, his eyes fear-widened. The governor of Shadark spun about, an expression of anger etched on his face. "How dare the pathetic wretch!" he bellowed.

From Krackit's still-warm corpse a pale effluence streamed into the air, taking on the vague semblance of a man. A mouth opened in its featureless face. Another piercing scream issued forth. A pair of weepy eyes snapped open and fixed on Magul. Taloned limbs slowly unfurled and stretched towards him.

Magul gave an involuntary gasp and raised his hands to protect his face from those claws. "Krackit's *dando*!" he cried.

Carad Thorn stepped in front of him. The hands recoiled. The creature let go a shriek as if its fingers had been burned.

"Fool!" Carad Thorn laughed. "As much a fool in death as in life! You've no power here, Spirit of Krackit! Indeed, you are trapped!"

Krackit's *dando* looked wildly about the chamber. Its shrieks were cries of terror and confusion. In the spirit's presence the floor and walls and ceiling began to glow. Previously invisible glyphs and symbols appeared on the cold bare stone, driving Krackit's ghost back to the center of the room and the space just above its former body.

No longer did it show interest in Magul or in Carad Thorn. It cowered upon Krackit's chest as if struggling to get back inside.

Carad Thorn laughed again. In this room he had murdered before. But only in this room. The spells that covered the surfaces of his laboratory, which indeed were deeply embedded in the stone, had taken years to prepare. Even so, he dared not test the strength of those spells too often. Only because he had received a final order from the Heart of Darkness had he done so tonight.

He went to a shelf and took down a wooden box fashioned like a small coffin. Opening it, he set it on the floor near Krackit's corpse. The *dando* shrieked again and darted about the chamber looking desperately for a way out. Bright blue lights flared wherever it struck the walls as it sought desperate escape.

"Into your coffin!" Carad Thorn ordered. He pointed a finger, and the ring upon it glowed with the same azure fire as the glyphs.

Krackit's *dando* gave a long, despairing wail as its vaporous form grew thinner and thinner. It oozed toward the miniature coffin, hovered above it, and faded completely away.

Carad Thorn bent and slammed the small lid on the last echoes of a ghostly scream. He flipped a tiny metal locking bar over a metal ring on the side of the box and slipped a peg through the ring to hold it sealed. Then he sat it back on the shelf beside several other similar boxes.

"I chose well," he said with a satisfied smirk as he brushed his hands together. "Krackit's was a weak and timid soul." He clapped his servant on the shoulder. Magul's face was still pale and beaded with sweat. "Come now." Carad Thorn laughed. "You didn't think I'd let him get you, did you?"

Magul shook his head, drawing himself erect and meeting his master's gaze. "I have absolute trust in you, Lord," he answered. "I am yours to save as you wish." His glance darted toward Krackit's corpse. "Or to destroy."

Carad Thorn returned to the table where he had set the silver box before the interruption of Krackit's spirit. Wordlessly he closed the lid on the blood-soaked contents. "Follow me," he said, heading for the corridor. "This night's work is not yet done."

Magul obediently fell in step behind his lord. They hurried through the dark corridor without aid of a light. They both knew this palace's twists and turns as well as the lines on their palms. Up a set of stairs they rose, past an open window. The night's breeze blew in their faces, but neither stopped. Higher and higher the stairs carried them until at last they emerged on the highest roof of the palace.

Here the ruler of Shadark, southernmost of all the Dark Lands, held his outdoor courts beneath Thanador and Mianur, beneath the stars of Palenoc, in the winds of the world. On the far side of the roof, perched upon a small dais, stood Carad Thorn's black, high-backed throne.

There was no Thanador to brighten this night. There were only the sprinkling of stars and the pale blue ring of Mianur.

"Sit," Carad Thorn told his assistant. Generously, he waved a hand toward his throne. "You have often wondered how it would feel. For a few moments, at least, satisfy your curiosity."

Warily, Magul glanced at his lord, but he did as commanded and settled himself upon the great seat. Carad Thorn set the jeweled box with its strange contents on a small table beside the throne. A single silver goblet sat there, too, and a pitcher of wine. Thorn half-filled the vessel and raised it to his lips.

"I drink to you, King Magul," he said with more than a hint of mockery. He drained the goblet and wiped his mouth. Then he half filled it again. This time, however, he opened the box and added its bloody contents to the wine. He swirled them together, then passed the potion to his assistant.

"Now you drink to me, Magul," he ordered.

Magul hesitated as he peered into the cup from which he was expected to drink. "Lord, I . . ."

Carad Thorn frowned. "Come now, Magul. Don't

make a fuss. That is for men like Krackit. Not for men like you."

Magul continued to stare at the foul brew, his fear apparent. "Help me, then, Lord," he answered, summoning his courage as he brought the goblet closer to his lips.

Carad Thorn bent over his assistant and tenderly placed one hand behind Magul's head to support him. With his other hand he helped to raise the cup until Magul's lips were on the rim. Carad Thorn tipped the vessel ever so slightly, and Magul closed his eyes and drank, reluctantly at first, then willingly until the dark potion was gone.

Shadark's ruler cast the empty goblet aside, and it clattered on the rooftop tiles. Magul looked up into his lord's eyes. Carad Thorn leaned closer still and kissed his man on the brow. Their lips met. Clinging to each other, Thorn lifted his assistant from the throne and set him on his feet.

"With this kiss I rename you," Carad Thorn said in solemn tones. "Magul is no more. You are Cha Mak Nul."

"The Breath of Night," Magul answered, his voice no more than a whisper. "How long will I live, Lord?"

Carad Thorn smiled at his assistant. "You are dead already. So you have been from the moment you entered my service." He beckoned and led the way across the rooftop to a low wall. Together, they leaned upon the wall and stared outward over the darkened city of Pedrah.

"In the courtyard below," Carad Thorn said, "you will find a *chimorg*. Take it and ride through the Gray Kingdoms. Then set your course for the Domains of Light. Go where you will, or where the winds blow you, it matters not. Death will follow in your tracks."

"It is a hard road you set me upon," Magul said quietly.

"Have we not worked for this together?" Carad Thorn asked, placing a hand upon his assistant's arm. "Did we not labor over this physic side by side? Together this night we added the final ingredient—the warm blood of a man who has eaten corpse flesh."

"I did not know that I would be the Cha Mak Nul," Magul answered grimly. Yet, he drew himself erect and faced into the wind. "However, it is done. I drank willingly. There is no more."

Carad Thorn slipped a large ring from his forefinger. Even in the faint starlight the opal glimmered like liquid fire. "Take this," he said, slipping the ornament on Magul's finger, "to signify that you will always be my man."

"Your man," Magul answered glumly, turning his eyes up from the ring on his finger to the sky and Mianur's wispy light, "but her instrument."

A long silence hung between them as they gazed outward over the black rooftops of sleeping Pedrah. Finally, Carad Thorn took his assistant's hand and led him toward the staircase. "I will walk you to the courtyard," he said.

Magul's grip tightened around his lord's fingers. "Let your hand not leave mine until you have set me on the road." There was fear in his voice, but also control and determination.

Down the staircase they went together. The entire palace staff slept like the rest of Pedrah, and no one witnessed their passage through the gloomy corridors. Carad Thorn led the way, and Magul followed at his side like an obedient child.

They pushed back a stout wooden door and emerged onto a lawn of creeping thyme. A pair of sputtering torches shed pathetic illumination on the courtyard. From the thickest shadows a pair of burning eyes turned toward them. The creature to whom those eyes belonged plodded into the light, its ebon scales shimmering and its serpentine tail lashing back and forth impatiently. A rich herbal odor filled the air as gleaming black hooves crushed the delicate green carpet.

A stiff dorsal membrane rose from the crest between its ears and extended like a rigid mane down its neck to its powerful shoulders. A smooth black spike erupted from its brow, long as a man's arm and finely pointed. It was a horrible and mighty beast, a true spawn of the Heart of Darkness. But its most horrible feature was its eyes. Like pools of arcane flame they flickered and danced upon the *chimorg's* face, coldly radiant, and filled with the light of unholy intelligence.

"Mount your steed, my Cha Mak Nul," Carad Thorn whispered, freeing his hand from his assistant's grip. "Your road begins here, and your journey starts now." He moved to a marble bench near the door and picked up a pair of saddlebags. "Here is gold enough to keep you in luxury. Clothe and arm yourself as you will. Eat and drink. Take lovers as you choose. From this moment on all decisions are your own."

Magul accepted the saddlebags and approached the *chimorg*. The creature watched him with cool tolerance and allowed the bags to be placed across its shoulders. Swallowing, Magul drew a breath, then sprang upon the monster's back. It stood absolutely still and suffered its burden, though its eyes flared with a hateful indignation.

"I will not turn my back upon this beast," Magul murmured to his lord as he looked for someplace to put his hands. There were no reins. Finally, looking uncomfortable, he laid them on either side of the dorsal mane and balanced himself as best he could.

Carad Thorn put his hand on his assistant's knee and patted it reassuringly. "The *chimorg* will carry you into the Gray Kingdoms. Then you must make your own way. You needn't fear that it will harm you. It is her creature."

Magul looked down upon the ruler of Shadark. "As are you and I, Lord," he answered. "Her brand is on us all."

Carad Thorn's face settled into a stony mask, but his eyes betrayed resentment at those words. Yet, they were words of truth, no matter how they stung. "There is the gate," he said, pointing to an open portal on the north side of the courtyard. "Ride, my faithful. The world will shiver at your passing."

The *chimorg* turned and started for the gate. Carad Thorn walked along beside it. Magul stretched down his hand, and their fingertips brushed. "And you, my Lord," he whispered as the *chimorg* increased its pace and left Carad Thorn watching at the edge of the torchlight. "What will you do at my passing?"

Carad Thorn heard and answered in a whisper. "I will mourn," he promised. "I will mourn."

Chapter Three

MIANUR'S azure band arced across the black velvet sky from one horizon to the other. Palenoc's stars and strange constellations glittered around it like icy diamonds, lending beauty to the unfamiliar heavens. Their faint luminescence shed little light on the barren plain that stretched outward from the walls of Shadark's capital city.

From a hollow depression in the hard earth where he lay still as the night itself, Robert Podlowsky turned his gaze from the sky to the top of Pedrah's high rampart. With a gloved hand he adjusted the thin black scarf that masked his face, tugging it a bit higher over the bridge of his nose. It wouldn't do to breathe the fine dust and risk a sneeze. He pulled his close-fitting hood a bit lower as well, until it almost reached his eyebrows.

No watch fires burned atop the wall, nor did he see any lanterns or torches. Only long and careful observation allowed him to spot the four sentries on duty at this particular section. They moved quietly, dimly silhouetted against the starry sky, betrayed by their pacing, by small motions of an arm, or the turn of a head.

Shifting position, Robert rose out of the dust and crouched. Pursing his lips for a soft whistle, he glanced behind and to his left, then nodded with grim satisfaction. Not one of his company could be seen in the night.

Suddenly, a sound caused him to flatten against the earth again. He stared toward Pedrah as the clanking of chains and the creak of massive hinges shattered the silence. Farther along the wall to the right of his position stood the city's Dawn Gate. An ancient portcullis cranked upward, and huge iron-banded gates swung slowly inward.

A solitary rider thundered through the portal and down the lonely hard-packed road that led away from Pedrah. It was not the rider, however, that caught Robert's interest and caused his sharp intake of breath, but the rider's mount.

There was no mistaking the unnatural flames in the beast's eyes, nor the gleaming ebon spike that jutted from its brow. A *chimorg*! The creatures were the eyes and ears of Shandal Karg. What was this one doing in Pedrah? And with a rider, too. They rarely permitted men to ride upon their backs.

Robert waited, still as death, until the echoes of its hoofbeats faded and beast and rider were lost from sight. He repressed the slightest shudder and bit his lip. A *chimorg* in Pedrah. It couldn't bode well.

Still, there was no turning back now. He spied the guards again. They leaned over the wall, watching the rider, who would still be visible from their higher vantage. Moments passed, and finally the four relaxed again.

Robert rose swiftly, gave a low birdlike whistle, and raced across a thirty-yard span for the deep shadows at the base of the wall. In concealment once again, he flattened against the cool stone and calmed his breathing. A single bead of sweat purled from under the edge of his hood. He flicked it away with a fingertip and peered to his left.

Someone stirred in the shadows. About twenty feet away a black-swathed arm, barely visible, lifted in acknowledgment.

Robert gave his attention to the next part of his task. From inside his loose-fitting jacket he drew a small bundle. Quickly, he unwound the black wrappings to expose a pair of shukos, iron bands made to slip over his hands, fastened in place with leather wrist straps. They fit well over his gloves, and he turned his palms up to reveal the band's four clawlike spikes.

Next, he picked up the wrappings and tied them loosely about his sleeves.

Robert turned to face the wall. The shukos were climbing tools as well as weapons. The sharp spikes found easy purchase in the cracks and crumbling mortar between the great stones. Hand over hand, in practiced silence, he hauled himself higher and higher.

"Those spikers make my skin crawl."

Robert paused, holding his breath. The top of the wall was only a few feet away. The voice of a guard came from directly overhead.

"You're a damn fool to say so out loud," a second guard said gruffly. "*Chimorgs* aren't the worst of Her servants, you know."

A boot scraped on stone. Someone leaned on the parapet and stared outward. Gauntleted fingers curled over the edge.

Robert patiently wet his lips under his mask.

"Did you recognize the rider?" the first speaker asked.

Again came a gruff-voiced answer. "The way he passed through here like some *dando* was breathing down his neck?" There followed a hacking sound and another noise, like spitting. "I didn't see nothing, boy. Probably better if you didn't see nothing, too."

The guards' footsteps clapped softly on the walkway as they moved along. Robert willed his straining shoulder muscles to relax and resumed his climb, achieving the top of the wall a moment later. With an eye on the guards' departing backs, he slipped over the side and crouched.

He risked a glance to his left. No sign of Sulis Tel, but he trusted the Aegrenite to do his part.

He looked to the pair of guards again. With soundless stealth he pursued them. They had resumed their chat, making his job easier. When they paused again and leaned to relax against another section of the rampart, he rose up before them, seemingly out of the blackness of night itself.

The younger one had time to gasp in surprise before Robert drove stiffened fingers into his windpipe. The boy sank to his knees, wheezing for breath.

The older guard, though his eyes snapped wide with fear, reached for the wooden baton sheathed on his belt. Robert's right foot came up into an unprotected groin. The poor guard's mouth opened in pain, but no sound issued immediately. He bent forward, clutching himself, offering the back of his helmeted head for Robert's elbow.

The helmet was soft leather. No protection at all.

Robert whipped free the cloth wrappings he'd tied about his sleeves. Gentleness was not a priority as he bound and gagged the guards, then used their own belts to truss their feet. The first guard, the younger one, watched through teary, fearful eyes. Robert hesitated only a moment, then put the kid out with a quick punch.

With catlike grace he turned and stared back along

the rampart. From the ground he'd spotted four guards on this section of the wall. Now there was no sign of anyone else at all on the walkway. Cautiously, he rose to his full height and gave another low whistle. A low whistle answered. Farther back along the walk, Sulis Tel stood up.

The invasion of Pedrah had begun.

Robert slipped free of his jacket. Over one shoulder and across his chest he wore a coil of rope from which depended a small grappling hook. Securing the hook to the battlement, he cast the rope over the side. His companion did the same.

On the plain below, a host of human figures separated suddenly from the shadows and raced toward the wall. Robert crouched in concealment again, one hand on the hook until he felt vibration as someone below tested the rope. The hook held.

A moment later, a masked and hooded figure slithered over the wall and huddled down beside him, pausing long enough to regard the unconscious guards before merging into the gloom further along the walk. A second black-clad figure followed him, and a third and fourth. They moved soundlessly, as he'd trained them, and flattened themselves on the stone tiles or melted into shadows.

As he slipped into his jacket again, Robert studied the narrow interior courtyard below inside the wall. It was empty of any guards; nothing at all moved there. Small lanterns gleamed dimly from a few posts. He stared past that to the black shapes of the city's towers and minarets.

A dark-skinned hand brushed his shoulder. Sulis Tel's eyes bore into his above the top of the cloth mask. He hadn't even heard his friend approach. "The

Sharak-khen are ready," he said in a deep whisper. "As you say, *time to boogie*."

Sharak-khen. That was the name his company of men had given themselves. Brothers to Ghosts, it meant, and like ghosts they moved unseen and unheard through the night.

He had trained them long and hard, but to a good end. Each one had reason to hate Shandal Karg, and each had been touched by the long, evil hand of the Dark Lands. Robert had used that hate to forge them, to give them focus. To give them a purpose that suited his own.

He had another name for them, these fifty men who followed him, similar in sound, but different in meaning. They were his *shuriken*, and like that primary weapon of Earth's ancient ninjas, he would hurl them straight at the Heart of Darkness.

He leaned closer to Sulis Tel. "Where?" he whispered.

The Aegrenite pointed a slender finger. His black-skinned friend was the only one among them who knew anything of Pedrah. He indicated a sprawling three-storied structure barely visible in the gloomy distance. Robert could just make it out.

There was no more time to waste. The four vanquished guards were not the only ones who walked the city walls. At Robert's signal each of his *Sharak-khen* uncoiled kaginawas, twelve-foot lengths of line with tiny grapples. Robert had recently introduced them to it and to other weapons never before seen on Palenoc. Using the lines, they slipped down into the courtyard below. Those who reached the ground first moved swiftly to extinguish the few lanterns, plunging the courtyard into darkness.

Robert disdained a line. He jumped from the walkway to the ground below, rolling and regaining his feet. Sulis Tel imitated him and made something of a sweeping bow under Robert's stern scrutiny. "After you," he whispered with polite mirth.

As silently as their namesakes, the Brothers to Ghosts moved from the courtyard into the empty streets. They found themselves in the warehouse district. Barrels and boxes stood piled against old, weathered buildings. The streets were hard-packed earth, wide and lonely at this hour. Robert's company made rapid progress.

Abruptly, they stopped. A narrow stream flowed through the city, its banks lined with rows of lanterns hung on posts. Two sentries armed with staves, with whips and batons on their belts, stood a lackadaisical watch on a wooden bridge. They leaned on the bridge's railings and talked in low voices.

Crouched in the shadow of an abandoned wagon, Robert reached into a pocket sewn inside his jacket and extracted a smooth stone ball about the size of a marble. He held it up for Sulis Tel, crouched right behind him, to see. The black man nodded and produced a similiar stone.

With a gloved hand Robert pointed to himself and the guard on the right side of the bridge. He indicated the other man for Sulis Tel. Then he silently counted three on his fingers. He rose from hiding and gave a high whistle. The startled guards whirled in his direction.

Both missiles flew through the air simultaneously, and the sentries heads snapped back. Staves clattered noisily. One man fell to the boards and lay motionless. The other clung to the rail with one hand as he sank down clutching his face.

The *Sharak-khen* raced across the open ground.

Sulis Tel caught the conscious man in a choke-hold, applied pressure to the carotid artery, and put him mercifully to sleep before he could raise an alarm. Not that he could have raised a very loud one with his jaw broken where the stone ball had struck. The pair was bound and gagged and thrust beneath the bridge for safekeeping.

The company of black-clad men flowed on into the tanners' district. The smell of hides and dyes lingered unpleasantly in the air. The shops and apartments were dark and still, the occupants in slumber. Beneath a broad awning sat a caldron full of a foul-smelling brew. Scattered around it lay pieces of animal skins and piles of entrails. The night buzzed with flies as Robert passed by.

"The Street of Poisons," Sulis Tel murmured in his ear a few moments later as they reached the edge of a broad lane. The air smelled even worse here, and Robert tugged his mask a bit higher to block the stench of strange chemicals and stranger medicines.

As they were about to cross the street, a sound of gently shaken bells alerted them. The *Sharak-khen* dispersed, some melting into the shadows, some climbing with agile grace to the rooftops. Robert pressed himself into a doorway and pulled his hood lower to hide as much of his pale skin as possible. He watched through a squinting gaze, concealing even the whites of his eyes.

A squad of ten soldiers marched in crisp precision down the Street of Poisons. A pair of saffron-robed priests walked before them with a weird loping stride, their heads bobbing from side to side. Each priest carried in his right hand a torch to light the way. In his left each shook a three-tiered rack of bells to mark the cadence.

The strange procession moved on unaware that they were being watched. One by one the *Sharak-khen* slipped furtively across the wide road as the torchlight and the bells faded in the distance.

Every man made his own way now as they moved through more populated parts of Pedrah toward the palace. Sulis Tel stayed by Robert's side, but Robert was used to his presence, welcomed it even. From the first day of their meeting, the Aegrenite had appointed himself his leader's personal guardian and trained accordingly. In the process they'd become fast friends.

In this part of the city a few lamps burned dimly behind shuttered apartment windows, but none of the citizenry ventured abroad. Like most Dark Land cities, Pedrah enforced a curfew.

Sulis Tel tapped Robert's shoulder. They halted behind a low hedge that surrounded a broad, paved plaza stretching before the palace's Grand Entrance. Before a pair of soaring bronze doors a huge, Olympic-style torch stood. Its flames shed a flickering orange glow over a peculiar scene.

In three perfectly formed rows, guards knelt on the flagstones before the torch. They were naked from the waist up, their armor arranged in neat piles at their sides. With slender gold whips, they flogged themselves. A priest walked among them with a rack of bells. Each time he shook those chimes, the lashes fell.

More priests stood in a line before the torch. Each one clutched a leafy bough from which a single leaf was stripped off and cast into the flames as the priest passed by. After making his offering, each priest returned to the end of the line to await his next pass.

Robert watched, fascinated. It was all perfectly choreographed, every step, every movement, every stroke of the lash timed to the shaking of the bells. With reluctance, he left the scene. There was work to do.

Sulis Tel led the way as they skirted the edge of the plaza. On the east side of the palace a park was located just as the Aegrinite had said; at the back, was an orchard whose trees grew right up to the wall that surrounded Carad Thorn's elaborate residence.

In this park the scattered *Sharak-khen* gathered again. A few were already waiting when Robert and Sulis Tel arrived. The rest stole in in pairs and threes. For a short time the orchard seethed with shadows.

This inner wall was smaller than the rampart that surrounded the city. Ropes whisked through the air, and tiny grapples caught on the stone. Black-clad men climbed rapidly, dropped soundlessly on the other side, and coiled their kaginawas again.

Robert used his shukos. Sulis Tel climbed right beside him. As one, they swung over the top and dropped. A sweet, fresh smell swirled up to greet Robert. He glanced down at his feet and at a bed of trampled roses. It surprised him to find flowers in such a place.

He marveled at how easily things had gone so far. The city's defenses were nonexistent, its soldiers no more than ceremonial window dressing. Sulis Tel had assured him it would be so. Even in his own short time on Palenoc, Robert had learned a lesson. The Dark Lands were not ruled by force. They were ruled by fear.

An unshuttered window offered itself just twelve feet above the ground. Taking a kaginawa from one of his men, Robert crept forward and made a quick, skillful toss. The hook sailed through the dark portal. It made the smallest of sounds as it caught hold of the lower sill.

Sulis Tel caught Robert's arm with one hand as his other closed about the slender rope. Their gazes met only briefly. Robert frowned, but surrendered the line.

"That's a good little leader," the larger black man whispered, his eyes sparkling with amusement as if he could read Robert's expression even through the concealing mask. "I'm an expendable chunk of meat. You're not."

"Sweet of you to say so," Robert hissed.

The Aegrinite shrugged. "I'm a sweet kind of guy." He grabbed the line in both hands and began to climb. In no time he clambered through the window. Below, the *Sharak-khen* waited. After a few moments, Sulis Tel reappeared. He leaned out long enough to beckon the others.

A second kaginawa sailed through the window. Robert went next up the first line. By the time he slid over the sill another warrior was halfway up the other, and a third had started his climb at the bottom. So they alternated, working quickly.

The corridor beyond the window was narrow and unlighted. Robert could touch both walls by stretching out his arms. Sulis Tel led as they stole noiselessly down the passage. All of them had studied a crude map of the palace's design, but Sulis Tel knew it best, for he had drawn it from childhood memories.

The narrow passage merged with a larger one. Small oil cressets hung on chains from the ceiling, casting a wavering amber glow.

Sulis Tel held out a hand suddenly, stopping them before they could step into the light. A single pair of footsteps rang on the floor. An attenuated shadow slithered over the stone tiles.

Robert tapped a prearranged signal on the Aegrenite's shoulder. *One man—let him pass,* the signal instructed. Sulis Tel nodded even as he slipped a hand into a pocket on his sleeve.

The palace resident turned into their corridor. His head snapped up in surprise. Simultaneously, Sulis Tel flung a fine gray powder of ash and pepper. It streamed into the startled man's eyes, blinding him. Before the man could scream, Sulis moved in a swift blur, slipping a cord around the resident's throat, dragging him down to the floor.

In an instant, all struggles ceased. Sulis Tel unwrapped the cord as Robert knelt and pressed an ear to the still man's chest. "Alive," he murmured, rising.

Two of the *Sharak-khen* stepped out of darkness. They used knives to shred the man's dirty tunic into strips, with which they bound and gagged him, and then they dragged him back into the darkened passage.

"A servant," came Sulis Tel's annoyed whisper. "Hardly the game we came to stalk."

Robert put a finger to his lips and motioned for his friend to lead on.

The palace was eerily quiet. On the wide plains of Chol Hecate where he had trained his *Sharak-khen* these past months, Robert had grown used to open spaces. These walls oppressed him. The ceiling felt like a weight upon his head. The air was too still.

He forced such thoughts away and concentrated. A pair of shadows slipped down a side passage briefly and rejoined them. Nothing down that way. Someone quietly opened a door, explored an interior, and slipped out again. Nothing there. They turned into another, wider corridor where no lamps burned and followed it. The air began to smell of sweet, cinnamonlike incense.

The corridor bent at a sharp right angle, leading to

a passage that blazed with light. Sulis Tel held up a hand and everyone stopped. Alone, he crept toward the edge of the darkness, stretched out flat upon the floor, and peeked into the brightness.

A moment later, he returned. He held up two fingers, paused, then flashed all ten fingers three times—two men, about thirty feet away.

Robert frowned and felt for the potentially lethal spiked shurikens in leather sheaths strapped around his wrists. Unlike throwing stars, these were thin blades and went in deep.

Someone touched his hand before he could draw the weapons. In the faint light that leaked from the brighter corridor, he recognized the slender, fine-boned form of Ranye h'Tan, a young soldier formerly from the land of Chylas in the Domains.

Ranye tapped an authoritative finger on his own chest and rapidly began to shed his clothes, letting them fall in a pile at Robert's feet. When he was totally naked, without even mask or hood, he reached back and unloosed the band that constrained his long, thick mass of black hair. He shook it forward over his face and shoulders.

A mournful expression settled upon Ranye's face. He drew one shoulder up to his ear, leaned his head on it, and hugged himself. A pitiful mewl escaped his delicate lips as he eased past Robert and Sulis Tel toward the lighted passage. There, with sad, balletic grace, amid a swirl of hair, he sank to the floor. His body gave a shake as he sobbed.

Robert watched, mesmerized by Ranye's performance. He saw a woman huddled there, face hidden by hair, groin concealed by a carefully draped hand, body turned to reveal only that flowing hair, a small waist, one finely chiseled hip.

The guards played their roles as well. On cue, the pair rushed forward to investigate. Robert fancied he could almost read their minds as they stepped into view and bent over their naked visitor.

They were good-sized men and carried gold-tipped staves. From their belts hung coiled whips and the customary wooden batons of Dark Land soldiers. They were ill-prepared, however, assuming the meek figure before them no threat. One looked at the other with something of a leer.

Without warning, Ranye's right foot shot out. In one neat move he swept the ankles of the nearest man, who went down with a short squawk before his head hit the wall, then the floor.

A look of confusion flashed over the second guard's face. He brought his staff up in a horizontal defensive position. With lithe speed, Ranye caught the weapon, his hands between the guard's. Sinking suddenly backward, he pulled his foe off-balance, planted a foot in his stomach, and threw the startled Pedrahn.

Now the staff was Ranye's. He swung one metal-capped end and took the guard just below the earpiece of his leather helmet, ending any further conflict.

Robert gave an approving nod as the young soldier leaned the staff against the wall and hurried into his clothes. Four more *Sharak-khen* ripped strips of cloth from the guards' uniforms and trussed them before dragging them back into darkness.

No shadows hid them in this brighter corridor. Speed was their weapon now. Robert spun about on the balls of his feet in the direction the guards had come from. Then he stopped.

Sulis Tel stood about twenty feet down the way, his hands limp at his side, staring at a wooden sculpture that reminded Robert of the totem poles of the Northwest Indians of his own world. Six demonic faces leered out from the polished wood with open mouths and tongues that intertwined and tangled about the poles.

"This is my father's work," the black man whispered in a voice thick with emotion. He pointed to a matching sculpture farther down the hall.

But Robert's gaze was focused on a pair of gleaming doors between the two sculptures. The red-colored wood swirled with black streaks and grains. Slim bands of gold with silver inlays ran across the middles of both doors. Above each band ran a line of finely made silver runes in what Robert assumed was the Shadark language. He pushed against one of the large doors.

The sharp crack of a whip issued from within. A wisp of smoky incense wafted through the opening. Robert eased the door open just wide enough to allow a man entrance, no more.

Sulis Tel wasted no more time, but stepped immediately to Robert's side. For a moment the two men exchanged gazes, then Sulis drew a deep breath and nodded. This was it.

The Temple of Eternal Night.

They slipped into a vast, gloomy chamber. Rows of stout columns at the outer edges of the room supported a high, soot-smeared ceiling. The smell of smoke and incense nearly overpowered them. A rack of staves and batons stood by the door. Piled near it were pieces of armor, sandals, and items of clothing.

A towering idol dominated the temple from the far side. Carved from gleaming black stone, the statue stood with stern arms folded, its form concealed in the fluted draping of a stone cloak, its visage hidden beneath a stone hood. At its feet a pool of fire lit the sculpture with a sinister glow.

Robert tore his eyes from the idol as he crept past the rack of weapons and piles of armor. The temple crawled with shadows, and the columns provided ready concealment. Quietly, the *Sharak-khen* moved into the room with him, ranging themselves about.

Again came the sharp crack of a whip. Rows of naked men knelt on the hard stone tiles, backs hunched as they bent forward, their heads almost to the floor. Robert could see the angry red welts and fine trickles of blood that marred those broad, muscled bodies.

A naked priest moved among the supplicants, his expression serene; he carried a slender golden whip in his upraised hand. Without warning he brought the lash down on a random pair of shoulders. The man who received the blow flinched, but made no sound at all.

Sulis Tel touched Robert's shoulder and pointed to the idol. Then slowly he moved his finger about twenty-five degrees to the right and stopped. Sulis Tel swore there was a door there. Robert could not see it in the gloom, but he didn't doubt his friend.

To gain that door, however, they would have to cross the temple. He made a quick estimate. The temple supplicants were clearly soldiers; the weapons and armor that hung on the wall were testament to that. Their numbers were roughly the same as his *Sharak-khen,* but he also had the element of surprise.

He gave a short, sharp whistle. All around the temple black-garbed figures leaped out of the shadows.

The priest whirled about in amazement. He opened his mouth to scream as a small stone ball took him in the side of the head. He staggered, falling to his knees.

The supplicants jumped to their feet. Some ran for

the rack of weapons and found a line of *Sharak-khen* waiting to turn their staves against them.

One man broke for the door. A kaginawa flashed through the air, its line and small grapple entangling legs and ankles. The fleeing soldier crashed to the floor with jarring force and was reeled like a fish back into the temple before he could raise any alarm.

Robert reached into one of the numerous pockets on his sleeves as he stepped out of hiding. A large, powerfully built man scowled and rose up to block his way. Robert's hand flicked outward in a tossing gesture, and his foe froze in midstep, his jaw falling open as he stared at the tiny spiked caltrops that flowered on his chest and belly. Before he could utter a cry, Robert silenced him with a kick to the face.

The fight was swift and vicious. Soon, only a few low moans echoed around the temple. Choke holds or fists put a brutal end to those.

"Half of you remain here," Robert quietly instructed his men as he moved to the center of the temple. "Bind these Pedrahns securely, no matter their injuries. Then reclaim our weapons—shurikens, caltrops, lines, everything. Leave nothing behind that can be used again."

The rest followed Robert to the far side of the temple where Sulis Tel already stood waiting. "Just where I remembered it," the black man said. "A private access to the temple for the priests and for Carad Thorn himself."

It was a plain and unornamented door. Robert pushed it open and stared into a darkened passage. Again, he felt the strange weight of the palace crushing him. He glanced back at the idol whose glittering presence dominated the temple. He noted the suggestive swell of breasts and the subtle hint of feminine form beneath the hood and cloak.

Though it had no face, Robert knew whose image he beheld. A chill of anger shivered through him. It had to be the Heart of Darkness. In Shadark, as in all the Dark Lands, Shandal Karg was worshipped as a goddess.

Beneath his mask he chewed his lower lip and wished there were time to tear the damned thing down and smash it to rubble. "Break one of those staves," he whispered to Ranye h'Tan, who stood near his side. "Wrap some cloth around it for a torch."

Ranye hurried to obey.

"You hesitated in the corridor," Robert murmured to Sulis Tel.

"Well, just take me out in the woods and hang me," the Aegrenite answered.

Robert frowned. "I think I'm going to regret teaching you those kinds of colloquialisms."

From his fifth birthday to his ninth, Sulis Tel had been a slave in the kitchens of this palace. He had told Robert most of the story.

Raids into the Domains and the Gray Kingdoms for slaves were not uncommon, and Sulis's entire village had been taken. Most families had been separated and sold all over the Dark Lands. He did not, in fact, know what had become of his mother. But his father was a skilled artist, and artists were prized. Because such talent might be passed from father to son, a dealer had bought them as a pair.

His father had been put to work creating sculptures for Pedrah's temples and public buildings, work with which Sulis himself was allowed to assist. After less than a year, though, his father was crushed when a block of stone he was working on suddenly toppled.

The boy, who had so far shown no artistic ability, was sent to work in the palace's kitchens. It was there that Sulis Tel learned how the urine and excrement of the resident priests and nobles were collected each morning in huge earthern jars and carried through the Sundown Gate outside the city where they were ritually offered to the spirits of the river.

After much planning and years of awaiting his chance, the young boy concealed himself in one of the jars and managed to make good his escape. "When they poured me into the river," he had joked to Robert, "they just mistook me for another turd."

Robert put aside his memories as Ranye h'Tan returned with the torch. Its light spilled through the small, plain door to illuminate the darkness of the passage beyond.

"I've dreamed of this day," Sulis Tel confided quietly. He reached out and, with the spikes of the shukos he wore, carved parallel scratches deep in the door's face as if to leave his mark.

Robert took the torch and led the way into the narrow passage. The tunnel wound on for quite a distance before they came to a door. He pressed his ear to it and listened. A few faint voices in conversation could be heard. He stationed two of his *Sharak-khen* on either side of it. The rest moved on.

Abruptly, the passage ended. The light of the torch fell upon another plain wooden door. Robert put his hand softly upon it and pushed. It refused to give. He bent closer with the torch, discovering a fine space between the edge of the door and its jamb. There was no lock or keyhold. Latched, then.

He passed the torch back to Sulis Tel, then slipped one shuriken from a sheath on his right wrist. It was not a semban shuriken, a throwing star, but a single thin blade. It slipped easily between the door edge and the jamb. Cautiously, he worked the latch free, then resheathed his weapon.

Sulis Tel extinguished the torch. Robert eased the door open a quarter of an inch. A fine line of light showed around it. He put his ear close to the crack and listened, trying to distinguish the muffled sounds he heard within. He eased the door a bit wider, then he peeked into the room.

A puff of wind blew against his cheek from an open window. A cresset lamp suspended from the ceiling flickered in the new draft. The room was large, lavishly furnished with carved wooden chairs, a claw-footed table, desks, and trunks. A plush carpet covered the stone floor. A cold fireplace dominated one end of the room. On the elaborate mantel perched a smaller version of the temple idol.

A sharp gasp and a longer sigh of pleasure made Robert turn toward a side room as the rest of his *Sharak-khen* crept out of the passage. Someone leaped high and extinguished the cresset with a swift tap of a gloved palm. Another noiselessly closed the window's shutters. Two more took positions on either side of yet another door, which ostensibly led to the palace's main hallways.

A man's deep-voiced groan came from the smaller side room. Robert traded glances with Sulis Tel. There was no mistaking the sounds of lovemaking. He crept to the entrance to the bedchamber and paused. An oil lamp perched on a small table illuminated the scene within. A huge canopied bed was the room's only furnishing. A shimmering thin veil of gauzelike material draped the structure. Beyond it, the sheets churned.

Robert moved with swift, soundless steps. With one swipe of his left shuko he ripped the veil away and snatched off the top sheet. As he did so, a half dozen of his *Sharak-khen* surrounded the bed.

Carad Thorn looked up in surprised outrage as he rolled off a boy who couldn't have been more than twelve years old. Before the Pedrahn ruler could cry out, though, Sulis Tel barked a harshly whispered order in the Shadark tongue.

Dark eyes blazing with hatred, Carad Thorn rose up on one elbow. He glared at the Aegrenite, who stood just behind Robert's right shoulder. "You speak my language," he answered in a barely controlled sneer, "but with a Domain accent!"

It was Robert's turn to feel surprise. Carad Thorn spoke Guranian, which was the *lingua franca* of all the Domain alliance. "Good," he muttered, keeping his voice low. "It will make things easier if we understand—"

Before he could finish, the boy screamed and leaped at him, his tiny clawed fingers seeking Robert's eyes. Reflexively, Robert brought the edge of his hand up and batted the child down. But he had momentarily forgotten the shuko he wore. The iron band that encircled his hand connected solidly with the side of that small head.

The boy fell limp and unmoving on the floor, a trickle of blood pouring from a cut across his cheek bone.

Rage seized Robert. "You filth!" he hissed, glaring at Carad Thorn. He swung his hand, and the shuko's spikes ripped through sheet and feather mattress. "He's just a little kid!"

Carad Thorn crouched wolflike in his bed. The lamplight filled his eyes with a feral gleam as he met Robert's stare. Something else reflected that light, too. A tiny peridot, pale and sickly green in color, hung from a chain about the naked man's throat.

He clutched it suddenly as the *Sharak-khen* started to reach for him. At once the jewel began to glow with a nauseous light. The knuckles and bones of his fingers showed darkly through the skin as that light grew stronger. Then the glow encompassed his fist.

"Stupid Domain fools!" Carad Thorn cried triumphantly, "I'll shred your souls as easily as you did my bed!"

The weird greenish light surged outward. Robert felt its icy, chilling force sapping his strength and will. He tried to shut his eyes, hoping to shut out that evil glow, but couldn't. A frigid veil settled over his mind and enveloped his body.

He could barely see a few of his *Sharak-khen* on the other side of the bed. They stood like sculptures, captured by the same radiance that held him.

"You!" Carad Thorn gloated. Robert's vision began to blur. He felt, as much as saw, the Pedrahn's face close to his. Carad Thorn's mouth gaped like a black pit from which issued monstrous laughter. "If you've injured my little plaything, you'll take his place."

The peridot blazed with its cold fire. Robert felt his blood turning to ice. He screamed inside, not with fear, but with frustration, trying to focus some iota of his own willpower to resist.

Suddenly, Carad Thorn's laughter ceased. Robert felt the slightest thawing of the force that gripped him. As if from a far, far distance he again heard Thorn's voice.

"Your eyes!" The words were a hissed exclamation, tinged with fear. "By my Dark Lady! Your eyes!"

It was as if a spring wind had blew across his mind. Rime and ice cracked and gave way. Robert lashed out with the shuko's spikes, slicing through the chain around Carad Thorn's neck. Four red lines blossomed over the Pedrahn's bare chest, then began to bleed freely. Tiny golden links scattered over the bedsheet.

The glow vanished instantly. Carad Thorn howled with fear and pain, the concentration required to work his magic, shattered. He tried to jump up, but his feet tangled in the bedclothes, and he fell again. Blood splattered the sheets. He raised his fist. The ends of the severed chain dangled. He still clung to the peridot!

Robert threw himself across the bed, caught Carad Thorn's wrist, and twisted hard. Bone and tendon snapped. The peridot flew across the room and rolled under the table.

Sharak-khen piled on the bed, pinning Carad Thorn as he thrashed and struggled. Someone shoved a corner of the sheet into his mouth to prevent any further screams. Finally, Robert held the shuko's spikes just inches from the Pedrahn's eyes and snarled menacingly.

Carad Thorn grew still at once, his terror plain as he stared at those spikes and then at Robert. "No more noise," Robert ordered. Carad Thorn nodded agreement.

"Your eyes!" he whispered sharply when Robert pulled the gag free. "Who in Darkness's name are you?"

Robert motioned his men back and climbed off the bed himself. "Don't you recognize me?" he answered. "Don't you know me?"

Carad Thorn shook his head as he rose to his knees in the middle of the bed and cradled his broken wrist. "It's not possible," he said. "Not now! Not here!"

Robert glared at the cowering creature before him, feeling no mercy. He allowed himself to glance at the boy he had struck. Ranye h'Tan, kneeling on the floor, held the unconscious child in his arms and dabbed at the head wound with a wadded piece of the ruined bed veil. He gave an assuring nod. The boy would live.

Turning back to Carad Thorn, Robert slowly removed his mask. Then he put one hand to his hood and pushed it back. His prisoner gasped as Robert shook free a thick mass of blond hair. The lamplight shimmered on every yellow-white strand.

Robert noticed how his *Sharak-khen,* even Sulis Tel, stared, too. Suddenly uncomfortable, he pulled his hood back up.

"Eyes green with the coming spring," Carad Thorn mumbled dejectedly, automatically, as if he were reciting something he'd learned long ago. "Hair blazing like sunlight." He looked up at Robert again, and there was no doubt on his face. "You are the Son of the Morning."

"Pleased to meet you," Robert answered curtly as he masked himself again. "Ranye," he said, beckoning to the young soldier. "That was quite a gem you had," he continued, looking once more to Carad Thorn. "We've brought a gem, too."

Ranye h'Tan arranged the injured child carefully on the floor, then came to the side of the bed where Carad Thorn sat. From a pocket on his thigh he extracted a blue sapphire. Its facets gleamed as he placed it on his palm and knelt down directly before the man.

"Listen to me," Ranye said softly as he passed the stone slowly back and forth before the Pedrahn's eyes.

"You have only one salvation tonight. Only one way out of this room. Your safety lies within this stone. Look closely and you'll see it." Carad Thorn's gaze followed the sapphire back and forth. "Look closely," Ranye advised in subdued tones. "Look deeply."

Tears began to ooze down Carad Thorn's cheeks, but he looked, his gaze unwavering, locked on the gem.

Ranye continued to speak in the Domain tongue until the Pedrahn's eyes glazed over. Then gradually he slipped in words from his own native Chylas. Soon it was only Chylan he whispered. The words formed a repetitive pattern and created a quietly sibilant vibration. He sent the sound directly at the sapphire, which he now held so close to his mouth his lips seemed to brush it as he spoke. The jewel burned like a spark of intense blue fire. Carad Thorn's gaze fastened upon it.

Robert and the *Sharak-khen* watched, fascinated by something far beyond mere hypnosis.

A strange expression of peace settled over Carad Thorn's face. That eventually gave way to a totally blank look, and his tears stopped.

Ranye ended his chant. A few moments of silence passed before the young soldier moved. Slowly, like a flower curling its petals for the night, his fingers closed around the sapphire. He sat back on his heels, gave a sigh, and rubbed the bridge of his nose.

"Is it done?" Robert asked in a hushed voice.

Ranye h'Tan nodded and passed over the jewel. "Yes," he answered simply.

Robert carried the stone to the lamp and held it close to the light. Squinting, he stared into its glittering depths. At the very heart of that blue infinity pulsed a weak red spark. "You might want to see this," he said over his shoulder to Sulis Tel.

The black man took the stone from him, peered into it, and gave a grunt of satisfaction. "It's a happy homecoming after all," he muttered.

Robert took the sapphire back and squeezed it in his fist.

For a thousand years war had raged on Palenoc between the Domains of Light, who followed the Son of the Morning, and the Dark Lands under Shandal Karg's cold dominion. But it was an odd kind of war with odd rules. On a world where ghosts were real and vengeful, it was a dangerous thing to kill.

So Robert with his *Sharak-khen* had done something far worse. He had stolen an enemy's mind. Carad Thorn's body lived. But all that was truly Carad Thorn was now imprisoned in the sapphire Robert held in his hand.

Chapter Four

THE wind blew sharply across the rocky tops of the cliffs that formed the eastern bank of the wide Shylamare River. The rippling water shimmered with a horrible orange glow.

Nocturnal birds wheeled wildly across the sky, filling the night with a confusion of calls. Hordes of winged insects careened on waves of heat.

A thick veil of smoke shifted and swirled through the air, obscuring the stars and pale Mianur. Thanador floated like a sad and rheumy eye, sometimes bright and sometimes dim, sometimes barely visible at all. Smoke hung on the river like a wispy fog, climbed the cliffs, and rolled over their stony summits. It covered the soaring banks like a gray pall.

Abruptly, the birds scattered. Out of the smoke and darkness of the eastern night sailed a trio of dragons. The undersides of the beasts' powerful pinions shone with the steady glow of luciferase, and the light they gave off rippled over the land as they glided toward the cliff edges. Though huge, the creatures landed with startling grace and dipped their sinuous necks to the rocky ground.

Eric Podlowsky jumped from his saddle and walked to the very edge of the cliff. The blood drained from his face as he stared across the river where fire devoured acres and acres of cultivated cropland. The crackling roar of the flames reached him with muted power. The wind blew sharp and hot on his face; smoke filled his nostrils and stung his eyes.

A tall woman joined him, long dark hair streaming behind her until the wind abated a little. Her face was hard and set, yet a certain dim terror lit her eyes. Her slender hands curled into fists at her sides.

Eric knew what she was thinking. "Alanna," he said in a low voice husky with emotion, speaking her name as he took one of her hands in his. Together, from the safety of the high cliffs, they gazed into the inferno.

Six months before, in a distant forest on the border between Wystoweem and Chol Hecate, they both had lost loved ones in another fire. His brother, Robert, and his lover, Katherine Dowd. Alanna had been in love with Robert.

Neither of them had yet recovered from the grief.

A third figure joined them a moment later, a huge broad-shouldered man, fully a head taller than Eric's six-foot-plus height. He knelt down on one knee as his gaze swept back and forth along the river and over the fiery range.

"The reports were true," the big man said suddenly. "Can you see them?"

Eric nodded slowly. He had to concentrate and force his memories away, but he saw the same thing Valis did. Above the flames the air was full of tiny sparkling lights flitting to and fro. He might have mistaken them for ash, except they didn't rise. They hovered, swarmed.

"Fireflies," he muttered.

Alanna hissed. "Not ordinary fireflies. I know Dark Land sorcery when I see it. Chylas can't suffer these attacks much longer. And each disaster strikes closer to Guran."

The Shylamare River separated Chylas and Guran, though both nations were allies in the Domains of Light and stood against Shandal Karg.

"Chylas isn't suffering alone," Valis reminded her. "Aegren, Vormystra, Doven ... ," he named half a dozen other Domain allies, ticking each one off on his fingers as he spoke. "Crops have been wiped out, whole villages destroyed by winds, grain stores poisoned."

Eric interrupted. "That strange plague in the Gray Kingdoms. It's coming this way, too."

"She's getting desperate," Alanna snapped angrily. She walked a few paces along the cliff edge and kicked a loose stone over the side. "Her time is short. She knows the Son of the Morning is coming. She can read the signs."

The wind, unseasonably chill, shifted direction suddenly. A drop of water splattered on Eric's nose. A second struck him squarely in the eye. A fine drizzle began to fall, and he turned up the collar of his leather tunic. A moment more and the drizzle changed to a downpour.

Eric whirled about and ran for the shelter of his dragon's outstretched wing. *Sekoye,* he corrected himself. It only looked like a dragon to his earthbound brain. Safe from the rain, he reached out and stroked the great scaled ribs of his mount. "Not a pretty sight is it, Shadowfire?" he said to the creature as he stared at the fire again.

Alanna and Valis hurried to join him. Valis's short black hair was already plastered to his head. The opalescent glow from Shadowfire's wings lit their faces with strangely shifting color.

"Chylas's own sorcerers are fighting back," Alanna said as she crouched and gazed up at the rain-bloated sky, "trying to stop the fire from spreading and save whatever they can."

Valis gave a barely audible sigh. "They'll warp weather patterns up and down the entire eastern seaboard," he pointed out. His frown was disapproving, but he struggled with resignation.

A subtle movement far to his right along the edge of the cliff caught Eric's eye. A figure stood there, pale and ethereal. With a start Eric realized he could see the fire right through that form.

Eric pointed to the apparition as he nudged Valis. "Did you call him up?" he asked in little more than a whisper. No matter how long he'd been on Palenoc, ghosts still made him nervous.

"I lay such spirits to rest," Valis answered curtly. "I don't call them up."

"Good," Eric continued as he pointed to the left. "Then you didn't call that one up, either."

The second apparition was paler, thinner than the first. Older, Eric realized. Neither creature acknowledged the other's presence, nor the presences that watched them. They stood as if in utter solitude, oblivious to the wind and rain.

"This is haunted ground," Alanna murmured reverently as she pushed a wet strand of hair back from her face.

A shrill screech raised gooseflesh on Eric's arms, and every hair on his neck stood straight out. Shadowfire lifted his great head and gave an answering trumpet.

"What the hell was that?" Eric demanded of Valis.

"A banshee," his friend answered strangely, his

gaze sweeping around as if he could see things Eric couldn't. "The Dead are gathering."

Eric knew of banshees, though he'd never encountered one. That scream still seemed to echo inside him. Palenoc had many kinds of ghosts, all of which evolved and changed in a mysterious cycle he still didn't fully understand.

Without a word Valis started walking toward the cliff edge, ignoring the pelting rain.

"What are they watching?" Alanna questioned, her eyes still on the pair of apparitions.

"Let's find out," Eric responded.

Valis had reached the rim. The orange glow from the burning fields beyond the Shylamare made him a black silhouette. Eric and Alanna reached his side as he gave a shout. "Children!" he called.

Eric wiped at the rain streaming into his eyes. Far below, nearly a third of the way across the river, he saw a violent splashing. The reflection of the fire lent the water a bloodred sheen. Against that glow he could barely make out two small black forms. They were clinging to a bit of log, trying to flutter kick their way across the river from Chylas to the safety of Guran. But the current was clearly too strong!

"They're children!" Alanna shouted. "They'll drown!"

Eric wasted no time on words. He unsnapped a special pocket on his belt and snatched out a silver Hohner harmonica. Running back to Shadowfire, he blew a loud, wailing riff. The dragon lifted its head and bellowed in response, then stretched out its neck toward him.

From the pack behind his saddle he drew out a rope. Then, stepping into the stirrups, he mounted Shadowfire and blew another series of ascending notes on the gleaming instrument now clutched between his teeth. In response, the dragon sprang smoothly into the air and dipped over the rim of the cliff.

Eric blasted a frantic series of notes with the harmonica, and Shadowfire's great body shuddered with shared urgency as his music formed the bridge between their thoughts. While Eric hastily knotted one end of the rope around his saddle horn, his huge, majestic mount raced down toward the river and the desperately splashing figures.

The thick smoke stung his eyes as he neared the river. He could feel the searing heat of the flames on the wind rushing against his face. On the western bank of the Shylamare Chylas burned like a sea of fire.

The ever-shifting opalescent light from Shadowfire's wings cast a new glow on the churning river as the dragon sailed past the shore. Eric blew another riff from his harmonica. The dragon swept past the struggling children on their piece of flotsam and banked sharply. Shimmering wingtips nearly brushed the cliffs of Guran, and Eric clung to his saddle with knees and with both hands.

They arrived above the children once more. Shadowfire's pinions pounded the air furiously as they hovered over the river. In the center of the glow from the dragon's wings a pair of frightened faces stared upward—two boys. One of the children weakly waved a hand. The other screamed a note of terror that was abruptly cut off as a wave washed over his head.

Shadowfire's wings were creating a violent downdraft that made the river even more treacherous for the boys. Eric had to act fast. He threw the rope down to them, but the wind blew it out of their reach.

"Damn it!" Eric cursed as he drew the rope back up. Rain blew into his eyes, eliciting another curse as he carefully tied the free end around the leather boot on his left ankle. He slipped the harmonica back into its belt pocket and stroked his dragon's neck. "Okay, pal," he grumbled, "hold it steady, or you're gonna be looking for a new partner."

He threw his free leg over Shadowfire's neck and felt his stomach lurch as he lay facedown across the saddle. It hadn't been that long ago that heights had terrified him, and at moments like this, the old fear still gnawed at his resolve. He coiled as much of the rope in his hands as he could. Wrapping a little of the slack around his free foot, he eased himself off the saddle and into space.

His stomach lurched again. Clinging to the rope, spinning dizzyingly as rain and wind battered him, he swung back and forth on his line. Shadowfire fought to maintain a position above the children, but the rushing current swept them along, and the dragon tried to stay with them.

Eric bit his lip, resisting an impulse to close his eyes, and managed to stop his wild rotation. He slipped farther down the line. The coils tightened around his hands. He let them go one by one, descending to the end of his rope. Then he bent his left knee, curling his body into a ball while he still had rope to cling to. With a short prayer and a gasp, he let go.

The world spun crazily. Even through his boot the rope bit sharply into his flesh as his ankle took the entire weight of his body. He hung upside down, swinging in the air, arms flailing as he fought rotation. Gaining a measure of control, he locked one ankle around the other for added support.

High above through the smoky haze he spied the red-glowing wings of Mirrormist, Alanna's dragon. She could do nothing to help, though.

With one hand he cautiously retrieved his harmonica. The children were still beyond his reach, and the current was carrying them, not toward Guran, but farther downstream. He blew a high quavering note, and felt Shadowfire's thoughts merge with his own.

The dragon chased after the boys, and Eric put the harmonica away to free his hands. He could hear their small cries now, see the fear on their faces as they clung to the log with small, desperate hands. Shadowfire caught up with them and did a dragon's best to hover.

"Give me your hands!" Eric shouted, stretching his arms toward the boys. "Don't be afraid!"

One of the boys gave a powerful kick, fairly leaping out of the water for his hand. Eric groaned at the sudden increased strain on his ankle as his fingers locked around the kid's wrist. "Grab my arm with both hands!" he ordered the boy, who needed no further urging to obey. "Now you!" he called to the remaining child.

The second one hesitated. His young eyes gleamed in near panic as he stared wildly from the flaming banks of Chylas to the cliffs of Guran. "Look at me!" Eric ordered sharply. "Look at *me*!" He reached for the kid and missed. Then, with a frantic lunge, the boy grabbed him.

Shadowfire swept high into the air. The boys squealed with terror as they climbed toward the cliff tops. Eric gripped their thin arms with all his strength, praying desperately. The boys' struggling made his job all the harder. "Stop kicking!" he shouted uselessly over their squeals. They were too panicked to listen, nor did he blame them, for his own heart thundered with fear.

He shot a glance toward the sheer cliffs. The summit

never seemed so far away as it did in that moment. He squeezed his eyes shut, trusting to his dragon. "Hurry, Shadowfire!" The words hissed between his straining lips and were lost on the rushing wind. Yet, even without the bridge of music, he felt the dragon's thoughts as one with his own.

The wind ceased to roar in his ears. Eric opened his eyes and saw the ground beneath them. Shadowfire fluttered his massive wings and hovered once more, lowering them with surprising gentleness.

The boys collapsed beside one another on the grass while Eric, swinging in the air, wondered how he was going to get free of the rope tied around his ankle. His head pounded, and his joints burned.

Valis's knife suddenly sliced through the rope with a flash of silver. Eric barked a short, startled cry as he fell awkwardly, half on top of his big friend. The two of them collapsed beside the boys he had just rescued.

One of the boys scrambled up on his hands and knees, facing Eric with an excited expression as he started to speak. Eric interrupted him, fixing him with a stern gaze. Both boys looked about ten years old. They might have been twins.

"If you say, 'Gee, that was fun, let's do it again,' " Eric warned the boy as he untangled himself from Valis, "I'll pitch you back in the river."

Alanna and Valis sang to their dragons as they flew across the night-veiled landscape of Guran. Eric played an old blues tune on his harmonica. Between his thighs sat one of the boys, leather straps around his legs to secure him in the saddle. The second child rode with Valis.

The wind bit icily through Eric's wet leather garments, but soon they flew beyond the rain and smoke, and the fire that consumed Chylas disappeared in the distance. Thick clouds continued to obscure the sky, however, and there was no sign at all of Mianur or Thanador.

The glow of the dragons' wings colored the highest leaves in the trees below and lit the rolling ground. Mirrormist and Brightstar might have been a matched pair. The undersides of their wings shimmered with a soft greenish yellow radiance, entirely different from the girasol glow of Eric's own mount. The rise and fall of those mighty pinions caused the light to pulse with a strange beauty. But the greater beauty came when the creatures spread their wings and glided like cool comets across the night sky.

Soon a new glow lit the southern distance. The trio turned their mounts toward it, following a new bend of the Shylamare River until it emptied into the vast Great Lake. Eric played a new note on his harmonica. Shadowfire dropped suddenly, skimming the shoreline. The boy between his legs laughed and pointed to the skiffs and flatboats pulled up onto the beach, and at the larger ships moored farther out.

They passed above huts and small villages where watch fires burned, then over a bank of hills as they climbed up and down again.

Rasoul spread before them with breathtaking suddenness. Guran's capital city, even at night, shimmered magnificently, stretching from the glittering lake far back into the ring of hills surrounding it. Watch fires burned on the highest roofs and in the city's public squares; torches and lamps lit many of the streets.

In Rasoul Harbor great trading ships and smaller fishing vessels bobbed at their anchors and moorings.

Guy ropes hummed in the gentle night wind, and riggings snapped. Lanterns lit the piers and most of the ships, too.

Eric turned his gaze toward Sheren-Chad. No common watch fire burned atop the tallest structure in Rasoul. A massive globe of *sekoy-melin,* the luciferaselike fluid that coursed in the dragons' wings, illuminated the rooftop of that starkly soaring tower, which was home to all of Guran's dragonriders—*sekournen* in the Guran tongue—those who rode the great winged *sekoye.*

He felt a peculiar rush of joy at the sight of Sheren-Chad and knew it was Shadowfire touching him across the bridge of his music. Eric, himself, was more interested in the view to the south and east. He and his pair of comrades were not the only *sekournen* in the sky tonight. A trio of dragons approached over the Great Lake. Twice that number raced from the southern horizon.

He glanced upward. A host of *sekournen* circled high above Rasoul on watchful patrol.

Alanna and Mirrormist suddenly surged past him, heading straight for Sheren-Chad. A wall nearly five feet thick and just as high encircled the rooftop. Mirrormist extended taloned limbs, caught the wall and perched with folded wings. A moment later, the dragon extended its serpentine neck and Alanna dismounted. Mirrormist bid a trumpeting farewell to its rider, then swept away toward the distant peaks.

Shadowfire's wings fluttered massively, and claws scrabbled on stone. Hurriedly, Eric untied the straps from around his legs and the boy's. Alanna reached up to help the child dismount, then Eric sprang down to the roof tiles to join her. With a light riff on his

Hohner he said good-bye to his *sekoye* as it sailed after Mirrormist.

Brightstar caught the wall next, bathing the roof in the greenish light of his wings. Eric accepted the second boy as Valis handed him down, and the big man quickly followed. "A busy night," he commented grimly as he pointed to the dragons approaching from the east.

"Yeah, it's a real party," Eric commented sourly.

They turned toward the globe of *sekoy-melin,* which stood as a beacon on its huge metal tripod. Before they could approach it, though, a trapdoor cranked open in the space between the three stout legs. The light within spilled upward, and in the glow a silhouetted figure rose.

"Ola, amigos!" The figure hailed them with a wave.

Like Eric, Roderigo Diez was from Earth. The little Spaniard had stumbled through one of the mysterious gateways between Earth and Palenoc nearly twenty years ago, following the murder of his daughter, and had never gone back. Rasoul was his home now. A physician, he had worked his way into a position of power and trust within the Sheren.

With Alanna, Valis, and the two boys, Eric strode toward the trapdoor. The *melin* light from the beacon shone on Roderigo's head and pale face. Eric noted how drawn and weary his old friend looked.

"It has been a disastrous night," Diez confided as he led them down a short flight of stairs to the lavatorium beneath the roof. A series of small *melin*-filled globes mounted along the walls lit the chamber. Two long tables stood in the center of the room, and a trio of silent, white-robed attendants prepared basins of water, sponges, and towels.

"Cleanse yourselves," Diez instructed needlessly. It

was the tradition in most Sherens for *sekournen* to wash their bodies and don fresh garments upon returning. But there was a particular urgency in the Spaniard's voice. "Phlogis and the entire Tarjeel are meeting now in the Grand Sanctum."

He glanced at the two boys and summoned one of the attendants. "Where did you find this pair of tadpoles?"

"In the Shylamare," Valis answered, rumpling one of the boys' hair.

One of the two piped up suddenly. "We nearly got our tails cooked!" he shouted excitedly. He pointed to Eric. "But he saved us! It was great!"

"Great, eh?" Diez responded, turning a sardonic eye on Eric. "That no doubt explains your limp?"

Eric frowned sheepishly. Until Diez mentioned it, he hadn't noticed that, indeed, he was limping. His ankle was a bit sore as a result of his heroics.

"I'll look forward to the tale later," Diez continued. He beckoned to one of the attendants to take the boys away. "And we'll see what we can do about finding their families." He waved a hand toward the washbasins again. "But hurry now. Phlogis insists on seeing you immediately."

The three *sekournen* stripped naked. There was no sense of modesty in the lavatorium. They washed quickly but thoroughly, while Roderigo Diez and the remaining attendants assisted. Then they took fresh clothes of bleached white leather from wardrobes and shelves along the walls. Alanna tied back her long black hair with a leather strip.

"The Heart of Darkness is getting desperate," Roderigo Diez commented as he led them from the lavatorium and down a winding flight of stone steps where only the pale illumination of an occasional *melin* globe lit the way. "All reports indicate Chylas has taken heavy damage from fires. At the dinner hour Trilayn suffered the same massive devastation. In only hours its prime cropland, from the Broken Back Mountains to the sea, was turned into an ashen wasteland.

"Farther south, the same unnatural fireflies struck Prideet and Chule. The guardian sorcerers in both lands were able to destroy or turn back the swarms, but not before numerous villages were burned and lives lost."

Eric eyed the old Spaniard curiously. Despite the bad news Diez brought, there was a barely controlled exuberance in the man's voice, an excitement that seemed out of place. It grew more obvious as they descended the steps and emerged before the impressive wooden doors of Phlogis's Grand Sanctum.

Elaborate symbols painted on the doors reminded Eric of the Pennsylvania Dutch hex signs of his own world. He paused briefly to admire them, as he always did.

In that moment's pause Roderigo Diez caught his hand and squeezed it. Diez was normally a man of restraint, but a fervent, hopeful light shone in his eyes as he met Eric's startled gaze.

Before Eric could say anything, however, Diez let go of his hand and pushed open the great doors. "Come!" he urged as the massive portals swung easily open. "Come!"

A strange and ponderous gloom filled the windowless chamber, a darkness broken only by twin beams of scarlet light that speared upward from huge copper caldrons set next to each other on one side of the room.

In the center of the floor was a larger version of the symbols on the outer door. *Prekhits,* Guran's people called them—circles of protection. But poured gold formed the outer rim of this *prekhit.* Within it hundreds of jewels and precious stones lay embedded in the floor, sparkling and twinkling weirdly in the blood-colored light.

A creature floated in the center of the *prekhit.* Vaguely a man, its legs and feet dangled in the air as if it perched on some unseen branch. Sometimes the creature seemed no more than a shadow that disappeared in the chamber's deeper gloom. Sometimes it appeared pale and ancient, and its features seemed to shift and change in subtle and troubling ways that could not quite be described.

Only its red gaze was constant, and a potent, unrelenting wave of psychic anger radiated from this fearsome creation whose presence completely dominated the sanctum.

Phlogis was a *dando,* a vengeful spirit, slain by the Heart of Darkness over five hundred years before. Once, he had been the most powerful sorcerer in the ancient land of Dah Harag. Single-handedly, he had dared to oppose Shandal Karg's conquest of that land, and She had sent a black, icy fog to steal his life.

The Heart of Darkness alone could kill with impunity in this world where ghosts were real. Her spells and magics protected Her from reprisal. But Phlogis took a subtle course to revenge. Unable to strike back directly, he became the leader of Guran's *sekournen* and turned them into an effective force to thwart the schemes of his murderer.

"Blessed be, Son of Paradane."

Paradane was what the people of Palenoc called Earth, Eric's homeworld. A young, dark-haired woman greeted him formally, pushing back the hood concealing her face as she came toward him. A robe of soft white linen floated around her, stirring with her slightest movement. In the unnatural lighting Eric recognized Alanna's sister, Maris, who led the Tarjeel, Guran's Council of Guardians.

All twelve Tarjeel were present in the shadows and the gloom. They turned expectantly toward Eric and his comrades as Maris spoke again. "I'm so glad you've returned safely," she said, "but please, we must have your news."

"The northern fields of Chylas are all aflame," Alanna answered. The sanctum's acoustics were such that all within the chamber heard, though she spoke in a normal voice.

Maris clutched her hands together in prayer fashion, shaking her head regretfully. "Dismal tidings, sister, but not unexpected."

Roderigo Diez stepped forward. "I've already told them about Prideet, Trilayn, and Chule," he announced.

The Heart of Darkness knows her time is short.

Eric clutched his temple as Phlogis's thought-voice cut across his brain. It always felt like that initially. The *dando*'s thoughts, tinged with raw rage, were the telepathic equivalent of a buzz saw roaring in his ear.

"She makes her move on many fronts at once," Maris said, "with forces both mystic and physical. Four days ago soldiers from Durazador and Zorastor attacked Vanyel's eastern front."

Eric's eyebrows went up. Durazador and Zorastor were nations in an evil alliance called the Kingdoms of Night that once aspired to rival the Dark Lands. Vanyel was the southernmost member of the Domains and the most isolated. "I thought that alliance crumbled with the death of Keris Chaterit!"

Shandal Karg has restored the Kingdoms of Night

and set up her own puppet rulers to serve her bidding,
Phlogis informed them. *We battle once more on
many fronts.*

Roderigo Diez moved right to the edge of the gilt
circle and stopped. He gestured impatiently. "Excuse
me, my honored friends!" he said in a loud pleading
voice to Phlogis and the Tarjeel. "While this information is important, it is not why you asked me to bring
Eric here. I beg you; please tell him!"

Eric grew suddenly suspicious. He eyed Maris, then
turned to Phlogis. "Tell me what?" he demanded.

Phlogis's gaze flared with angry intensity. A cloak
of darkness seemed to enfold the *dando*'s form, obscuring from view all but those two glowing coals that
served him for eyes. Shadows suddenly filled the
room, and even the weird crimson light retreated from
the gilt edge of the *prekhit*.

Eric felt the creature's rage like an electric current
on his skin.

Then Phlogis regained his self-control. The shadows
retreated, and the light returned to what passed for
normal within this special sanctum.

Listen carefully, Son of Paradane, Phlogis began.
There was a tense edge to his thoughts. They scraped
the surface of Eric's mind like a carefully handled
razor. *Two months ago some force dared to attack the
governor of Shadark in his own palace in Pedrah.*

Eric raised one eyebrow at such news. The tactics
of the Domains were purely defensive. They fought to
hold territory against the Dark Lands and never
launched incursions of their own. "Successfully, I
hope," he answered curtly.

Quite successfully, came Phlogis's grim answer. *By
all reports, Carad Thorn was left a mindless husk. But
there is more, Eric Podlowsky.*

Roderigo Diez sighed wearily and whispered to Eric. "This is the problem with ghosts, *mi amigo*." He rolled his eyes and gave a weary sigh. "Living men may age and die in the time in takes ghosts to come to the point."

Valis overheard and stifled a snort of amusement.

If Phlogis had heard, he gave no indication of it. *One month later,* the spectral figure continued, *a similar attack transpired in Kardoom. That state's governor was left in the same condition. Two weeks after that, in Nazrakh—*

"Somebody's turning Shandal Karg's glorified henchmen into zombies," Eric cut in. "More power to them, I say. It's about time somebody stuck it to that bitch."

The members of the Tarjeel looked at him with stunned expressions. Maris gave a small gasp of shock and made a warning gesture in the air.

Eric frowned, mildly irritated by the council's reaction. "Sorry," he grumbled. It was forbidden to speak out loud the true name of the Heart of Darkness. That he did so sometimes in private with his friends did not excuse him in a formal session with the Tarjeel. He looked to Phlogis again. "So, how'd you learn all this, and what's it got to do with me?"

"We have spies, Eric," Maris answered, lifting her head proudly. "Men and more. Phlogis is not the only spirit who seeks revenge on the Heart of Darkness."

Phlogis's thoughts came ice-tinged. *Do you still think your brother survived the fires of Chol-Hecate?*

Alanna stepped suddenly forward. "Robert?" she cried. "You think he has a hand in these attacks?"

Eric's breath caught in his throat at the mention of his brother's name. For a long time he had hoped that somehow Robert and Katherine Dowd had both managed to escape the disastrous forest fire that had separated them all on the border between Chol-Hecate and Wystoweem. Six months had gone by since then. In that time Eric suddenly realized that he had, in fact, given up such hope.

At the same time, he knew that Alanna, who loved his brother, had never lost hope. He glanced at her now. Her expression was bright and grim at the same time, almost frightening in its intensity.

"I searched the ruins and the surrounding countryside for weeks," he reported in a voice thick with emotion. A vision of Katherine Dowd's face flashed across his mind as he spoke—Katherine, who'd loved him since they were children. "The devastation was awesome. There was no way they could have escaped the flames."

"We never found any trace of them," Alanna interjected hotly, reminding him that she had also helped search. She turned from Phlogis to Eric. "We escaped. It's possible Robert did, also."

Eric's brow creased with pain, a stinging in the corners of his eyes. "In those flames bodies would have been ..." He couldn't finish the sentence.

He thought he'd put his grief away, but it was still with him as strong as ever—grief and more. For surviving when his brother and lover had not, he felt a consuming guilt.

We think Robert Podlowsky lives, Phlogis stated. *We think he is leading this invisible force that has so far destroyed three of her most powerful allies. Not just governors, mind you, but sorcerers as well.*

"Why?" Eric shouted, enraged that Phlogis might hold out such a hope to him without proof. He wanted it to be true. He wanted his brother to be alive, and Katherine, too. But he needed more than just words and suspicions, even from Phlogis, before he allowed himself to believe.

The thoughts of the *dando* leader shivered through the sanctum. *Show it to him.*

A councilman whose face was concealed beneath his voluminous hood strode toward Eric and held out an object wrapped in gleaming white silk. As he put it into Eric's hand, however, the crimson light seemed to dance on it, staining the fabric the color of blood.

It cost a good woman her life to bring this to us from Nazrakh, Phlogis reported as Eric slowly unwrapped the delicate material. *But she placed it into the hands of another before she died. That one carried it by foot across the deserts of the Dark Lands and the mountains of the Gray Kingdoms until he reached Domain territory. A* sekouren *courier brought it the rest of the way to place it in Maris's hand.*

Eric let the silk wrapping fall to the floor. Revealed in his hand was a thin sliver of edged metal. A cold chill crept up his spine, followed by a barely contained rush of hope.

A shuriken. Thoughts racing, he turned the narrow blade over and over in his hands.

Small and simple though it was, such a blade should not exist on this world of Palenoc. No warrior carried edged weapons of any kind into combat, not even the Dark Land soldiers. The fear of killing was far too great.

Valis bent closer for a better look. Alanna's eyes lifted up to meet Eric's. They both knew the truth.

Robert was alive.

Chapter Five

THE sun fell slowly and gracefully behind the western hills of Karakis. Alizarin streamers stretched across the sky like fingers poised to pull down the curtain of night.

Katherine Dowd stood at the mouth of the cave that was her home and watched the last hours of daylight fade. She was tired and dirty, and her clothes were no more than rags. Yet, she felt completely at peace.

As it grew darker, she dared to venture outside. The cool breeze felt as good as a shower. She smiled and thought of her own world, of New York and the Catskills and a small town called Dowdsville. She thought of showers and baths and scented soaps and oil beads.

She gave a little laugh, a soft tinkling sound, sweet as wind chimes, as she chided herself. Such luxuries had little to do with her present reality. She padded quietly up the hill. The grass, still warm with the day's heat, tickled her bare feet. The trees rustled, and crickets began their lullabies.

At the hill's summit Katherine sat clumsily, folded her legs under her, and turned her face to the bejeweled heavens. How quickly the Palenoc nights came on, she reflected. Her gaze swept over the darkening hills. The deepening shadows seemed to whisper to her. Off to her right a thin, trickling waterfall, barely aglimmer with starlight, murmured.

For a while she could sit here and think of the beautifully forested slopes of her beloved Catskills where she used to hike and wander, where all her favorite times and many of her favorite memories were centered. She remembered nights spent on her back porch, staring at those legend-haunted peaks as she listened to the rustle of the pines and maples, the creak of her swing, the muffled voices of children playing hide-and-seek down the street.

She thought of Eric Podlowsky and smiled. In her mind's eye she saw him, a huge man in his postman's uniform, muscled legs revealed in blue shorts, a hat cocked on his head, a leather bag on one shoulder. On her days off from the library, he would pass her box on the picket fence and bring the mail to her door, and sometimes they'd exchange a surreptitious kiss before he went on with his rounds.

Of course, there were other times, too, times when they couldn't stand the sight of each other. But those memories were too faint to cling to now.

Eric was gone, lost months ago in the great fire with his brother, Robert, and she was left alone on this strange world called Palenoc with no way home.

Well, not quite alone. She put one gentle hand on her swollen belly and smiled wanly. "You would have liked your daddy, baby," she said softly. "He was an ass sometimes, like all men. But his heart was bigger than the sky."

She glanced up again. The stars glittered like diamonds. It would be an hour yet before Thanador rose over the hilltops with tag-along Mianur. Plenty of time to sit and quietly tell her baby stories of a world that seemed farther and farther away and more and more like something she had dreamed. Had there ever really been a place called Dowdsville?

A subtle movement off to her left caught her eye. She jerked around sharply, then relaxed. A pale young woman stood silently watching her from between a pair of slender trees. Her face wore a sad expression, and her eyes were luminous. A ghost, Katy realized, more specifically a shade, a harmless wandering soul.

Nor had the shade come alone to this isolated hilltop. Katherine glanced slowly around. Scattered shyly and at a respectful distance among the trees on this summit, a small host of phantoms attended her. They no longer frightened Katherine as they once did. She was used to them, even felt a strange empathy with them.

It puzzled her, though, that these spirits took such an interest in her. They had provided a weird sort of comfort and companionship on her long journey across the Dark Land nation of Chol-Hecate where she'd lost Eric and Robert. Now that she found herself in Karakis in the Gray Kingdoms and too pregnant to continue her trek to Guran, they yet remained with her. Sometimes, only one or two appeared when she found herself alone. Sometimes, like now, many clustered around, silently observing her every move.

Farther down the hillside another shadow stirred. From the way it moved, it was plainly no ghost. Katherine froze, daring not even to breathe as she hugged her arms protectively over her belly.

A scrabbling figure limped into view, one arm in a makeshift sling. He was no more than a tousle-haired boy. Even in the darkness his face appeared flushed with excitement.

"Sparrow!" Katherine hissed sharply. "You scared

the living hell out of me!" She wasn't angry at the boy, though, but at herself. For nothing more than a sunset, she had put herself and her child at risk by wandering away from the cave when the hills were full of raiders and Dark Land soldiers.

"What's hell?" Sparrow whispered back, his eyes fixed expectantly on her face. "Another of your wonderful stories?" He had a vast curiosity about the world she came from, a world his people called Paradane.

"Never mind!" she snapped sternly. "What are you doing sneaking out of the cave?"

"Matterine sent me to fetch you," he answered with a defensive tone. "Everybody knows you sneak up here."

She didn't miss the veiled, mildly petulant accusation in the word "sneak." His pouty expression caused her to smile secretly. Sparrow was one of her favorites among the children of the Kirringskal. Of course, she tried not to let him know that.

"She says you'd better come quick," Sparrow continued, his eyes growing wide again as he remembered the message he was supposed to bring her. "Crow and Falcon found a man in the village. A Darklander. They brought him here."

Katherine Dowd caught Sparrow's offered hand and let him help her to her feet. Pregnancy made her awkward. She was six months along, by her own estimate, but it felt like ten. Still, she descended the hillside as fast as she could manage.

"He's got the sickness," Sparrow supplied as he preceded her.

"And they brought him into the cave?" Katherine snapped.

Sparrow didn't answer. A pair of men armed with

staves stood outside the cave entrance, watching the valley below. "A Darklander?" Katherine said to them, and they both nodded. Shaking her head in consternation, she strode inside.

Matterine stood waiting with an oil lamp to light the way. "Was he alone?" Katherine asked hurriedly as Matterine led her deeper into the darkness of the cavernous space. "What if someone's looking for him?"

Matterine stopped and pushed back a strand of iron gray hair as she regarded Katherine. The lamplight made her old eyes gleam. "He had the sickness," she answered crisply. "No one's going to look for him." She beckoned and led the way again. "Besides, he's not a warrior."

The tunnel turned sharply and opened into a wide, domed chamber. Perhaps twenty people huddled in the shadows, all that remained of the Kirringskal. The few pitiful belongings they'd been able to salvage lay scattered around. A small fire burned on a stone shelf, providing warmth and a yellowish light.

The Darklander reclined on a pallet of blankets in the center of the cavern. A pair of women bent over him, pouring water over his lips. A feverish sweat dampened a once-handsome face made gaunt by the disease. His black hair hung in wet ropes. Despite the sweat, he trembled, wracked with chills.

"Can you help him, *Shayana*?" Matterine asked quietly. "Not even a Darklander should die like this."

Katherine chewed a corner of her lip and let one of the women help her kneel down beside the Darklander. She noted his garments—expensive leather and silks ruined with filth. On his left hand he wore a ring, an opal that glimmered with fantastic fire, despite the dirt caked in its elaborate gold setting.

Adjusting her swollen body as comfortably as she could, she leaned close to him. "Where are you from, Darklander?"

His eyes struggled to focus on her face. His cracked lips quivered as he spoke a few barely audible words in a language Katherine couldn't understand.

Matterine bent closer and spoke in the same tongue. The Darklander answered weakly. "He's come a long way," the old woman reported. "From Pedrah in the land of Shadark."

Katherine touched the sick man's cheek. His skin felt paper thin and radiated heat. Beneath his sweat-saturated garments he was little more than bones.

"I found him in the ruins of the village, *Shayana*," said a deep voice just behind Katherine. "He was slumped over the well, too weak to scoop a drink of water with his hand."

She glanced over her shoulder and nodded to Falcon, one of the few Kirringskal hunters to survive the surprise raid on their village by black-masked Chols two nights ago. "He's dehydrated," she said. "But for you, he might have died of thirst with water inches from his lips."

"We scavenged a couple barrels of grain, too," Falcon continued as he looked past her to stare at the Darklander. "There'll be food soon."

"Any sign of the Chols?" she asked.

"We saw no soldiers," the broad-chested hunter answered, "but Crow spied a pair of *chimorgs* in the next valley just before dusk."

Katherine cursed silently and turned her attention back to the Darklander. "Ask him his name," she murmured to Matterine. As the old woman spoke, Katherine stooped and placed a wet cloth on the Darklander's head.

With painful effort he shaped the words. "Cha Mak Nul."

Katherine raised an eyebrow. Matterine looked back at her and shrugged her thin shoulders. "Cha Mak Nul," the older woman repeated. "He may be from Shadark, but that's the ancient high tongue of Srimourna."

Katherine frowned at the mention of that dreaded land. "How about if I just call you Mac?" she said to her patient.

The Darklander closed his eyes as he turned his head away. The tip of his tongue licked weakly over his lips.

The rest of the Kirringskal crept out of the shadows to gather around. Women, children, and the few remaining men all shuffled closer and formed a curious ring around Katherine and the Darklander. Sparrow broke through the ring with a cup of water carried carefully in his good hand. Wide-eyed, he offered it to her.

Katherine brought the cup to her lips and paused as she surveyed their expectant faces over the earthen rim. These were decent people, she reflected, kindhearted people, and it pained her that so many of their friends and relatives had been dragged away to the slave pens or starvation camps by the Chols and other Darklanders like the one before her. They knew little of violence, these Kirringskal, but they took care of each other, and they had taken her in as one of their own.

Now they had brought this one, this Shadarkan, home like a stray injured kitten, no matter that he was an enemy and a follower of the Heart of Darkness, or that he carried a horrible disease that had already ravaged much of the Gray Kingdoms.

She closed her eyes and pressed her palms together. In little more than an instant they became hot in a manner she did not yet understand. With a strange new inner sight she could see an azure glow surrounding her hands, a radiance that no one else could see. She could not say how she knew what to do, nor why; without further thought she reached out and placed her right hand on the Darklander's head, her left on his stomach.

The gentlest of sighs escaped his lips as he lay unresisting beneath her touch.

The glow spread from her hands, becoming a blue fire that slowly engulfed the Darklander. Pale energy rippled over and through him, sparking and flaring with pinpoint brilliance. He trembled beneath her touch and sighed again.

Then the energy faded, and Katherine's hands were cool once more. For a moment she sat perfectly still, frightened by this unexplainable power of hers. A sudden fatigue washed over her, just as it had when she drove the sickness from Matterine's body and when she healed Sparrow's crushed body after the raid.

Falcon caught her as she slumped sideways, and he held her in strong arms until she recovered enough to sit with little assistance. When Matterine pressed the cup of water to her lips again and urged her to drink, Katherine obeyed meekly.

"How is he?" she managed after a second swallow.

Matterine took the damp cloth from the Shadarkan's head and pressed the back of her old hand to his brow, then to his cheek. "The fever has eased," she reported.

Katherine shook her head wearily. "It wasn't enough," she said. "I wasn't strong enough."

"Patience, *Shayana*," Falcon told her with a supporting arm still draped around her shoulders. "Let it take several times, just as it did with Matterine. As it did with Sparrow. The Darklander is out of danger for the moment. Do more when you are able."

Katherine experienced a twinge of guilt as she glanced at Sparrow and the sling on his small arm. "I have to finish with you," she murmured as the first edges of unwanted sleep reached out for her.

The boy smiled so easily. "You put me back together again, *Shayana,*" he answered as Matterine drew him into a motherly embrace. "Like the Humpty-Dumpty story you told me." He slipped his injured arm from the sling and flexed it stiffly, completely unaware that she'd changed the ending just for him. "This will finish healing now on its own."

The Shadarkan who called himself Cha Mak Nul gave a soft groan. "He's sleeping," Matterine reported.

"Me, too," Katherine Dowd whispered as her head rolled back onto Falcon's shoulder.

The days turned gray and damp. Katherine watched from the mouth of the cave or, sometimes, from her favorite spot atop the hill. It was dangerous to venture outside, however. The Dark Land raiders had apparently moved on, but the Kirringskal hunters reported numerous sightings of *chimorgs* in the woods.

Matterine had directed the women in the weaving of a vine-and-grass curtain to disguise the cave entrance. With *chimorgs* so close no cooking was allowed. The beasts' sensitive snouts would detect the smoke and aroma. Only the small fire on the rock shelf was permitted, to provide a minimum of light and warmth. The people ate handfuls of uncooked grain, and the hunters brought back only roots and tubers and berries that could be consumed raw.

The baby inside her body began to kick. Katherine sighed uncomfortably and leaned against the cave wall while she held aside the grass curtain with one hand so she could continue to peer out. "Be still, little one," she whispered, placing her other hand on top of her belly. "You're in too big of a rush!"

"Are you keeping careful watch, *Shayana*?"

Sparrow crept up out of the tunnel darkness and grinned at her. His arm was no longer in the sling, and his limp was gone. Silent laughter sparkled in his young eyes, and that made Katherine's heart light. Wherever the strange healing power she seemed to wield came from, she blessed it for letting her save this little boy.

"Just breathing the fresh air, Sparrow," she answered. She didn't try to explain how she hated the cave and the darkness. She could almost feel the crushing weight of the earth over her head. When she let herself think about it, her chest tightened and her breaths turned shallow and labored. The fear was not so bad as it once was, though. Palenoc had changed her in lots of ways, and this was not the first cave she'd been forced to use for shelter. Still, she spent as much time outside as safety and wisdom allowed, or lingered near the mouth, like now, with her eyes on the far horizon.

"Does he ever answer you?" Sparrow asked abruptly. He leaned close and put his ear to Katherine's belly.

She smiled softly and patted the boy's head. His hair was silky and jet black. Even in the thin, gray light that seeped through the curtain, it gleamed. "I'm not sure," she told him mock-seriously. "All his kicking might be a code."

Sparrow seemed to accept that as a straight answer. He nodded sagely and stood back. He then turned away from her and gazed through the gap in the curtain. A light mist, not quite a rain, fell from the iron gray sky. The hills beyond looked lush and green and moist, and tendrils of fog slithered through the valley below.

"I wish we could go outside," the boy said.

Katherine didn't answer as she slipped an arm around his shoulders and drew him close again. She pushed the curtain a bit wider so they could both look out together.

She wondered when it would be safe for the Kirringskal to leave the cave and begin to rebuild their homes. She wondered about the villagers the raiders had dragged away, those who would probably never see homes and families again.

Eric had told her about the Dark Land starvation camps where captives were imprisoned and allowed to die very slowly. It wasn't murder, and it wasn't violent, so few ghosts were created, and fewer still of the vengeful kind called *dandos*.

It had taken her time to understand this strange world and its ghosts. When most people died, their souls ascended quietly to Paradise, a place of rest, before ultimately becoming part of something called *Or-Dhamu*, a kind of collective spiritual consciousness.

But when violence or sudden accident resulted in death, the soul refused to rest. A *dando* would haunt its murderer, or an *apparition* would linger at the scene of its death. Over time both of these could change—evolve—into other kinds of ghosts. A *dando* unable to obtain revenge might become an *ankou*, a malevolent spirit possessed of tremendous, but completely unfocused power. They might, over time, further evolve into *screamers*, or *banshees*, or *leikkios*. *Apparitions* might slowly turn into *shades* or *chills*.

There were still other kinds of specters and phantoms, an entire evolution in the afterlife. She didn't understand it all and wondered if she would ever understand.

Far down the hillside Falcon appeared, staff in one hand, his game bag slung over one shoulder. He was soaked to the skin, his long hair plastered to his face and shoulders. He hurried up the slope, his head turning from side to side as his watchful gaze swept around.

Katherine pulled the grass curtain aside to allow him entry.

"A miserable day, *Shayana*," he muttered as he shook himself and unslung his bag. "Charberries," he said to Sparrow as he dipped his hand into the bag and pulled out a couple of plump black berries. He popped them into Sparrow's eager mouth, then passed him the bag. "Take them to Matterine," he instructed, and Sparrow obeyed, disappearing swiftly down the dark tunnel.

"How's the Shadarkan?" Falcon asked when they were alone.

"On his feet," Katherine answered with a small sigh of weariness. "Barely."

Together they walked away from the cave mouth to join the others deeper inside. "Be careful around him," Falcon warned in a quiet voice. "He looks at you strangely. He notices your hair."

Katherine frowned as she ran one hand over her red mane. Her hair color was unknown on Palenoc. For most of her trek across the Dark Lands she'd kept it hidden under a hood. Here, among the Kirringskal where she felt safe, she hadn't bothered. "Maybe I should cover my head again," she suggested.

Falcon shrugged. "Why hide what he's already seen?" he answered pragmatically. "Just be careful,

Shayana. This Darklander watches you all the time, every move you make. I know, because I watch him."

Katherine pinched his biceps through the wet sleeve of his shirt. "You're better than a big brother. I'm grateful for all you and your people have done for me, you know."

"It's we who owe you gratitude, *Shayana*," he answered firmly.

"*Shayana* again!" she responded, changing the subject. "I've asked you before what that's supposed to mean. My name is Katherine. Or Katy to my friends."

Falcon only smiled and kept silent. But a few paces later, he volunteered, "It means little mother."

They reached the inner cavern, and Falcon strode to the fire to warm himself. He leaned his staff against the shelf and peeled off his damp shirt. His eyes went straight to the Darklander.

The man who called himself Cha Mak Nul sat up on a rough pallet not far from the fire. He held a small bowl of grain just under his chin. Using only his fingers to eat, he lifted a few hard kernels and placed them on his tongue. His gaze, however, was fixed on Katherine.

She went to him. "You're looking better," she commented, keeping her voice low.

Not far away, Matterine overheard. She smiled at the small girl-child to whom she had been telling a story, smoothed the child's hair, then put her down from her lap. Rising, she came to Katherine's side. "You want me to translate, *Shayana*?"

Katherine nodded.

Gathering her skirts, Matterine squatted before the Darklander and spoke to him. His answer was little more than a morose whisper. When he finished speaking, he stared down at the ring on his finger. The fiery opal flashed brilliantly even in the dim light.

Matterine eyed the ring and its wearer as she spoke over her shoulder to Katherine. "He says he was supposed to die. We've interfered and prevented him from fulfilling his duty."

Katherine raised one eyebrow. "Well, excuse me all to hell," she said. "Tell him there's a tall cliff down by the waterfall, and when he feels strong enough, he's welcome to jump off it. It'll be quicker than the sickness."

She started to turn away, leaving Matterine to translate, but the Darklander stopped her with a rush of words that was aimed over the old woman's head directly at her.

Katherine waited expectantly, but Matterine seemed reluctant. "What'd he say?" she pressed.

Matterine wrapped one arm around her knees and pushed back wisps of gray hair with her other hand. "He wants to know how you saved him," Matterine said hesitantly. The Darklander leaned forward, listening intently, his gaze fixed on Katherine's face. Matterine swallowed, continuing. "He wants to know if you used crystal"—she hesitated and swallowed again—"or if you used blood magic."

Before Katherine could react, Matterine suddenly stood to block the Darklander's view. "I don't like this question," she said sharply, "nor the way he looks at you, *Shayana*." She turned suddenly, seized Mac's bowl, and set it aside, scolding him as she pushed him back down on his pallet. "You should not be sitting up," she said, throwing an extra blanket over him. "Shadarkan you may be, and a grown man as well, but when I tell you to rest, I mean rest."

The Darklander started to protest, and Matterine

let fly a string of words in his own language as she shook a finger at the end of his nose.

Katherine left them to argue and drifted to the far side of the cave where she dipped her hand into a barrel of fresh water and sipped from her palm. Then she dipped in both hands and laved her face. The cool contact refreshed her.

Sparrow tugged at her elbow. "Falcon said to give this to you." He handed her a bowl with a sticky, orange root in it. It smelled honey-sweet, and a small wisp of steam rose from it. She glanced in surprise across the cavern to Falcon. He had violated his own rule and warmed it by the fire for her!

She strode to the fire and handed the bowl back to him. "I won't eat hot food until all the Kirringskal can," she said firmly.

He pushed the bowl back into her hands. "You need the nourishment," he insisted. "It was no great danger to warm a single root. And it is already done."

Katherine glared stubbornly and thrust the bowl at him again. Falcon locked his hands behind his back, his expression just as stubborn.

"Well, all right, then!" Katherine snapped. "I'll eat it. But not until it's turned stone-cold." She stuck out her tongue triumphantly and went to her own pallet where she kept her few personal possessions in an old worn backpack in a shadowy corner near the tunnel. There she gathered her blanket and draped it around her shoulders, then sank down against the wall and placed the bowl at her feet to let it cool. She glanced at Falcon to make sure he was watching.

But Falcon was watching the Shadarkan. The Shadarkan was watching her.

Chapter Six

DEEP in the bowels of Boraga, Gaultnimble walked softly, his velvet-slippered footsteps making not the slightest sound. A tiny oil lamp cast a dim pool of radiance against the nearly impenetrable darkness that filled the ancient passages. Rather than holding the lamp high, the dwarvish little man hugged it close to his chest and shielded it jealously with one hand as if he were trying to hoard the light.

Stopping suddenly, he cast a furtive glance over his shoulder. The light shone on his sallow cheek, revealing a black bruise along the high bone. Ever so slightly he turned and moved his hand from the lamp, allowing the edge of the light to creep back up the way he had come. His lips parted with a barely uttered gasp of fear.

Then he grinned with relief. A yellow cat came padding out of the gloom. Tail high, it rubbed against his ankle and purred, then circled his feet, weaving between them, rubbing, until he bent down and ran his hand over its soft head and along its furred spine. Arching its back to meet his touch, it purred more loudly.

Gaultnimble's fingers curled tightly around the cat's throat. He lifted it until only its hind feet remained on the floor. Its wide green eyes gleamed fearfully in the lamplight. "*Shhhh,* little Pusskins!" he whispered sternly to his pet. "Not a sound tonight."

The cat swiped at the back of his hand. Its claws drew a fine line of blood from the yellowish, tissue-thin skin. Gaultnimble released the animal and licked appreciatively at the tiny wound. He grinned again and tickled the cat's pink nose with a fingertip. "Behave yourself, you little bitch," he warned in a silken, half-playful murmur. "Remember, you've got four more kittens."

Rising, he cast a final glance along the way he had come. Nothing back there but his tiptoe footprints and the fainter marks of Pusskin's paws in the thick pounce. With the cat following, he moved on.

A low keening issued abruptly from the darkness ahead. Gaultnimble froze, the hair prickling on the back of his neck. The sound rose to a sharp wail, eerily subsided, then swelled once more. *A banshee?* Gaultnimble wondered fearfully. But his mistress had renewed and strengthened her wards, driving all the ghosts from her palace. It surely couldn't be a *banshee.*

Tiny legs quivering, Gaultnimble mustered his courage. Step by step he crept toward that dreadful sound. Without warning something brushed across his face. The lamp's flame flickered crazily and threatened to go out. He bit his lip to keep from crying aloud with fright even as he cupped one hand protectively around his small light.

Pusskins padded right by him with an air of unconcern and disappeared beyond the wavering circle of illumination.

The keening rose yet again. And again something brushed his face and his throat, too. His heart skipped a beat. Then he clapped a hand to his mouth to stifle a nervous laugh. Immediately, however, he used that hand to shield his flame again.

The wind! Somewhere ahead a window must be open. It was only the wind whistling through one of the narrow crenellations! So certain was he of his deduction that he ran on tiptoe until, indeed, he came upon the portal. It was twice as tall as he, but only as wide as his diminutive shoulders.

Perched on the sill, Pusskins licked one paw and mewed.

"Don't laugh at me, kitty," Gaultnimble whispered softly. "Your soft hide would make a fine pair of gloves."

The cat hopped down and paced the floor as Gaultnimble set down his lamp. The bottom of the window stood as high as his chest. He had never before heard the wind sing like that through a window, and curiosity seized him to view what lay beyond that opening. With an effort he hoisted himself up and leaned his elbows on the sill. His toes kicked and scrambled at the wall as he squeezed his shoulders through the narrow crenellation. A moment later he hung halfway out and looked around.

The wind sang again, snatching the cap from his head, sending it sailing high into the air, spinning and tumbling on the currents, and when the wind died just as suddenly, it fell with floating grace down, down, down into the black and yawning depths of Srimourna's great canyon.

Gaultnimble caught his breath as he stared into that abyss. Boraga extended deep within the canyon walls just as it soared high above them. From the unfathomable depths, his gaze traveled up the canyon's far wall, and he stifled yet another cry before it could quite escape his lips.

The shadow of a monstrous hand hung upon the opposite wall, an ominous warning telling him to stop, to turn back. But it wasn't a hand, he told himself, reasoning hastily and licking his lips. It was only the sillhouette of Boraga's five towers. The moon, Thanador, must be in the western sky. It was the moonlight—that's what it was!—that created that huge shadow.

He turned his gaze toward the sky even as the wind rose again and whipped about his face. Against the black night he spied a peppering of stars and the faintest edge of Mianur's blue ring.

The cat, forgotten, stretched upward and nipped at his ankle, and Gaultnimble's heart lurched again. "Don't do that!" he scolded in a hiss as he dropped to the floor. The cat ran to the edge of the light, sat down, and stared at him.

The little dwarf paused long enough to glance back up the corridor, but blackness had thoroughly filled the wake of his small light. He picked up his lamp. Pusskins fell in beside him and rubbed up against his leg. Together they continued on, leaving the window and the mournful singing of the wind.

The passage descended suddenly in a flight of stone steps and joined with another, smaller tunnel. Gaultnimble lifted his lamp a bit higher. The cat never strayed far from the little man's feet now. Its tail lashed back and forth, and it paused frequently to look up at him with a luminous gaze.

Finally, the tunnel ended. The fragile light fell upon a plain, unornamented door with a silver ring tarnished almost black for a handle. The wood of the door felt damp and moldy as Gaultnimble placed his palm against it and gave a timid push.

The creak of old hinges sounded unnervingly loud

in the subterranean quiet. An uncontrollable shiver seized Gaultnimble as he watched the door swing halfway open, then stop. The blackness beyond appeared densely solid. Even the lamplight seemed reluctant to cross that threshold. Pusskin curled up behind the little dwarf's feet and peered between his ankles.

A bone-numbing cold exuded from the room into the passage. When Gaultnimble dared to let go of the breath he'd been holding, it came out as a white, steamy cloud. When he inhaled again, the frigid air raked his throat and lungs.

The cat leaped up and ran ten paces back down the corridor and hunkered down in the gloom, eyes staring, ears twitching, hind legs quivering as if it were deciding whether to flee even farther.

"Coward," Gaultnimble muttered scornfully, drawing courage from the animal's retreat. He looked at the door and chewed his lip. He looked at the threshold. He looked at his feet. Lips trembled. "Move, legs," he said in a nervous whisper.

Slowly, obediently, one foot lifted from the floor and stepped over the threshold. Gaultnimble swallowed as the other foot followed. He was inside. No turning back now, not that he'd ever intended to turn back. He raised the lamp and peered around the edge of the door. Almost of its own accord, the door swung wider.

The light suddenly fell on a glittering white coffin, the only thing that occupied the room. Gaultnimble caught his breath again, and his heart thundered in his chest. "Hello, my friend," he murmured softly.

He allowed himself a small, terrible grin as a measure of his fear left him. An expression of purest malice and unquenchable evil slowly lit up his round face, and the lamplight danced in his eyes. He put one hand to his cheekbone and touched the tender bruise that extended from the corner of his right eye to his ear.

Did his mistress think she was clever to conceal the coffin so deep in the rarely visited levels of the keep? Gaultnimble smirked. He was more clever, and he was persistent. Patience, he told himself, was his greatest virtue.

For nearly a year the coffin had rested in Boraga's throne room where his mistress could fawn or gloat over it, until, without word or warning, on a full-moon night She decided to hide her favorite trophy. No amount of prodding or teasing from her fool could convince her to reveal where or why. She had her reasons and her secrets, was all She would say.

Well, so did Gaultnimble. He began his own quest, and after weeks of cautious, room-by-room searching, he stood before the coffin once again.

He crept on tiptoe to the coffin and placed a fingertip against it. Flesh tingled at the contact. The coffin was ice, white and shimmering. Raising himself as tall as he could, he studied the seamless construction in the lamplight.

Without warning, Pusskins bounded up onto the top of the coffin, settling inches from Gaultnimble's face. The startled servant barely stifled a terrified outcry. Fear turned to rage. That a mere cat should scare him so! He drew back his hand and knocked Pusskins across the room. The cat screeched as it twisted desperately in midair to land on its feet, and sped out the door.

Gaultnimble stared after the little beast, his heart hammering. Fear filled him again. He ran to the door, half afraid he would see her stalking down the passage, coming for him. He touched the bruise once

more. Nothing She had ever done to him would match
what She would do if She caught him here.

Half frantic, he pushed the door shut, all but for a
small crack, then ran to the coffin. Perched on a bier,
it was too high for him to work. He set the lamp on
the floor and spent a few desperate moments attempting with his meager strength to push and lift one
end. If he could get the coffin onto the floor . . .

It wouldn't budge. It was as if coffin and bier were
all of one piece, and all his efforts were in vain. Gaultnimble cursed silently and rubbed his half-frozen
hands together, his mind racing. At last, he grabbed
up the lamp. If he couldn't bring the coffin down to
him, he'd go up to the coffin.

Stretching up on tiptoe again, he set the lamp near
the coffin's head. He caught the edge with his fingers
and opened his mouth in a soundless scream at the
cold, shocking contact. He muscled himself off the
floor, his feet kicking at the air. One velvet slipper
flew across the room to fall softly in a corner. Still, he
struggled, grunted, and groaned, and managed at last
to haul himself atop the coffin.

Kneeling upon it, he shoved raw, tortured fingers
into his mouth as tears spilled down his cheeks. Then
he sat up stiffly, his face hardening. His life was nothing now. It would be less than nothing if he failed to
finish his task.

Ignoring the cold that stabbed through his trousers,
through his socks and one slipper, ignoring his fear,
he reached inside his waistband and brought forth a
tiny blade. The lamplight gleamed on the razor edge
as he held it up. Without hesitation he raked his
thumb along it. Thick blood welled up.

"I love to receive pain, Mistress," he mumbled to
himself as he pressed his thumb to the coffin's lid and

drew a peculiar line with his own life fluid. "But little do You know how I love to give it." He drew another line, then paused to squeeze his wound, to call up more blood for his artwork.

He scooted around the sides of the coffin as he painted an elaborate pattern in scarlet on the shining white ice. Three more times he sliced his fingers, opening new fountains for his palette.

When it was done, he returned the blade to his waistband and brought out a second tool, which he held up to his eyes—a delicate silver hammer, crafted by his own hand from melted dishes and vessels he had pilfered from the palace, a hammer that had never struck a blow.

He laughed lowly to himself. How She would wonder in the nights to come where he had learned this magic! Never, never would he tell. It would be his secret forever. She would demand to know, and he would laugh. But he would never tell, and thus would he torment Her.

He touched a finger to the hammer's flat head, depositing a single drop of ruby blood. The tool seemed to tingle in his hand as if it were coming to life within his grasp!

His gaze fixed on the exact center of the pattern he had made on the coffin lid. "May your pain be long and personal, my most deserving Mistress," he murmured with a smug grin. He raised the hammer and swung it down with a crashing blow.

The impact brought no sound at all. It was as if the darkness sponged up every vibration. Gaultnimble's head snapped up in surprise and disbelief. Disbelief swiftly gave way to terror. He stared at the hammer, then dropped it. He regarded the pattern made from his own blood.

Something was wrong! The lid had not shattered. Her spells still held this cursed box sealed!

He had doomed himself, and all for nothing!

With a shriek of despair he leaped off the coffin, leaving behind his hammer and lamp and one velvet slipper. As swiftly as his stunted legs could carry him, he flung open the door and ran into the darkness. The passage echoed with his moans and whimpers.

Pusskins uncurled from a corner on the outer side of the door and padded softly after him with an air of feline superiority.

Inside the room the lamp continued to burn. Then, in the silence, came a sound, a short, sharp crack. A dark crevice formed along one line of Gaultnimble's pattern. A second fissure, then a third. Suddenly, cracks radiated across the lid, and a piece of the coffin fell suddenly inward.

For a long moment there was no other sound except the hissing of the slowly burning wick.

A pale hand reached up through that icy fissure.

Chapter Seven

ROBERT tossed back the last of his second club soda and wiped a trickle of perspiration from his brow. The bar was warm and crowded tonight. People squeezed by one another, exchanging grins and barely audible apologies. Everyone was in a good mood. Why not? The whole weekend lay ahead.

In the farthest corner of the bar someone plunked merrily on an old grand piano. A small throng had gathered around the player, and a dozen voices all strained toward the high notes of Weber's "Music of the Night."

From the basement of the bar rose a different kind of music. A heavy disco backbeat filtered through the floor and up the ominous-looking black spiral staircase that descended from a shadowy corner back by the coat check.

An odor of stale sweat lingered in the air, mixed with the auras of amyl and butyl nitrates, the diverse sweet smells of alcohol, colognes, and aftershaves, and dominating it all, the usual fog of tobacco. No matter how many times the door opened and new customers entered, fresh air simply refused to cross the threshold.

Robert loved the place. He was riding high on life, and the party atmosphere suited him. His new book,

A Pale Knock, was sailing toward the best-seller lists, a first for him. And he'd just returned from nearly a year's worth of travels in the Far East. His foot tapped on the rail in time to the beat that vibrated up through the floor. He felt like dancing and glanced toward the spiral staircase.

A touch at his elbow made him turn. He smiled at his friend and soon-to-be roommate. "Great crowd tonight, huh, Scott?"

Scott nodded, but a touch of weariness showed in the sag of his shoulders as he leaned on the bar. Sarasota was his hometown, and he hadn't yet adjusted to the pace of New York life.

"Okay," Scott said suddenly. "How about if I move in next Saturday. That'll give me time to fly home and settle things in Florida." He grinned nervously as he stirred the ice in his bourbon and water. Then he looked up suddenly, and the grin turned into a laugh. "We had a great time in China, didn't we? How different can New York be?"

The bartender reached for Robert's empty glass. "Another?" he asked, half shouting over the crowd. Robert shook his head and pointed to Scott's glass. "Two more of those," he said. He didn't drink much, but now that Scott had agreed to move in, he felt like a drink to celebrate.

The bartender brought the drinks. "Hey, you guys twins or something?" he asked as he took the bills Robert offered.

It was a question they'd been asked before. Robert and Scott looked at each other. Scott's blond hair was straight while Robert's was curly, and in the bar lighting no one could tell that one had blue eyes and the other green. But otherwise, they might well have been twins.

"My brother!" Robert shouted, clutching one hand melodramatically over his heart. "He's come back from that bitch he married!"

"Siamese twins," Scott explained with a straight face. "Joined at the apartment."

"Sounds like a kinky arrangement," the bartender answered, pushing Robert's money back before he walked away to serve another customer. "On the house this time."

Robert took a gulp of the strong-tasting bourbon. The vibration coming up through the floor tickled his feet. He glanced at the staircase again, then at his watch. It was nearly midnight—time to dance.

"You go ahead," Scott said. "I think I'll head back to the hotel and pack." He lifted his drink again, adding, "I hate early flights."

Robert clapped his friend on the shoulder. "Hey, the sooner you leave, the sooner you'll be back." He swallowed the contents of his glass and set it down. "I'd better get out of here, too." He glanced wistfully at the staircase. With a sigh he pushed away from the bar. "I can still get a little writing done tonight."

They elbowed their way through the crowd and out the door. The fresh evening air felt like a slap in the face as they stepped out into Grove Street. A taxi moved toward them. "Want to ride?" Robert asked.

"Give me a break," Scott said good-naturedly. "It's all of a couple blocks." He nodded in the direction of Washington Square. The rooftop of the Washington Square Hotel was just visible over on Waverly Place. "You have farther to go, though. Take it if you want."

The cab whisked on by. Robert shook his head as he stared after it. "Nah," he said with a shrug. His apartment, soon to be *their* apartment, was up in Chelsea. It was easily walkable, and he could use the exercise as well as the air. The bourbon had left him with a mild, unwanted buzz.

Scott glanced up and down the street, then held out his hand. "Thanks for putting up with me, Polo," he said sincerely. He always called Robert by his pen name. "New York's been a great capper to our trip. I'll be back as soon as I can."

Robert took Scott's hand in a firm grip, and the gesture became a quick embrace. Scott returned it, then stepped back, looking embarrassed as he glanced at the people who walked around them on the sidewalk.

"Hey," Robert reassured him, "this is the Big Apple. Nobody cares." He slapped Scott on the arm and started walking backward with a jaunty step. "Call me before you leave for the airport," he instructed.

"Sure," Scott answered as he stood in the light from the bulb above the bar's entrance and gave a short wave of farewell. The wind ruffled his hair and the sleeves of his white cotton shirt.

Robert sighed again as he turned and started up the street, an acute sense of emptiness and loss filling him with every step. He thrust his hands into the pockets of his Levi's and increased his pace, taking long strides, ignoring the signal as he crossed to the next block. He hoped Scott could wrap up his affairs in Sarasota quickly. Meanwhile, there were plans to make; for one thing, he had to clear space in the apartment for another person.

A loud pop halted him in midstep. He whirled around as two more pops followed the first. Staring back down the sidewalk, a cold chill crept up his spine. On the opposite side of the street, a woman shrieked. Shouts of warning and fear rose in the night, and a man dragged his wife down behind a car, covering her head with a protective arm.

Scott lay unmoving on the sidewalk, not ten feet from the bar entrance. Five rough-looking punks stood around him. The one with the gun bent down and felt for a wallet, his eyes wide and desperate as his friends shouted at him to hurry, man!

Robert screamed. Then he began to run. The punks saw him and shouted a warning. The one with the gun looked up in panic and squeezed off a shot before his friends deserted him and sped off like frightened mice. He followed right on their heels and they all vanished around a corner.

One knee of Robert's jeans ripped, and cold cement scraped his bare skin as he fell beside Scott's still form. A huge red wetness was rapidly staining Scott's white shirt; his blue eyes were open and frighteningly empty. Robert screamed again, his hands clenching into fists as people emerged from their hiding places and customers streamed from the bar to see what had happened.

Scott's eyes fluttered open. "Polo . . ." he said, and a stream of blood gurgled from the corner of his mouth. Then those eyes misted over, and his head lolled to the side.

"Go after them!" Robert cried, staring up at the swirl of curious onlookers. "Stop them!" But the crowd only murmured and whispered, pressed fingers to mouths, and shook heads. *I'll go after them, then,* he swore to himself. The punks had worn jackets and gang colors, and one face, at least, was burned in his memory. *I'll go after them myself,* he swore again as he slipped an arm under his friend's shoulders and cradled him. *Just as soon as I get Scott home.*

The owner of the bar and the doorman bent down

beside him and tried gently to pull him back. Someone was speaking to him. Then a pair of cops bent down beside him, and the world was flashing with red light.

Robert looked up again, strangely in a world of his own where no sound seemed to exist. His gaze fastened on a word above a doorway. The name of the bar: *The Monster.*

He laughed. Then a wave of pain, deeper and colder than any pain he had ever known, swept over him, drowning his senses, all reason, and he screamed again. . . .

A black hand clamped hard over Robert's mouth, stifling the scream. Robert clutched at a wrist, his eyes snapping wide, his mind filled with disorienting images. Then, in an instant, he remembered where he was.

"You cried out in your sleep," Sulis Tel explained, removing his hand.

A dream, Robert realized. *The same dream.* He rose on one elbow and rubbed a hand over his eyes. His cheeks were moist as if he'd been crying. He wondered if Sulis Tel had noticed?

Slowly, he sat up and brushed the dirt from his sleeves and out of his hair. The hard, dusty ground had been his bed while the sun sank from the sky. The first stars shone in the deepening twilight. Neither Thanador nor Mianur were up yet.

"You dreamed of your friend again," Sulis Tel murmured as he pushed a stoppered bottle into Robert's hands.

"Scott," Robert said distantly as he pulled out the stopper. "Scott Silver." He took a quick drink and looked away.

Images from the dream still haunted him, and he

experienced a shuddering chill. At least he had awakened this time. Sometimes in a longer version of the dream he would stalk the Village streets night after night in search of the gang leader who had gunned down his friend. He would find the punk in a quiet, garbage-strewn alley. He would coldly and methodically beat the punk to death and leave him lying in the stink and the darkness.

He would awake in a cold sweat, sit up shivering. Tonight, though, it had all seemed so much more intense. He had actually screamed. If Sulis Tel hadn't stopped him, he might have jeopardized the lives of his men.

Robert got up suddenly and walked up a slight incline to the edge of a high, rocky scarp. Far below, the city of Abalon squatted like a slim black spider on the flat plain. Shadows from the surrounding hills closed in upon it like a threatening fist.

Sulis Tel crept to Robert's side. He opened the folded blanket that Robert had used as a pillow and draped it around his leader's shoulders. The air was warm enough, and the act was no more than a gesture. The black man wisely knew it was a different kind of cold that chilled Robert Polo.

"Come away and rest," Sulis urged quietly. "There are others watching the city."

"I can't sleep," Robert answered as he drew the blanket closer around his shoulders. Nevertheless, he turned his back to Abalon and started down the incline again. "Too many dreams," he mumbled. "Too many memories." After a pause, he added, "Too much to do."

At the bottom of the slope a caravan of seven wagons waited in the gathering gloom. The *garouns,* huge, oxenlike creatures that pulled the wagons, had been unyoked. The beasts stood hobbled, munching on the sparse grass or merely resting.

Most of the *Sharak-khen* slept on pallets around the wagons. Only six men stood watch around the perimeter. More guards would have looked suspicious. The wagons bore the markings of Chol merchants, and everyone dressed appropriately. To the outward eye it looked to be a quiet caravan, camped for the night. Thus had the *Sharak-khen* made their way undetected through Dark Land territory, striking time and again, seeming to vanish.

Out of the corner of his eye Robert caught a flicker of movement. He stopped in his tracks and stared. Off to his left beside the boll of a long-dead tree stood a pale, featureless shape. An *apparition,* he realized uncomfortably.

"I still haven't figured it out," Robert murmured to himself.

Sulis Tel overheard. "What is that, Son of Paradane?"

Robert frowned as the apparition turned his way, seemed to study him for a moment, then faded from view. "I killed Kajin Kasst," he said in a low voice. His gaze remained locked on the spot where the *apparition* had been, but his thoughts turned back to the Chol leader.

Kajin Kasst called himself a prince of Chol-Hecate —how Robert cursed his memory. Kasst was largely responsible for the deaths of Eric and Katherine. For that reason alone Robert hated the man. But when Robert finally caught up with the prince, almost by accident, Kasst was leading a troop to Chols who were escorting captured Domain soldiers to the starvation camps.

To free those soldiers, Robert fought and killed

Kasst. Some of those liberated captives swore allegiance to him and became his *Sharak-khen*.

"I killed him," Robert repeated. "Where's his ghost? It's been months and months. Isn't it supposed to seek revenge?"

The black man grinned. "Maybe this is his revenge," he said. "The suspense is killing you."

Robert gave him a sidelong glance. "You and Scott would have gotten along great," he said with a hint of distaste. "Same sick sense of humor."

Sulis Tel turned serious again. He pointed to the guards and the sleeping forms around the wagons. "They think it is because you are the *Shae'aluth*," he repeated. "No ghost can harm the Son of the Morning."

"I'm not the *Shae'aluth*," Robert said.

Sulis Tel scratched his chin and studied the darkening sky. The first stars were beginning to peep through the clouds. A pair of birds gyred playfully overhead, appearing out of place in the otherwise bleak landscape.

"Wake everyone quietly," Robert instructed as they reached the wagons, "and gather on the field. It's time to prepare."

Sulis executed a short bow and Robert slipped into the back of one of the wagons. The *Sharak-khen* had set this wagon aside for his private use, but he preferred to sleep on the ground as they did, to walk beside them as they traveled during the day, to take his meager meals with them.

Alone as the heavy curtain closed, he found himself shivering. There was no lamp or candle to give him light, nor did he want any. Slowly, he untied his belt and slipped out of his dirty black clothes. The garments were actually the captured uniforms of Chol soldiers stripped of all rank and insignia, and they reminded him again of Kajin Kasst.

Naked, he rubbed his hands together, half expecting to find them slick with blood. But it was not Kasst's death he found himself comtemplating. It was the street punk's, the basher who had killed Scott Silver, for it was no dream that he had hunted the bastard down, broken him bone by bone, and finished him in that black alley.

His shivering increased as he tried to push the memory from his mind. He had delivered justice. What he had done was right, he told himself, just as killing Kaast had been right. Yet, in his heart, he couldn't make himself believe it.

Worse, he now suspected that Scott wasn't dead at all, but alive somewhere in Palenoc. If that was true, then how could he even pretend to justify his action? If Scott was alive, Robert had avenged himself by taking an innocent life. The thought ate at him like slow-working acid.

A small table stood beside the narrow, unused bed. Robert groped for a leather thong he kept there and tied back his hair, which had grown quite long during his time on Palenoc. Quietly, he knelt on the hard floor, rested his hands on his thighs, drew a slow breath through his nostrils, and tried to empty his mind.

It was a futile exercise. With a sigh he finally got up and chose fresher garments from the piles of black Chol uniforms scattered carelessly around. He sniffed them and grunted. He couldn't call them clean, but they didn't smell as bad as the ones he'd just discarded.

As he slipped into the trousers, he became aware he was no longer alone. From the corner of his left eye he spied a pale, barely visible figure just behind him. *Another* apparition, he thought, turning. *The second one tonight. Why are they so restless lately?*

But this was no ordinary ghost.

"Scott!" The cry hissed through Robert's teeth as he turned and recognized his visitor. His hands passed through air as he tried to grasp his friend.

Scott Silver raised one hand as if in supplication. Thin, bloodless lips moved weakly, but no sound issued forth. His emaciated form flickered and faded as it tried to manifest in the wagon's darkness. His hand clenched into a tight fist, and a small white light shot like lancets from the spaces between his fingers. For an instant he strained for substantiality. But the light shriveled, and Scott Silver disappeared.

Robert shot out a hand in a vain attempt to pull his friend back from oblivion.

"Polo!" Sulis Tel whipped back the curtain over the wagon's entrance.

Robert jumped again as he heard the name by which Scott Silver had most often called him. But he could tell by the expression on Sulis Tel's face that the black man had not seen the visitant.

Ranye h'Tan and several others stood behind Sulis. Beyond them, Robert could see men moving about the encampment restlessly.

"What is it?" Robert asked sharply. Sulis Tel stepped out of his way as he bent to peer outside. The entire camp was awake and on its feet. All eyes were trained on the western sky.

"Storm moving in," Sulis Tel answered. "Fast."

Dim flashes of lightning skipped along the horizon, lighting up the billowing clouds, turning their dark shapes into great jack-o'-lanterns that leered momentarily and winked out. An unnaturally cool wind blew veils of dust into the air. The wagons creaked and rocked on their wheels. The smell of rain hung like a heavy perfume.

No trace of Thanador or Mianur showed in the heavens. Nor would they this night.

Robert heard the drawn-out, lowing call of the *garouns*. The beasts were only hobbled. He worried that thunder might frighten them. "Tie up the animals," he instructed. "We can't waste time chasing them down if they panic."

Sulis Tel gave the order to another man as the first fat raindrops splattered on the earth.

"What of our mission?" Ranye h'Tan asked. The wind surged suddenly, turning his long black hair into lashing snakes.

Robert thought of Scott Silver, and his mouth set into a grim line. "We go," he said. "This storm will give us added cover. Spread the word to arm."

"We're leaving now?"

Robert nodded and turned to reenter his wagon where his own weapons were waiting. Then he turned back. "Ranye," he called.

The slender Chylan whirled with a dancer's grace. "Yes, ghost-brother?"

"Bring me the soul-jewels."

Ranye sped away, the ground turning to mud beneath his racing feet. Robert watched until the young man disappeared behind another wagon, then he turned his gaze toward the advancing clouds.

A violet flash lit up the darkness. The air crackled, and thunder wracked the night. The storm was on top of them.

Robert went inside long enough to pull on a thin, black tunic and slip into the harness that held his escrima sticks, slender dowel-like rods about two feet in length. They nestled comfortably between his shoulder blades. Next he pulled on a lightweight jacket of the same dark fabric. The jacket was lined with hidden pockets, each containing a special surprise. He belted it snugly. Finally, he pulled on a concealing hood and bound a black mask over his lower face.

The *Sharak-khen* waited for him. Like silent statues they stood on the plain beyond the last wagon, oblivious to the rain, clad like their leader. Lightning illuminated their stark sillhouettes as the wind swept over them. As one, they bowed when Robert approached.

Robert raised his arms above his head and crossed them at the wrist. The ghost-brothers did the same. He lowered his arms to forty-degree angles, and so did they. He brought his palms together, then moved his hands and fingers through a series of intricate gestures, each with its own meaning—*purpose, focus, strength, indomitable spirit.*

Lastly, he clenched both fists over his chest, knuckles touching, and drew them slowly apart. Ranye had taught him this gesture. It had but one meaning—*Death to the Heart of Darkness.*

Robert walked to Ranye h'Tan. "You have it?" he asked needlessly.

The Chylan took a small leather pouch from his belt and placed it on Robert's palm. Robert loosened the strings and poured out three sapphires of various sizes. They glimmered sharply in the lightning strikes, and deep in each of their faceted cores a red spark burned.

Shadark, Kardoom, Nazrahk. Three times his ghost-brothers had struck at the allies of Shandal Karg. Three times they had stolen the souls of her governors and sealed them in jeweled prisons. Tonight, they would strike again.

"You have a fourth stone prepared?" Robert said.

Ranye h'Tan nodded. "I've been polishing and shaping it for days." He extracted another sapphire from under his belt and held it up.

As lightning danced across the sky, Robert looked toward the horizon. Rain rilled down his face, but he ignored it. "The Tarjeel of Chylas must have been fools," he said. "Why did they never make you a *sekournen*?"

"Don't blame the councilors," Ranye answered without bitterness. "I'm tone-deaf. I can't bond with the *sekoye* because I can't make music. And this gift of mine . . ." he shrugged and followed Robert's gaze to the skyline. "Stealing souls. It has no good use."

Robert closed his fist around the stones and squeezed until he felt their sharp edges bite into his palm before he poured them back into the pouch. "We've found a good use for it," he said, pressing the pouch back into Ranye's hand. "I want you to bury these somewhere," he said suddenly. "Don't let anyone see you, and never tell anyone the location you choose."

Ranye nodded. "I'll plant them deep," he promised, clutching the pouch to his heart. Then, without warning, his face paled, and his eyes glazed over.

"What's wrong?" Robert asked.

"Call it a vision," Ranye answered in a softer than normal voice, "though I don't believe in visions. But from these evil seeds, a greater evil will grow. A Tree of Souls and Jewels, whose roots will strangle this land, until you return one day to chop it down." His voice faltered. "I will not see that day, Robert Polo."

Before Robert could answer, Ranye turned and ran away from the camp. Startled by the strange pronouncement, Robert shivered as he watched the Chylan's retreating form through the rain.

Sulis Tel spoke up suddenly at Robert's right-hand side. Robert hadn't heard him approaching.

"With all respect, little leader," the huge black man said with a hint of impatience, "it's wet."

Robert glanced up at his tall friend. Only Sulis's eyes were visible under his concealing garments, but he stood with his arms folded over his chest, one foot tapping in the mud and the vaguest impression of a grin beneath his mask.

"Time to boogie?" Robert asked, forcing a half-hearted smile, knowing how the Aegrinite loved such expressions.

Sulis moved one hand to reveal a small semban shuriken clasped between the first two fingers. With dexterous skill he flipped it over each of his knuckles and back again, like a magician doing coin tricks. "Your Paradane colloquialisms are so colorful," he said.

Robert and Sulis led the way up the long slope to the escarpment that overlooked the valley and the city of Abalon. It was a small city, barely more than a town, with no defensive wall. But at the edge of Abalon sat a single-storied, white stone villa, where Abakhet, governor of this land called the Grieve, took his frequent vacations.

They descended the escarpment swiftly, but with extra care. The rain made the footing treacherous, but all the ghost-brothers reached the valley without injury. Halfway across the valley, they paused to regroup, and Robert discovered that Ranye had caught up with them. The Chylan executed a curt salute and nodded his head to indicate he'd accomplished his task.

On Sulis Tel's advice, Robert chose two men to run the point. The pair jogged off through the rain while the rest of the *Sharak-khen* followed at a slower, more cautious pace.

The storm, which had moved so swiftly before, seemed trapped above Abalon, and it struggled with a fury to escape. Thunder shook the ground, and jagged lightning stabbed at the rooftops. Rain fell in wind-driven sheets. Perhaps it was the shape of the valley, Robert thought, that kept the storm from moving on.

A twinge of grief touched his heart as he thought suddenly of Eric. Robert knew nothing of geology or weather patterns or that kind of thing. Eric, though, would have paused in the heat of battle to explain inversion layers, downdrafts, wind shears, and such.

He missed his brother, but he shook himself to clear his mind. Too many old memories haunted him to-night when he should be focused on the present and the task at hand.

The scouts returned. The streets of Abalon were empty, they reported. The rain was keeping every-one inside.

Robert bit his lip and stared at the sky. Lightning flashed in vivid purple colors, strange lightning, such as he had never seen on Earth. For some reason it made him think of Scott again and the rays of white light that had shot between the fingers of his clenched fist.

What did it mean?

It meant to press on, he decided grimly. To find Scott if he was alive and free him. Or to avenge him if he was dead.

Blasts of thunder heralded their arrival as the *Sharak-khen* entered Abalon. As the scouts had said, the streets were empty. A few lamps shone through the cracks of tightly shuttered windows. A dog slunk miserably across the road, eyed them, and cowered between the side of an old barrel and the wall of a house.

Though the city lacked fortification, a low wall surrounded Abakeht's villa. A man standing on the shoulders of a partner could reach the top, and so the *Sharak-khen* clambered over. Robert joined his hands and boosted Sulis Tel, who, from the top of the wall, pulled Robert up. Together they dropped inside. The pounding rain drowned the sounds of their squishy landing.

A searing flash of lightning made them freeze. For an instant the sky turned stark white. Serpentine bolts ripped across the heavens in a fantastic and terrifying display. An electric crackling filled the night. All around the villa's broad lawn black-clad men stood starkly revealed with weapons in their hands.

Robert muttered an inaudible curse and gave the silent signal to attack. But as his ghost-brothers started forward, a figure rose slowly from the shadows near a flowering bush and moved to intercept them. Something gleamed in his hand.

A sword, Robert thought with amazement. But the weapon had not been developed on Palenoc! Then lightning flashed again, and he saw it was not a sword, but a long kitchen knife.

Another figure shambled from the concealment of a doorway. Yet a third rose from out of a flower garden. Another crawled from behind an ornamental well. The door to the villa opened, and a host of foes surged into the courtyard. The gateway to the outer city also swung inward, and scores rushed in.

Men and women and children clutched knives and rakes, the broken handles of hoes sharpened to deadly points, scythes and clubs and chains. The entire city had been hiding and waiting for them, waiting to protect their governor.

A violet bolt lanced across the sky and reflected in hundreds of staring eyes, eyes empty of life. Robert felt a numbing sickness. "Revenants!" he cried.

"Abakeht knew we were coming!" Sulis Tel hissed as he drew a shuriken from a pocket in his sleeve. It flashed like a star in his fist as lightning rent the night again.

"Not Abakeht," Robert said bitterly as he cast another swift glance at the sky. "That's not thunder you hear, my friend. It's the beating of a heart—the Heart of Darkness. She's murdered the entire city, and set their animated corpses on us!"

A hail of stones suddenly pelted them. Robert spun about as he threw up an arm to protect his head. A sharp pain shot through his raised forearm. More foes stood atop the villa's wall, hurling rocks and worse. A hayfork streaked through the air. A ghost-brother screamed and stared in disbelief at the three wooden tines that perforated his chest as he fell.

"They mean to kill us!" Sulis Tel shouted in horror as if he couldn't quite grasp the concept.

"Then let's do it as we do it on Paradane!" Robert answered.

The odds were overwhelming, but he pushed that thought out of his mind and leaped forward. A tall revenant lunged at him with a rake. Robert brushed it aside with a sweeping block and caught the haft with both hands as one foot swung around and sank into his enemy's stomach. Completing the spin, he brought the rake, which was now his, down on the creature's skull with a force that shattered bone and wood.

A stone glanced off his shoulder. Ignoring the pain,

Robert whirled, spied the thrower, and sent the broken rake handle hurtling like a spear. The slow-moving revenant clutched the shaft that suddenly protruded from his throat, then fell backward off the wall.

"Don't hold back!" Sulis Tell shouted. "They're already dead! Their *shaas* have already left their bodies!" The huge Aegrenite held a foe in a tight headlock. Even as he urged his ghost-brothers on, he gave a powerful grunt that snapped bone. The revenant collapsed at his feet and thrashed helplessly on the ground.

Robert stood paralyzed for a moment as he watched. The revenant didn't die. It was already dead. But with its neck broken, it couldn't get up, either. The realization hit him full force.

He whirled again and watched his first foe climb unsteadily to its feet. Despite a crushed skull it lumbered toward him once more, its outstretched hands grasping.

Robert sidestepped and with a powerful yell smashed the stiffened edge of his hand against the creature's neck. It fell, and before it could get up again, he jumped on its spine with both feet. The sound of bone breaking was like thunder.

The monster writhed and groped toward Robert's foot with one hand. It was all the more terrifying, because it made no sound. None of them did; they were corpses, animated by the power of Shandal Karg.

But there were screams. His men were struck down by stones, dragged down by numbers, impaled on farm implements and kitchen tools. All their training suddenly counted for nothing against such an unnatural force.

He had thought to strike a blow at Shandal Karg, but this time he had led them into a trap.

Half his ghost-brothers were down already. Across the lawn Ranye h'Tan fell, dragged down by the weight and fury of six monsters.

Robert felt a strange, cold darkness spread through him. Like a small, black flower, it blossomed in the shadows of his soul, enfolding petals around his mind and heart. "So be it, then," he murmured as he ripped away his hood and shook free his blond hair. A circle of empty-eyed creatures closed about him. He drew the escrima sticks from his harness and settled into a defensive cat stance. Blood filled the night with a coppery smell. He blinked rain from his eyes.

It was not to the revenants he spoke, but to another, who he knew, somehow, was listening. "Let's dance, you fucking bitch!"

Lightning raced across the clouded night, and the sky crackled. It was the sound of her laughter.

Chapter Eight

THE huge chamber swarmed with souls. Pale, nearly transparent *shades* wafted among the basalt columns. *Chills* rode the drafty currents of air. *Leikkios* shimmered and danced in the darkness. *Poltergeists* flew madly about, finding nothing to seize upon. Brooding *dandos* and *ankous* lurked in the deepest shadowed corners. The walls echoed the desperate, bone-freezing screams of *banshees*.

In the faint greenish light of the *leikkios*'s ghostfire, slender, long-fingered hands moved over a crystal caldron. One long nail dipped into the water that filled the vessel and seemed to draw an invisible line from one side to the other. Tiny ripples dashed against the caldron's lip. The nail withdrew from the water.

The hands disappeared for a moment, then reappeared, moving with purposeful grace above the caldron, seemingly disembodied in the gloom. Grains of a fine powder made from crushed human bones slithered down from those hands and settled upon the ripples like snowflakes.

The crystal caldron began to glow with its own soft azure radiance. The *dandos* and the *ankous* roused themselves from the shadows and slipped closer. The *shades* forgot their own sorrowful self-pity and felt the first stirrings of curiosity. The *leikkios* ceased their shimmering and dancing and were drawn slowly, like moths, to the new light. The screaming of the *banshees* subsided to a fearful whimpering. Even the *poltergeists* seemed to lose their manic energy and drew nearer.

The luminous surface of the water then began to dim and brighten, dim and brighten, sometimes the whole surface, sometimes only pieces of it, as if clouds rolled above it, obscuring sunlight that was not there.

The ebb and swell of that radiation revealed the form of Shandal Karg. Layers of night-black gowns draped all but her face and hands. Tight folds hooded even the proud bounty of her hair. The slender ebon horn that rode her brow like a crown, however, could not be hidden.

The gold-colored jelly of her eyes gleamed, and the black, feline slits of her pupils narrowed to needle thinness as She stretched her hand over the caldron. Her lips parted ever so slightly, and breath fled streaming from her mouth to brush over the water.

The ripples became waves that smashed the caldron's inner sides and threatened to leap its confines.

Stepping away from the vessel's azure light and back into the embracing gloom, Shandal Karg wrapped her arms about Herself and paused. Then She spoke in a low, rich voice, every word tinged with a seductive edge that had nothing to do with the message. "My precious beauty," She said, "tell your brothers the time is now."

In the farthest part of the chamber where the blackness was thickest, a *chimorg* took a single step forward, its hooves making a crisp sound. Its eyes snapped open, though it had not been asleep. Twin spots of red flickering flame burned upon its scaled face and reflected along the length of the spike that jutted from its bony forehead.

Muth-errrrrrr. The thought hissed from the monster's brain, and there was a sick kind of affection in it.

"The spell is nearly cast," said Shandal Karg. "Our forces are marshaled and waiting. Let them wait no longer. Rasoul must fall."

Razzzz-oul muzzzt fall, the beast echoed obediently. It blinked. The fires of its eyes winked out momentarily, then flashed again. It spoke, but this time there was some hesitation in the thoughts it sent. *Know how to killlll uzzz, they dooo,* it said. *Muth-errr, why you neverrr telll uzzz we can die-eeee? Why you neverrr sssay more than* sssekoye *can hhhurt usss?*

The corners of a rose-red mouth turned upward in a patient smile. "Because, my precious beauty," Shandal Karg answered, "it is so unimportant. I made you. You are my creations, therefore my children and my joys. But you are also my tools. A well-made tool will serve a long time. But on Palenoc only I will live forever."

Another half-muttered voice spoke suddenly.

"Lying whore."

Shandal Krag turned from the *chimorg* to gaze into the blackness high above the caldron. She raised a hand and drew it down slowly, and as She did so a long rope whose far end might have been affixed to the rafters or to the black nothingness descended. Dangling by his ankles from the near end, wrapped in cocoonlike bonds, was the dwarf-sized Gaultnimble.

"What did you say, little man?" asked the Heart of Darkness, her voice a cool challenge.

Hanging upside-down as he was, Gaultnimble forced a broad smile. Behind his jovially mocking answer, however, quavered a note of fear that his outward demeanor could not hide. "I said my ankles are getting sore, my Queen of Pain," he said. "You know

how I love it when you play with me like this." He
stared down at the caldron full of thrashing water roil-
ing directly beneath him. His bald head, without its
jester's belled cap, gleaming in the blue radiance. In
obvious discomfort, he licked his lips and tried to mus-
ter some enthusiasm. "This is a far, far better game
than we have ever played before."

"A better and bigger game than you know, little
Gaultnimble," Shandal Karg purred. "Your poor
fool's mind can barely conceive."

She turned back to the *chimorg*. "You know my
will," She said. "Inform your brothers. Let no other
goal fill our hearts this night but to destroy Rasoul.
That city is the very heart of the Domains of Light.
Once it is gone, that alliance will crumble." Her hands
curled suddenly into fists, and her coldly beautiful face
contorted in an expression of pure malice. "Then I
can give full attention to finding and destroying the
cursed *Child*."

We are yourrr obediennnt toolllzzz, Muth-errr, the
chimorg answered. It bowed, stretching out its front
legs and lowering the tip of its horn almost to the
floor. Then it rose and clopped out through an unseen door.

A host of *poltergeists* surged after it and latched
onto the door with their energy. The door shook suddenly on its hinges, opened and slammed and slammed
again, raising a terrible noise. That set the *banshees*
off with screams that threatened to rend the very
stones of Boraga.

"Enough!" the Heart of Darkness cried out in angry
frustration. She raised her hands, the folds of her
gown sliding down nearly to her elbows, and strained
at the air as if pushing at an invisible barrier.

The *banshees* screams turned to whimpers again.

The *poltergeists* and *chills* streaked toward the perceived safety of the ceiling and the rafters. The other ghosts retreated watchfully into the shadowed gloom and became silent.

"This is your fault, you miserable, slant-eyed dwarf!" She shrieked.

She drew back her hand and smashed it savagely against Gaultnimble's head. Helplessly bound, he grunted loudly in pain. The force of the blow set him swinging back and forth like a pendulum over the caldron, spinning wildly.

"You can't drive them out, Mistress." Gaultnimble laughed as he swung back and forth, a high, hysterical note in his laughter. His left eye was rapidly swelling from Shandal Karg's blow. "Your powers are weakening. The *Child* is already in the world!"

The Heart of Darkness glared, then calmed herself and struck a regal posture. "Not yet, my diminutive fool. There is still time to prevail."

Even in his topsy-turvy predicament, Gaultnimble mocked her. "You may hit me again, Dark Lady. You may slit my belly and drain my blood as you do Pusskins' kittens . . ."

"Yes," agreed Shandal Karg with a cold nod. "I may. You released the cursed Paradane from his prison."

Gaultnimble bucked his body as he tried to stop spinning. He looked like a larva wiggling on the end of a silken line. "Nay, Sweetness!" he lied. "Not me! The *Child* is to blame! Your power ebbs as he grows stronger. The seals on the Silver Man's icy coffin dissolved just as the wards that protect your very house are dissolving. Look around this, your throne room! The souls of your victims are thicker than flies!"

The Heart of Darkness reached out and caught

Gaultnimble's head between her hands, stopping his motion. His gaze was on a direct level with hers. He tried to flinch away, but She held him firmly, forced his mind to open to her prying will.

"Really, Mistress!" he protested unconvincingly even as his struggles ceased. "I'm innocent!"

Shandal Karg said nothing. Her catlike pupils contracted almost to invisibility. Long-nailed fingers touched either side of the dwarf's frightened face. "I'll rip the truth from your lying mind, you traitorous little toad," She hissed.

For long moments She gazed straight into his eyes, forcing his lids to remain open with the balls of her thumbs. Her body grew increasingly rigid. Beads of sweat popped out on Gaultnimble's brow.

With a sudden scream Shandal Karg flung her victim away, and he went swinging wildly at the end of his rope. "You resist me!" She cried. "You dare!"

"Playtime!" Gaultnimble shouted with a crazed cackle. "And the curtain goes up on a whole new act!" He bit down hard on his lip, and a bright red flower blossomed around his mouth with petals that spread rapidly over his inverted face. Laughing, he spat a great bloody wad. "There's power, power, power in the blood!" he sang, "wonder-working power!"

The blood acted as an acid. His ropes smoked and snapped. At the apex of his next swing his bonds broke, and Gaultnimble hurtled gracelessly through the air, arms and legs thrashing for some semblance of balance. He hit the floor hard, banging his head. Then he jumped to his feet and ran.

The ghostly spectators came alive with excitement. The *banshees* began to scream. The *poltergeists* ricocheted like pinballs among the chamber's columns.

Like shooting stars the *leikkios* flew to the farthest end of the throne room.

Suddenly, illumined by the *leikkios*'s light, a huge golden door shone forth. On its gleaming surface dozens of elaborate *prekhits* were painted in black blood, all in careful order and position. The door rose to twice a man's height. The *leikkios* strained to burn brighter, as if to light Gaultnimble's way, and the *poltergeists* seized the golden ring set into the door and rattled and shook it in desperation.

Shandal Karg put on a tiny smile, but there was no mirth in it, only deadly cold amusement. Placing one foot against the crystal caldron before Her, She pushed it over. The churning water inside rushed out over the floor, a greater quantity than the caldron should have held. It spread with amazing swiftness, overtaking her rebellious jester.

The thin tide touched the heel of his felt slipper then surged around him. For an instant he continued to run, splashing, slipping. Then he began to slow. His movements turned sluggish. Finally, he stopped.

The *banshees* fell silent. The *leikkios* dimmed, and the *poltergeists* frantically scattered.

"Uh-oh," Gaultnimble muttered nervously. He turned slowly to face his mistress. "Is this the end of poor Gaultnimble?"

Like an infinitely elastic serpent, the broken end of the rope from which he had depended moments before began to grow and lengthen. It touched the wet floor and slithered like a water snake toward him, causing ripples that disappeared into the darkness. The rope curled about his ankles and knotted itself.

The dwarf was jerked off his feet. His head cracked sharply on the floor. A long, terrified wail escaped his throat as the rope dragged him back toward the overturned caldron, then up into the air again.

Once more he hung upside-down, eye to eye with the Heart of Darkness.

"You're wet," She said.

"My bladder," Gaultnimble answered, giving the closest thing to an apologetic shrug he could manage in his inverted position. "No control over it at all lately." He forced a sheepish grin and licked a tongue over his still-bleeding lip.

"Don't you love me anymore, my tiny yellow-skinned worm?" Shandal Karg asked. She caught a drop of his blood on one pale fingertip and put it in her mouth. "Would you flee my service back to the misery you knew on Paradane?"

Gaultnimble shrugged again as he turned his head slightly and glanced toward the far end of the chamber. A few *leikkios* still seemed to linger there, and the golden door with its sealing wards barely glimmered. "Home sweet home," he said with exaggerated wistfulness. "Zhejian Province wasn't really such a bad place until all those stupid missionaries arrived and ruined it. I made a nice living picking pockets in Hangzhou."

"You hurt me in my heart of hearts, Gaultnimble," Shandal Karg said. She shook her head, wearing a pouty look. "That you could even think of leaving me!" She caught him by the shoulders and turned him around and around, winding him up, winding the rope which bound him. Then She let him go.

"Whoaaaa!" the dwarf shrieked, flinging out his arms as he spun with dizzying speed until the rope unwound itself.

Shandal Karg folded her arms over her breasts and merely watched until he stopped spinning. "I see so much now," She told him, her voice purring. "These little magics that you so amateurishly display. It was you, my sweet, attentive little jester, who told Scott Silver the secret of the golden door."

Gaultnimble forced another grin, showing all his teeth, and shook his head back and forth. "I'm innocent, Queen of Night," he insisted.

Shandal Karg struck the end of his nose lightly with a finger. "Because of you, Robert Polo nearly escaped me. My greatest weapon against the *Child*, and he nearly slipped through my fingers." She hit his nose again. "Because of you."

Gaultnimble's grin disappeared, and his hands clenched into fists. His voice turned suddenly venomous. "Didn't I go through the gate between the worlds for you and fetch him back? You gave me the Silver Man's face and shape so I could trick him. You promised me I could keep that shape, and that I'd be a dwarf no longer. You broke your promise!"

She hit his nose a third time, silencing him. "Now, because of you, Scott Silver has escaped me again with stolen magics at his command." She glared at her helpless servant. "Magics you must have taught him, Gaultnimble!"

Gaultnimble began to tremble, and suddenly tears flooded his eyes, tears of rage from pent-up years of humiliation. He answered in a high-pitched scream. "And I hope he chokes you with them, you stupid, wretched cow!"

The Heart of Darkness threw back her head and laughed. "You pathetic pimple! Don't pin your hopes on your Silver Man. He was never more than a hostage—Robert Polo's lover. As long as I had him, I had the ultimate means of control over the man who would slay the hated *Child* for me."

Gaultnimble hawked and spat a wad of bloodly saliva on Shandal Karg's breast. It smoked and steamed on the fabric of her black gown, then fizzled out. "Well, You can't control him anymore!" the little dwarf shouted defiantly. "I set the Silver Man free, you hear me? I set him free!"

The Heart of Darkness smiled with evil tolerance and patted her servant's cheek in a gesture that mocked affection. "It's no matter," She said, her voice a purr once more. "There wasn't time or reason to tell you, little insect." She paused, and her hand lingered tantalizingly on his face before withdrawing. "Robert Polo is mine. He has been mine for a long time."

Gaultnimble's jaw went slack and all hope left him. "What of the other brother?" he asked after a moment.

Shandal Karg bent and gripped the sides of the crystal caldron. With easy effort She set it upright on its three gleaming legs. "Eric Podlowsky is no longer of any consequence."

Gaultnimble licked his lips again. The flow of blood there had nearly ceased. "And the Dowd woman?" he pressed.

Shandal Krag hesitated and seemed to lean for the briefest instant for support on the caldron's edge. "Nor is she of any importance," She said at last. "Palenoc is a big world. Let her be lost in it, She is not a player in this game."

A *chill* dared to venture near the Heart of Darkness, and her last words issued forth in a vaporous cloud. Shandal Karg batted at it with the back of her hand as if the bothersome spirit were no more than a fly.

"I will have a housecleaning, yet," She swore. "But first, back to business."

She stretched out her hand. All the water that had spilled out on the floor began flowing backward toward the caldron, up its polished sides and over its rim. Every drop oozed back, leaving dry tiles. Only moments more, and another miniature tempest raged within the caldron's confines.

"With storms and fire I've wracked the Domains of Light," She intoned as She stared at her handiwork. "The plague of the Cha Mak Nul has laid waste the Gray Kingdoms. Only the city of Rasoul remains unscathed. It is time for that to change."

Within the caldron winds blew upon the water, and great waves splashed back and forth. The caldron itself flashed deep within its facets as if with lightning.

Once more, the souls of the dead in all their various forms dared to draw near to witness the deed of magic.

"A sea storm," Shandal Karg murmured, "is only the beginning. But wait." She paused, her face showing pretended surprise. "Where are the ships? What is a sea storm without ships to wreck?"

She looked to Gaultnimble, and suddenly he knew why he was suspended above the caldron. Her magic required blood. How much this time?

From her sleeve She withdrew a slender shining needle half as long as her forearm. "It cannot be a mere scratch this time, little half-a-man. You have betrayed me, and I am minded of a saying on your world, one you have often voiced—*If an eye offend thee, pluck it out.*

Gaultnimble screamed and thrashed his hands in an effort to keep Her at bay.

"Be still!" She hissed, and Her will clamped down upon him like a vise even as his own garments began to twist and tangle around him until he was as good as bound once more.

He swallowed, helpless. "This will hurt me more than it will you," he stammered.

She gripped his face with one hand. Though he squeezed his eyelids shut, it was to no avail. She shoved the needle straight into his right eye. He screamed again, a long, agonized wail that set the *banshees* off in sympathetic chorus.

Blood and jelly leaked out, ran down his face, dripped, and splashed into the caldron, forming a fleet of round, shining droplets that valiantly rode the crashing waves only to be dashed and broken apart.

"There," Shandal Krag sighed as She licked the needle clean. "There are my ships!" She made a pouting face as She watched the droplets fall, only to be consumed by the tiny storm. "Oh, the poor ships," She moaned. "The poor ships! Gaultnimble, look!"

But Gaultnimble could not hear Her for his screaming.

Chapter Nine

ERIC lay on his back on the cool stone floor of Phlogis's sanctum. His right hand rested at his side, but his left rested upon his heart. In his left fist he clutched a small piece of tourmalated quartz. The stone pulsed with a white radiance that matched the beat of his heart. Slender spears of light shot outward between his clenched fingers.

Relax, Eric Podlowsky. Phlogis's words rasped through a dim corner of his brain, filtered somehow, as if coming from a great distance. *Let the sound of your heartbeat stimulate the natural vibrations of the crystal. See the stone in your mind. Shut out all other thought. See only the crystal.*

Eric gently closed his eyes. It was easier than he thought it would be, picturing that splinter of quartz shining in a dark void. It rotated slowly like a misshapen planet spinning in a starless space. His awareness of the floor against his spine and under his head faded away. He felt incredibly light, unbound by gravity.

In that void the mesmeric beat of his heart was the only sound. But it didn't come from him. It came from the crystal. He seemed to draw nearer and nearer to it, as if he were flying and the quartz drawing him.

Its spinning slowed, and so did his own sense of

motion. Finally, both stopped. The stone merely hung in the void, shedding its light as if it were the lone sun in an undiscovered universe. He floated before it, fascinated and uncertain.

Now it is a door.

Was that Phlogis's thought or his own? Eric Podlowsky couldn't tell anymore.

A door into the Dream Stream where all things are possible, said the voice inside his head. *Your shaa has left your body and stands poised upon the threshold.*

The voice paused. Eric waited for further instruction, all his attention focused upon the gleaming door, for that was how he perceived it now.

When you cross into the Dream Stream, the voice continued, *think then of your brother. Fill your mind with him. Will and desire, and the strength of the bond between you may show you where he is now.*

"May?" Eric murmured, his gaze fixed upon the door. A slender crack widened in its shining face. The door was opening for him.

Nothing is certain in the Dream Stream, Eric Podlowsky. But your love for Robert is strong. It may guide and protect you.

Eric frowned. " 'May', again."

No response came.

The crystal doorway divided neatly down the middle, and the two halves swung outward. Beyond lay a blackness even deeper than the void where he floated. Once he passed over that threshold, he was on his own. A place of beauty, Phlogis had called it, and of danger. A place where all things were possible.

He swallowed. If that was where he had to go in hope of finding Robert, then so be it.

Suddenly, he flew again. Straight through the open doorway he sailed, then beyond.

He knew at once he wasn't alone. He could see nothing, but he sensed other presences with a strange acuteness. Ghosts, probably. Perhaps other seekers like himself. The Dream Stream was a plane where a living man's soul, his *shaa,* could interact with the spirits of the dead.

He put aside such thoughts. He was here for one purpose only, to find his brother. He didn't understand this place, but he knew what he had to do. "Bobby!" he called, filling his mind with thoughts of his brother.

He began flying again, slowly, tentative and directionless. Something brushed up against him, and something else fluttered across his face with the whispery touch of a spider web. The presences he had sensed. Phlogis had warned they might try to distract him.

"Bobby!" he called again. He visualized the thought spreading in all directions like a wave. He glanced back at the door. It remained hanging in space, half open.

Again something brushed against him. "Get away!" he hissed. In the Dream Stream thought was power. As if a bomb had gone off, he felt the annoying presences scatter.

All but one. It brushed his face again. Thought was power, Eric reminded himself. He visualized a shield around his body and used it to push the presence away. "Bobby!" he called, returning to his task of finding some trace of his brother.

The presence pushed right through his shield and touched his face again. "Get away from me!" Eric shouted, swinging the thought as if it were a club. The presence merely brushed it aside.

Eric recoiled, sensing the centered power behind the almost casual deflection of his thought-attack. Here had been engagement and exchange, and without knowing it, he had lost! *Ippon!* Full point to his foe.

Something began to take shape in the space before him. The presence assumed a form. At first its features were blurred. Still, Eric thought he recognized it.

"Bobby!" he shouted.

"No," the presence answered. It looked up at him with eyes of aching blue. "I am Scott Silver."

Eric was puzzled and distrustful. Phlogis had warned him. Maybe this was just a distraction to keep him from finding Robert. "Bobby's friend?" he said. "But how—"

"There's no time," the form claiming to be Scott Silver interrupted. "I entered the Dream Stream in hopes of making contact with someone in Rasoul. I never dreamed it would be Polo's brother."

Eric felt some of his distrust slip away. *Polo.* Bobby had told him once that Scott always called him by his pen name.

"You've got to go back," Scott Silver continued.

"The hell I will," Eric answered. 'I'm here searching for my brother. He's in trouble, I know it. And if he's not, I don't doubt he will be soon. He's got the knack for it." He peered uncertainly at the figure before him. Amazing, he thought, how much it resembled his brother. "Are you Scott Silver's *shaa*?" he asked. "Or his ghost?"

A faint wisp of a smile flickered over the figure's face. "I'm alive, Eric. For the moment, at least. But I bring a warning. You've got to go back and warn Rasoul."

"Warn them of what?" Eric snapped. He had no intention of returning. He thought he'd made that clear. Finding Robert was his paramount concern.

Scott Silver put out his hand. Eric felt himself being

gently pushed back toward the crystalline door. "Stop!" he demanded. But the force of his will was as nothing against Scott Silver's, and he began to fly back toward the threshold.

"Tell them," Scott Silver shouted after him, "the Heart of Darkness will attack Rasoul. Tell them to prepare, if it's not too late already!"

"Don't push me away!" Eric screamed in frustration. "My brother!"

With a final mighty shove Scott Silver propelled Eric back through the doorway. "I'll find him." Silver's last words followed Eric like a distant echo across the threshold. "I love him, too."

As if invisible hands had reached out and seized them, the crystal doors slammed shut.

"Goddamn you!" Eric shouted again, but this time his voice ricocheted off the stone walls of Phlogis's sanctum. He sat up angrily, finding himself back in his own body. "Phlogis!" he cried.

But the *prekhit* where the old *dando* should have been was empty. The sanctum doors were also thrown wide. Eric cursed as he leaped up, and he threw the bit of tourmalated quartz into the darkness above the strange and elaborate device. If it fell or struck the opposite wall, Eric couldn't tell. No sound resulted, no clatter or rattle. That fact sobered Eric.

Then from somewhere he heard vague screaming, not from one voice, but from many. Turning, he exited the sanctum's great doors and ran into the corridor.

The hallway was empty. Still the screams persisted. Racing up a flight of stairs, he found a narrow window at the next landing and stared outward.

The scene beyond the Sheren walls was chaos. A herd of *chimorgs* thundered down a street. People ran before them, crying in terror. Huge black hooves trampled human flesh. The triumphant bellowing of the black-scaled monsters chilled him to the bone.

He ran back down the stairs, through the hall, and down another flight to his own quarters. He thrust a hand beneath his mattress and drew out two wooden canes from where he'd hidden them weeks ago. Then he ran back into the hallway.

The Sheren seemed utterly empty. He headed for the rooftop, taking stairs two and three at a time, finally springing up through the open trapdoor beneath the great globe of *sekoy-melin* that served as a beacon to Sheren-Chad's dragonriders.

Dragons filled the sky, circling and swooping, their wings only half-luminous in the early evening sky. Clad in flowing white robes, Maris and Rasoul's eleven other councilors stood positioned in a ring around the great rooftop. Eric called her name, and she turned. "What's happening?" he demanded as his fingers fumbled at the special pocket sewn onto his belt. He drew out the polished Hohner harmonica he kept there.

Maris was tense, but calm as befitted the Tarjeel's leader. A high wind stirred her dark hair and set her garments to snapping crisply. "Hundreds of *chimorgs* charged into the city from the north and south." She took his arm and drew him to the south side of the rooftop. In the distance a huge fire burned, its glow in turn coloring the twilight clouds so that the sky itself seemed on fire. "The granaries," she said. She led him to the western side. "And more fires in the Fishermen's Quarter."

"Why didn't someone wake me?" Eric cursed.

"We tried," she answered flatly. "You were too deep in the Dream Stream."

He put the harmonica to his lips and blew a screeching series of notes up and down the instrument's range. A mental bridge fell into place, and immediately he felt Shadowfire's thoughts next to his own and knew the great beast was already in the air, racing to his call. He climbed on top of the wall that encircled the roof and shoved the wooden canes down the back of his tunic to free his hands. The wind buffeted him, but he never glanced at the ground far below.

Shadowfire appeared in the east, his massive wings beating in rapid time, the faintest opalescent glow lighting up the undersides as he flew through the deepening twilight.

"Taedra carry you in her wings," Maris said, "and all of us this night."

Eric clenched the harmonica between his teeth, blew another long note, and hurled himself in swandive form out into the air. Shadowfire folded his wings and plummeted. A long, sinuous neck slid beneath Eric. Hands grasped the horn of the saddle encircling that neck. For a precarious instant Eric dangled in space, but quickly he muscled himself up into the saddle and slipped his feet into the stirrups.

Sheren-Chad was already far behind them. Eric played a wild series of notes, and Shadowfire turned southward toward the burning granaries. Once, he had played actual familiar songs on his harmonica, but now he no longer knew what he played. Music simply flowed through him, as sure and strong as the bond he shared with his *sekoye*.

The fire was much worse than he had guessed from the Sheren's rooftop. The granaries were totally destroyed, and with them food supplies for the winter ahead. Flames spread rapidly among the shops and apartments in that quarter of the city as well. As high as he was on his dragon, he could hear the screams of Rasoul's people. Faced with the choice of remaining in burning buildings or confronting the *chimorgs* that raced through the streets, many panicked and ran blindly.

Eric cursed and turned Shadowfire toward the Fisherman's Quarter. There, too, flames cut through the old buildings like scythes through dry grass.

But here, squads of *Kur-Zorin,* Rasoul's regular soldiers, harried the *chimorgs* with fishing nets and ropes. As Eric watched, a clutch of women, hidden on a smoking roof, threw down broad sailcloth as if it were a net, ensnaring and blinding a *chimorg* as it charged a pair of soldiers. The pair turned and began to beat the beast with the staves they carried as the women cheered.

"Break off its horn!" Eric shouted uselessly from the sky. Then he blew another note on the harmonica. The battle was on the ground, not in the air. At his musical command, Shadowfire swooped low toward the fighting, and Eric prepared to jump off.

Suddenly, another dragon flew wingtip to wingtip with his own. Eric recognized Mirrormist by the amber glow of his wings, and his gaze met Alanna's just before he jumped. He heard her high soprano voice as she commanded her own beast. Then she landed in the street behind him, rolling on her shoulder, getting to her feet, and running to join him.

A *chimorg* charged down the street, the strange flames of its eyes streaking behind it like twin heat trails.

"Get down!" Alanna cried, tackling Eric and driving him into the dirt.

An instant later, a huge shape passed above them, Mirrormist with his wings folded tightly against his body so he could fit between the buildings. A pair of talons seized the *chimorg*. The dragon's shrill cry of triumph mixed with the *chimorg*'s terrified bellow. Wings spread with a bright amber-golden radiance as Mirrormist took flight again and carried the monster into the air. Then, with an almost casual effort, those great claws flexed, ripped the *chimorg* in half, and let the separate pieces fall.

"Ugh!" Eric commented as he picked himself up and found his harmonica where he'd dropped it in the dirt.

"Nice to see you, too," Alanna said as she whipped out a small blowpipe from inside the black leather tunic she wore.

"That won't do any good against the *chimorgs*," Eric reminded her. "I've got something that will." The two canes stuck up from the neck of his tunic. He drew them out and offered one to Alanna.

"A big stick?" she scoffed. "Am I supposed to goose them into submission?"

"It's called a *shinobe-zu* on my world," he answered, grinning at her sarcasm. He gave one end of the cane he held a sharp twist, and exposed a long length of gleaming metal blade. "I had these made in secret," he told her. "One for me, and one for Bobby."

She stared at the weapon she held, reluctant and fascinated. Slowly, she opened it and drew out the sword.

Eric knew what was on her mind. "We're not using these on people," he reminded her. "They're for *chimorgs*."

Alanna shot a look around, biting her lip. Flames rippled along the roof of the apartments on their right. From the next street came the sound of screams and combat. "Let's go," she said.

Eric shoved the harmonica back into his belt pocket and ran after her, gripping the *shinobe-zu*. In the next block they found a dozen *Kur-Zorin* struggling to control a netted *chimorg*. The soldiers had three ropes on the beast, and still it slung grown men around as if they were toys.

"Take off the horn," Eric told Alanna as he thrust the sheath end of the cane into his belt and advanced toward the monster with the upraised blade. Firelight danced along the keenly forged edge. He crept in among the struggling soldiers, and when the beast swung his way, the sword flashed downward.

The horn spun away end over end and landed in the dirt. Black blood spurted from the severed stump on the *chimorg*'s brow. The monster reared, bellowing with pain and rage, jerking three of the *Kur-Zorin* off their feet and dragging them. Two more men jumped on one of the lines, but one of the soldiers cleverly looped one rope around the *chimorg*'s rear ankles, and when it reared again, it toppled over.

Men and women, even children, who had been watching in terror from the windows of their burning homes, suddenly streamed into the streets to join the *Kur-Zorin*. They piled on the fallen *chimorg*, which was still tangled in nets and ropes.

"Tshai!"

At Alanna's shout everyone fell silent. All eyes turned toward the female *sekournen*. In one hand she held the *shinobe-zu*, but in the other she held the unicorn's horn. Even the monster stopped its struggling and seemed to stare at her. Its great chest labored, and its breath came like the wheezing of a forge bellows.

Without another word she raised the horn. The light of the fires gleamed redly on her black leather garments, and a hot wind lifted the strands of her hair. The same light shimmered on the horn, turning it into a tongue of flame as she dropped the *shinobe-zu* and seized it with both hands. Her eyes flashed. With a fierce cry she drove the horn deep into the *chimorg*'s heart.

The beast screamed and thrashed with such power that everyone leaped back. For a moment it found its feet and took a faltering step, but the nets and ropes only tripped it again, and it fell with ground-shaking force on its neck. A moment more, and it was dead.

Alanna took up the *shinobe-zu* again, freed the shining blade, and thrust the wooden sheath into her belt.

A loud trumpeting sounded eerily around the city, the cries of *chimorgs,* as if they sensed the death of one of their own, not at the claws of dragons, but at the hands of humans. Anger and deep despair filled the sound.

Eric glanced at the sky. Dragons circled everywhere, some with riders, others without. Like herons catching fish, the fabulous *sekoye* dipped and dived, snatching *chimorgs* into the air and ripping them apart in their huge talons.

Then, without warning, the sky changed. Black clouds rolled in with impossible swiftness to blot out the few twilight stars. The wings of the dragons glowed brighter and brighter as the darkness deepened, and the fires that spread through the city reflected angrily on the stygian canopy.

A deafening blast of thunder rent the air. A bolt of red lightning stabbed earthward to lick at a wall. Brick and mortar exploded.

At the same time, one of the *Kur-Zorin* gave a

shout. "The ships!" he cried, pointing down the street that led to Rasoul's harbor. "The ships!"

Eric and Alanna ran to the man's side and stared. "Damn!" Eric cursed. "Come on!" With Alanna hard on his heels, he sped down to the wharves. Bodies littered the road, but no *chimorgs* challenged them now.

Rasoul's commerce fleet was in flames—the fishing fleet, too. Tiny black canoes, driven by black-masked warriors glided among the anchored vessels. Fiery pitch-balls streaked through the night, igniting sails and rigging.

Eric cursed again, feeling helpless and inadequate as he watched a terrible tragedy unfold. Alanna's hand closed on his arm and squeezed. Their gazes met, and for the first time he thought he saw a hint of fear in her eyes.

Then, staring past his shoulder, she paled. "The Sheren!" she screamed.

Lightning ripped open the night again, a great ball of glittering force that rippled across the black heavens only to crest unexpectedly against some unseen barrier before it could touch the soaring tower. A serpentine bolt followed it only to splinter in a crackling display against the same barrier.

Sheren-Chad remained untouched.

"It's Her," Eric murmured coldly. "She's come to finish the job personally."

"She can't!" Alanna cried. "She's tried before. The people can stop Her!"

He knew what she meant. Once before, Shandal Karg had dared to attack Rasoul. The people had a song, though, an anthem that was in reality a powerful protective spell. He had watched them turn out into the streets, watched them line their rooftops and lift their voices to repel her attack.

He and Robert had joined their voices to those of Rasoul's citizens, and he remembered how, in that moment, for the first time in years, as song filled his throat and something much greater filled his heart, he had at long last felt truly part of something, felt like he really belonged somewhere.

But this was not that time.

"Look around," he said stonily to Alanna. "The people are panicked. She planned well this time. The *chimorgs* put us off balance while her soldiers burned the granaries and fleets and set fire to the city. Scott Silver tried to warn us."

Alanna blinked. "Robert's dead friend?"

There wasn't time to explain. A pair of *chimorgs* charged out of an alley toward the wharves. Eric shoved his way through the surprised *Kur-Zorin* and ran to meet the monsters. His blade flashed, and a horn went spinning. The *chimorg* screamed and reared, spraying black blood everywhere. The wharf shook as its hooves smashed downward on the rough planks. It shook its mane and reared again, then ran away, shrieking in pain.

Eric turned toward the second beast, but Alanna was already there. With a high-pitched shout, she swung her sword. The first blow cut deep. The horn cracked and broke, sagging at an angle. The beast snapped at her with its powerful jaws. Alanna danced lithely aside and swept the blade around in a powerful backhand stroke with barely a pause. The horn flew high into the air.

Nets flew from three different directions, ensnaring the creature. Armed with a club, a brave *Kur-Zorin* leaped on its back and rained blows on its head as, with hooves enmeshed, it stumbled and finally fell. A dozen men surrounded the monster, attacking it with clubs and fists and fishing pikes. Someone snatched up the horn and drove it repeatedly into the *chimorg's* breast.

A blast of lightning turned the world white. Eric clapped a hand over his eyes. Sparks and miniature stars swam in his vision. When he could see again, he stared toward the tower, and what he saw sent fear lancing through his heart.

She was there. Her form floated high in the night, a giantess that rode the clouds and spawned the deadly lightning, framed by a fiery ring filled with a blackness blacker than the sky itself. Her hair lashed in the wind, and her eyes burned like the eyes of her creations, the *chimorgs.*

"Phlogis!" Alanna shouted, pointing with her sword.

The *dando* was barely visible high above the Sheren rooftop. He floated in the air, surrounded by some astral version of the *prekhit* in his sanctum and by a twinkling ring of precious jewels and crystals. His form, too, was swollen to gigantic proportion, yet Shandal Karg dwarfed him.

Eric slammed the blade of his *shinobe-zu* into its cane sheath. "He can't fight her alone!"

"He's not alone," Alanna reminded him, a note of quiet fear in her voice. "The Tarjeel is up there, too. My sister, Maris, is up there."

"It won't matter," Eric said. "They won't be strong enough without the city behind them."

Alanna stood frozen for a moment, her gaze fixed on the drama over Rasoul. Another white blast of lightning wracked the darkness. A crystalline-colored bubble seemed to twinkle around the tower in response, but the form of Phlogis doubled over as if in pain, and the bolt sheared through the bubble.

A horrible crack split the side of Sheren-Chad.

Eric felt a cold hand around his heart. Alanna's mouth gaped as she prepared to scream. But she didn't scream. She sang.

Gather people! Stand together!
Darkness has no power here!

Eric despaired. It was too late, and the people were too panicked. But Alanna's hand sought his and gripped it. He stared at her, shaking his head. Still, compelled by her faith, he began to sing.

In that instant he felt Shadowfire in his mind. The dragon was high over the Great Lake, circling the burning ships, blood on his claws and on the claws of other *sekoye*. Eric watched through Shadowfire's eyes as one of the winged creatures swooped low and crushed a canoe full of black-masked warriors with its great tail. Eric sang.

Join hands and raise your voices!
Filled with Light, we have no fear!

Shadowfire turned away from the ships and flew inland toward the shattered tower. Alanna tugged at Eric's hand. The *Kur-Zorin* squad sang with them now, and some of the fishermen and women, too.

Alanna led the way up the street, singing at the top of her lungs. People who cringed fearfully in the shadows, wiped their faces and stepped out nervously to join them. Others stole warily out of their homes or out of the ruins of their shops. Their band grew, and their voices became a chorus. A layer of harmony rose over the melody, then another wound over and around that.

> *Men and women, little children!*
> *We are not afraid tonight!*
> *The smallest of us is a fortress!*
> *Stand as one against the Night!*

They marched through the streets toward Sheren-Chad. Lightning rattled the sky, and the wind scorched the air with the heat of the fires that ravaged the city. Rasoul's people came anyway, by twos and threes, raising their voices high. Another squad of *Kur-Zorin* ran up from the Scholars' Quarter, and when they neared the Temple of Taedra on its high knoll, Roderigo Diez came down, leading the priest-healers.

Still, there were those who did not come. Eric saw them, huddled fearfully in the alleyways, in the broken doorways of their apartments, dirty and soot-covered, clutching wounds or bent over bodies of their loved ones. Their eyes were the eyes of the defeated, without hope.

Eric swallowed and gazed over the great chorus that surrounded him and realized what a pitiful, ragtag little band it really was. As many as they were, they were too few.

And yet, there had come no other blast of lightning.

"Listen!" Alanna cried, squeezing his hand, though her words were for their entire band. "Listen! The *sekoye*!"

A high, loud trilling filled the night. Above the tower Shadowfire and Mirrormist flew with a score of other dragons. And more came to join them from all corners of the city, from over the Great Lake, from the mountains in the east. Around and around they flew, circling the Heart of Darkness in her ring of fire, and the trilling grew louder.

And suddenly hope flooded Eric, for he knew what the sound was. He heard it with his ears, but more, he heard it through the bond he shared with Shadowfire.

Singing! The dragons were singing!

Gather beings! Fly together!
Darkness has no power here!

The form of Shandal Karg wavered for an instant. Then She threw back her head and screamed in anger and frustration.

Eric freed himself from Alanna's grasp as they approached the mouth of an alley. A woman huddled in the shadows with two children, a small boy and girl, under an arm. He took her hand and the hand of the little girl and urged them into the street. "Sing," he whispered to the child. "It makes the fear go away."

The little girl trembled, but she sang. Her mother and brother sang, too.

The Heart of Darkness screamed again. Lightning flashed wildly in all directions. A dragon's wing exploded, and the beautiful creature plummeted. But it was only a final, vengeful spasm of power. Shandal Karg began to fade. Her form grew tenuous, like a thing of smoke, and the wind blew her away piece by piece until only her ring of fire remained. At last, that also faded and died.

The form of Phlogis slumped and seemed to melt back into Sheren-Chad.

A great cheer went up from the people, but Eric fell quiet. He stared at the great crack in Sheren-Chad, then at the thick clouds overhead that still redly reflected the fires raging through Rasoul. He took out the silver harmonica from its special pocket and put it softly to his lips and blew a quiet, sustained note. He felt Shadowfire's mind next to his, and invisible wings of comfort enwrapped him. He blew another not, then a slow, mournful riff.

Alanna touched his arm, and Roderigo Diez was suddenly before him. "The look on your face, *mi amigo*," he said with a worried expression. "What are you saying to that dragon of yours?"

Eric gazed toward the sky. Shadowfire gyred gracefully around the rooftop of the shattered Sheren, listening, waiting. "On Paradane we have an expression," he answered finally, taking the harmonica from his lips and tapping it lightly on his palm. "Don't get mad." He raised it once more and blew another, sharper note before continuing. "Get even."

Chapter Ten

KATHERINE sat alone in her favorite place on the hilltop above the Kirringskal's cavern. The wind whispered softly around her, rustling the leaves and rippling the grass. Billowy clouds crawled lazily across the bright afternoon sky, and birds fluttered in the limbs above her head.

A sense of loneliness teased her heart as she lay back in the tender grass and folded one hand under her head. A sigh escaped her lips. She would have welcomed Sparrow's persistent questions and demands for stories right now, or even the company of her ghostly companions. But Sparrow with the rest of the Kirringskal males was making preparations to rebuild the village, and daylight kept the ghosts away.

She put one hand on her swollen belly and sighed again. "Well, I have you, little one," she murmured.

After a time she struggled to sit up again. By her side was a scarred and worn backpack she had brought with her from her own world. It contained her few possessions. Among them was a dog-eared paperback, Robert Polo's last novel.

"*A Pale Knock,*" she read aloud, pronouncing the title slowly. "Palenoc." She patted her belly again. "You don't think it's a coincidence, either, do you, baby? Robert had been here before."

That was a growing conviction with her. She'd lost count of the number of times she'd read the book now, but with each reading she discovered something new, became more and more certain that Robert was somehow describing, in a veiled and metaphorical way, elements of this strange world.

She opened the book at random. Though fiction, ostensibly a genre horror novel, Robert had made extensive use of verse. Her gaze settled on a couplet that ended one of the chapters.

Now lay me down and close my eye;
Straight to Darkness's heart I fly.

Those words tumbled over and over in her mind. She closed the covers, frowning, wondering, as strange and dangerous thoughts took form. They were not new thoughts, however. Daily, as she turned the pages of Robert's book, a fear grew within her. She turned to yet another chapter's end and read.

Despairing, yielding all control,
The Hand of Darkness holds my soul.

Katherine closed the book again, set it on the grass, and stared at the garish cover. *A Pale Knock* was a story about child abuse and the ghosts who come to deliver a young boy from his abusers. There were passages so poignant they made Katherine's heart ache, and scenes where she simply cried, knowing the emotional price Robert must have paid to write them.

Yet, there was more to the book than the story, she was convinced of that. Too many elements were descriptive of this other-world called Palenoc. The title, for one thing. Ghosts. The frequent references to the Heart of Darkness or the Hand of Darkness.

Katherine laid a hand upon the book and gazed toward the western hills and the horizon beyond. "Despairing, yielding all control," she spoke slowly, "the Hand of Darkness holds my soul."

The child within her belly stirred.

"You know what I'm thinking, don't you, little one?" she said to her unborn baby. "There's no more sickness here, and the Kirringskal are rebuilding their village." She braced an elbow on a knee and rested her chin in the palm of one hand. Her gaze strayed back to the book. Her mind churned with thoughts of Robert and his tale and what it all meant.

She needed to know the answer. She had thought to stay here with Matterine and Sparrow and Falcon and have her child safely by a fire with friends to look after her and her newborn. That was the rational thing to do.

She gave a sigh. In fact, it was what she *was* going to do. Robert was dead, she reminded herself, and she had a new life to look after.

But someday ... someday ...

She returned Robert's book to her backpack with ritual care. Years as Dowdsville's librarian had instilled in her an almost religious respect for books. Wearily, she wrapped her arms around the pack and hugged it to her. Inside were the few things she treasured, some from her world, some from this. Memories, mostly, and one or two practical items.

Abruptly, she felt a presence. The sensation startled her. She hadn't heard anything, and none of her natural senses had alerted her. She simply knew she was no longer alone. She even knew where. . . .

"Mac?" she called, casting a look over her right

shoulder. The Darklander stood half hidden behind a tree not ten paces away. He had lost weight during his illness, and his face was gaunt, though strangely handsome. Matterine had cut his black hair and shaved him, but a fine black stubble lined his jaw.

Cha Mak Nul stepped away from his hiding place and strode toward her. A smile blossomed upon his features as he spoke softly musical words in a language she didn't understand.

But despite the pleasing tone of his voice, a wave of hostile emotions engulfed Katherine. Without knowing how, she sensed evil behind that smile and knew the treachery he planned. Too late, she saw the rock he held as he swung it over her head. Desperately, she tried to scramble up, but her big belly made her slow and clumsy. She raised an arm, ineffectually, hoping to ward off the descending blow.

Pain flashed against her skull. "Baby ..." she sighed. Then darkness.

Katherine woke, her head throbbing. One side of her face felt swollen, the skin drawn painfully tight over the line of her left cheek to just above her eye. Strips of cloth bound her wrists and feet. A gag filled her mouth.

She lay on a soft carpet of grass in a thick grove of trees. Through the branches she noted an unfamiliar configuration of hills that loomed on both sides of the grove. Mac must have carried or dragged her to this small valley and away from the Kirringskal's cave.

At the sound of rustling, she craned her neck and tried to look around. Not far away, Mac worked hurriedly, twisting grasses into cords to bind leafy branches between two stout sapling poles. Attracted by her movement, he paused in his labor and glared at her.

The gag prevented her from speaking. She fumed, cursing inside. She'd never felt so helpless. Even if she could work her bonds loose, what could she do? She couldn't run in her pregnant condition. Fighting him was not even a possibility.

She tried to relax for the moment. All she could do was hope some opportunity would present itself. Surely the Kirringskal would miss her, and they'd note the Darklander's absence, too. Falcon would look for her.

All she could do was wait. Wait, and wonder why Mac had grabbed her. What was his motive? Of what possible value could she be to him?

She closed her eyes. There were times she wished she'd never left Dowdsville. Something, after all, could be said for a dull little librarian's job in the most boring one-horse town on earth.

Mac carried his construct over and dropped it beside her. She recognized its purpose immediately and gave a little groan. Mac bent down and half rolled, half lifted her onto a stretcher-style bed of limbs and leaves that was scratchy and unpleasant. Passing a stout vine across her middle, he tied it to the poles on either side to secure her. Then, much to her surprise, he bent and recovered something from the ground—her backpack! She hadn't noticed it lying just above her head. He dropped it beside her on the crude rack.

He stared at her briefly, then examined her bonds. Satisfied, he lifted a thicker, braided vine tied with thick knots to the tops of the poles, put it over his shoulder, and began to drag her over the ground.

The ends of the poles cut furrows in the earth and

gave Katherine hope. They made a clear trail for Falcon to follow. Mac dragged her across the valley and up a long slope. She had to admire the Darklander's strength and determination even as she hoped he'd slip and break a leg.

At the bottom of the next hill a shallow river flowed. Katherine smelled the water long before they reached the shore, and realized how thirsty she was. Mac eased her conveyance to the ground and slipped out of the harness-vine. His tunic was torn where the rough vine had rested on his shoulder, and raw flesh showed undeerneath.

Grunting, she nodded toward the river. Mac glanced suspiciously around, then removed the gag.

"Buy me a drink, big boy?" she said in a sarcastic tone. Then, remembering he didn't understand her language, she added sweetly, "You ugly jackass."

Mac's brow furrowed, and he answered in his own incomprehensible tongue. Plainly, he didn't understand.

"Water," Katherine said. "Watch me now, you stupid bastard." She licked her lips and turned her gaze toward the sun-dappled river. "Water," she repeated.

Abruptly, Cha Mak Nul got up and stripped a broad, rubbery leaf from a bush near the bank. Folding it, he dipped it into the river and carried it back to Katherine.

"Well, what do you know," she said with a wry face. "You do have more brains than a vanilla wafer. I was beginning to wonder." She lifted her head and opened her mouth while Mac held the leaf to her lips. The cool water bore a sweet minty taste imparted to it by the leaf.

Her thirst quenched, she leaned back. Casting the leaf aside, her captor grabbed the ends of the poles

and dragged her toward the water. She started to protest, then bit her lip. Mac might decide to replace the
gag if she made too much noise.

The Darklander waded in until he was waist deep
in the river, and he pulled the rack in after. Katherine
felt a moment of panic as the water surged up around
her, but the primitive construction quickly stabilized.
Raftlike, it floated on the surface.

Again, Mac slipped the braided vine over his raw
shoulder, but this time he walked beside his captive,
guiding the rack with one hand as they moved
downriver.

Privately, Katherine despaired. There were no
tracks now for the Kirringskal to follow. With a light
current to aid him, Mac made far better time, too. She
glanced at her pack to make sure it hadn't washed
overboard.

She was thoroughly miserable. The strips of cloth,
pieces of her own dress that bound her wrists and
ankles, chafed. The sun beat mercilessly down on her
face and neck, and she was soaked from her dunking.
Water swirled up through the rack and over its sides
as well, keeping her soaked. Unable to convince the
Darklander to stop, she was forced to wet herself, and
the urine odor lingered.

The sun began to sink ever so slowly. Shadows
stretched dark fingers across the water, and the visible
sky turned a bloody red. Mac's eyes darted from side
to side, watching the trees, the banks, and the evening
birds that glided among the high, overarching
branches.

Katherine groaned softly. The baby in her body
stirred restlessly, kicking and nudging. She folded her
bound hands over her stomach and stroked her palm

lightly over the wet fabric of her skirts. "Give me a break, kid," she murmured, "please."

Mac clapped a hand over her mouth and glared with hard, dark eyes. In a low voice he whispered an incomprehensible warning. He took his hand away, his fingers leaving white marks on her cheeks.

"The stork that brought you into the world should have been arrested for smuggling dope!" Katherine hissed.

His lip curled in a vicious snarl. If he couldn't understand her words, he clearly understood her tone of defiance. He raised a hand to strike her.

A shrill scream ripped the air with soul-chilling effect. The blow never fell. The blood drained from Mac's face as he stared toward the riverbank.

Katherine turned toward the sound, too, every nerve taut, goosebumps livid on her flesh.

The sun behind the hills and evening fully upon them, there was nothing to see on the banks except the trees and bushes. The wind stirred the leaves and set the branches to swaying. There were no birds now.

"A *banshee*," Katherine said quietly, her gaze combing the nearest bank. The scream had seemed to emanate from there. But *banshees* had no form. They were ghosts who manifested only as screams, men or women who had died particularly horrible deaths. Some said a *banshee*'s scream was but an echo of their last terrible moment of life, that their souls became the final sound that left their dying lips.

If she could not see it, though, Katherine felt its presence with the strange, inexplicable awareness she seemed to have developed. The *banshee* was not alone, either. Other things were out there, all crowding near the riverbank, all watching.

The Darklander swallowed nervously and lowered

the hand with which he had been about to strike her. He avoided her gaze and, gripping the side of the rack, propelled her through the water again at the best pace he could manage.

The sunset colors faded from the sky, and night crept in like a wary thief. Cha Mak Nul began a low-voiced chant, barely a whisper, with his eyes turned upward. Katherine noticed how he clenched one hand over his heart.

Praying, she realized. *He worships the Dark.* A songlike quality to his mutterings made her wish she could understand him.

Pale light shimmered through the trees as Thanador slowly rose. The moon, a swelling crescent growing toward fullness, silvered the leaves and grass. The river's gently rippling surface sparkled under its radiance.

Katherine gazed toward the shoreline again. Hundreds of ghosts walked there now, moving soundlessly, invisibly, through the trees, following the edge of the water. And their numbers were growing. They were no more than vaguely felt presences, yet they were there, and she could feel them watching, following.

She thought of Falcon and wondered if he was following, too. She couldn't guess how far from the Kirringskal cave she had come, but it was a goodly distance, she was sure. Falcon would have a hard time tracking her in the darkness.

Mac's prayer-song ended. At the next bend in the river he stopped and gripped the sides of the rack. His gaze darted along both sides of the river, and he licked his lips. When he turned and spoke to Katherine, his words rolled like a muffled echo over the quiet water. He paused as if expecting an answer, then shrugged. Moving to the front of the rack, he threw the thickly braided vine over his shoulder, grabbed the ends of the poles, and headed toward the shore.

Suddenly, Katherine lurched sideways, and only the restraining vine across her chest prevented her from being dumped into the river. Mac cried out as he slipped in some mud and went under. He came up sputtering and cursing.

Despite herself, Kaltherine gave a little laugh. "Karma in action," she said aloud. "Not the slipup I'm hoping you'll make, though." She glanced at her backpack again, making sure it was still there.

To her surprise Mac answered, not with a blow, but in a tone that matched her own for sarcasm.

"Oh yeah?" Katherine said. "I wonder if you can understand this?" She raised the middle finger of her right hand and smiled.

Mac glared at her, then scowled and shook his head in apparent disgust. He grabbed the rack's poles again and dragged it up a muddy slope to the shore, where he lowered it to the ground.

Katherine tried to sit up, but the Darklander pushed her back down. His gaze locked with hers for a moment, and she saw a warning there. He put his hand on her swollen belly.

Though bound, she lashed out angrily, knocking his hand away. "Keep your hands to yourself, buster," she said, drawing one arm protectively across her stomach as she glared at him.

Cha Mak Nul did not back away. He spoke sternly and pointed at her belly again. Then he reached for her hands. Again, Katherine tried to jerk away, but this time he caught her wrists and held them in an iron grip. His fingers went to the wet knots of her bonds. A moment later, her hands were free.

"Am I supposed to say thank you?" she asked,

meeting his gaze as she rubbed her chafed wrists. "Get fucked." She reached down to untie her ankles, no easy thing to do, considering the size of her belly.

Mac caught her shoulder, though, and held up a warning finger. Again that long, stern gaze and muttered words in a language she didn't speak.

She understood, though. "Don't worry, scumbreath," she said. "I'm not going to run away in my condition. I'll be as docile as a lamb." Putting on another of her big, false-hearted smiles, she leaned back on her hands and shifted her feet toward the Darklander.

Mac pursed his lips thoughtfully, then began to untie the strips of cloth.

"Of course, as far as I can tell, you don't have lambs on Palenoc." She smiled again with that same dripping sweetness, reached for her backpack, and hugged it to her body.

Mac stepped back, glaring at her before he turned away and began to gather bits of bark and fallen branches. He put them in a pile and used his hands to clear an area of earth around the kindling. Then, scooping handfuls of mud from the riverbank, he built a low, circular wall, making a neat firepit.

Katherine watched him work for a few moments, then ignored him. Loosening the strings of her backpack, she pulled out some items. Fortunately, the pack was waterproof. Her copy of *A Pale Knock* was undamaged. Rolled leather trousers were in good shape, too, but with her belly so large, she could no longer get into them.

Her hand closed on something else, a small black rectangular object. She looked up to make sure Mac wasn't watching, then drew it out quickly and thrust it out of sight under the edge of her skirts.

She smiled to herself as she put one hand over her belly and rested the other on the hidden weapon. With the Omega stunner in her possession she felt much more secure—forty-five thousand volts more secure, in fact.

She only hoped the batteries were still good.

The baby inside her kicked. Katherine closed her eyes and squirmed a bit until the child grew still again. When she opened her eyes, she bit her lip. The ghosts were much closer now. They stood among the trees and bushes or on the riverbank. A pale, drawn figure of a woman stood at Katherine's right side. Another figure, a grizzled old man, loomed over Mac.

Mac didn't notice. He went about his work. On a piece of bark he made a small pile of dry leaves and grass. Next, he positioned the point of a stick upon the bark and began to roll it vigorously between his palms.

He had no awareness at all of the presences surrounding them, Katherine realized. Only she could see them. Or sense them. That was a better word, *sense*. All her senses seemed to be expanding in ways she didn't understand. Not only could she sense ghosts, but other things, too.

She gazed toward the opposite bank of the river. Over there, somewhere in the darkness, was the ancient remnant of a Gateway to Paradane, to her own Earth. She didn't know how, but she knew it was there. She could feel the weak seepage of energy. For a thousand years the Gate had been dying, and it was dying still.

How could she know that, she wondered. She turned her face up toward the spectral figure beside her. "What's happened to me?" she whispered. If the figure could respond, it chose not to.

She turned back toward Mac. He was still struggling

to start a fire in his pitifully primitive fashion. Katherine muttered a disgusted curse. Reaching into her backpack again, she drew out a Bic lighter. "Try this," she said. She flicked the mechanism, raising an inch-high flame.

Cha Mak Nul's eyes widened in surprise and fear, and he leaped back from his firepit. Katherine muttered under her breath as she shook her head. "What a wimp," she accused. "Some kidnapper." She released the mechanism, and the flame disappeared. Then she flicked it twice more, showing him how it worked, before she tossed it to him.

The fear left his face. He studied the lighter with genuine curiosity, quickly learning to operate it.

"Yeah, you're a regular Einstein," Katherine complimented. "Now get a fire going so we can dry out." She patted the hidden Omega stunner. "And later, if you come very close, I'll show you something that will really light your fire."

In no time Mac had a campfire going. He slipped the lighter inside his waistband and fed bits of twigs and leaves into the flames. The blaze grew brighter. The ghosts seemed to withdraw a bit, but not far. Vacant, hollow eyes glimmered redly with the fire's glow.

In the distant woods another light began to shimmer. And to the right of that, yet another light. Startled, Katherine twisted around to find two more lights like tiny flames dancing in the gloom.

Mac saw them, too. "*Leikkios*," he said grimly.

Leikkios. She knew that word. A *leikkio* was a spirit that appeared as a spot of light to lure unsuspecting travelers from safe trails to more treacherous places. Robert had told her once about his encounter with a *leikkio*, how it had tried to trick him and nearly caused him to fall into a deep, abandoned well.

Mac scowled and uttered a harsh command. In the long days she'd spent nursing him in the Kirringskal cave, Katherine had learned to understand just enough of his language to catch the word "sleep." He was ordering her to sleep while he squatted by the fire and kept watch.

"Sending me to bed without supper, eh?" Katherine muttered.

Mac snapped at her again, then looked away and moved closer to the fire. He stared into the flames and seemed to forget her. A strange, lost look came into his eyes. He held up his left hand and took off the ring he wore. The opal shone like a star as it caught the light. He put the ring back on and whispered something that sounded like "Thorn."

Strange feelings of loneliness and uncertainty swept over Katherine, emotions she realized with a start originated, not with her, but with the Shadarkan. Somehow, in some empathic manner, she suddenly shared what he felt, and what he felt surprised her.

She tasted his dark love and the powerful longing he felt for someone far away. She drank of other emotions, too, of rejection and hurt and fear, but also of determination. She understood none of it. It was insight she didn't want into this man, who had kidnapped and abused her.

Katherine tried to shut it off, but instead she drew closer to him. His emotions, even his thoughts, became clear to her, as if something were sucking the two of them together, merging them into one being.

"Get out of my head!" she screamed suddenly, clapping her temples.

Her outcry shocked Mac from his reverie. Unaware of what had happened, he shot a suspicious look across the fire. "Be silent, woman!" he ordered, half rising from his crouch.

She understood his command just as clearly as if he'd spoken plain English, though she knew he hadn't. There was no time to be surprised, though, no time to react to this fantastic development.

Without warning the campfire seemed to explode in his face. Burning sticks flew into the air, smoke and hot sparks spiraling upward. The Darklander screamed and fell backward, clutching a burned hand. A fiery branch flashed upward from the fire straight for his head. Cha Mak Nul barely dodged it.

Katherine put a hand to her mouth. She couldn't see the *poltergeist*, but she could sense it. She could also sense the anger it directed at Mac. The trees shook, showering them with leaves and acorns, and the protective mud wall around the fire blew apart, splattering them with filth.

"Stop it!" Katherine screamed, panic filling her throat. Flaming brands and hot ash streaked around the camp as if juggled by hundreds of invisible hands. Her mind suddenly filled with visions of another fire, the great forest fire that had taken the lives of Robert and Eric.

Cha Mak Nul stumbled across the camp, reaching for her, shouting at her. The *poltergeist* flung itself around the clearing, hurling anything it could move. Mac caught her arm roughly and yanked her to her feet.

At first Katherine barely responded. In her mind she was transported to another time and place, where the woods were burning, and Eric, lost somewhere, was screaming her name. She had to get to him. "Eric!" she cried. She had to reach him, find him, save him from the fire.

But someone was preventing her.

Wildly, her gaze unfocused, she lashed out at Mac with one fist, striking his face. Then, before he could recover, her other hand came up, clutching the Omega stunner. She slammed it against the Darklander's side, barely aware of her actions.

A flash of light and a sharp, electric crackle, then Cha Mak Nul dropped like a puppet whose strings had been cut. For a moment he lay still, then his muscles began to twitch, his arms and legs to thrash.

Katherine emerged from the madness of her vision and saw what she had done. For an instant she hesitated, uncertain of her next move. Then she bent and snatched her lighter from the Darklander's waistband. "Thief," she muttered breathlessly. Grabbing her backpack, she ran toward the trees.

The woods were dark. She couldn't run fast in her pregnant condition, but maybe she could hide far enough away that Mac wouldn't find her when he recovered. Then she could make her way back to the Kirringskal or some other place where she might find help.

All around, the ghosts retreated into the deep woods as if encouraging her to follow. Even the *poltergeist* was gone. Katherine crashed into the underbrush, moving as swiftly as she could manage, her heart pounding in her chest.

Abruptly, she stopped.

Even in the forest gloom there was no mistaking the creature. Katherine stared at a pair of burning eyes, feeling all hope drain from her.

Beneath an ancient tree, not ten paces away, stood a *chimorg*.

Chapter Eleven

REMEMBER.

Robert retreated farther inside himself and tried to shut out her voice. All was darkness and cold. He didn't know where he was. *No!* he cried in soundless defiance. *Get out of my head!*

Laughter, cruel and softly seductive. *Remember.*

Robert tried to put up walls against her voice by focusing his thoughts on something else. *Left upper level side block. Right middle cross block. Horse stance and left middle punch. Right punch and pivot.* He concentrated, visualizing each movement.

Gankaku. She spoke the Japanese name of his favorite training kata and laughed that feathery laugh again. *Or in your own language, Robert, "Crane on a Rock."*

He screamed inside, unable to hide his secrets from her. *Leave me alone!*

He felt a sensation, like a hand upon his chest, though he knew even that was in his mind. *Crane on a Rock,* She repeated in taunting fashion. *Crane on a precipice. Be careful not to fall, little Crane.*

The hand pushed. Robert fell and fell, tumbling through a vast black hell. He tried desperately to summon his courage. This wasn't real, he told himself, but his heart hammered harder, faster, until pain flared in his chest. His mouth opened, but still he held back his screams. Head over heels he spun helplessly, falling, falling. He squeezed his eyes shut—or imagined he did—

And screamed. Fear and terror won out at last, and all his walls of resistance exploded with soul-shattering force. His entire being became one long shriek.

Through his screams he heard Her speak again. *It's all in your mind, Robert Polo*, she said. Her voice sounded like cracking ice. *But your mind is my playground. Want to play, little boy?*

"No!" he cried aloud, his voice sounding small and alien.

No! She cried, mocking him. Then her tone changed, and her words stung like whiplashes in his brain. *So many delicious memories and fears to choose among!* She said. *What a cornucopia of guilt you are!*

The dark void changed. Suddenly, there was sky, gray and wet and oppressive. There were trees and earth. There was hard rock, treacherous, slippery. He continued to fall, and the flesh on his palms ripped as he tried to find a grip and stop his plummet. Something knocked the breath from him. He tried to protect his head from the mountain slope's sharp projections as he rolled and tumbled; then his left leg struck a rock, and white-hot pain flared in the bone just below his knee.

He came to rest on a stone outcropping. A red haze slowly lifted from his vision. Just below the knee his leg hinged at a peculiar angle, and a spur of bone jutted up through the skin. Blood oozed from dozens of cuts and scrapes, and for a moment the world slipped out of focus. He fought to stay conscious.

Seconds ticked by, measured by the distant pounding in his head and the strangely muffled throb in his broken leg. An eerie calm settled over him as he thought he must be dying. He stared at the sky, seeing shapes in the clouds, and smiled weakly as dragons took form—Chinese storm dragons riding the winds. They smiled down at him.

He was back in China's Zhejian Province. He'd been climbing Hengshan Mountain before his fall, and now his leg was broken.

He remembered.

Robert craned his neck back, trying to see the incline down which he'd fallen, but a shadow fell across his face as someone bent over him. He looked up into the blue eyes of Scott Silver.

"Polo!" Scott shouted, flinging down his pack as he knelt at Robert's side. Scott's face was pale with fear as one hand stroked reassuringly through Robert's hair. "Hang in there, buddy!" he urged. He reached for his pack again. "I've got the first-aid kit right here. Then somehow I'll get us off this damned mountain!"

Robert raised one shaking hand and tried to touch his friend. "Scotty . . ."

Darkness swirled around Robert again. Scott and the mountain melted away as the air took on a sharp chill. Through muted senses, he perceived the icy touch of chains encircling his limbs. He seemed to be spread-eagled horizontally in the air, suspended in some kind of sling. ". . . help me." His words barely sounded in his own ears as he finished his plea, and his unsupported head sank back.

Tears leaked from his eyes. He clung as long as possible to the image of Scott's face. "I remember," he confessed in a defeated whisper, knowing how it would please his tormentor.

You are such fun to play with, Polo. Her voice was velvet, and She stroked him with her words, touched him in impossible places. *A seething mass of conflicts and denials—I could feed on you forever.*

Robert felt cold hands on him, and this time he knew they were real hands, but he could see nothing in the darkness. He realized he was naked, and the hands were exploring him in ways they shouldn't. "Don't touch me!" he screamed, writhing violently against his chains.

Sweet puppet. Her sigh of pleasure filled his mind, smothering all other sensation except his awareness of Her. *Here is one of my favorite memories. Shall we live it again?*

Once more, he began to tumble through the darkness. "Please!" he begged, hating the whimper in his voice. "Stop!"

Don't quit on me now, little Polo, She said laughing. *As you would say, "It's showtime."*

Pinpoints of light perforated the void and resolved themselves into street lamps, car lights, office windows, neon signs, storefronts, a hot dog vendor's sidewalk cart, a magazine kiosk. The constant din of the city assaulted his ears, and its smells swirled around him like a miasma.

"New York," Robert muttered, recognizing his surroundings. He glanced up at a nearby street sign, Grove Street, and his heart shriveled in his chest. "Not again!" he cried in despair.

Crack! Crack! Crack!

The gunshots echoed like thunder in his brain. He raced up the sidewalk, past people crouched fearfully between parked cars, past shoppers huddled open-mouthed in doorways. On the sidewalk ahead a circle of youths stood. Robert's gaze fastened in horror on the smoking gun, the gang colors and insignia on a leather jacket, and the face of the punk who held the weapon.

The gang broke and ran as a siren screamed suddenly in the night, but Robert didn't chase them. He stared down at Scott Silver's still form and watched spots of blood blossom on his friend's white shirt like roses opening their petals. Robert sank to the sidewalk, feeling the knees of his jeans rip, the harsh scrape of cement on his bare flesh. "Scott!" he cried, his hands clenching into fists.

Her voice sighed in his mind. The city faded even as Robert reached down to gather Scott in his arms. All was darkness once more.

The flavor of your despair fills me, She murmured. Her words were thick with an almost sexual satisfaction. *Do you remember nights later how you stalked and killed your lover's murderer with your bare hands? Shall we relive that one, too?*

"I remember!" Robert shouted, hating the hot tears that stung his eyes. He thrashed against the unseen chains binding him, but he knew he was weakening, not even trying to throw up walls to shut out the hateful sound of her voice. "I remember everything! Why are you tormenting me?"

Because it's fun to abuse you, Robert Polo, came the answer. *You owe me some amusement for the difficulty you have caused. But you do not remember everything. In time you will.*

He felt her fingers in his mind, a prickling inside his head, rifling his memories like cards in a Rolodex. "No more!" he begged. "I don't want to remember!"

He plunged again through a deep, stygian well.

A dim red glow slowly alleviated the darkness. Wisps of smoke curled up from braziers, and a whiff of jasmine incense tickled his nose. He found himself in a vast chamber. Rows of fat painted columns supported the low ceiling, and a huge wooden sculpture of the Contemplative Buddha dominated one wall. Behind it rose an elaborate mural portraying mountains and clouds and dancing wind dragons.

Robert's gaze turned to the opposite wall and a huge golden door.

"We shouldn't be pissing around down here," Scott Silver whispered earnestly in his ear. "They only let us stay because of the storm." His gaze roamed around the chamber and settled on the Buddha sculpture. He shivered. "It's like we're violating a church or something."

Robert glanced at his friend as the two of them crouched in the shadow of a pillar. He leaned out and took another look around the chamber—no sign of the priests who had given them shelter. The temple was unearthly quiet.

Earlier that day he and Scott had climbed Hengshan Mountain to see the legendary Suspended Temple, but a ferocious storm had come up, nearly blowing them from the mountain several times. At last they'd made it to the temple gates, where the priests, usually reluctant to admit visitors, had taken them in and provided them with sleeping mats for the night.

"I want to look around!" Robert insisted, reassuring himself again that they were alone. The hour was late, and he guessed most of the priests were asleep.

Scott caught Robert's arm. "Our hosts asked us to stay in our rooms. We should honor their request, not sneak around like this."

"All right, all right!" Robert snapped, jerking his arm free. "We'll go back." He jerked his thumb toward the golden door. "Right after I see what's through there. Do you have any idea how few Westerners have ever seen what we're seeing?"

Scott gave an exasperated sigh and followed Robert.

The door stood perhaps twelve feet high. A solid sheet of hammered gold covered it: dragons, unicorns, and other strange creatures stood out in relief on the shimmering surface. Robert ran his fingertips along it.

Despite his misgivings, Scott's face was awe-filled. He laid a palm on the door and lovingly stroked it. "I didn't know there were unicorns in Chinese mythology," he whispered. "Nothing like the European beasts, though. These look almost sinister."

Robert didn't answer. His hand found the golden ring at the left side of the door.

Scott touched Robert's shoulder and pointed upward. "There's something written over the jamb. Can you read it?"

Robert let go of the ring and stepped back. A line of characters painted above the door was barely visible in the glow from the braziers. "I speak the language a little," he answered, "but I can't read it."

Scott frowned. "Looks like some kind of a warning."

Robert grinned and seized the ring again. "You've been reading too many of my books."

"It just feels . . ." Scott hesitated, shaking his head. ". . . wrong."

Robert pulled the door open. Despite its size and obvious age, it swung easily on its hinges. "What the hell is that?" he asked quietly as Scott moved closer.

The room beyond was totally dark but for a tiny greenish light that appeared impossibly far away. Robert started across the threshold. Again, Scott caught his arm. "Not so fast, Polo," Scott urged. "It's blacker than a bat's asshole in there."

Robert eased his arm free and fixed his gaze on the minuscule light. "This bat must shit emeralds," he said. "Come on." Scott muttered a curse as they both stepped inside the darkened room.

The green pinpoint of light shone steadily before them. Before they took five steps, Scott leaned close to Robert's ear. "Polo, we're just begging for trouble—"

Robert interrupted him. "Hey, it's moving!" he said suddenly breathless. "It's—"

In an instant green fire engulfed them. Robert felt as if the skin was blasted from his bones. Pain, worse than anything he'd ever known, filled him. Yet, before he could voice a scream, the flames vanished, leaving him with nothing worse than a tingling sensation that faded as quickly as the flames. He looked at Scott. Neither of them said a word; they just stood with their mouths agape and slowly looked around.

They were no longer in the Suspended Temple. Wondrous as that place was, it could never have contained a chamber like the one in which they found themselves. Immense, fluted columns of marble soared upward toward an unseeable ceiling. The floor, too, was fashioned of highly polished stone. A golden door nearly identical to the one they had come through stood open behind them. As they watched, it closed, seemingly of its own accord.

At the far end of the chamber, a throne carved from black onyx glimmered in the moonbeams that penetrated from an open balcony. A vaguely feminine figure half reclined there. It sat up with sudden interest, and a cascade of black hair spilled forward, revealing a shining length of horn that jutted upward from a pale brow.

Suddenly, Robert couldn't breathe. He reached out

to grab Scott's hand, but his friend faded away. Vertigo and darkness swallowed him again, and he found himself once more suspended in chains. He screamed in frustration, filled with a grinding sense of despair as Scott slipped from his grasp again, and he found himself once more a prisoner in Shandal Karg's chamber of horrors.

The touch of the chains was like ice on his bare wrists and ankles. His limbs felt stretched almost to the breaking point. As before, he could see nothing, though he was sure his eyes were wide open.

Our most treasured remembrances, She said, *are such delicate and elusive things.* Her voice inside his mind was like the whisper of the winter wind. It blew through his memories, stirring them like dead leaves. *Is the past a little more clear to you now?*

A strange numbness threatened to overcome Robert. "I've been to Palenoc before," he said. He'd suspected it, but now he knew it was true. A wave of weakness swept over him. Unconsciousness loomed, a welcome blackness deeper even than the darkness which surrounded him. "God help me, I've been your prisoner before."

Her laughter shrieked through his brain. *Don't faint, little puppet,* She said. *We have much work to do and many lessons to learn.*

Robert trembled, and fear swelled within him again. Still, he tried to resist it. "I escaped you once!" he shouted. "I'll do it again!"

She laughed again. Then her words scraped over his mind like dull razor blades. *You never escaped me, puppet. Even as you fled back through the gate of Paradane I placed a dark seed deep in your mind, erasing your memories of Palenoc, but ensuring your return.*

"Only my conscious memories," Robert muttered

in abrupt realization. "My book, *A Pale Knock*, it's all there. Just in coded, subconscious form."

Memories twisted and perverted, the voice responded. Robert felt invisible fingers sorting through his memories again, choosing, discarding. *In your tale an evil woman tries to kill a child. But it is not I who shall kill the* Child, *Polo*. She paused, and the silence hung like an icy sword about to fall. *It is you who shall kill the* Child.

Robert's head snapped back as if he'd been struck in the face. "I remember!" The words ripped from him like a scream. Then, swallowing hard, he tried to regain a semblance of calm. "You did something to my head—programmed me. I'm going to kill the Son of the Morning."

I would have sent you back to Paradane even if you had not tried to run away, She said. *I can sense all the gates between Palenoc and Paradane, Polo, no matter where they are, and I put that information in your brain. Your programming, as you call it, was complete. I would have sent you home. Then you would have returned to Palenoc, a seeming innocent, through the gate in the mountains near Chalosa, practically in Rasoul's backyard. And those trusting fools would have taken you to their hearts—exactly as they did—never suspecting that you were my weapon.*

Robert stopped trembling and sagged in the embrace of his chains. His mind raced with thoughts and memories, realizations, fears, and recriminations. "The program was complete?" His question was a barely audible whisper.

Invisible strands of something like hair slithered around his fingers and manipulated them. *My poor puppet*, She sighed with a mock-sympathetic tone. *You are the perfect killer, Polo. You need no weapon. You have physical skills never seen on this world and so much pent-up rage needing release. All I had to do was maneuver you close enough, like a piece on a chessboard. Then, when the hated Child was born, you would have been there, and one blow from either of your hands would have murdered all hope for the Domains of Light.*

"Damn you!" Robert thrashed uselessly against his bonds. "I'm not a killer. I'm not!"

A savage, catlike hiss filled his mind. Without warning, as if the chains that held him had suddenly dissolved, he fell again through the vast, smothering darkness toward some moment in his past.

"I won't play this game," he started to say. "I'm not your puppet."

But those thoughts faded before they actually took form. The darkness shifted and reformed itself into a familiar Greenwich Village skyline. Robert looked up, scanning the rooftops, then peered up and down Christopher Street, making sure no one was in sight. For a moment he leaned against the wall of a closed florist shop. Then he turned cautiously into a dirty, garbage-strewn alley.

Sweat poured down his face. He was breathing hard from the chase, his heart pounding. Now, though, the chase had ended. He knew this neighborhood and this alley, and there was no way out for his prey.

An aluminum trash can overturned at the alley's far end, and a human cry followed.

A streetlight at the mouth of the alley shone faintly behind Robert. It stretched his shadow out before him in grotesquely elongated fashion, and the very edge of its black shape touched a form sprawled on the pavement among the refuse. A leather-jacketed young punk scrambled desperately to his feet as Robert came closer.

"Use your gun," Robert said in a low voice. "Please."

From under the leather jacket came the metal gleam of a pistol—the same gun the kid had used to kill Scott Silver. Robert sighed with satisfaction as he brought his left foot up and around in an inside crescent kick. The weapon flew toward the other side of the alley. "Thank you," he said.

The frightened kid stood frozen before him, the deer caught in headlights. Then Robert's eyes narrowed as he noted the red bandanna tied to a metal ring on the jacket sleeve and the gang insignia painted on the shoulder. Something went cold inside him. This kid was nearly his own age.

For more than a week Robert had hunted and stalked this piece of subhuman garbage, waiting to catch him alone. Now he took a moment to study Scott Silver's murderer. He turned his head and spat in disdain.

"Who are you, man?" the punk demanded in a panicked, high-pitched voice. "What do you want? You're meat if you mess with me, man. I got friends!"

Robert's left foot came up again. The punk's head snapped back, and he crashed backward, falling on the overturned aluminum can, making a terrible racket. Robert didn't care; he didn't look around to see if the noise had attracted anyone. The punk rose shakily to his feet, blood flowing from both nostrils.

The sight meant nothing to Robert. He'd seen blood—Scott's blood. Putting his whole body into the blow, he struck with a palm-heel smash. Fragments of teeth flew, and the punk crashed backward into a wall.

Dazed and driven by fear, he turned and tried to climb it, so desperate was he to get away.

Robert advanced and grabbed a handful of jacket. The punk screamed, whirled, and swung wildly at Robert, who countered with a knife-hand block and forefist strike to the lower ribs. The punk's eyes widened with pain. As he sagged to his knees, he reached out with one hand and clutched at Robert's trousers for support. Robert caught the hand and twisted. Cartilage snapped and bone broke. The punk started to scream again, but Robert's knee stopped his mouth.

Robert stepped back for a moment. The whimpering form at his feet made a pitiful effort to crawl away. Robert watched him, allowing him to make a little progress, noting the bloody slime trail the worthless little slug left on the pavement. Then, with a few quick steps, he straddled the punk, caught a handful of hair, and pulled the kid's head back until their eyes met. Then, with unfeeling precision, he broke the neck of Scott Silver's murderer.

Robert turned up his left palm and stared at the pale red scar that paralleled his lifeline, barely visible in the light from the alley entrance. It was the mark of the blood-bond he shared with Scott. He put the hand to his mouth and kissed the scar.

The darkness of the alley closed in on him and became a void. Falling and falling, all emotion numbed, he waited to be caught by his chains and to hear the tormenting sound of her voice.

You hated him because he killed your lover. Her whisper rasped through his mind. He flinched inside, and cold tears seeped from his eyes, spilled down the sides of his face, and dripped away into whatever pit yawned beneath him. "Stop using that word!" he screamed, struggling violently against his chains.

Her laughter gave way to purest, dripping scorn. *You pathetic fool! Your refusal to face and accept yourself made it so much easier for me to shape you into what I wanted you to be.*

"I don't understand," Robert said through quiet sobs. "How could that punk kill Scott? You wanted me to remember, and I do. Scott didn't escape back through the gate with me. He's still here."

Pain blossomed deep inside his brain, a tiny, gnawing pain that promised to grow worse. She was inside his head again, crawling through him like a worm through old meat. Once more, he fell through a long darkness to relive yet again that moment in the alley. Bone broke under his fists, the smell of blood filled his nostrils, and he dealt death with a soul-chilling joy.

He found himself once more in his web of chains.

You hated him because he killed your lover. Her whisper rasped through his mind.

"Yes," he answered coldly. Somehow, he felt Her smile with satisfaction and knew he had pleased Her.

You are full of hate, my puppet, my Polo. Her voice was almost a purr now. He felt hands on him as he had before, many hands, dry, cold hands. They stroked his naked body as if he were a cat while She continued to purr in his brain. *You blame yourself because Scott Silver is dead.*

"Yes," Robert murmured. A weird iciness was growing deep down inside him. Pieces of him were turning numb. Though all he could see was darkness, he tried to close his eyes and discovered he couldn't. His lids were staked open with tiny sticks. He didn't care, feeling almost sensual pleasure in the realization.

You hate yourself, She said, *and your life, which has been filled with nothing but pain and deception and denial.* Her voice was sympathetic, consoling. It seemed to cradle him in his turmoil.

"Yes," he admitted.

The invisible hands massaged him now, touched him in private and shameful places. He could do nothing to prevent them, nothing to save himself. Though his eyes burned from crying, his tears ceased. His mouth elicited a low moan. As if it were no longer quite his own, his traitorous flesh began to respond to those unseen caresses.

You despise yourself and your perverted desires.

She knew all his horrible secrets, his sins, the things that had tormented him all his life. Why deny it any longer? It was time to face the truth. "Yes," Robert said. His voice changed subtly with his answer, taking on a harder edge.

You hate your brother because he would reject you if he knew of your lusts.

"Yes," Robert confessed.

You hate your father for what he did to you when you were a child, because his desires are even more twisted than your own. You hate your mother because she knew and turned a blind eye to your pain.

"Hate," Robert said. "I hate You for making me remember these things and for showing me myself."

It is good to hate, Polo, She said softly. *Hate is the scalpel with which I shape and mold you. I am the only one who cares about you, Polo. You are important to me. I will give you a new life and a new purpose. I will be your family, and you will give me your loyalty.*

Robert groaned low in his throat as the hands moved swiftly over him, and his body found orgasmic release. He screamed, and his flesh shuddered. Every nerve ending burned as if stripped raw and touched with fire. Moments later, the hands that manipulated him withdrew, replaced by mouths and tongues that licked and lapped at his unresisting form until they promised to ignite that fire again.

I will teach you pleasure, Polo. Her voice was almost a lullaby in his head. It soothed him even as it terrified him. *I will teach you pain. Then I will teach you the pleasure to be found in pain.*

Robert turned his head slowly from side to side as the harsh bite of his chains and those softly, hungrily devouring mouths overwhelmed his senses—and more, his fears. Barely audible words came out of his mouth. "Teach me."

Then you will show your gratitude for my lessons, She said, her voice stroking him as if he were a helpless kitten clutched to her breast. *You will kill the cursed* Child, *the Son of the Morning. Even now my forces are scouring the land for Him.*

The darkness seemed to lift a little. Like a man in a drugged state, Robert tried to look around. There was no source of light at all. Yet, with a strange new vision he could see the shadows that moved around him, whose mouths so pleasured his body.

They were not shadows, but revenants. He knew now why the mouths were so cold, the tongues so dry and rasping. They belonged to the same animated corpses that had killed his followers and captured him. He should have been horrified, but there was a nightmarish eroticism in the discovery.

You will also kill Eric Podlowsky, that thrice-cursed fool, who stumbled upon a thousands-year-old secret and revealed it to my enemies. My chimorgs, *my children, cry out for his blood.*

Robert felt as if he were dying by slow degrees. He tried to remember his name, where he was, why he was here, but nothing came to him.

The revenants began to touch him again. With a sudden tension on his chains his legs were drawn apart. He sighed and surrendered himself to yet another invasion.

The echoes of her words filled his head. With the faintest fading portion of self-awareness, he tried to turn away, to look inside himself, to see what changes She had wrought in him. All he saw was a cold, black void.

Finally, he stopped looking.

Chapter Twelve

GAULTNIMBLE scratched around the edge of his new eyepatch as he watched his mistress from a gloomy corner of the throne room. Silently, he crept out of his hiding place and crouched down behind a fluted, marble column. He peeked around, jerked his head back nervously, then peeked again.

Shandal Karg sat motionless on her onyx seat. A faint azure light rose up from two crystal caldrons arranged before her, giving her skin an icy cast.

Gaultnimble eased toward the next column, slipping even closer to the throne. Letting out a slow breath, he leaned on the column and prepared to steal another look. A piece of marble crumbled suddenly at his touch. Bits of stone clattered on the floor, followed by a crash as a larger section fell away and shattered.

The dwarf's heart nearly stopped. He covered his head protectively with his arms, cringing, as he waited for the angry sound of her voice.

Silence.

Perplexed, Gaultnimble uncovered his head and looked up. The falling stone had not disturbed his mistress; She hadn't moved at all. A strange look was frozen on her face. Though She appeared to gaze into one of the caldrons, her eyes seemed vacant.

He stepped nervously from the concealment of the

column into plain sight. Still, She didn't move. Emboldened, he waved his arms and jumped up and down, drawing no reaction. He stuck out his tongue, shoved fingers into his mouth, bugged out his one good eye, and made a horrible face.

"Knock, knock," he whispered in a singsong manner. "Anybody home?"

Shandal Kark made no response.

With growing confidence Gaultnimble tiptoed toward the low dais where the throne sat. Stepping between the caldrons, he stopped at the bottom of three stairs that led up to the throne. There he made another face to mock his Mistress. Finally, he turned around, dropped his trousers, and showed Her his bare backside.

"I've never found you so personable, Divinity," he muttered when even these deeds drew no reaction. He pulled his clothes together and climbed the three steps to the top of the dais to take a position by her side. He waved a hand before her unseeing eyes.

Indeed, no one was home.

He sang close to her ear, improvising a rhyme:

"The Child is leeching your power, you stupid cow—
Keep and column crumble around you now.
Merrily, merrily Night gives way to Morn,
A queen's gaze falls upon an empty bourn,
A Heart grows still as another Heart is born."

Gaultnimble grinned at his cleverness and turned toward the pair of caldrons.

Sometimes there was one caldron, sometimes two. Sometimes there were three, but he had never seen more. His Mistress claimed to have fashioned them centuries ago with her own hands and baptized them with her own blood. Like pets they waited invisible until she conjured them forth to serve her needs.

In the rightmost caldron, various scenes and landscapes rolled upon the water, as if seen through an eye that ranged freely around. It was searching, he realized, searching for the *Child* called the Son of the Morning. Fields, woodlands, rivers, mountains all flowed by, interspersed with scenes of villages, towns, and far-off cities. The eye roamed through congested streets and stinking alleyways, peered into hovels and homes.

Gaultnimble watched, mesmerized by the parade of images. Suddenly, he gave a sharp shake of his head and forced himself to look away. His gaze fell upon the other caldron. At first he frowned. Then his face took on a coldly calculating look.

There upon the still waters floated the image of Robert Polo. It seemed his Mistress had once again captured the luckless boy. Gaultnimble descended the three steps and leaned on the caldron to study the vision of the naked young man, who hung spread-eagled in a webwork of chains, an expression of pain and confusion on his dirty, tear-tracked face.

"Where?" Gaultnimble said softly.

Abalon, the caldron whispered in a voice like the swaying of reeds in a marsh pond.

"So that's where you've gone, you great whore," the dwarf said over his shoulder to the unmoving form of Shandal Karg, "through the Dream Stream, like a spider, to suck and feed on your victim."

As he turned his attention back to the caldron, a slight ripple shivered across the water. One image diffused and faded, and a new scene rose from the caldron's depths to the surface.

A barely adolescent Robert Polo lay sprawled on a

rumpled bed in a dimly lighted room, a look of terror on his child's face. An older man—his father, to judge by the resemblance they shared—slapped him sharply across the mouth and ordered silence with a stern wag of a finger as he bent over the boy and slowly unzipped his trousers.

Gaultnimble watched the little play to its conclusion and, stepping back, wiped a bit of saliva from the corner of his mouth. Before his pounding heart could calm itself, another ripple disturbed the water. Again, the images shifted, and a new tableau began. He leaned closer, the better to see what was already perfectly clear.

This time Robert Polo and the Silver Man made love to each other on an isolated beach. The setting sun painted their bodies scarlet and made a glittering bed of the sand beneath them. Robert flung back his head and cried out with pleasure, seeming to stare wide-eyed directly out of the caldron and straight at Gaultnimble. The dwarf barely dared to breathe as he witnessed their passion.

Without warning the scene stopped only to begin all over again. Gaultnimble licked his lips as Robert Polo flung back his head and cried out with pleasure exactly as he had done before. Only this time the Silver Man, bending over Polo, snarled suddenly and slapped him harshly across the face. The passion in Robert's eyes turned to a familiar childlike terror.

Gaultnimble stepped back again, nearly stumbling on the bottom stair, his one eye narrowing with thought as he realized what he was seeing, Robert Polo's memories. Shandal Karg was drawing them out one by one, forcing him to relive certain moments, then changing and reconstructing them. She was, in essence, re-creating Robert Polo.

"How you abuse and mistreat your toys," he murmured as he walked up the steps to stand beside his Mistress again. He touched the eyepatch that covered his ruined eye and thought about cutting her throat—an entertaining, but pointless fantasy. The Heart of Darkness could not be slain so easily or so casually.

He hated Her. How many promises to him had She broken, how many lies told? Many were the indignities She had visited upon his body, too many to count, too many to even remember.

Gaultnimble put his mouth close to her ear, and again he sang, but this time his voice was a sharp hiss.

> *"I despise*
> *your empty eyes,*
> *your barren thighs—*
> *your breasts are breeding grounds*
> *for flies."*

Robert Polo's suffering was nothing compared to his. For more than half a century he had amused Shandal Karg as her fool. In return, She had taught him pain and shown him the pleasure in pain—an important and worthwhile lesson, to be sure, but not one that excused her casual cruelties. He raised his hands, fingers extended, and groped toward her throat only to stop himself before actually touching Her.

"I wonder, my Queen of Night," he whispered as he walked in a circle around Her, "how well You have learned your own lesson?" He reached out to touch the slender horn that sprouted from her forehead, but again he stopped himself. The slightest disturbance to her body might draw Her back, and she would be angry at his interference.

Gaultnimble glanced toward the caldrons again,

then all around the vast chamber. The ghosts were gone for the moment. He could sense his Mistress's wards, exceptionally strong, holding them at bay. Even so, the spirits of Palenoc were near, pressing to get in, and the wards were weakening.

Descending the steps once again, he made a gesture that he had seen Shandal Karg make many times, and the eastern wall disappeared, revealing a balcony. A chilly wind blew through the chamber, but Gaultnimble took no notice. He walked outside to gaze over the black landscape of Srimourna, and a low chuckle escaped his lips.

His Mistress had no inkling of the true power he had gained in his years of servitude. Even a fool could learn at the feet of Shandal Karg, and he had wasted no opportunity. Who, in fact, *was* the fool? Her schemes and plans absorbed all her attention. She paid no attention at all to the small bits of magic he displayed, even failed to notice how he kept himself younger than his natural years.

He stared out across the vast, yawning canyon where a small herd of *chimorgs* wandered on the far rim, eyes shimmering. Most of their brothers and sisters were searching for the *Child*, but a few remained close to Boraga to serve as messengers and couriers, or in any other capacity Shandal Karg might devise.

He gazed beyond the *chimorgs* with a farsighted vision his Mistress didn't know he possessed. Night smothered the blasted landscape. In the distance the black peaks of the Krael Mountains rose up sharp as needles to prick the star-flecked sky.

Stretching out his right arm, extending his hand, Gaultnimble gazed through outspread fingers. For a moment that hand seemed to glow as if it were covered with a glittering, icy rime, and the fingers stiffened and turned white as icicles while the air filled with a hissing and crackling like the sound of glaciers breaking apart on the far northern continent.

"I will set my handprint on this land," he murmured to himself. "Eric Podlowsky discovered one of your secrets, Mistress. But I know a greater secret."

The wind wailed suddenly from the canyon depths, snatched his fool's cap from his head, and sent it spiraling out across the night. *Two caps lost now,* Gaultnimble thought with a wry frown. The same wind swept into the chamber and whistled teasingly around the fluted columns, filling the air with a new sound that was disturbingly like laughter.

"Mock me now," Gaultnimble said smugly, lifting his face to the night. "What is a poor fool to the mighty wind?" He paused, then laughed deep in his throat before he turned and walked away from the balcony. Inside, he waved his hand again, and the wall reappeared solid and thick and more than enough to keep out a mere wind. His tongue shot forward and curled down to touch the point of his chin. He brushed his hands together as if to rid them of dirt. "And so Gaultnimble deals with the wind."

As he waddled back toward the throne and the still figure of Shandal Karg, his eyes narrowed again. He climbed two dais steps and gazed down into the left caldron. Robert Polo lay on a mountainside, his leg horribly twisted, a splinter of bone protruding just below his knee.

"How long has She been doing this to him?" the dwarf said aloud.

Long, came the caldron's whispery answer.

Gaultnimble kicked the crystal vessel and scowled. "Hours, days, weeks, months, years, or centuries, you inarticulate, good-for-nothing chunk of cheap crockery!"

The caldron might have been pouting in the space of time before it answered. *Days.*

The dwarf lifted his nose, indignant in his triumph. The stupid caldrons gave one-word answers only, for the spirits that Shandal Karg had imprisoned within them were old and recalcitrant, unwilling to give useful information easily. Sometimes they just had to be put in their place.

"If you knew whom you were dealing with ..." he said.

Both caldrons whispered as one—*fool.*

"Bah!" Gaultnimble spat contemptuously in both vessels before striding down from the dais and across the chamber floor. Head lifted just a bit too high, he walked slowly, pretending he was dragging the great train of a regal robe.

Before he exited, he turned once more toward the Heart of Darkness and made a sweeping bow. "There are spirits even older than you, Divinity," he murmured, straightening. "They know such wondrous secrets."

He glanced toward the ceiling, then to all the dark, shadowy corners of the chamber. When he focused his vision just so, he could see the wards his Mistress had formed to keep her visitors at bay.

"You shouldn't be rude to your guests," he said. Reaching into a pocket, he extracted a handful of crystaline powder made from finely ground amethysts. With a broad motion he scattered it about.

Nothing happened at first. Then all around the chamber the wards dissolved in a twinkling of violet light.

Gaultnimble jumped up and down, giggling with

glee and clapping his hands. *But*, he told himself when the initial excitement was past, *it is better now to make a hasty retreat before She returns.*

He stepped over the threshold into the corridor that would take him deep into the bowels of the five-towered keep, but he cast a glance over his shoulder and smiled to himself.

Ghostly forms bled slowly through the throne room's walls and ceiling and up through the floor. Hands emerged, grasping, from the stone. Faces and arms thrust out from the columns. Eyes burned hungrily in the gloom-filled corners. A *banshee*'s song came down from the rafters.

Gaultnimble laughed and went to feed the cat.

Chapter Thirteen

O N a sea of darkness a pair of bodies writhed in sexual pleasure. Both faces were hidden beneath a cascade of long, black hair. The woman rode the man; her hands pinned his naked shoulders as his body arched against her. Muted gasps and plaintive moans rose from his lips. His head began to whip back and forth, and he screamed. It was not a sound of release, but of pain and terror.

The woman bent forward suddenly, her mouth fastening on the man's neck. He screamed again, then grew quiet. When the woman sat up, two thin, crimson streams flowed from a pair of wounds on his carotid artery. As if unconscious, his head lolled to the side.

The man was Robert Podlowsky.

The woman brushed the hair back from her face, turned, and smiled with evil mirth, her mouth and chin slick with blood. Her lips moved slowly.

I have something you want, She said coyly. *Come and take him from me—if you can.*

Eric Podlowsky sat bolt upright on his hard pallet, a short cry bubbling past his lips as he flung back the single coverlet. His heart hammered in his chest, and sweat drenched him. He got to his feet and stared as he tried to calm himself.

Small campfires dotted the gloomy shore as far as he could see. Sleeping forms, huddling beneath blankets near the fires, stirred uncomfortably on the sand. They were Rasoul's newly homeless. With no other place to go, hundreds—perhaps thousands—had retreated to the beaches. A few people drifted restlessly, unable to sleep. From here and there came snatches of soft conversation.

A harsh wind rattled the trees lining the beach and sent leaves swirling into the clouded night. The surf pounded like a massive drum. A thick fog bank approached from far over the Great Lake, promising to enshroud the shore sometime within the next hour.

On the pallet beside his, Alanna suddenly awoke. The huge crack in Sheren-Chad had made the tower unsafe until repairs could be made, and most of the city's *sekournen* were sleeping somewhere on the shore among the rest of the city's newly homeless.

"Eric, what is it?" Her voice betrayed her fatigue. She rubbed one hand over her eyes as she regarded him while her other hand stole toward the *shinobe-zu* concealed just under the edge of her blanket.

"I had a dream," Eric said quietly.

Alanna paused and licked her lips. "The Heart of Darkness?" she finally said.

Eric nodded. Those he trusted knew how Shandal Karg sometimes haunted his dreams. It had been a while since She had come to him in such a manner, however. A chill crept up his spine. "She has Robert."

Alanna didn't question him further. She brushed hair back with one hand and began to fold her blankets.

He watched her work, knowing without needing words what she was feeling. Her motions were crisp, tightly controlled, all evidence of fatigue gone as she perfectly matched the blankets' corners and made impeccable folds. But when she was done with that and reached again for the *shinobe-zu* where it lay on the sand, he saw her knuckles go white as she gripped it.

He bent, picked up his own *shinobe-zu* from the rumpled pile of his blankets, and touched her shoulder. "Alanna," he said softly, "I should go alone."

She raised her head slightly to stare outward across the black water, and her hair spilled forward to conceal her face. 'You do what you must, Eric," she said without looking at him. "But before you, after you, or with you, I am going to Boraga."

She straightened, turned, and held the *shinobe-zu* across her thighs in both hands. Their eyes met, and for an instant Eric wondered if, under other circumstances, Alanna might have fallen in love with him instead of with his brother. Then a wave of shame washed that thought away as he remembered Katy Dowd.

"I don't suppose there's any point in arguing with you?" he asked.

An ever-so-slight grin lifted the corners of her mouth. "Is there ever?"

Eric chewed his lips as they maintained that eye contact. Neither seemed willing to break it. Now, he realized, was the time for truth between them. "You love my brother very much," he finally said.

It was her turn to pause. "When I thought he had died in the fires of Wystoweem, I wanted to die, too," she answered at last, unable to disguise the regret in her voice. "But I didn't. I survived." She hesitated again and swallowed. "That same night of the fire—before it all broke loose—we had some time to ourselves. He talked about Scott Silver, and I realized then what Robert wasn't prepared to admit to himself.

Scott Silver had his heart, and I never would." She turned and looked Eric straight in the eye, drawing her shoulders back and lifting her chin as a wistful smile flickered over her face. "I'm a big girl. I can handle disappointments."

"You don't have to come with me," Eric said. "You're crazy if you do."

She waved a hand back up the beach toward the ruins of Rasoul. Perhaps a third of the city had burned to the ground, and another third had been damaged beyond safe habitation. Plumes of gray smoke continued to drift upward into the heavens, and a sooty pall hung in the air.

"The Domains of Light have lost," she said. "Our world is dead, and Shandal Karg has won. But if I have to lose, I'd rather go down spitting in her eye. And just maybe, if She blinks, you can jerk Robert out of her clutches and get him back to the safety of your world. It's not much of a chance ..." She shrugged, and her grin returned. "But as your brother would say, *what the hell.*"

A lone, feminine form wrapped in white cloaks strode down the shore from the direction of Rasoul. Small, bare feet padded through wet sand, and the foam-flecked waves that rolled up around her ankles lapped at the hems of her garments. She paid no attention. Her gaze seemed to roam over the sleepers higher on the beach.

"Maris," Alanna said with quiet recognition.

Alanna waved to draw her sister's attention as she and Eric started toward the councilwoman, picking their way quietly and carefully around the campfires and outstretched bodies until the three met close to the waterline. Here and there a head lifted nervously to watch them pass. Someone else coughed and shifted, restlessly turning away from them. Most continued to sleep undisturbed.

Maris raised her hands and touched her sister's palms in hasty greeting. "You'd better come quickly," she said in a tight whisper as her hood fell back to reveal her worried expression. "Something is happening to Phlogis."

Eric and Alanna glanced at each other, then sped toward Rasoul, leaving Maris to follow at her own pace. They reached the charred ruins of the wharves where blackened spars and timbers jutted up from the water and the shore at odd angles. Most of the Fishermen's Quarter was gone. Smoke still rose from the half-standing shells of a dozen warehouses.

Throughout the city pairs of Kur-Zorin wandered, carrying wooden buckets, watchful for any small spark that might threaten once again to grow into flames. Outside the Temple of Taedra, which had thankfully remained untouched by the fire, lines of citizens sought healing for burns or other injuries incurred during the invasion or in its aftermath.

Sheren-Chad stood like a proud but wounded creature keeping watch over the corpse of the city. The encircling wall and the massive wooden gates stood black with smoke, and the courtyard was littered with rubble that had fallen from the gaping rent in the upper portion of the tower.

No one stood guard. Eric pushed open the tower's main doors and peered inside. No torches or globes of *sekoy-melin* lit the dark interior, and he hesitated on the threshold.

Alanna squeezed past him impatiently. "This way," she said, setting a course through the blackness.

They began climbing steps that spiraled upward higher and higher. Dust and fallen plaster made the air thick and unpleasant to breathe, but they hurried as swiftly as they could. At one point, perhaps halfway up, they paused. A portion of the Sheren's wall and a section of steps had been blown away by one of Shandal Karg's bolts. The wind whipped around Eric as he stared outward, openmouthed.

"Stay close to me," Alanna said, taking his hand as she led the way. They pressed their backs against the inside wall. A bit of jagged stone ledge, barely wide enough to accommodate their feet, was all that remained of the next ten steps. They inched upward, mounting each fragment and pausing to test the next.

Eric wondered how Maris had ever descended from Phlogis's sanctum. *The same way*, he realized. Though she was a councilor and not a warrior, Maris was every bit as courageous as her sister, Alanna.

They made it to the next safe section of the stairway. The rent in the outer wall, however, continued upward for two more levels. From that point on the tower seemed to lean at a suble angle.

The sanctum doors stood open. Eleven white-robed members of the Tarjeel gathered within, silent and grave-faced. Valis was there, too.

Phlogis's pale form hung still in the air as if crucified on an invisible cross. The golden boundary of his *pre-khit* burned with a shimmering fire, and the gems within it shone like tears. He lifted his head as Eric pushed into the room, and old eyes opened.

Tami, Namue rana Sekoye, he said, his thoughts brushing through Eric's brain like wind-driven leaves. *Hello, my Brother of the Dragon. Hello—and farewell.*

Eric felt his heart lurch. "Farewell?" he said. "Where are you going?"

Phlogis smiled weakly. His pale form was fading, becoming more tenuous. *I don't know*, he said. *I am being* . . . He closed his eyes and was silent for a moment. *Drawn.*

"Can you resist?" Alanna asked. "We need you, Phlogis. Rasoul and the Domains need you."

Eric cast a glance at Valis, who stood behind him now. The big *sekournen* shook his head and said nothing.

I cannot resist, Phlogis answered in a strange calm, *but I've lingered long enough to say this to Eric Podlowsky.*

Phlogis's gaze fixed on Eric, and for the first time Eric realized there was no wave of anger emanating from the *dando* and no psychic pain in their mental contact. Instead, there was—serenity.

Phlogis spoke again, his thoughts seeming farther away than before. *Look for Robert Podlowsky in Boraga. Your brother lives.*

"I know," Eric said. "Shandal Karg has him."

Alanna slipped her hand inside his and squeezed.

Phlogis allowed a soft sigh. *I have seen him through the eyes of other spirits, Eric. He is not a prisoner. She has turned him to her will. I know now that he has always had her mark upon him.*

Eric's heart lurched again, but he refused to believe. "You are wrong, my friend," he said.

Phlogis shook his head. *Beware of your brother,* he warned. Closing his eyes, he smiled strangely, and his head lolled to the side. *I must go,* he said. *I am going.*

"Where?" Alanna demanded.

I don't know.

Eric took a step closer to the fiery circle. "Will you be back?"

I don't know.

Valis's deep-voiced whisper came over Eric's shoulder. "Is it all over, Phlogis? Have we truly lost all?"

There was a long pause.

I don't know. Then Phlogis opened his eyes once more and looked at Eric. His lips moved, and he manifested a true voice, something he only rarely attempted. "*Si mayan mai Mianur-kolu,*" he said. "May we meet again on the bridge that leads to Paradise."

Phlogis faded away like a wisp of smoke in the darkness. The circle of fire around his *prekhit* flickered and died. Even the stones and gems inside the device seemed to lose all luster. Only a dull red radiance rising from within a pair of weird caldrons on one side of the chamber provided any light, and that, too, seemed to be ebbing.

For a long time silence filled the sanctum.

Eric slowly turned to the other councilors. "I must also leave you," he said.

"You can't save your brother," one of the councilors said quietly. "We have a world to think about."

Valis walked softly across the chamber toward the door. "What good is saving a world," he said, "if you can't save your own brother?"

"You are *sekournen,*" said Maris, gathering her white cloaks about her as she entered the sanctum. "We need you here to fight off any new attacks and to help rebuild the city, not off on a mission for which there can be no hope."

Alanna walked toward the door, too. When she reached Valis's side, she paused and glanced toward Maris and the other councilors. She raised a hand to the small silver medallion that she and all *sekournen* wore at their throats. With small effort she broke the chain and let the medallion fall to the floor. Valis did the same, and the two of them left the sanctum.

Eric felt the councilors' cool stares upon him. "I've come to love your people," he said, "your city, and your cause. But this time, finally, Robert comes first. I'm sorry."

He touched his own silver medallion. His was more than just an adornment. It was the key that allowed him to move between this world and his own. That meant nothing to him now. He had already lost Katy Dowd. Without Robert there would be no going home.

He broke the chain and dropped the cartouche beside the other two.

Alanna awaited him in the hall beyond the sanctum. "Can we call the dragons from the rooftop?" he asked.

Valis nodded. "The great *sekoy-melin* globe has been shattered again," he said. "Glass is everywhere. Part of the rampart is also rubble. But it might bear the beasts' weight."

Alanna led the way up the stairs to the lavatorium on the next level. She pushed the door open with the *shinobe-zu*. Several small globes of *sekoy-melin* still shone in their mounts. The others lay broken on the stone floor. "I'm going to change," she announced, going to one of the many shelves of clothing and seizing fresh black leathers. "I will not fly all the way to Srimourna with trousers full of sand."

Eric also began to change. He'd been wearing the same garments since the fire two days ago. Besides, a set of shiny black leathers would fit his current mood.

Valis crossed to the far side of the lavatorium and opened the door to a weapons locker. "What should we take?" he asked.

Eric placed his *shinobe-zu* on a table and poured water from a pitcher into a washbasin. As he was about to splash his face, he paused thoughtfully and wondered aloud. "What weapon do you use against a woman who can shatter moons?"

Leaning forward, he dipped his hands in the cool water and laved it over his eyes. Then he began to pull on the fresh clothes he had chosen. The soft *se-koye* leather felt good against his skin, and he found a sense of calm greater than he had ever known. He didn't know what lay ahead, but he was going to get his brother.

He picked up his *shinobe-zu*. Valis still stood beside the weapons locker empty-handed. "Take this," Eric said, tossing the sword-cane to his friend. "I won't be needing it."

Alanna whirled around with a shocked expression, one hand on her own *shinobe-zu*. "What will you use for a weapon?"

"The only thing that matters in the end," Eric answered. He tapped a finger over his heart.

They climbed the last flight of steps to the rooftop. The door was wedged partially open, and they forced it the rest of the way by hand. The tall iron tripod, which once had held the great globe of *sekoy-melin*, was a twisted, half-melted piece of wreckage. Splinters of sparkling glass scattered about the roof were all that remained of the globe.

Some of the Tarjeel councilors followed them to the roof, but they kept their distance, making no further attempt to stop the dragonriders, unless they expected sullen and accusatory looks to achieve what Maris's pleas had not. Eric stubbornly turned his back to them, but one white-robed old man came to his side and, saying nothing, placed a pack near his feet.

Alanna glanced at the old man with a raised eyebrow as he solemnly rejoined the other councilors. She knelt, loosened the pack's drawstrings, and peered inside. "Food," she said, drawing the strings tight again, "for a few days, anyway."

Eric took out his harmonica and tapped it on his palm as he stared toward the distant mountains. Nestled among those ancient, weathered peaks was the Valley of Beasts where Shadowfire waited for his call. Putting the instrument to his lips, he drew a deep breath and prepared to blow a riff.

"Wait, my friend."

Eric knew the voice of Roderigo Diez. Though he was impatient to be away, he lowered the harmonica and turned as the old Spanish physician pushed through the councilors and approached him. Diez's robes were dark with dirt and blood, and he looked near exhaustion, like a man who'd gone without sleep much too long.

"I couldn't get here soon enough to say good-bye to Phlogis," Roderigo Diez said, clutching at Eric's hand and pressing it between his palms. "I would be sad if I missed saying good-bye to you." Diez paused as his gaze locked with Eric's. "We didn't get along when we first met, but I've come to think of you and Roberto as sons."

Eric's mouth felt suddenly dry. He freed his hand from Roderigo Diez's grip and awkwardly embraced the old Spaniard before stepping back. "You should get some rest," he said with gentle concern.

Roderigo Diez shook his head. "There are too many injured," he said. "The Temple of Taedra has been turned into a hospital where anyone who can manipulate healing crystals is hard at work, and with the medical skill I learned on Earth, I am doubly needed."

Eric frowned. "You still need rest—"

Roderigo Diez pressed his fingers against Eric's lips,

silencing him. "We both do what we must," he said firmly. "Is this not true? We are slaves to our hearts."

Eric gazed toward the mountains again as he thought of the long journey before him and the confrontation at the end of that journey, and he understood Roderigo Diez better than ever before. "You've never really told me how you first came to Palenoc," he said without looking at his friend. "When I return, you owe me a tale."

Diez said nothing. His gaze fell on the harmonica in Eric's hand, and a distant look came into his eyes as if he were remembering things from long ago. Diez, the harmonica's original owner, had carried the instrument with him from Earth to Palenoc many years before. He had given it to Eric.

" 'De Guella,' " Roderigo Diez said quietly. "Do you know it?"

Eric thought for a moment, then blew the opening strains. He lowered the harmonica, nodding as he recalled the song and the legend. "The song General Santa Anna ordered played day and night during the seige of the Alamo," he said.

"Twelve days and nights," Roderigo Diez said as he, too, turned to stare toward the mountains. "The same number of days and nights it will take you to reach Boraga in Srimourna." His voice became tight and grim. "Play it, Eric. Play it, and when you reach Boraga and rescue Roberto, take one of those swords you've made and cut out the Heart of Darkness."

Roderigo Diez turned abruptly away from Eric and said his good-byes to Alanna and Valis. A moment later he was gone on his way back to the Temple of Taedra to minister to the city's sick and injured.

Eric tapped the harmonica on his palm as he wet his lips. Then from the silver Hohner "De Guella" flowed forth, called by some "The Throat-Cutter's Song," and by others, "No Quarter." Roderigo Diez had chosen the song well, for at Boraga no quarter would be given.

He stopped playing. "Are you with me, my friends?" he asked Alanna and Valis. As he spoke, he recognized within himself a strange and dreadful calm. Faced with the certainty of death, he found no fear of it; where hopelessness might have been, he found more than hope. He found faith.

"I am your right hand," Alanna answerd with ritual solemnity.

"I am your left hand," Valis said, closing one fist tightly around his *shinobe-zu.*

Eric cast a final glance at the gathered councilors near the rooftop stairway. Maris, Alanna's sister, was not with them. Somewhere, within the Sheren or without, perhaps at the Temple of Taedra or in the gritty streets where smoke from the ruins still drifted, she would be back at work, trying hard to help her people, trying to save her city.

These other councilors, he knew less well. They watched him numbly as if he were their last hope, and he was leaving. *Abandoned*, he thought with a twinge of guilt, remembering they had just lost Phlogis, too. *They look abandoned.* Still, they were good people, and soon enough they would pull themselves together.

We do what we must.

"*Hala namue shi hami rana sekoye,*" Eric said. "My brother and sister of the dragons, learn this song." The Hohner wailed. The strains of "De Guella" soared outward from the high roof of Sheren-Chad over the ruins of Rasoul, and with it this time went a mental summons.

Valis's voice wove a deep, rich harmony around the

harmonica. In only moments, after a single hearing, he seemed to master the subtle complexities of the tune.

Out of the mountains a glittering light appeared, moving with dazzling speed, like a white-hot star, streaking across the night toward Rasoul. Behind it came another light, a spark of wildfire, whose speed was nearly the equal of the other. Eric watched the first and felt Shadowfire's mind reach out to his across the bridge of music. The second light, he knew, was Brightstar, Valis's *sekoye.*

Alanna listened to the harmonica with her eyes closed. Then she took up the song in a high soprano, seizing the melody from the small silver instrument, bending, shaping, and making it her own. The harmonica had sounded grim, mournful. Her voice was angry, full of challenge.

In response to her call, Mirrormist rose above the peaks, shining like a golden-amber star. But Mirrormist did not come alone, and the sky above the mountains was suddenly full of shimmering dragononwings, all turning toward Rasoul.

Alanna sang, her head thrown back, the wind sweeping her hair, as she called, not just to Mirrormist, but to every wild dragon. From the Valley of Beasts the creatures came, from the high mating nests in the most distant peaks, from the warm, sandy shores of the eastern ocean beyond.

All over the city Rasoul's citizens briefly forgot their misery and suffering to gaze up in wonderment. Never before had they seen such a gathering of dragons. The city was bathed in *sekoy* light. In some places rooftops and ruins seemed on fire for a second time.

The darkness of Palenoc throbbed with the wardrum beat of countless wings while Eric, Alanna, and Valis mounted their beasts. A seeming wave of fire gathered over the tower—fire and thunder. Yet, as it swept westward, it could not drown out the song so many swore they heard that night.

"De Guella." No quarter.

Chapter Fourteen

HOLDING her breath, afraid to move, Katherine stared at the huge black beast before her. Its eyes burned and smoked with a flickering light that shimmered on the scaly face and stiff, razor-sharp mane, as well as on the length of smooth horn that sprouted from its brow. Regarding her, it snorted and stamped one hoof, carving a deep gouge in the earth.

Her finger hesitated on the trigger of her stunner, but an electric jolt wasn't going to hurt this monster. Her other hand tightened on the straps of her backpack. Heart hammering, she glanced to the right and started to run.

The *chimorg* charged after her. In the darkness it was hard to choose a course. Limbs scratched her face, and her skirts caught on bushes, but the crashing of those deadly hooves drove her on.

The *chimorg* trumpeted. Katherine gave a cry and ducked around a fat tree and sank back against it, clutching her belly. Pain shot down the sides of her bulging midriff and down her back. Her breath came in gasps. The *chimorg* shot past her hiding place and whirled to face her again, its eyes burning hotter as it gave another loud trumpet.

Katherine screamed with surging panic as the backpack slipped from her grasp. The *chimorg* snorted and shook its great head. She felt the rough bark of the tree at her back as the beast pressed toward her, felt the heat of those arcane eyes as that horn settled ever so gently, menacingly, on her left breast, felt its breath scorch her skin.

Then, suddenly, she felt far more. Buried in her backpack was a useless wand of quartz crystal and a small blue sapphire on a broken chain, gifts from a long-dead friend named Salyt. Katherine had treasured them for the memories they represented. Within the nylon pack they flared with life.

And still she felt more. It was as if her senses were expanding outward at an incredible rate, and she had no control at all. The flow of the *chimorg*'s blood and the beat of its heart—she felt those. Insects burrowing unseen in the grass, birds mating in their nests, the roots of trees pushing ever deeper into the earth—all these things she sensed and became part of. The earth beneath her feet pulsed as with a living heartbeat.

A shining, crystalline light flooded her vision, and yet in a manner she couldn't explain she saw the *chimorg* and the woods and the night around her. Rising out of the earth, twinkling sparks danced like fireflies. First one, then ten, then hundreds and thousands, they filled the darkness with a silver shimmering, and still they multiplied.

Soundlessly, the forest floor cracked, and a lacework of narrow fissures ripped open the ground. Beams of blinding radiance lanced upward, bathing everything with a pure white glow, expelling the darkness. The air itself seemed to shine and burn.

The light touched the *chimorg*, and its scales and horn and mane glittered with an incandescent beauty. It whipped its head back and forth and lashed its serpentine tail wildly, crying in terror like a thing trapped, facing its own doom.

Then, just as the ground had done, the *chimorg*'s skin seemed to crack open, and the light poured in to fill the beast. Its screaming ceased immediately. The light shifted and coalesced into dazzling streamers as it invaded the creature through every crack and orifice. The streamers became tiny stars and fireflies again. Straight to the *chimorg* they flew, and the *chimorg* stood still as it absorbed them.

The night became normal once more.

Katherine let out a sharp breath as she tried to grasp what had happened. There were no cracks in the ground. It might all have been a grand hallucination, except some part of her still sensed the huge deposits of crystal buried deep in the earth for miles and miles around, raw energy that she had somehow tapped.

The *chimorg* sank at her feet and wept, sounding disturbingly like a child. It no longer offered any threat. Shifting its head, the creature brushed her foot with the tip of its horn. No cracks showed in its hide, no wounds of any kind. Fire still filled its eyes, but there was a new quality to the light.

Her back to the tree, Katherine sat slowly beside the *chimorg*. Tentatively, she reached out and touched its neck. At the slightest contact, she pulled her hand away as if expecting to be burned. The *chimorg* gave a great sigh and stopped weeping. Hesitantly, she reached out to stroke it again, and it trembled at her touch.

Tears flowed down her face, but the emotions that brought them were the *chimorg*'s. She shared the creature's feelings, startled by both its intelligence and the depth of its understanding. The light had burned out the darkness in the monster's heart and severed the bond of evil that held it enthralled to Shandal Karg. For that freedom, the *chimorg* felt joy.

Yet there was sorrow, too. It considered Shandal Karg its mother, and with new eyes and clearer wisdom it realized all she represented and felt repulsion.

With that discovery, the sorrow Katherine felt became her own. The *chimorg* really was no more than a child, a child in need of comfort and solace. She lay down beside it and put an arm around its neck, careful of its sharp mane, which was really more of a membranous dorsal spine.

The quiet of the woods closed in around them. After a while the insects began to sing gently again, and the wind whispered through the leaves.

Giving the *chimorg* another pat, Katherine sat up and dragged her backpack closer. The omega stunner lay nearby on the grass. She recovered it and slipped the belt clip over the waistband of her skirts.

Abruptly, the *chimorg* lunged upward to its feet and shook its mane. It moved a few nervous paces away and stopped. Looking over a shoulder, it regarded Katherine and lowered its head before returning to stand before her.

A movement to her left drew her attention. At first she thought it might have been Mac trying to sneak up and grab her again, and one hand went to the stunner, but it was only a ghost watching her with dull eyes.

The baby inside her began a gentle kicking, and she put a hand upon her belly as she peered deeper into the woods. Once more, the night was full of ghosts, all of them watching her. She no longer just *sensed* them. She could see them now, those with any form at all.

She rose uneasily to her feet, using the tree for support. Her body felt larger than it should have been, and she cursed her clumsiness and lack of stamina. By her calculations she was only into her seventh month, yet the baby was so active and her stomach so swollen she felt like a blimp.

"And worse," she added aloud, "you're talking to yourself again. What I wouldn't give to just wake up back in Dowdsville and find this was all a weird, junk food–induced dream." She stooped, grabbed the nylon backpack by a single strap, and slung it over her right shoulder. "Now that you mention it, Katy Dowd, you'd give a lot for a cheeseburger, fries, and Coke right now. Or a hot shower. Or an hour with your feet up before the television set." She paused and licked her lips as she regarded the flame-eyed *chimorg* and the host of spirits to whom she seemed to be so fascinating. "I miss my waterbed," she muttered under her breath.

She couldn't stay where she was. The stunner's effects wore off within twenty minutes or so, and Mac would be recovering by now. With the *chimorg* following docilely, she started off through the woods. Pale shapes drifted through the trees on either side, ahead and behind, walking or floating, unhampered by branch or underbrush as they kept pace.

Night came on very quickly, and the woods became so dark she could barely see the black trees and limbs that blocked her way. She thought of the Bic lighter in her backpack, but she didn't dare use it to make a torch. In the sky Thanador would be nearing fullness, but the moon was not yet up, and the leaves, though it was autumn, were thick enough to blot out its glow.

She tried to sense where Mac might be, but her newfound awareness had contracted once again, and try as she might, she could not force it to expand. Whatever this strange power was that she possessed, she apparently could not control it. She could see scores of *shades* and *apparitions* that accompanied her and even sense the invisible *chills* and *poltergeists*. Otherwise, she had only her eyes and ears to rely upon.

She hadn't gone far before her condition compelled her to rest. Leaning against a tree again, she clutched her stomach with one hand and her lower back with the other and gave a low groan. A vague nausea plagued her, and hunger gnawed.

Her ghostly companions had stopped, too. They drifted closer, perhaps to see what was the matter, perhaps impatient to continue. Some of those dead, staring eyes fastened upon her belly.

Though she would have liked a few more moments of rest, Katherine tightened her grip on her backpack's strap and started off again. Like soundless guards, the ghosts retreated to the flanks once more.

Sharp pain caused Katherine to yelp and jerk away from a barely visible briar. Blood, thick and black, poured from a scratch on the back of her left wrist, but as she watched in dumbfounded amazement, the flow ceased, and the wound knit itself back together.

She touched the bruised and swollen side of her face where Mac had struck her with the rock. There was no pain there, no tightness of the skin, no tenderness.

A disquieting fear set her to trembling. It was too much strangeness in one night, too much for her to cope with. A scream bubbled up in her throat. She barely held it back, biting her lip until she tasted blood. That, too, healed.

She stared at her wrist, then slowly lowered her

arm. "Don't think about it, Katherine," she told herself in a low, uneasy voice. "Just put one foot in front of the other and keep moving." She no longer cared where she was going or in what direction. All that mattered was putting distance between herself and Mac.

The *chimorg* snorted suddenly and walked a few paces ahead of her before pausing and sniffing the air. It bobbed its head up and down, stared at her with its burning eyes, then walked on a few more paces.

"All right, all right, I'm coming," Katherine muttered, quickening her step, for the beast plainly wanted her to follow.

They emerged from the woods onto a riverbank. She couldn't tell if it was the same river she'd rafted on all day or a different one, nor did she care. The *chimorg* went straight to the edge and lapped greedily at the water.

"Hey, fella, save some for me," she said. Dropping the backpack, she knelt gracelessly on the shore, heedless of the mud, and cupped some water in her hand. It tasted sweet and cool. She cupped another handful, held it up, and let it trickle down her throat and into her tunic.

She sat back on a grassier part of the bank and sighed wearily. Above the river stars sprinkled a thin ribbon of sky. Though still no trace of Thanador, the very edge of pale Mianur shone over the trees.

For a moment everything shifted in and out of focus, and her head rolled forward. Then it jerked upward again, and she sat straighter, forcing herself to stay awake and alert. She didn't dare sleep until she was farther away. Awkwardly, she got to her feet, feeling like a whale, aching all over.

The *chimorg* watched her. She could read nothing in

those alien eyes, yet behind them she sensed patience, even sympathy. The beast walked slowly toward her, then folded its legs and settled to the ground at her feet. It made no sound, but twisted its head and looked at her once more, waiting.

Katherine hesitated, torn between fatigue and fear. She was so tired she could barely walk. But did she dare try to ride such a frightening creature? And if she dared, could she do so in her pregnant condition without hurting herself or her child?

She gazed back the way she had come into the darkness of the forest. Mac was back there somewhere. She had no doubt he would be searching for her. Whatever his reasons, the Shadarkan had gone to too much trouble to capture and drag her away from the Kirringskal to just let her walk away. What would become of her and the child if she let herself be recaptured?

Recovering her backpack, she turned toward the *chimorg* again. Its scaled hide gleamed with the firelight from its own eyes, and its horn seemed to shimmer. But her gaze fastened on the mane. Cautiously, she put out a hand and touched it, feeling the cool, oily sharpness of the spiny membrane. The *chimorg* allowed her touch without flinching.

"Do you have a name?" she wondered aloud as she stroked the *chimorg*'s neck and the crown of its head. "I'll call you Kailuun. That's the Guran tongue, but in my language it would mean Darkstar. Either way, it suits you."

Hiking up her skirts, she put one leg astride the *chimorg*, taking care to avoid the razor edge of its mane as she lowered herself into a comfortable position. She marveled at the strange reptilian texture of its skin. "Kailuun," she whispered, awed by the creature's power and beauty.

In one smooth, rippling motion the *chimorg* lunged to its feet. Katherine braced herself on her hands, taking as much weight as she could off her pelvis, yet the breath hissed between her teeth, and pain flashed up her lower back. As if he understood her distress, Kailuun stood perfectly still.

"No sweat," Katherine said as the worst of the pain ebbed, but she didn't know if she was reassuring the *chimorg* or herself. She drew several deep breaths and let them out, then adjusted her position, finding better balance as she strove for something approaching a horsewoman's perfect seat. When she was ready, she muttered, "Hi ho, Silver."

The *chimorg* remained still.

Katherine swallowed, then nudged gently with her knees as she placed one hand softly on the creature's neck beside its mane. "Kailuun," she whispered.

The *chimorg* followed the bank of the river, moving at a slow and cautious pace as if it was aware of the baby she carried. At first Katherine continued to try to support her weight on her hands, but gradually she settled back. The pain she expected did not come, and there was something soothing about the easy rocking motion of the ride.

To either side of the river, deep in the woods, small candlelike lights appeared among the army of spirits that continued to march along with her. *Leikkios*, Katherine realized calmly. She no longer held any fear of the ghosts. Why they followed her, she didn't know, but she was convinced they meant her no harm.

A *banshee* cried somewhere in the distance ahead, and another answered.

Kailuun snorted nervously, though he didn't falter

or change pace. Katherine stroked his neck. "They're only singing," she said to the *chimorg*. "I just never understood their music before."

A weird serenity fell over the woods. Mianur glimmered like a pale icy mist directly over the river, and the first hint of Thanador's light shone above the trees on the far bank. A cool breeze set the leaves to murmuring, while a pair of owls called softly to each other. A doe, up to its hooves in mud on the other shore, paused from drinking to watch her go by. Katherine could barely see the creature, but she sensed its timid heartbeat and the hot, vital life in its body as if it were her own.

"Matterine told me a story once," she said quietly to Kailuun, talking to keep herself awake. "An old Kirringskal folktale, actually. She called it *The Child Who Loved the Deer*, and it took place a long time ago when another great plague swept through the Gray Kingdoms."

She continued to stroke the *chimorg* as she told the story.

"We must leave our village," the Kirringskal leader told his people, "and go high into the mountains until this plague is past and the land is pure again."

The Kirringskal took nothing with them but a few weapons and some cooking pots and made the long trek to the Baran'Dur Mountains, traveling only at night so that the disease could not follow them.

But the plague was crafty, and to show its contempt for the Kirringskal leader, it waited until the villagers made a new camp high atop Moondust Mountain; then on that very first night it struck the leader's beautiful young daughter, Fawn. She burned with fever, and her father and all the Kirringskal flung up their hands with grief, for she was a much beloved child. All night they mourned outside the hut they had made for her from branches and leaves and wild grasses.

But in the hour just before dawn, Fawn struggled up from her bed and went outside. Fever sweat ran down her flushed face and her eyes were wild, but she reached out her hand and smiled as if seeing something no one else could see.

Her father and the villagers rushed to her side. "It's a deer," the daughter exclaimed in a weak voice. "A beautiful white deer!"

The father shook his head as he led her back to bed. "No, my precious child," he said, thinking her delirious, unable to hide the tears that ran down his face. "There are no deer on Moondust Mountain."

"But there is, Father," Fawn insisted. "It's come to save me. It's the angel of the Son of the Morning!"

The father stayed beside his daughter, holding her small hand, until she fell into a restless sleep. The moment he turned his back, however, she awoke, slipped outside, and cried, "There he is. There is the white deer who will save me!"

At dawn an old woman came to sit with Fawn while her father went outside, sat down among his people, and wept openly. From inside the hut, off and on all day, Fawn's sweet little voice called out. "The white deer will save me!" Meanwhile, the day became night, and the campfires burned, and Fawn became sicker. At midnight, when Mianur and Thanador were both high above the mountain, she cried out again, but this time her voice was full of pain and fear for the white deer to save her.

Fawn's father rose from his place beside the campfire, and all eyes in the village turned toward him. He had not slept, and his despairing face was so pale, his eyes so glazed, that more than one of the Kirringskal thought that he had caught the plague, too.

He no longer cared about being the leader; he cared only for his daughter. He went in to her bedside, kissed her hands and her forehead, stroked her shiny black hair, and brushed away his tears. Then without a word to anyone, he left the hut and the village and ran down the mountainside.

There were no deer on Moondust Mountain, but in the woods that filled the valley where the Hummingh River flowed there were deer. Fawn's father made his way there, walking all night without rest or food.

In the gloomy twilight of approaching dawn, he reached the riverbank and examined it carefully for prints and deer-sign. Satisfied, he rubbed himself with leaves and grass to hide his human stink, then made a hasty noose from narrow vines and climbed into a tree to wait.

Just at dawn, when the pink fingers of morning still seemed too weak to pry back the night, a fine stag and his doe wandered out of the woods to drink from the river. The father held his breath, his noose ready, and when they passed right beneath him, he cast it—and missed.

Stag and doe sprang into the trees. With a heartbroken cry the father leaped from his hiding place and ran after them. Faster than he had ever run before—perhaps faster than any man had run before—he plunged through bush and thicket, leaping and dodging all obstacles with an agile grace. The doe darted unexpectedly to one side, taking another course, but his eyes were fastened on the huge stag. Its tan skin was not white, but it was very pale.

Driven by desperation and his love for his daughter, he caught the stag. Throwing his arms around its neck, he dragged it down to the ground. It fought, kicking and writhing, but he locked his legs around its body while his hands locked on those great horns. With all his strength he gave a sharp jerk and snapped its neck.

"Oh, Great One," he said, weeping as he prayed to the stag's spirit. "Forgive me for this offense, but my daughter cries out in her fever for the white deer, and she is dying. If I cannot make her well, I can make her happy in her last moments."

He got to work then, breaking off a piece of the stag's horn and sharpening it on a rock until he had a keen edge. With his new tool he sliced open the animal's belly and carefully removed the hide, head, hooves, horn, and all.

"Forgive me for not eating you," he told the deer when he was finished. "You would fill the bellies of many Kirringskal, but I have no way to get you home."

The day was nearly passed. Fawn's father carried the stag's fine pale skin back to the river and washed out the blood as best he could before rolling it and tucking it under one arm. He glanced up at the sky, measuring the westward course of the sun. He had far to go, so he began to run, thinking not of the fatigue in his legs or the stitch in his side, but only of his daughter.

It was past nightfall when he walked into the new village atop Moondust Mountain. All seemed quiet. The campfires burned, and the villagers milled about outside his hut.

"Is my Fawn still alive?" he asked his friends, barely able to speak, he was so out of breath.

They nodded, but their faces were grave. "She calls out for the white deer," said one in a sorrowful whisper as he eyed the bundle the leader carried under his arm. "Over and over."

Her father unrolled the skin and threw it around himself like a cloak. "And she shall have him," he answered, adjusting the stag's head upon his own. The firelight shone on the antlers. He got down on all fours and crawled inside the hut and straight to his daughter's side.

The old woman who sat with Fawn gave a startled gasp and leaped up, knocking over a stump of wood that had been placed there as a stool. Others peered in through the doorway to see that would happen.

Fawn's face was to the wall, but at the commotion she turned slowly. Her glazed eyes lit up, and a pitiful smile blossomed on her gaunt face. "White deer," she said, her words barely audible, "You've come to save me."

She put out a trembling hand and touched the stag's face. Wet, gleaming eyes turned up toward her as her head sank to the side and life left her body.

Fawn's father let out a cry of grief as, kneeling, he clutched the stag's hide around his shoulders. "Let this skin enfold me, change me into the beast whose life I've taken. My own has no meaning now, for my child is dead!"

Of course, he did not turn into a deer, and he gave up the leadership of the Kirringskal, for he had promised to lead them away from Plague if they left their homes and possessions and followed him to Moondust Mountain, but Plague had followed them.

However, on very rare occasions, even Plague has a heart. Ever present in the village and all through the Gray Kingdoms, it had witnessed what Fawn's father had done to bring his little girl happiness in the last moments before it claimed her, and Plague was so moved that it promised, whenever it walked the land again, it would pass by the Kirringskal.

Katherine patted Kailuun's neck as she finished the tale. Massaging her back with one hand, she tried to adjust her position a bit. She was growing increasingly uncomfortable and thought she must get down soon and walk or rest.

"When Matterine first told it to me, I thought *where's the magic in that*? Folktales are supposed to have magic, and he should have turned into a white deer." She ducked below a limb and glanced at the following ghosts. "Then I realized the magic was in the caring—and in what he did out of love for his child."

She paused again thoughtfully. "You know, several of the Kirringskal were sick with this new plague when I arrived, but not one of them died from it." She tapped the *chimorg*'s back a couple of times and twisted uncomfortably. "Stop, Kailuun," she said. "I've got to get down."

With uncanny understanding, Kailuun stopped and knelt carefully so that Katherine could get off. Her legs were wobbly, and oh how she had to find a bush to relieve her bladder! When she'd done that, she sank against a tree and folded her hands over her belly.

"This is your fault, kid," she said wearily to the baby inside her. "I used to run miles and hike mountain trails for fun. Look what you've turned me into, a blimp with no energy. If your daddy could see me now."

Her mouth drew into a taut, sad line as she thought of Eric. His face floated in her mind, and his touch seemed to linger warm on her skin. She recalled their last night together when they made love on the ground beneath a huge tree and made the baby she now carried. She still heard his voice sometimes, and impulsively she would jerk around to look for him, then remember that he was dead.

What did death mean to an earthman on Palenoc? she wondered. The ghosts stood patiently, motionlessly, watching and waiting all through the forest wherever she looked.

"Eric?" she called in a soft voice that was half hope and half fear. "Are you out there?"

No answer came back, and tired as she was, Katherine got to her feet. "Just a little farther," she told Kailuun, touching his flank affectionately as she took the lead. "Then maybe I'll be tired enough to just fall asleep and not remember anything."

Not far ahead another river joined the one they were following, and she found herself stranded on a point of land with the choice of either going back or fording one of them. Neither seemed particularly dangerous, but she decided to follow the new river back upstream a short distance in hopes of finding a narrower point to cross.

With Kailuun right behind, she wandered perhaps a hundred yards before stopping. Thanador's effulgent light shone through a gap in the trees, illuminating a dark bridge that spanned the water.

"Maybe our luck is changing," she said to Kailuun as she headed for it.

The bridge was an ancient construct, suspended by cables and weathered ropes, its timbers stout but rotting. More than a few of its planks were gone. The road that led to it had long since been swallowed by the woods.

"I think I'd rather get wet than trust my life to that thing," Katherine said disappointedly. "Once we're on the other side, I'll build a fire with my lighter, and we'll call it a night." She turned to face Kailuun. "My new friend, will you please carry me once more?"

The *chimorg* bowed down and allowed her to mount. Pain rose like a slow wave through Katherine's body, but she sucked down a breath and held it as Kailuun strode to the river's edge and waded into the chilly water. With a strong swimming stroke, he made for the far bank.

Back on shore, the ghosts following Katherine had stopped. They would not cross running water. They stared after her with abandoned expressions, and Katherine felt strangely sick at heart for leaving them. What do they want of me? she wondered.

Suddenly, she heard a shout. Cha Mak Nul stood near the bridge, glaring at her. The Darklander had managed to trail her after all, even in the night. She put one hand on the stunner clipped to the waistband of her skirts, and her heart sank. The water was over the *chimorg*'s back and swirling around her waist. Her weapon was submerged, the batteries no doubt rendered useless.

"Kailuun, go!" she urged, and the *chimorg* redoubled its efforts to reach the far shore. Once they made the bank, the *chimorg* could easily outrun Mac. She'd just have to bear the pain.

But Mac wasn't ready to give up. Cursing her again, he ran across the bridge.

Then he screamed. A gray, amorphous shape flowed up from the bottom of the bridge through the cracks and gaps left by the rotten planking and blocked the Darklander's way. A sound like the wailing of an infant filled the air as the thing took on a vaguely humanoid shape. Tiny arms totally out of proportion to the rest of its mass sprouted and reached toward Mac.

An invisible force lifted him off his feet and tumbled him head over heels into the air.

His screams turned to helpless shrieks of terror. The shape gestured again. Stones tore themselves from the ground and flew straight at Mac with bone-breaking fury. Branches broke and ripped away from the trees, flashed toward Mac, lashed and whipped him, cutting his clothes to shreds, splitting his flesh.

Suddenly, Katherine's senses began to expand again. She touched Mac's mind, and his panic nearly overwhelmed her. She shared his pain, experiencing every lash and blow. Her throat turned raw from his screams.

But she shared something else, too. Another mind was there, primal and undeveloped and angry. *A baby*, she realized, recoiling in horror, *the ghost of a murdered infant, enraged because it had been deprived of life.*

Eric had taught her about the ghosts of Palenoc. *Utburds,* he'd called these unfortunate spirits. Unfocused in their rage, they were ruthless and difficult to lay to rest.

Reeling, she fell from Kailuuun's back. The water swept over her head, filling mouth and nose. Her skirts and backpack started to drag her deeper, but she fought to regain the surface, her mind still bound with Mac and his attacker.

Sputtering, gasping, she got a grip on Kailuun's mane. The sharp membrane cut stingingly into her palm, but she hung on, and the *chimorg* swam for shore. As soon as her feet touched bottom, she let go and stumbled to the bank, collapsing in the mud.

Blood pouring down her arm, she rolled over and thrust her injured hand toward the bridge. "Stop!" she cried desperately. She wanted only to be free from the Darklander, not to see him dead. "Stop it!"

Again, something inside her seemed to open up and send shoots deep down into the earth to tap undreamed-of power. The river's surface began to burn with rippling white flame. Without warning, bands of light surged up from the mud and arced above Katherine, and radiant ruby sparks flashed out of her bleeding wound to fly in dazzling orbits around and around her.

The *utburd*'s primal mind finally took note of her. A word that was half plaintive cry brushed against her thoughts.

Maaa-ma?

It released its hold on Mac. The Darklander fell to the planking. The boards cracked and splintered under his weight, and pieces fell into the river. Barely conscious, Mac scrambled for a grip on the old wood. Then with a despairing cry, he fell through.

Kailuun plunged into the burning water and swam toward the Darklander. The flames had no heat. They were energy she somehow conjured from the river's mineral content—how, she didn't know.

The *utburd* continued to call in her mind, *Maaama? Maaa-ma?* She heard its wail, tasted its confusion and the heartbreaking hurt that drove it, and she began to weep. Her own pain no longer mattered. Katherine got to her feet, slipping in the mud as she scrambled ashore, and ran as quickly as her awkward body allowed to the end of the bridge. Despite its dangerous condition she gripped a cable at the side and took a cautious step toward the creature.

The bridge creaked ominously, a vibration passing through the boards under her feet. Still, she ventured farther. The bands of light surrounding her lit up the black, weather-beaten structure, showing the holes and weak spots. Below, the river continued to burn.

Katherine held out her arms and folded them over her breasts as if she were holding a baby that she rocked back and forth. "Peace, little one," she said softly, tears streaming down her face, for she still shared its misery. "You're not alone anymore. Come to me. Come to me, and let me hold you."

The *utburd* moved hesitantly toward her, then stopped. Slowly, its anger ebbed from Katherine's awareness, but still she felt an overpowering sense of confusion and hurt. Clinging to the bridge's support cable, she walked to meet it. The bridge swayed and shivered, but she no longer hesitated.

The light surrounding her touched the *utburd*, and its shape began to change. Its ugliness dissolved, and she realized it was never more than an illusion, a reflection of the child's own self-perception.

A naked little boy-baby sat crying in the middle of the bridge, its pudgy legs folded before it, its dark, round eyes locked on Katy. Its hands reached for her. *Maaa-ma?*

Forgetting her safety, Katherine gathered the child in her arms and hugged it to her, setting her cheek next to its face. Then she kissed its eyes and nose and chin, cooing, "Yes, baby, yes. It's all right now." She hugged it again and rocked it as her light swirled around them both. "You poor baby," she continued. "I'll never let anything bad happen to you again. I'll take you home with me and love you, love you, love you."

The baby raised one fist, then its fingers opened to touch her face. Its little hand slid down her chin and throat, lingering on her breast. Its crying subsided to only a whimper. Then that, too, ceased. Dark, innocent eyes closed.

Like dew in the sunlight, the child faded from her arms. Only a spirit, it was peaceful at last.

Katherine bit her lip and trembled. Her light faded, and below the bridge the surface of the river turned normal once more. She gazed into the sky as if she could see that tiny soul rising toward heaven. She couldn't, of course. They didn't believe in heaven on this world, she remembered. They believed in Paradise and something beyond called *Or-Dhamu*.

Inside her body her own baby kicked against her right side, then settled down. Katherine felt bathed in serenity, free from fear or despair. She wiped her face; there was no more need for tears. Grabbing the bridge's suspension cable, she made her way back.

But before she reached shore, she stopped and stared at her palm. The cut from Kailuun's mane was already closed. The scar vanished as she watched.

Katherine closed her eyes for a moment and covered her swollen belly with both hands. "I thought I was doing all these wondrous things," she whispered in sudden understanding. "But it's you. It's not my power. It's yours."

The child inside her turned restlessly.

Chapter Fifteen

THE sun stung Eric's face, and the wind whipped his hair as Shadowfire carried him through the midday sky. Seven days of swift flight had brought them far across the Sinnagar continent, but he felt bone-tired, and when he played his harmonica, he could sense even his dragon's fatigue.

The landscape below rolled and rippled, on fire with the red and orange colors of late autumn, the soil bearing a sharp reddish cast. The sun glinted on a range of low hills. Nestled among them in a sprawling valley lay a small, blue lake.

Eric twisted in his saddle; Alanna and Mirrormist trailed on his left. With a gesture he indicated his intention to land. Valis and Brightstar were farther off to his right, but he had no doubt the big *sekournen* would see them and follow.

Taking out his harmonica, he blew the opening strains of "De Guella." Shadowfire's mind brushed against his own, and the dragon knew his desire. One wing dipped. Eric gripped his saddle with his knees as he continued to play. The ground came up at a dizzying rate, then suddenly they were skimming the lake's silvery surface. Shadowfire's tail cut a wake through the water, throwing a wet spray high into the air.

Through their bond, Eric felt his dragon's laughter and turned to see the reason. Alanna had followed too close behind, and Shadowfire had playfully drenched her with a wall of water. Despite his weariness, Eric laughed, too.

They touched down on the farthest shore. As soon as Eric dismounted and put away his harmonica, Shadowfire crawled back to the water's edge and submerged half of his great bulk. The dragon expressed his satisfaction in a high-pitched trilling that reminded Eric of a cat's purr.

Mirrormist and Brightstar settled to the earth moments later. After Valis and Alanna removed their saddle packs, both beasts joined Shadowfire in the lake. Brightstar folded his wings tightly against his body and dived beneath the lake's surface, only to rise again in a rippling, sinuous movement and sink once more out of sight like some monstrous sea serpent of legend.

Alanna carried their meager sack of supplies. The food that the councilor had provided was long since gone. The sack contained only a few pieces of bread and cheese they had picked up in a village along their route and some roots and tubers Alanna had harvested from the ground at their last stop.

"I'm in a mood, Eric Podlowsky," she grumbled, dropping the sack at Eric's feet. Her hair hung in wet ropes, and her garments were soaked. Black circles ringed her eyes, her face pale and drawn from fatigue. "You're teaching that dragon of yours nasty habits, and don't think I won't find a way to pay you back."

Eric hid a grin as Valis joined them.

"You're all wet," Valis said with a straight face. He turned to Eric. "There's plenty of daylight left. Why did we stop?"

Eric shrugged. "On the seventh day, even the Lord rested. We won't be serving Robert or ourselves if we reach Boraga exhausted. There's water here to drink, and we can probably catch some fish for a decent meal. After a good night's sleep we can start again tomorrow." He gazed back toward the range of hills, shielding his eyes against the sun. "Any idea where we are?"

"Bastra," Valis answered, "on the western most edge of the Gray Kingdoms." He pointed toward the hills. "Not far beyond those peaks lies the Dark Land nation of Shadark, and beyond that ..." he hesitated, as if debating whether or not to say the word out loud ... "Srimourna."

Eric nodded with satisfaction. It would not take them twelve days to reach Boraga as Roderigo Diez had said. By pushing himself, his friends, and the *sek-oye*, he had shaved perhaps two days off the Spaniard's estimate. They had slept very little, flying night and day, sometimes tying themselves to their saddles so they could grab short naps safely.

He looked around for Alanna. On the shore's edge she had already slipped off her clothes and eased into the water to swim. Eric scanned the shoreline, alert for any danger, and noticed a copse of trees right down at the water's edge about a hundred yards to his right.

"You any good at spearfishing?" he asked Valis.

The big dragonrider wrinkled his brow as he frowned. "Jab a fish with a sharp stick? In the water? While it's moving? I've never been desperate enough to try."

Eric put his hand on the *shinobe-zu* that Valis wore under his belt and slowly reclaimed it. "Think you're desperate enough now?" he asked, giving the cane a twist and exposing an inch or so of the blade as he glanced toward the copse of trees.

Valis put one hand to his stomach, and a thoughtful gaze settled on his face. "If I have to eat one more root that Alanna's dug out of the dirt, I'll throw up."

Eric closed the cane again and twirled it on the tips of his fingers baton-style as he started toward the trees. "Then follow me, old chum, and I'll teach you one of my favorite survival games. If we're lucky, we'll have something better to eat than roots."

The copse was surprisingly gloomy, the trees close together and the autumn leaves still clinging to the branches, blocking the sunlight. In very little time Eric found two tall, straight saplings. He felled them with a pair of perfect swordstrokes and quickly stripped away the branches.

"The next part is trickier," he told Valis as he began sharpening one end of the first sapling. "Once you get a good point, you have to notch it just right, or the fish will wiggle off." He looked up at his friend and grinned. "Assuming you're fast enough to skewer one in the first place."

Valis was gathering wood kindling and pieces of dried bark to build a fire. A sharp movement caused the leaves to shiver in the branch directly above his head. The *sekournen* gave a strangled yell; his armload of wood flew in all directions as he clutched at a slender brown line that coiled around his throat.

In less than an instant Valis was jerked off his feet. His toes kicked at the ground; his eyes bulged and his face purpled. With another jerk the brown line dragged him higher still.

Eric shouted. Dropping his nearly completed fishing spear, he leaped, swung his blade, and severed the brown line. Valis crashed to the ground, sputtering and gasping for breath as he ripped at the writhing coil still encircling his neck.

Eric stared in disbelief. A terrible hissing sounded in the thick leaves above. The severed line thrashed back and forth, spewing a dark ichor as it withdrew upward.

It wasn't a rope at all, but a living creature.

Before he could recover from his shock, something leaped at him—claws and teeth, a long, scaled body. Too late, he brought his weapon up, but the creature's weight smashed into him, and the *shinobe-zu* went flying from his grasp.

Eric hit the ground on his back. Through a haze of stars, he stared desperately up at the huge lizard on top of him. A red tongue lashed at his face, stinging his cheek. Teeth sought his throat, and Eric smelled the beast's fetid breath. Without thinking, he swung his fist with all his strength, straight for the monster's snout. At the same time he brought his knees up under its belly and heaved, flinging it in one direction as he rolled in the other.

Its hissing filled the small copse. Eric looked wildly around for his sword, spied it, and lunged.

Inches from the weapon, something snapped whip-like around his neck. With constricting force it jerked him backward before he could grasp his sword. Lights exploded behind his eyes, only to be drowned in a red fog.

Again the air filled with hissing and sharp claws scrabbling. The pressure on Eric's windpipe ceased. The coil around his throat quivered, twitched, and fell away.

Half in a panic, Eric scrambled to his knees. Valis then pulled him to his feet, bloodied sword in hand. Before them, mere yards away, repillian eyes gleamed angrily, and powerful muscles gathered. With an astounding leap the beast sprang for the nearest tree. Its claws digging deep into the bark, its color darkening to form a nearly perfect camouflage, it hissed again and spat at them, lashing the air with a bleeding tail that was still twice the length of its four-foot body.

Eric dived for the nearly finished spear and hurled it with all his might. The creature emitted a high-pitched scream as the shaft of wood impaled it. In a spasm of pain it fell to the ground again, and Eric leaped upon the spear, driving it completely through the monster's back and into the earth. In a fury he tried to push it deeper still until the wood snapped in his hands.

Heart pounding, breath ragged, he stepped back and stared at the struggling beast. The thrashing of its limbs rapidly ceased, but the length of tail coiled and uncoiled like a scorpion's. Finally, the tail curled once more, uncurled, then lay on the ground like an old rope.

"What the hell is that?" Eric asked, casting aside the fragment of spear he still held. He wiped a warm and sticky ichor from his face with the back of his hand, feeling sick in the pit of his stomach.

Valis rubbed the red welt around his neck, and answered hoarsely, "A *kinoit*." In your own tongue, a Gallows Lizard." He paced a wide circle around the beast and prodded it with the tip of the sword. "Too bad about your fishing spear," he added.

With a wry face Eric examined the scratches the *kinoit*'s claws had made on his leather shirt. "I never really cared that much for fish, anyway," he said, venturing a bit closer. "This thing was planning to make a meal of one of us. I think we should return the favor."

With Valis carrying an armload of wood and kindling for a fire, Eric dragged the dead *kinoit* back to the lakeshore by what remained of its tail.

Alanna sat by the water, dressed again, combing her fingers through the tangles of her wet hair. She looked up when she saw them coming, her eyes focused on the huge lizard. "What a pair of happy-looking hunters," she said. "Did you boys have a good time?"

"Game was a bit scarce," Eric answered offhandedly, dropping the *kinoit*'s tail and wiping his hands on his sleeves as he continued with a straight face. "But we were ferocious and triumphant. Would you mind cleaning and gutting this for us? The rest is woman's work from here."

Alanna flashed a pretty smile, turned to her opposite side and gathered a handful of a green, seaweedlike moss she had collected from the lake and spread on a broadleaf. Still smiling, she flung it at Eric, and it splattered on his chest. "Have a little garnish with your lizard," she said with an innocent expression.

Valis sat down with a stick and a dry piece of bark and went to work building a fire. In a short time a small flame began to grow. Quickly, he fed handfuls of grass into it, then larger pieces of bark and wood.

Alanna stood over the dead lizard with the blade of her *shinobe-zu* in one hand. "Would you like a drumstick, dear?" she called to Eric. The sword flashed up, then down, in one smooth movement. She bent and picked up a bloody leg.

Valis put on a subtle grin as he glanced at Eric. "Can she cook, or can she cook?"

With the fire going, Eric spitted several pieces of *kinoit* meat on a stick and carried it to the lake where he vigorously rinsed away the blood. When he was satisfied, he returned to the fire. Valis had driven two forked sticks into the ground on either side of the flames. Eric balanced his spit upon them, and they stood back to watch the roasting of their dinner.

A sweet odor rose in the air as the chunks of meat popped and sizzled. The joking ceased; they waited in silence, impatiently staring.

Eric's mouth watered. More than ever, he was aware of the emptiness in his belly. The waiting was too much for him. He butchered several more chunks of meat from the *kinoit*'s carcass, then rinsed and spitted them so they would be ready to go on the fire when the first ones came off.

"Time to feast," Valis announced when their dinner was sufficiently cooked. He slipped off his shirt and used it as a pot holder to lift the spit. After waving it in the air for a few minutes, he offered the pieces of meat.

Alanna had gathered several rubbery broadleaves to use as plates. Carefully, each dragonrider stripped a piece of steaming meat from the stick onto a leaf.

Eric blew on his to cool it and licked his fingertips, which were slightly burned. He didn't care. As soon as he dared, he lifted the meat again and and bit into it. Hot juice dribbled down his chin; he just flicked it away and chewed. "It's like gator," he said, but neither of his friends paid him any attention.

When they had stuffed themselves on *kinoit*, they lay back in the grass side by side and patted their stomachs contentedly. "That was wonderful." Alanna sighed. "Sorry I hit you with the kelp."

Eric, eyes closed, answered in his worst, most menacing German accent. "Don't worry, woman. You will pay in ways you cannot imagine." He didn't even realize that he had answered in English, not in the language of Guran, and that she hadn't understood him.

The words had come out in a mumbled slur, anyway, for sleep was upon him.

Eric awoke to a gentle shaking. Alanna bent close over him, speaking low so as not to awaken Valis. "Shadowfire is gone," she whispered.

Rubbing his eyes, Eric sat up slowly. Twilight filled the sky, and black clouds rumbled across the eastern heavens. The shadows of the mountains at their backs stretched across the lake. Someone had kept the campfire going, but the flames were low, and the coals glowed redly.

Mirrormist and Brightstar were curled up on the shore, half in and half out of the lake. Their great heads rested on the ground, and diamond-faceted eyes blinked lazily. Their soft, purrlike trilling, along with the lapping of the water, made a soothing sound in the gathering darkness.

"I woke up, and he was gone," Alanna said again. "I thought you'd want to know."

Eric wrapped his arms around his knees, hugging them to his chest as he craned his neck and scanned the sky for his dragon. *His dragon.* Shadowfire would certainly laugh at that.

"He may just have decided to stretch his wings," Alanna said reassuringly.

Eric nodded, but he slipped the Hohner harmonica from the pocket on his belt and wet his lips with the tip of his tongue. Softly, he played the opening notes of "De Guella." The quivering music rolled over the lake, and Mirrormist and Brightstar stopped their trilling to listen.

Abruptly, he put the instrument down. He got to his feet, turned, and gazed toward the mountains. The last gasps of sunset colored the spaces between the peaks with a dull, bloody glow, but the peaks had surrendered to the night.

"He's on the other side of the mountains," Eric said quietly. "Something's got his attention."

A powerful wind at his back nearly blew Eric off his feet. Without any warning Brightstar climbed into the sky, wings beating in a powerful rhythm that carried him swiftly toward the mountains.

Alanna whirled toward the lake, singing out in a sharp soprano voice. Mirrormist, on the verge of flying after Brightstar, folded his wings again and turned disappointed eyes toward his rider.

Valis sat up, awakened by the commotion. "What's happening?" he asked.

Eric didn't answer. He wet his lips again and raised the harmonica. The music flowed from him, opening the bridge between his mind and Shadowfire's.

The distance between them didn't matter. Alanna and others had remarked on the unusual nature of the bond he shared with the *sekoye*, a bond stronger, different, than that experienced by most other *sekournen*.

Eric had never told them how different, choosing to keep a secret to himself. Music was more than just a bridge over which he and Shadowfire could communicate. It was a bridge Eric had learned to cross.

He closed his eyes, embellishing the melody as he played, and felt his mind draw near to Shadowfire's. The dragon's senses were alien to Eric, frightening at first, confusing. A mountain breeze blew chill upon the leathery hide; he felt he could clench and unclench his talons on a stony perch. Still, he continued to play his harmonica.

Through music, it *was* possible for him to be in two places at once.

A powerful blood lust, barely held in check, burned in his brain. Images began to play behind his shut lids as he saw what Shadowfire was seeing. *Chimorgs*— scores of them, running down a steep-walled valley toward an unsuspecting village. After them came a squad of black-armored soldiers, bearing whips and batons and nets at the ready on their shoulders.

A pair of women, working late together in the fields, dropped hoe and basket and ran. A pair of *chimorgs* charged toward them.

Shadowfire swept into the air and raced from his mountain perch toward the valley, trumpeting a shrill challenge as he extended his talons. For an instant Eric thrilled at the rush of wind beneath his wings even as he urged Shadowfire to wait. The dragon pushed his rider away.

Eric's eyes snapped open, and the music ceased. He spun toward Alanna, screaming, "Get us to the other side of those mountains! Quick!"

Alanna wasted no time with questions. She sang to Mirrormist and ran toward her *sekoye* with Eric right behind her. The dragon stretched out its neck, and she flung herself into the saddle, tied narrow straps of leather around her thighs, and drew Eric up behind her. "Hold tight!" she warned.

Valis sang out, calling Brightstar back before the dragon had gone far. Brightstar let out a trumpeting cry, barely touching the earth before his rider leaped into the saddle.

"Tschai!" Alanna called to Mirrormist. Then her voice rose in her own version of "De Guella," and her dragon surged upward. The wind whipped at Eric, threatening to snatch him from the dragon's neck, but he clung to Alanna, his hands locked around her waist.

Side by side, the two dragons flew, racing toward

the mountains as Eric pointed the way over Alanna's shoulder past the peaks, then diving toward a valley where a terrible sight awaited them.

Shadowfire's angry screams echoed against the hills, and his massive pinions cut wakes through the tall grass and fields of grain as he swept from one end of the valley to the other. In each set of talons he held a writhing *chimorg*. With a twitch of those huge claws, he crushed them and hurled the corpses into the field below.

Chimorgs and soldiers ran in all directions. The ground was littered with torn and flattened corpses. Shadowfire screamed again, then swooped upon yet another *chimorg*, seized it in both claws, and ripped it into bloody halves as if it were tissue paper. Then with unerring aim he flung one of the halves at a fleeing soldier.

Eric blew a note on his harmonica, not to stop Shadowfire, but to let him know he was no longer alone.

Valis and Brightstar screamed at the same time. The big *sekournen* leaned down against his dragon's neck as Brightstar folded his wings and plunged straight for a panicked *chimorg*. Brightstar lashed out with one swift claw, and the *chimorg* went flying, its neck bent back against its body.

Mindful of her passenger, Alanna held Mirrormist back from the battle. There was little left to do, anyway. The rest of the *chimorgs* and soldiers had escaped into the hills and the surrounding woods.

"Take us down to the village," Eric said to Alanna. "I want to know what warrants such a large raiding force."

Alanna sang, and Mirrormist dropped gently onto a narrow roadside that was no more than a pair of wagon ruts and stretched out his neck. Alanna and Eric slid to the ground.

A few men and women stood in a wary pack at the edge of their village, eyeing the dragons and the newcomers. One of the men started toward Eric, meeting him halfway.

"Are those real *sekoye*?" he asked in broken Domain patois, staring at Brightstar as he settled to earth beside Mirrormist.

"Of course they are," Eric said. "Haven't you ever seen dragons?"

The villagers shrugged. "They're trampling our crops."

Another man came up behind the first. "Shut up, Kestrin. These strangers and their beasts saved our lives." He spoke in perfectly accented Guranian and raised his hands, palms outward toward Eric. "My name is Trake, and I believe this is the proper Domain greeting?"

Eric smiled and touched his palms to the new man's. The other villagers ventured closer now, some slipping around Eric and Alanna to greet Valis and to get a better look at Mirrormist and Brightstar.

Shadowfire continued to fly in ever widening circles over the valley, a protective, watchful angel, the undersides of his wings burning with opalescent fire as the evening grew darker. Even without the bridge of music, Eric could sense the pride and determination that filled his *sekoye*.

He turned back to the villagers. "Why did the Darklanders attack you?" he asked.

"Shadarkans," Trake corrected. "A nation of madmen at the best of times, but they're even worse since the theft of Carad Thorn's soul has left them leaderless."

"They wanted our children," a shy young woman said, peering around Trake. Her eyes were wide and frightened like a deer's as she clutched a newborn baby protectively to her breast.

Trake caught Eric's arm. "Why don't we talk over wine," he suggested. "We seldom get strangers in this isolated corner of Bastra. Let us show you some courtesy."

"No wine for me," Eric said, "but for my partners if they like. We can't stay long, but it's always good to make new friends."

Half the villagers stayed to admire the dragons, but the other half followed as Trake led the way to his home and threw open the front door. As many menfolk crowded in as the space would allow, leaving the women to gawk from outside through the door and windows. Eric, Alanna, and Valis were given stools at a crude wooden table.

"Forgive me, but I have no wife," Trake said, "so I must serve you myself." He disappeared into a back room and returned with several jars of wine and wooden cups that he set before them. "Don't worry, don't worry," he said to Eric, "I haven't forgotten you." Once more he disappeared only to return with another jar. "Cool water from my own well out back," he said grandly.

The three *sekournen* offered thanks as Trake filled their cups.

"So," Eric said as Trake pushed his cup toward him, "tell us more about the Shadarkans."

Kestrin leaned against the wall right behind Eric. "Those filthy Darklanders have been raiding all the villages. They say they're searching for the Green-Eyed Child . . ."

"The *Shae'aluth*," Trake explained. "In the Darklands they call him *Na-kaya Amun.*" He made a bow and smiled broadly. "I spent three years of my youth on a trading ship working the coast from Eden to Guran."

Eric raised his cup, but before he could drink, Alanna lashed out and knocked Valis's cup from the big dragonrider's hand. Leaping to her feet, she flung the contents of her own cup in Trake's face. Staring at her, Eric sniffed the contents of his own vessel and set it back on the table.

"The best poisons and potions in the world are made in *sekournen* Sherens," Alanna shouted scornfully as she dashed her cup on the floor. "Did you really think we wouldn't detect your drug?"

Scowling, Valis seized one of the wine jars and sniffed it. Then he grabbed the jar of water and raised it to his nose. *"Pritikit,"* he said, naming the chemical as his face clouded with anger.

Kestrin threw his arm around Eric's neck. A pair of men grabbed for Alanna. Four men flung themselves at Valis and dragged him to the floor. Ropes appeared as if from nowhere.

"Interesting brand of courtesy you have here," Eric muttered. He smashed his head back into Kestrin's face. The man grunted and stumbled back, clutching a ruined nose. Standing up, Eric grabbed his stool and swung it in a wide circle, driving back the men who sought to take Kestrin's place before he cracked it across the back of one of Alanna's attackers.

Alanna smashed her heel on the toes of her other would-be captor, then flung the table on its side into the path of two others who came at her. The *shinobe-zu* came out of her belt. Without drawing the blade, she spun it like a short staff and dropped another villager.

A man charged Eric from the right. A short, sharp chop across the windpipe sent the man gasping to his knees. A stool came flying through the air, straight for Eric's head. He caught it nonchalantly and redirected it into the face of still another foe, who went staggering back into a cold fireplace amid the crash and clatter of pots and pans.

"Stop! Stop!" Trake cried suddenly, waving his arms from a safe corner. "You'll wreck my home! Stop, I tell you!"

The village men—those who could still stand—reluctantly obeyed. Trake ventured out toward the center of the floor and glared at the five men piled on top of Valis.

"Get off him!" Trake shouted, grabbing one of the men by the shoulders and pulling him back. "Let him up! It's over. We failed."

Scowling, the villagers released Valis.

"I was almost free," the dragonrider said to Alanna.

"I'm sure you were," Alanna answered with a straight face.

Trake shrugged and forced another of his smiles. "We're farmers, not fighters," he said.

"I'm sure you are," Alanna said.

Eric gazed around the room, alert for any further hostility. "Do you want to tell me what that was about?" he asked.

Alanna tapped the *shinobe-zu* on her palm. "Or shall we beat it out of you?"

"Down, woman," Valis muttered.

Kestrin wiped blood from his nose, his face smeared with it. "We were going to trade you!" he grumbled.

Trake opened a small chest, took out a soft towel, and offered it to Kestrin for his nose. "When I saw three *sekournen* walking into our arms," he explained as he moved about the room, helping his friends and neighbors to their feet, "I had the idea we might capture and trade you to the Darklanders in exchange for leaving us alone." He shrugged again. "Some ideas are good ones, and some obviously are not."

Eric shook his head. "Get away from the door," he instructed a pair of men who blocked the way to the outside. When the men obeyed, he indicated to his friends it was time to go.

"We're desperate people," Trake said suddenly. "We have four newborns in this village! The Shadarkans will be back! They'll scour the countryside to find the *Green-Eyed Child*!"

"None of your children have green eyes," Eric answered coldly.

Kestrin spat at Eric's feet. "Darklanders never go away empty-handed," he said. "They take your grain or your livestock. They rape your wives. They burn your crops or your home because it amuses them."

Another man spat. "What do they know of our pain or our lives?" he questioned. "They're safe with their pretty *sekoye*."

Alanna's breath hissed between her teeth as she spun and slammed the back of her hand across the speaker's mouth with force enough to topple him. Then, pointing to Eric with the end of the *shinobe-zu*, she spoke in a deadly quiet voice. "He lost his lover, fighting the Chols." The cane's tip moved toward Valis. "He lost a young partner fighting the Kingdoms of Night. Don't speak to us of safety."

The man she had struck glared at her from the floor as he wiped blood from his mouth. "And what have you lost?" he dared to ask.

She returned his glare as she shoved the *shinobe-zu* back through her belt. "My femininity," came her sarcastic answer as she strode through the doorway, "and my patience with people like you."

Valis followed her.

"Thanks for the hospitality," Eric said caustically to Trake. "I'll be sure to recommend your town to my friends."

"What do we do about the Shardarkans?" Kestrin shouted, clutching the towel to his face. "They'll be back!"

Eric forced a look of concern. "You probably shouldn't be here," he said. "I wouldn't be."

He left Trake's house and walked down the village's only street. Alanna and Valis were with their dragons already. A small gathering of women and children watched at the edge of the village. None of them spoke as he passed, but one young boy clutched at his trouser leg. Eric paused long enough to rumple the boy's hair and hope that his parents were smart enough to heed Eric's advice. Then he left the villagers behind and joined his friends.

Shadowfire still circled overhead. Eric took out his harmonica and called to his mount. In moments the dragon landed beside Brightstar and Mirrormist.

"Do you think the *Child* really has been born?" Valis asked in a low voice.

"I don't know," Eric said, tapping the harmonica thoughtfully on his palm. He gazed back toward the village. Some of the men had joined their women and children to watch from a safe distance. "I'll tell you what else I don't know," he added. "Sometimes, my friend, I don't know which of us is from the crazier world."

"The *Shae'aluth* is no longer our concern," Alanna called as she mounted Mirrormist, a hard, unpleasant edge in her voice. "Finding Robert is."

She began to sing a now familiar song.

Chapter Sixteen

KATHERINE held Mac's head in her lap and tried to make him comfortable. Kailuun had saved him from drowning and had dragged him onto the muddy shore. His injuries were extensive, and she could not seem to turn off the awareness that allowed her to share his pain. He shivered violently and rolled frightened eyes up to meet hers.

"*Shayana*," he murmured. "*Na-kaya Amun.*"

Katherine barely heard. She pressed his shattered left hand between her own hands, causing him to cry out, but a pale blue light and an intense warmth flowed around her fingers and up his arm halfway to his shoulder. Scratches and cuts on Mac's wrist, forearm, and elbow sealed and vanished, and the bones in his hand knit back together again.

Mac's eyes fluttered and closed as he lapsed into unconsciousness.

Katherine bit her lip in dismay. She could sense Mac's broken bones, internal bleeding, and damaged organs. She did her best to heal each injury, but deep inside him she found something that surprised her—plague.

But she had already driven that from his body in the cave of the Kirringskal! She rubbed her hands together and drew a deep breath, then touched him and concentrated. Once more the disease retreated from her energy, but the moment she took her hands away it began to grow slowly, inexorably, within him again.

No matter how she wrestled with it, each time she turned her back, the plague returned, tiny and weak, but growing.

"What are you?" she whispered, taking Mac's head between her hands, regarding him with new suspicion.

His eyes fluttered, and he answered hopelessly, "I am the Cha Mak Nul."

As had happened once before, he was speaking another language, and yet she understood him in her mind. Putting one hand on her belly, she swallowed. "Cha Mak Nul?" she said uneasily. "I thought that was your name."

His lips trembled as he tried weakly to tap his forehead. "Because we are sharing thought," he said, "I know you are trying to drive the plague from my body." He shook his head ever so slightly. "You can heal my outward symptoms, but nothing can drive out the disease; it is bound to my life force."

Katherine brushed a wet strand of hair back from his face as she struggled to understand the meaning of his words. "Magic?" she said, feeling acknowledgment take shape in his mind before he found his voice.

"It is the Cha Mak Nul," he said. "I am the Cha Mak Nul. While I live, I will spread disease." He rolled his head to the side and lifted his hand. His gaze fastened on his opal ring. He spoke again with a strange sadness. "I am what my master made me."

"You were taking me to your master," she asked softly, "weren't you?"

A slight nod of his head on her lap was her answer. "He would have been proud of me," he whispered.

"He would have loved me for bringing him a prize such as you. Perhaps"—he hesitated, swallowing with difficulty—"perhaps he would have taken this cup from me, and I would not have had to drink this death."

Katherine bit her lip again as she began to realize the enormous decision confronting her. She looked back over her shoulder to Kailuun, as if the *chimorg* could help her, but though he stood watching, eyes burning with patient fire, she knew the decision was hers alone.

"What would your master want with me?" she whispered.

Mac lowered the beringed hand and closed his eyes. "You are the *Shayana*," he answered. "The mother of *Na-Kaya Amun*—the one your people call *Shae'aluth*."

"That's crazy," Katherine said too quickly.

He coughed suddenly, and a fine stream of blood bubbled over his lips and down his chin. He tried to wipe it away, but Katherine, using a corner of her sleeve, was faster.

"You know it is true," he said when he could speak again, "just as you know the powers you control are not your own. I realized it when I saw you give healing in the cave. Only the Son of the Morning can heal without crystals or blood. The Kirringskal knew it, too, so they called you *Shayana*, Mother of the *Shae'aluth*."

He twisted in a spasm of pain. Katherine gave a sharp intake of breath, feeling the splinter of bone that perforated his left lung as if the injury were her own.

"Not much longer now." The words squeezed between his clenched teeth as his agony eased a bit.

Katherine clenched one fist, her mind filled with

doubt and turmoil. She had healed his outward injuries—the cuts and most of the broken bones—but the internal injuries were killing him. Those, too, she could heal, but not the plague. If she saved his life, he would spread the disease, and others would die.

Yet, how could she let him suffer? She wasn't God, and she couldn't choose between life and death. She had power, though, however she had come by it, and she could heal. That simple fact left her no choice at all.

Hesitantly, her fist unclenched. She opened her hand, feeling an increasing warmth in her palm as she reached toward his heart.

Mac caught her wrist and held it with surprising strength.

"Shayana," he said with pleading eyes, "give me something else, something not even Carad Thorn could give me." Trembling, he raised the hand with the opal ring and pointed overhead. Through the trees, Mianur's ring was faintly visible. "The Bridge to Paradise," he said. "You can give me peace, *Shayana.* I have no wish to wander Paradane like these unhappy souls."

She followed his gaze and realized that Mac saw the ghosts at last. They watched from the trees, from the silent, dark places. *Apparitions* crowded the bank on the far side of the river. Some, having found their way to the bridge, crossed wistfully over. Other spirits were emerging from the woods at her back to swell the ranks of her unnatural army.

She stroked Mac's forehead and rocked him gently. "This day will you be in Paradise," she whispered.

With fading strength he reached up and laid one hand on her swollen middle as he once more closed his eyes. He never opened them again, and sometime before morning, Katherine, her mind still touching his, shared the experience of his death.

For a long time she sat there, unable to weep, unwilling to move. Then she eased away, laying his head carefully down. With her bare hands she began to dig in the mud until she had a hole deep enough. She rolled Mac in and covered up his grave.

She wanted to bathe and cleanse away the filth from her body, but she could no longer bear to stay in the shadow of the bridge or near the mound of earth she had made.

She touched Kailuun's shoulder, and leaning on the *chimorg* for support, they started downstream.

The dawn of morning sent a shimmer through the eastern trees. Her ghostly entourage slipped further and further into the shadows, avoiding the lengthening light as long as they could, fading away as the morning grew brighter.

The woods seemed suddenly empty and lonely. Katherine touched Kailuun again for reassurance as she stopped and turned her face to the warmth of the sun. The trees swayed softly, and the leaves rustled.

With no idea where she was or where she was going, aching in every part of her body, fatigue at last overcame her. The bank was no longer mud, but inviting grass and fallen leaves. She managed to quench her thirst at the river, then stretched out on her back in the shade of a bush and allowed sleep to claim her while Kailuun stood guard.

She awoke without feeling rested. The sun had moved past the zenith, destroying her shade. It streamed down through a gap in the trees, baking her in her clothes, which were clammy with sweat and mud and grime.

Clutching the small of her back, she struggled to her feet. Nearby, Kailuun emerged from a thicker part of the woods and snorted a greeting. She didn't wonder where he'd been as she wiggled out of her boots, tunic, and skirts and kicked them into a pile at the water's edge. Her red hair was a tangled mess full of knots and twigs and leaves; she couldn't even get her fingers through it. Her arms and legs were smeared with filth.

Making her way to the shore, she sat down painfully on the bank and slipped into the water. Goose bumps rose on her flesh; she hugged herself and shivered, but forced herself to wade deeper into the cold river until she was submerged up to her breasts.

Bending her knees, she tilted her head back and allowed the water to rise to her neck. Gradually, she adjusted to the chilly temperature, which soon soothed away the aches and pains and lifted her spirits. She gave her body a much needed scrub, pausing to laugh at a bird that landed on a close limb and chittered at her.

"You'd like to make a nest in this, wouldn't you?" she said, giving her hair a tug. "Or maybe you thought it *was* your nest." She took a breath and bent forward to begin the task of washing the wild mass, thinking that if she'd had a pair of scissors, she'd have cut it off and have done with it.

When her ministrations were finally complete, she reached for the pile of clothes and scrubbed them, too, casting them ashore on a grassy spot when she was satisfied with each garment. Then she waded ashore, smiling with childlike glee at the squish of mud between her toes, and hung each item on a branch or bush to dry in the sun.

Her stomach rumbled, reminding her that she was

famished. She found nothing to eat, however, no berries in the bushes, no fruit in the trees. To ease her hunger, she drank deeply from the river, filling her belly with water. Perhaps later she'd have better luck at finding food.

Cooled by the breeze, she settled down in a patch of direct sunlight that streamed through the trees, rejoicing in its warm touch on her bare skin, and began to disassemble her stunner. The interior mechanisms seemed dry enough. She spread the parts on the ground to dry as she examined the small nine-volt battery and found no obvious damage.

With a sigh of satisfaction she reassembled the weapon. Pressing the trigger resulted only in a dim flash; the battery, though intact, didn't have much power.

Her back no longer ached, but her breasts felt heavy and sore. She checked her garments, finding them still damp, and decided to dress anyway. Close by, Kailuun watched her, and when she picked up her backpack by its straps, the *chimorg* knelt down.

Katherine settled herself carefully astride the monster's back. Kailuun rose and began to follow the riverbank at a leisurely pace.

"On the road again, baby," Katherine murmured, placing one hand on her stomach. "Just can't wait to get on the road again."

But where was she going? She could wander for days, even weeks, around the Gray Kingdoms without encountering a homestead or a village. Her time was near; she could feel the baby stirring and growing restless inside her. The thought of having her child alone in this wilderness was not a pleasant one.

The river abruptly changed its course, turning southwestward. The opposite bank became a soaring range of scenic cliffs, crowned with sweeping trees whose leaves burned with the colors of autumn. Huge white birds glided above those cliffs and over the river. Katherine spied several large nests in the cracks and crannies of the bare stone face.

Beautiful, she thought, finding a deep peace as she watched the birds' flight.

Without warning, a sharp wind rustled the trees, and a shadow blotted out the sun. A huge dragon skimmed the edge of the cliffs, pale gray against the blue sky, sunlight glimmering on its wings. Another came behind it. Still another pair of dragons sailed past, following the course of the river.

Kailuun moved to a place of concealment in a thick cluster of trees, leaving Katherine to stare through leaves and branches as scores of dragons darkened the sky overhead. Her gaze followed their swift westward flight, and her heartbeat quickened. Never before had she seen such a gathering; it fairly took her breath away.

They flew in no particular formation. Some skimmed the tops of the trees, ripping away leaves in their powerful wake, while others appeared small and distant against the high clouds. The white birds that inhabited the cliffs scrambled to get out of the way, taking refuge with their mates in their nests, filling the air with indignant, high-pitched cries.

Katherine urged Kailuun to follow, but only when the last dragon passed beyond sight would the *chimorg* venture out of hiding.

As they resumed their plodding trek along the riverbank, Katherine wondered at the dragons' purpose. Wild *sekoye* seldom ventured this far into the Gray Kingdoms, or so she'd been told. But these were all clearly headed in the same direction, flying as fast as wings would carry them.

Into the Dark Lands, she realized with a sudden chill. Palenoc was still a world torn by war, and some inner instinct told her she had just witnessed the prelude to a coming battle.

The thought seemed to drain her of energy, and of hope as well. At a word Kailuun stopped and let her dismount. Her back ached again, and a fine line of pain ran down the side of her belly. Worse, the baby was playing soccer with her bladder.

"Give me a break, kid," she muttered, lifting her skirts as she headed for the bushes.

When she had relieved herself, she began to walk along the riverbank. Kailuun preceded her, picking the best course, leading her around obstacles. Her legs felt rubbery, and she paused often to catch her breath.

A strange stillness filled the air. No wind shook the leaves; no birds fluttered in the sky. Even the river had turned placid.

She regarded herself in the water's mirror-smooth surface and recoiled. It was not her own face she saw reflected there, but another. A dark-haired woman with lips red as blood and a slender horn sprouting from her brow stared up from the depths. Eyes blacker than space swept back and forth as if searching. For a brief moment those eyes seemed to focus on Katherine, but they turned away again without seeing.

Shandal Karg.

Trembling, Katherine clapped a hand to her mouth to keep from whispering that name aloud. How she knew the identity of that face, she couldn't say. Yet she knew!

The image in the water faded as those eyes continued to range back and forth. When it was gone, Katherine stepped quickly away from the bank and leaned against a tree, gasping, trying to calm the rapid beating of her heart.

When she was able, she moved from that spot as swiftly as she could, half running through the brush and undergrowth, batting back the limbs and branches that scratched at her face and clothes. It was not a pace she could maintain, though, and finally she sank to her knees and wept with great, wracking shudders, letting fear and misery overcome her.

When the tears were finished, she wiped her face with her sleeves, drew a deep breath, and sat back on her heels. There was no point in crying, but there was no harm in it, either. With a sigh she struggled up and looked around for Kailuun. The *chimorg* waited quietly at a discreet distance.

She took a step, then groaned as something cramped deep inside. She bit her lip and waited for it to pass, resolving not to ride the *chimorg* anymore. Gingerly, she took another step, then another.

The sun slipped slowly from the sky, and a soft, hazy twilight stole across the woods. Wisps of fog began to curl and eddy up from the water; tendrils of gray vapor crawled over the banks and along the forest floor.

Bone-tired, cramping with almost every step, Katherine pushed on until she thought she could go no farther. Still, she forced herself a few paces more. Then, pausing, she put one hand for support on Kailuun's shoulder. The *chimorg* stood absolutely still.

She had reached the edge of the forest, and the landscape changed dramatically. The south bank of the river was still a range of towering cliffs, but the north bank had become a rolling plain.

A few paces to her right, the first ghost of the eve-

ning, a pale *apparition*, drifted out from behind a thick
boll to regard her with dull, ancient eyes.

Behind the ghost, a pair of *leikkios* twinkled like
fireflies.

Somewhere near, the first *banshee* howled.

"My fan club's back," Katherine said through
clenched teeth to Kailuun. "My personal following
of Deadheads."

More ghosts emerged from the woods, following her
as she advanced into the clearing. They spread out in
no particular formation, moving before and beside and
behind her. Some looked like shadows that flowed
over the earth; some resembled pale, sad reflections
of men and women; some were transparent, substance-
less, nearly invisible in the patches of fog; some appeared as real and tangible as she.

"That's not saying much," she muttered, "considering I'm half dead."

She clutched her stomach as another spasm seized
her. The breath caught in her throat, and her eyes
snapped wide. That spasm was followed by another,
then another, each causing her greater pain.

At first she'd thought the cramps were symptoms of
her hunger, but she could no longer deny reality. Even
though, by her estimate, it was much too soon, she
was in labor.

She tried to stay calm. Maybe it was a false labor;
what the heck did she know about pregnancy, anyway? Another spasm wracked her. It sure didn't feel
fake! What should she do? Sit down? Lie down?

Swallowing hard, fighting panic, she went to work.
At the riverbank she began to pull up handfuls of
grass, which she piled and made into a soft bed by
spreading one of her skirts over it. The spasms didn't

stop; she worked through them, pausing when the pain was too great, and resuming as soon as it eased.

She tried to think of things she'd need. Fire came to mind. There were plenty of dead sticks and branches nearby. She gathered them in bundles and stacked them near her makeshift bed. From her backpack she took the Bic lighter. Fearful of a grass fire, she scooped a shallow pit with her hands.

The contractions came faster. Sweat beaded on her face as she concentrated on her preparations. In a short time she had her fire going.

Hot water, she thought. *In the movies they always have hot water.* She had a fire, and she had water. But she had no vessel, no pot, no pan. Looking around, she reached for her backpack and upended it, spilling the contents, shaking it to make sure it was empty. Next, she took off her underskirt and ripped it into rags. Carrying the strips to the river, she soaked them, rinsed them until they were reasonably clean, and put them wet into the pack. It wasn't hot water, but it was the best she could manage.

"What next, Kailuun?" she said with surprising calm to the *chimorg*, who stood by watching. "Something to cut the umbilical cord." She glanced around, wincing at another spasm, for something that would serve as a tool. She had no knife in her pack, nothing with a suitable edge.

Her gaze fell on the slender quartz crytal wand, a treasured memento, given to her by a dear friend named Salyt, who had died to save Katherine's life many, many months ago on the Nazrit Plain in the Dark Land nation called Chol Hecate.

Katherine had thought the wand's energy was spent, leaving it useless, but in her first encounter with Kailuun she had felt it flare to life, along with another jewel in her backpack, along with all the buried crystalline for miles around.

Bending awkwardly, she picked the wand up. What did she care if a piece of crystal was alive or dead? She knew as much about Palenoc magic as she knew about pregnancy. Whatever the wand's potential, right now she needed a cutting edge, and the crystal was going to provide it—she hoped.

Down along the river she'd seen a fist-sized rock. Finding the stone again, she got down on her hands and knees. The effort cost her acute pain. "Not yet," she said through clenched teeth. "Hold on, baby. I'm almost ready, but not yet."

Seizing the rock, she smashed it down on the wand. Splinters of quartz flew in several directions. When she lifted the rock, however, she nodded with satisfaction. The wand had broken along a cleavage line, leaving sharp edges.

She returned to her camp and set the new cutting tool close to the fire. The meadow was full of ghostly spectators now. The night sparkled with the lights of *leikkios*, and the grass rippled with the movements of *poltergeists*.

Katherine eased herself onto her bed of grass, half blinded by a rush of tears as the contractions intensified. Desperately, she unwrapped her undergarments and cast them aside. But for her boots and tunic, she was naked in the cool night. She glanced worriedly at her fire, fearing her little pile of wood would soon run out.

Another contraction brought a short scream. She bit her lip, and the cry became a whimper as she sank flat onto her back.

Katherine Dowd.

Was it the wind that called her name? Katherine

struggled up onto one elbow and peered around. It couldn't have been the wind, for there was none.

A second cry escaped her lips, and her back arched suddenly as the flesh of her belly rippled.

Katherine Dowd.

Was it her imagination? There was something vaguely familiar about the voice. "Who's there?" she cried, twisting onto her side, the better to look around.

The ghosts were drifting closer, gathering around her in a huge, crowded semicircle. In the air, watching from high above her, she sensed the invisible spirits, too—the *chills, poltergeists,* and *banshees.*

The night came alive with a strange chorus as one by one the *banshees* raised their voices, hundreds of voices, then thousands, weaving harmony with no melody. Never had Katherine heard such music! It almost drowned the scream of her next contraction.

The *leikkios* began to swirl and dance to the song of the *banshees.* Countless tiny lights rose flickering toward a central point above Katherine where they seemed to merge into one brightly shining mass that bathed the meadow in a pure radiance.

Katherine's belly convulsed, and she screamed again. Biting her lip, she fought to rise. Gaining her feet, she straddled the soft bed of grass and squatted down.

I am with you, Katherine Dowd. You will not go through this alone.

Her face contorted with pain and concentration, Katherine looked up. Through narrowed, tear-filled eyes, she recognized a gaunt, nearly forgotten face and gasped. "Phlogis?" she whispered. "What are you doing here?"

Phlogis smiled at her from the other side of her fire. *I have come to witness the birth of the* Shae'aluth, *Katherine Dowd,* he said solemnly. *All the ghosts of Palenoc have been drawn here to bear witness.* He stepped unharmed through the flames and came to her side. *The hour of dawn is at hand when Morning will overthrow the Darkness.*

Katherine turned her face upward to the new star that shimmered above her; she heard the *banshees'* chorus.

"This is bullshit," she hissed through her pain. "I'm no fucking Madonna! This is Eric's baby. Eric's and mine!" Her head snapped back with the force of her next scream. Her entire body seemed on fire; her breaths came in rapid gasps.

Phlogis's spectral form knelt down before her, and wide, dark eyes locked with hers. *The* Shae'aluth*'s spirit has chosen you to give Him flesh again,* he said, his words brushing in gentle wonderment over her brain. *A Daughter of Paradane is the* Shayana—*I knew you were special from the moment I saw you.*

Katherine forced words out. "If you can manifest real speech, Phlogis," she said, "I'd welcome the sound of another voice. Otherwise, shut up and get out of my head, because I'm kind of busy!"

"I can manifest more than just a voice," he answered in the language of Guran. He reached out, offering her his hand for balance and for support. When she caught it, it was quite tangible.

It was no time for amazement. Another scream ripped from her, and she freed her hand from Phlogis's grip to catch her child as it entered the world. All bloody, she tied the cord with a strip of cloth and picked up the broken wand and sliced through the cord. With other wet strips of cloth stored in her backpack, she cleaned her child and herself.

The *banshees'* singing rose to a fever pitch. Her baby, however, had not made a sound. Lying back on her grassy bed, cradling the child in her arm, she felt its little heartbeat and the soft tickle of its breath against her breast.

When she turned slightly, the light from the *leikkio-star* shone full upon its face. The child did not blink or shy away from the light, but turned its eyes up toward it.

Green eyes.

"Eric's eyes," Katherine whispered.

Phlogis shook his head. "The eyes of the *Shae'aluth.*"

The blue ring of Mianur rose above the trees. All over the meadow, the ghosts raised their arms in a supplicating gesture and melted away.

"Where are they going?" Katherine asked, hovering on the edge of exhausted sleep.

"To Paradise," Phlogis answered. He gazed down upon the *Child*, and an eerie, loving light lit up Phlogis's face. Gone was the *dando*'s anger that once had driven him. "They have witnessed the birth of the *Shae'aluth*, and they are free," he told her, "no longer bound by old grief and pain to this world."

"Are you going, too, Phlogis?" she asked, her words slurring.

"Not to Paradise, Katherine Dowd," he said. "But to another place. I have a new purpose now. Yet I will stay to watch over you while you sleep."

Katherine gently hugged the new life in her arms. Her beautiful baby smiled at her. She desperately wanted to stay awake and count fingers and toes, goo and gurgle and do all those things that made new parents look so silly, but all she could manage was to smile back, nod, and close her eyes.

A gentle shaking woke her. She blinked as she wakened to the bright light of day, realizing even before she was fully alert that something was dreadfully wrong.

Her baby, Eric's baby, was gone!

In a panic she sat bolt-upright, ignoring the pain such an effort brought, and her vision focused on a bearded black face that hovered over her. Without hesitating, she lashed out with a palm-heel strike, catching the stranger on the chin, sending him toppling backward. She scrambled for her stunner, but couldn't find it among her scattered possessions. She grabbed for the broken crystal wand with its sharp edge and brandished it.

"Where's my baby?" she demanded, turning to face the stranger. "What have you done with my baby?"

He sat up, rubbing his chin as he grinned strangely at her. "I don't know anything about a baby," he said in accented Guranese. "Where did you learn to hit like that? With a little power behind it, you might have hurt me."

Katherine looked around wildly. Kailuun was gone as well. Two more men with staves for weapons stood at ease behind her, looking scruffy and filthy, as if they'd traveled a great distance on foot.

"Rook and Kasteen," the black stranger said, making introductions. "My name is Sulis Tel."

Katherine lowered the sharp piece of crystal as she realized these men meant her no harm, nor had they stolen her child. "The ghosts," she said, her heart sinking as she stared toward the forest. "Phlogis—he must have taken my baby!" Shaking with fear and rage, she screamed her next question. "Why?"

The one called Sulis Tel stood up and stepped toward her. Confused, her thoughts racing, she warned him back with a threatening wave of the crystal.

Then the world began to swim crazily. Her vision

blurred; the crystal fell from her limp grasp as she sank sideways. Strong arms caught her and eased her onto the grass pallet. Sulis Tel stripped off his tunic and draped it over her naked loins.

"Rinse this in the river," he said, tossing a bloody strip of cloth to the man called Rook.

"It has to be her," said the third man, Kasteen, as he bent down to peer over Sulis Tel's shoulder. "Her hair—no one born of Palenoc has hair of such a color. It's just as he described her. And she spoke of Phlogis."

Katherine trembled uncontrollably, all the strength gone from her limbs. Rook returned and wiped her face with the cool, wet cloth before he folded it and placed it upon her forehead. She tried to sit up again, but Sulis Tel pushed her gently back.

"Be still," he ordered. "It's plain enough you've had a rough time." He adjusted the wet cloth on her brow again, fingering a strand of her red hair as he did so. He looked to his two friends, then back to Katherine and asked, "Are you Katherine Dowd?"

Her eyes shot open, and she stared at all three men, who were now kneeling down beside her. Rook was examining her stunner, which he'd found in the grass, while Kasteen riffled through the worn pages of Robert's novel. "Who are you?" she demanded.

Sulis Tel licked his lips before answering. "We were friends," he said slowly, "of *Robert Polo Namue Rana Sekoye.*"

"All that remains," Kasteen added with a weary note as he dropped the book on the ground, "of the *Sherak-khen,* his soldiers."

"Robert?" Katherine said, her heart filling with new hope. "He's alive? Where is he?"

The three men exchanged dark looks. "We walked

into a trap," Sulis Tel explained with an uneasy shake of his head, his eyes half closed as if he were in the grip of a powerful memory. "Many of us died. We don't know what happened to Robert." He swallowed and stared toward the remains of her campfire. "If he's lucky, he's dead. If not . . ." He shrugged, trying hard to hide a turmoil that raged inside him.

In that gesture Katherine found a man she knew she could trust, and any doubts about these three strangers vanished. "I'm Katherine Dowd," she said. *"Hami Rana Sekoye.* How did you find me?"

"We saw a strange star in the sky last night where we were camped," Kasteen said.

"It wasn't a star," Sulis Tel said, frowning. "Though I'm damned if I can say what it really was. We broke camp anyway and followed it all night until, just moments before dawn when the star, or whatever it was, vanished." The black man's frown turned into a grin. "You're kind of a mess, Katherine Dowd, and you don't look like you've eaten for days. How is it you're not dead, as Robert believed you were?"

She could barely answer. Her mind churned with thoughts of her missing baby. Haltingly, she told her story, feeling a measure of strength returning to her limbs as she talked, then retold it, filling in detail, as all three strangers sat enrapt.

When she finished, Sulis Tel leaned forward and patted her shoulder sympathetically. "If Phlogis has stolen the *Child*, as you believe, there's nothing we can do here. Even though he's only a spirit, his power is too great." He hesitated, searching the faces of his friends before continuing. "We were returning to our respective homes," he said. "Instead, we'll take you to Guran. If there are answers to this mystery, you'll find them in Rasoul at Sheren-Chad."

Katherine nodded. A small, inner part of herself still danced on the edge of hysteria. "Could we search the woods, first?" she begged. "Kailuun's gone, too. Maybe I was wrong about him. Maybe he dragged my baby off." She burst into tears again as she tried to sit.

Once more, Sulis Tel pushed her softly back. "We'll search," he assured her, and the other two nodded agreement. "We'll hunt, too, *Shayana*. You need to eat and rest. The Domains are a far distance, and you'll need your strength. We'll linger here a day or two until you're ready."

Slumping back on her bed, Katherine closed her eyes. These men were friends of Robert's, and she trusted them. *Robert is alive.* The thought played over and over in her head. Sulis Tel said he was dead, but she had thought so once, too, and been wrong. *And if Robert is alive, perhaps Eric is also alive.*

She clung to those thoughts as she rolled over on her side, folded her hands, and hid her face from her new companions. Eric and Robert *had* to be alive! Though it was no more than a hope, it was all that filled the emptiness inside her, all that stilled the tiny voice that told her, no matter what, she would never see her baby again.

The thought hit her like a hammer driving a nail through her heart. Sitting up, she stared toward the forest and reached out with her senses in a desperate effort to find her baby, but those powers had never truly been hers. They were the baby's, and somehow, while she carried him in her body, she had shared them.

Sinking again on her pallet, trembling, she pressed an ear to the ground. She could no longer sense the growing things there, no longer feel the insects that crawled in the grass or the birds that chirped in the trees at the forest's edge.

She was alone again. Sulis Tel and Kasteen hovered at the forest's edge, crouching low to the ground as they hunted for Kailuun's tracks or some sign of her baby. Rook was busy filling water bottles at the riverbank. Only by rising on an elbow could she see him.

Drawing up her knees, she curled nearly into a fetal ball, feeling as if she'd been struck deaf. One hand clutched at the blades of grass beside her makeshift bed and ripped them slowly from the ground as, despite her sternest intentions, she wept again.

Chapter Seventeen

SCREAMING in frustration, the Heart of Darkness rolled on the floor before her throne, beating her fists and kicking her heels against the marble tiles to vent her rage. Sparks flew up from the impacts of her blows, and cracks radiated like zigzagging snakes over the stone.

"The cursed *Child*!" she shouted to the walls as She rose. "The arrogant brat dares to challenge me!"

She jerked her head toward the single crystal caldron that glowed below the dais. A sea of hair swirled wildly about her face, so savage was her motion. Her lips parted in an angry, animalistic hiss, and with three swift strides, She reached the vessel, braced her hands on its rim, and stared within.

The view reflected in the mirror-smooth waters ranged about like an all-seeing eye as, empowered by her spells, the caldron searched the world. Forest, plain, and mountain—village, town, and city were revealed to Her. The advance of her armies through the countryside, the stealthy questing of her *chimorgs*—but no sign of the damnable infant who would usurp her power.

Already She felt herself weakening with each passing instant, like a flower wilting in the heat, like meat rotting from the inside. With a shriek She strained against the caldron and heaved it over sideways. The crystal shattered; water splashed over the floor, pushing the fragments and gleaming splinters before it like a tide.

A gray, misty *shade* rose up from the caldron's fractured base, taking a vaguely human form. With a scream of fury that matched Shandal Karg's, it extended clawlike hands and flung itself at Her.

High above, from the darkness that cloaked the hidden rafters of the throne room, came a sudden *banshee* chorus. The bleak, gloomy halls of Boraga echoed with its volume. Simultaneously, scores of *leikkios*, appearing as if from nowhere, swarmed in the air like vengeful glowing wasps.

The Heart of Darkness was not distracted. With a snarl and a gesture, the air turning suddenly icy, She froze the *shade* in the middle of its murderous leap. With a sweep of her hand She sent the *leikkios* crashing like tiny shooting stars into the four walls.

She turned back to the treacherous *shade*. The hapless spirit hung in midair, trapped like a fly in amber by her power. "For five hundred years, imprisoned in my caldron, you served me," She said bitterly. "Now serve oblivion."

On the *shade*'s pale face, shining eyes snapped open where there had been none before. Its fingers flexed, desiring her throat.

The Heart of Darkness recoiled in surprise, and a flash of fear passed over her face before her expression hardened again. The efforts of the *shade* were small and struggling as it resisted her power, but it remained suspended, helpless.

"Stupid spirit!" She cried. "Look at me and tremble. By the power of the blood that flows in my veins, my will is Rule in Boraga." Razor-sharp nails sliced open her palms as she clenched her right fist. With a flick of her wrist She flung crimson droplets at the misty form. Each red pearl blossomed into arcane flame, and the *shade* burned. Its shrieks filled the great hall.

"Here is one soul that will never reach Paradise," the Heart of Darkness shouted over the din to the multitude of ghosts that her power still kept at bay, "and will never know *Or-Dhamu*. I have destroyed it as I will destroy you. As I will destroy everything!"

The *banshees'* angry screams drowned out her hateful words as the *leikkios* swarmed toward her face and eyes, and *chills* whirled around Her, generating such intense cold that a fine, white rime instantly coated her skin. Throughout the throne room, *shades* and *apparitions* suddenly appeared from the darkness and shambled toward Her, reaching with grasping, malformed hands.

The Heart of Darkness threw back her head and laughed. "I told you before," She said, raising her hands. "Get back!"

But they pressed on, defying her power. A *poltergeist* dived invisibly from the rafters, snatched a chunk of plaster from the floor near one of the pillars, and hurled it. Shandal Karg reeled as the stone struck Her in the shoulder and sent Her toppling.

Sprawled amid the folds of her gown, the Queen of Night looked up with a heart full of fear. Sensing her weakness, the spirits fell upon Her, pulling her hair and ripping her clothes. They tumbled Her like a helpless doll on the floor, caught her arms and tried to rip them from the sockets.

Her hand closed on a fragment of the shattered crystal caldron, and its jagged edge opened her fingers and thumb as She squeezed it. Blood flowed richly into her palm, then down her arm.

The spirits shrank back as the Heart of Darkness struggled uncertainly to her feet, holding the bloody piece of crystal before Her like an amulet against her attackers. "Blood and crystal magic at my command," She raged, "and it is barely enough to expel this undead rabble!"

Her lips curled back from ivory teeth as She gave a sharp, serpentine hiss. The throne room's eastern wall exploded outward in a shower of stone and dust. She aimed the crystal toward the rafters. Shrieking, the *banshees* dived through the gaping rent and flew far into Srimourna's star-speckled night.

Dripping with blood, the crystal began to exude a red glow that, like a living force, sought out the ghosts and drove them from Boraga's confines to hurl them into the vast black abyss beyond. The screams and shrieks and wails died away, and, for a brief while, the keep knew silence.

The Heart of Darkness lowered her arm. Her head rolled forward wearily, and her shoulders slumped. Its work done, the red light was absorbed back into the crystal, returning the throne room to its accustomed gloom. The crystal slipped wetly from her fingers and shattered into tiny splinters.

From a darkened corner came a soft, mocking laughter. "You're an over-the-hill whore who has turned her last trick," said a cold voice from the shadows.

The Heart of Darkness drew Herself slowly erect, straightened her shoulders, and lifted her head. Her hair seemed to arrange itself stylishly, and the rips in her tattered gown drew together, forming whole fabric that clung to the seductive curves of her body. "I have more tricks up my sleeves, sweet puppet," She purred, turning, "than there are beats left in your fragile human heart."

Gaultnimble waddled forward, leading Robert Polo by a leash attached to a leather collar that encircled the earthman's neck, his only clothing. He had been washed and scrubbed, groomed like a prize animal prepared for show, but though a leather strap bound his hands, his lips wore a smirk.

"Shall I kneel and bow my head to the floor?" Robert Polo asked, matching her purr. "Fall over on my back and throw my legs to the wind?" His gaze roamed up and down her figure. It was not lust that gleamed in those emerald eyes, however, but unveiled contempt. "In what position would my Mistress like me?"

A delicate hand, bloody no longer and without even a trace of a wound, tapped lightly upon a silken-covered thigh. "Heel," She murmured.

Gaultnimble dropped his end of the leash. Stepping away, the little dwarf tugged uncomfortably at a corner of his eyepatch and kept an uncharacteristic silence.

Robert Polo moved boldly forward, his eyes locked with Hers even as he bent his knees. His face mere inches from her hand where it still rested on her thigh, he leaned forward without asking and licked her leg, leaving a wet trail on the slick cloth. "Woof," he said, turning his gaze upward to her face once more. "May I say you have a beautiful horn?"

"So do you, my pet," She said, letting her gaze roam down his flat belly as She lightly patted his head. Her fingers lingered, lifting a strand of his blond hair, and her expression turned solemn again.

"Remind you of someone?" Robert Polo asked, deliberately taunting.

She dug deeper into his thick hair and jerked his head back sharply. Her face came down close to his. "I've left you a measure of will and self-awareness," She hissed, "because I want you to realize how completely you are mine."

"I am completely yours," Robert Polo said in mocking, mechanical tones. "Beat me, whip me, make me eat the dirt between your toes."

Gaultnimble snickered, then took another quick step farther away. With hands clasped behind his back, he stared toward the ruin of the eastern wall with sudden, intense curiosity.

"I shall have no other mistresses before me but my Mistress," Robert continued in a sneering voice. "My Mistress is a vengeful Mistress. Seek ye the way of my Mistress."

Gaultnimble sidled closer to the Heart of Darkness and reclaimed his end of the leash. He gave it a little shake, snapping the leather in Robert's face. "He misquotes a religious text from his world," he explained in conspiratorial tones.

Robert snarled viciously. "Shut up, you little abomination!" He then appealed to Shandal Karg. "Send him away. Why do you keep this troll around now that you have me? To satisfy another of your kinky pleasures?"

The Heart of Darkness climbed the three steps of the dais and settled Herself regally upon the onyx throne. "He is my fool," She said patiently, adjusting the folds of her gown. "You are my hound."

"I was raised by missionaries," Gaultnimble whispered to Robert Polo. "You are unwise to mock Her."

"How can I not mock Her?" Robert Polo answered

without bothering to lower his voice. "She has made me in her image."

On her throne Shandal folded her hands and pressed her fingertips together. The chamber's gloom seemed to gather about Her as She closed her eyes.

"What's She doing?" Robert whispered suspiciously to Gaultnimble. Though his hands were bound, he grabbed his leash and gave it a jerk. Gaultnimble nearly toppled against Robert, but he kept his grip on the leash, nonetheless. With Robert kneeling, they were nearly eye to eye.

The dwarf pointed to a dim corner of the throne room, and Robert had to lean to see around a column. Barely visible but for its glimmering eyes, a *chimorg* stood in an archway.

"They're speaking," Gaultnimble explained, tapping his temple with a forefinger, "in here. The beast won't come any closer—it's afraid of you."

Robert looked sharply at the dwarf. "Afraid of me?" he said. "How do you know?"

Gaultnimble's face paled, and he shot a glance at the Heart of Darkness. "She thinks I'm an insignificant nothing," he answered finally in the lowest of whispers, "so She doesn't realize I've learned to hear the *chimorgs* a little."

"Foolish little fool," said Shandal Karg, rising from the throne and descending the dais steps. She walked right by Robert and Gaultnimble without giving either a look. "Of course I realize. In the Greater Game, it simply doesn't matter. You simply don't matter."

Delicately, She picked her way among the rubble of the blasted eastern wall. A wind swept in through the gaping hole, swirled her gown around her ankles, and teased her hair as she stared outward. At the smallest gesture of her right hand, the rubble and the remains of the wall disappeared.

"My hound," She said, inclining her head toward Robert. "Heel."

Gaultnimble released the leash as Robert rose from his knees and went to stand obediently at his Mistress's side. She touched a razor-sharp nail to the leather straps around his wrists, and the bonds fell away. Then she led him out to the marble balustrade at the balcony's edge. There She slipped an arm about his shoulders, drawing her pet close.

The heat of Robert Polo's mortal body shot through her cold form like a flare. Though She had a heart and blood flowed in her veins, there was no warmth in Her. That, She leeched from other living things— like Gaultnimble's kittens. The sensation, though, was druglike, and She rarely indulged her craving.

A sigh of satisfaction escaped her parted lips as She let go of her pet and sidled a few paces along the balustrade. Again, her gaze turned outward. Across the canyon's black gulf, on the far rim, herds of *chimorgs* milled about restlessly. Thousands of eyes shimmered like small stars fallen to earth. As if sensing their Mistress, they turned toward Boraga and grew still.

"My children," She whispered, not out of love, but with pride in her handiwork and the evil they had wrought. For a brief moment She allowed herself to remember the names of twelve loyal generals who had offered themselves for transformation into creatures of her design. These thousands upon thousands of *chimorgs* were their offspring, and more still roamed the world, all serving her will.

The names came back to Her like voices out of the distant past and formed soundlessly on her lips. Faces, too, floated in her memory, but those She pushed away. Those were the old, mortal images. She preferred to think of gleaming scales and shining horns and eyes of cold fire.

The Heart of Darkness abruptly put her memories away. She had not come out here to admire her children, but to share a message with Robert Polo. She lifted a graceful hand, pointed to the distant eastern horizon, and said, "What do you see, my pet?"

Robert Polo placed his hands on the balustrade as he glanced toward Thanador's effulgent light, the pale ring of Mianur, and the dark clouds that raced across both. Leaning farther out over the uncertain rail, he then gazed into the yawning abyss.

"Above or below," he said, shrugging as he straightened, "this is not my kingdom. Survey it yourself."

"This is not a hound, great Queen of Terror." Gaultnimble laughed, doing a little jig as he crept up behind them. "This is an insolent pup!"

Shandal Karg turned slowly toward Robert Polo, and in her cold-eyed gaze burned the same eerie fire that lit the eyes of the *chimorgs*. "I like his insolence," She said. "I already own a toadying sycophant."

"I am your hound," Robert Polo said coldly as he turned his gaze toward the dwarf. "Your killer. Let me kill this one for you."

The Heart of Darkness pursed her lips thoughtfully. "You may not kill him," She declared at last. "However, you may put out his other eye."

Gaultnimble screamed and ran back into the shadows of the throne room as fast as his malformed legs would carry him. Robert Polo started after him, but before he'd gone two steps, Shandal Karg laughed and cried, "Heel."

Polo returned at once to her side, his leash trailing loosely from the collar around his neck.

"Good hound," she said, rumpling his blond hair, brushing her fingers through it. "Obedient pet. Climb up on the balustrade for your Mistress."

Robert Polo stared at the narrow marble rail. It was as high as his waist, but he lifted one foot, set it in place, and stretched out his arms for balance. With no regard at all for the abyss below, using only the strength in his right thigh, he pressed himself up, set his left foot in place, and stood, perfectly balanced on a surface no wider than her hand.

"One foot," the Heart of Darkness commanded.

Without hesitation Robert bent his right knee slightly and raised his left foot. "Crane stance," he said with a calm sneer. Suddenly, his right foot shifted, and his left leg shot out and remained rigidly in the air. "Side kick." Without lowering the leg, he straightened his upper body, reached out with his left hand, and caught his heel. He raised the elevated leg even higher until his foot was above his shoulder, above his head. "Ballet," he said.

The Heart of Darkness studied her pet closely. The wind teased the end of the leash that hung from his collar, but he stood solid as a piece of sculpture, awaiting her next command. If She ordered him to jump, She had no doubt he would obey.

And yet it was She who stood at the brink of doom. Staring past Polo, past the canyon's rim, past her *chimorg* children, She saw what no other eyes could yet see: a trio of dragons sweeping over Srimourna's border, skimming the blasted mountains and black-water rivers, lighting the petrified forests with the dazzling fire in their wings.

Like a cracked cup slowly draining, She felt the loss

of her power, and for a disconcerting instant, it was She on the baluster, not Robert Polo.

"Why don't you fear falling?" She asked coldly.

Robert returned to the crane stance position, all his weight still one on leg. "I've danced on more edges," he answered disdainfully, "and stared into deeper abysses in my life than You have power to imagine. Why should I fear falling?" He hesitated as the muscles in his right leg began to tremble visibly. "I've considered jumping too many times. You know that, but You don't understand it. For all your magic, for all your centuries of life, You can't understand it. You have no soul."

Shandal Karg knew the truth in his words. His inner despair—the pain he had hidden even from himself—was what made him such an easily malleable puppet. Still, She felt vaguely dissatisfied. The taste of his pain was not sweet.

"Come down," She ordered. "Go and dress youself appropriately, for we shall soon have guests."

"Anyone I know?" her pet asked offhandedly as he jumped down to the balcony and entered the throne room.

She said nothing, but waited until She was alone. Once more She glanced toward the horizon. The dragons were closer now, coming fast. She went inside, leaving the wall open, and climbed the dais to her onyx throne.

Something stirred in the shadows near the archway where the *chimorg* had been earlier. She whirled around, catching movement in the corner of her eye, glaring, but saw nothing.

"Damn ghosts," she muttered. "You can't hide from Me in my own Keep."

Settling upon her throne, chin in hand, She studied

the shadows cast by the many columns as Thanador's light poured in through the space where the eastern wall had been. She loathed the light. Nevertheless, She left the space open as a courtesy to her soon-to-be guests.

"Come to me, Eric Podlowsky," She whispered, beckoning toward the opening. "Your little brother was much too easy, and Scott Silver was no challenge at all. Give me a real game."

As She leaned her chin in one hand and waited, her gaze swept around the chamber. The ghosts crept back in twos and threes. She felt them with weakened senses, but no matter. They were insignificant creatures.

Chapter Eighteen

SHADOWFIRE soared through the night, wings burning with shimmering opalescence brighter and more colorful than Eric had ever seen. Knowing, as Eric knew, the impossibility of surprising the Heart of Darkness, the dragon instead proclaimed its coming with a fantastic display of light.

"De Guella," nearly unrecognizable, blasted from Eric's harmonica in angry, powerful strains. He played like a wild man as the wind whipped his hair and snatched at his garments, the bleak landscape rushing beneath. The ground, illuminated by a hugely shining Thanador, seemed cursed and lifeless, scarred with shadows.

Mirrormist and Brightstar surged up on his left and right, wings burning nearly as wondrously as Shadowfire's. The roar of the wind in Eric's ears muted the voices of their riders, but Alanna and Valis leaned forward aggressively in their saddles, like racers charging the finish line. Alanna thrust a finger toward the ground, pointing as she sang, and as Mirrormist dipped his left wing toward the south, her partners followed.

A huge black crack split the crust of Palenoc's surface. Turning, they sailed above its eastern rim. Thanador's light spilled over the canyon's edge, revealing the banded strata of the vastly awesome walls in shades of gray and white and black. The canyon's bottom could not be seen, but a glimmer of silver suggested a river flowed there.

However like his own Earth's Grand Canyon it might have seemed, no mighty river had carved this geological marvel. In shattering the moon, Mianur, Shandal Karg's magic had produced an unexpected and dreadful backlash. This fissure was one result of that magic, and her keep had nearly toppled into it, taking Her along.

The lifelessness of the land for hundreds of miles around was another result.

Shadowfire raced to take the lead again as he opened his great mouth and let out a trilling cry. Without warning he began a shallow, swooping dive, extending his talons.

On the ground below, exposed by the light from the dragons' wings, a herd of *chimorgs* fled in terror. Bonded with Shadowfire, Eric felt a startling murderous rage as his dragon spied the unnaturally spawned monsters, whose very creation mocked the great *sekoye* of the Domains. Looking at the *chimorgs*, the dragons saw darkly twisted, perverted versions of themselves, and it burned like fire in their hearts.

Eric blew sharply, furiously, on the silver Hohner harmonica. The *chimorgs* were unimportant now. Boraga was their target, and the Heart of Darkness. He blew again, a demanding riff, and this time Shadowfire responded by folding his claws against his body. Spreading his wings as wide as possible, the dragon flattened out of his dive and skimmed just above the panicked herds of *chimorgs*, drawing a measure of satisfaction by driving the terrorized beasts before him.

In the southwest, on the opposite rim of Palenoc's

great canyon, the black towers of Boraga rose suddenly like the fingers of a massive, opening hand. In Thanador's bright light, the walls of the great keep gleamed like volcanic glass. Upon the tallest of its pinnacles, the azure arc of Mianur seemed suspended like a cosmic scale in balance.

"De Guella" flowed from the Hohner, but it no longer sounded like an angry challenge. Eric played with a wary caution as he and his friends drew closer. On the ground, the herds of *chimorgs* still ran in heart-pounding fear, but even Shadowfire lost interest in the creatures as he turned toward the keep.

Boraga—the Throne of Darkness. Around that ponderous structure sprawled stark and crumbling ruins, all that remained of Tul Srimourna, the shadow-haunted capital of all the Dark Lands until it was flattened by the same quakes that had created the abyss. The Heart of Darkness had saved her keep, but she had lost an entire city.

A dim, amber light showed through a balcony opening high on Boraga's east side, but with Valis and Alanna flying close at his side, Eric flew a slow circle around the keep. The towers, so tall and ominous, seemed without opening. In fact, except for the balcony, there appeared to be no gates or doors or windows anywhere.

As Eric guided Shadowfire toward that pale, lonely light again, he wondered if it was by design or accident that Shandal Karg's only apparent view to the outside world looked across the gulf and away from the ruins of Tal Srimourna. Standing on that balcony, She would not be troubled by a view of even a single toppled stone of that long-dead city.

The only light, dim though it shone, was an obvious invitation. Eric flew by it once, and the glow from

Shadowfire's wings trailed eerily like a shimmering shadow on the glass-smooth stone. Unable to see far into the room beyond the balcony, he turned and glided past a second time, gaining no more information, half expecting an attack. None came. He had no doubt, however, that somewhere within, the Heart of Darkness watched and waited.

The balcony was too small for Shadowfire to land on, yet it was clearly the only entrance they would be offered. He glanced over his shoulder. Alanna and Valis hung back, giving him room, waiting to see how he would proceed. As he turned his dragon yet again, he put away his harmonica, then stroked Shadowfire's neck affectionately.

"Taedra," he murmured as he prepared to make another pass by the balcony. "You're no goddess— just an ideal of perfection on this crazy world. But if you do exist, then please let me do this right." He paused, swallowed, then added, "Because a mistake at this point is really going to play havoc with my self-confidence."

Untying the restraining straps around his thighs, Eric clutched the front edge of his saddle and freed his feet from his stirrups. Shadowfire swept slowly toward the dim light as Eric pulled himself into a precarious crouch. The wind rushed past his ears and snapped his sleeves. His heart hammered, and his mouth went dry as he bit his lower lip.

Shadowfire flew closer to the balcony than on any previous pass, folding his wings tightly, gliding, practically falling past the marble rail.

Eric flung himself into the air.

For a terrifying moment he thought he'd misjudged. The black, yawning abyss seemed infinitely wide and deep and the balustrade an impossible fingertip's reach away. Then his feet struck the solid stone of the balcony's floor, but with such momentum and at such an angle that he pitched full-length on the tiles, avoiding injury with a last-minute, clumsily executed forward break-fall.

He looked up, then pulled himself cautiously to his feet and rubbed a bruised elbow. He found himself in a huge chamber filled with narrow columns. Torches mounted in sconces on some of the many marble shafts provided poor, smoky illumination that created as many shadows as it chased away. Thanador's bright moonlight seemed to stop at the threshold as if it were reluctant to follow him inside.

He took a wary step forward, then stopped as a golden light flooded the entrance. Out of the glow of Mirrormist's wings, Alanna somersaulted, clutching her *shinobe-zu* in both hands, her legs tightly tucked against her body as her black hair whipped around. She landed with feline grace in a low crouch, perfectly balanced on her feet, her eyes narrow and bright with excitement, as her dragon banked sharply away.

Beyond the balcony Brightstar hovered, wings burning with the colors of living fire. Valis, though large and powerful, lacked Alanna's athletic skills or Eric's crazy daring. Unloosing himself from his saddle, he crawled along his mount's slender neck until he lay nearly flat on the creature's head. The dragon's wings pounded the air as it fought to hold its position before the balcony. It stretched its neck over the balustrade, and Valis dropped off.

"Good thing a stealthy approach was never part of your plan," the big man grumbled as he strode to Eric's side. He rested one hand on the tip of the *shinobe-zu* under his belt as his gaze swept around the chamber.

"Maybe we should have told Alanna," Eric whispered, inclining his head toward their partner. She stood with her back pressed flat against one of the columns, peering out around it, before she slipped noiselessly to another column and peered out again.

Soft, feminine laughter issued from the darker end of the chamber.

Eric stiffened, then forced himself to relax as he turned casually toward the sound. He steeled himself to speak as he took his first steps in the direction of that laughter. Then another, far more familiar voice caused him to pause again.

"Bees to the honey; mice to the cheese. Ally, ally, oxen free."

He could not see his brother, for darkness and shadow still cloaked the far end of the room. Yet he knew Robert's voice. A chilling quality rang in that little rhyme, though. For an instant he tasted the fear he had struggled hard to repress.

"Bobby?" he called, keeping his voice calm as he slowly strode toward the darkness. "I've come to take you home."

The gloom slowly parted like a curtain drawn back by unseen hands. Eric couldn't say how. There was no new source of light, nor did the torches burn brighter. He stared toward the revealed dais and the onyx throne. Sprawled upon it in seeming languor, draped in gowns of shimmering black fabric, the Heart of Darkness sat smiling at him. She ran a small pink tongue over her upper lip.

Eric's heart thundered in his chest as he gazed at Her. She was beyond beauty. Her eyes were like dark, gleaming stars, her skin pale and smooth as ivory. His mouth went dry as he took in the lines and curves of her body, watched her breasts rise and fall as She breathed, imagined the perfumed scent of her hair beneath his stroking touch. An erotic thrill awaited his fingers sliding along the length of horn jutting from her brow.

Valis touched his arm, and Eric jerked as if awaking from a dream. A cold anger and a colder fear filled him as he realized Shandal Karg had tried to ensnare him with some subtle wile—and nearly succeeded. Glaring, he steeled himself to resist any more of her mind games.

Shandal Karg frowned at her failure, and the room itself, as if in sympathy with her moods, momentarily darkened. Then She gave another little laugh. "Welcome to my home," She said. "It has been a long time since Boraga has had so many visitors at once. I am warmed by your presence." Her gaze turned toward some columns on the right side of the room, and She called, "Come out, little girl, come out."

Eric clenched his fists. "Where's my brother?" he demanded.

"Hidey, hidey, all in free," Shandal Karg said as Alanna stepped out from behind one of the marble pillars. Her voice, though, was a perfect imitation of Robert Polo's voice.

Eric realized he'd been tricked yet again. It hadn't been his brother's voice he'd heard earlier, only this creature's mockery. His anger surged, and he lunged toward the dais.

The Heart of Darkness raised a hand. Eric froze in midstep, held by an unseen force.

"You Sons of Paradane have no sense of humor," the Queen of the Dark Lands said, lowering her hand as She adopted Robert's voice again. "Would I make you come all this way if your brother wasn't here?"

"Stop that," Eric said, released from whatever force had held him. Hearing Robert's voice from her mouth filled him with cold nausea, but he regained control of his temper and made no further unwise advance toward the throne. "It's obscene."

She pressed the tips of her fingers together thoughtfully and spoke from behind her hands as She regarded him through narrowed lids. "You do not know what obscenity is," She said softly. "I shall relish showing you."

"I haven't come here to fight," Eric responded.

The Heart of Darkness lowered her hands. "Then why did you come, *Namue Rana Sekoye*?"

"To trade," Eric answered quickly. "My life for my brother's. Let Robert leave here with my friends"— he gestured toward Valis and Alanna—"and I'll stay willingly to take his place."

High, feminine laughter echoed throughout the chamber. "Willingly?" She cried. "Sweet fool, did you expect that any of you would leave here?" Clutching the armrests of her throne, shaking her head slowly, She rose and glared at him. "You have caused me too much trouble, Eric Podlowsky, and harmed too many of my children. No man or woman on this world knew how to slay my *chimorgs* until you revealed the secret. I will not forgive that."

"Then punish me, let Bobby go!" Eric shouted.

"I don't wish to go, big brother."

Robert stepped calmly out of a patch of shadow in the farthest corner of the room behind the throne. There was no doubt to Eric that it was his brother, but there was an unsettling coldness in Robert's eyes, in his whole expression. He wore black leather trousers and boots and some kind of studded harness over his thinly muscled chest, and on each arm a studded leather bracer. A black collar encircled his neck.

Though he moved with Robert's grace, his bearing possessed an unfamiliar arrogance.

"I finally know my place," Robert continued as he mounted the dais to stand beside the throne where he extended his hand for his Mistress to accept. Her fingers curled around his. "I belong here now, to the Heart of Darkness. My heart is as black as hers; my soul is black." He gazed about the chamber, then back to Shandal Karg, who squeezed his hand. "Here, I am at home."

Gleaming silver flashed through the air. The bare blade of Alanna's *shinobe-zu* struck Shandal Karg through the heart with force enough to hurl Her back against the onyx throne. The hilt quivered between her breasts; the metal length protruding from her back scraped against the onyx.

"If the heart offend thee," Alanna said grimly as she stood clutching the wooden sheath, "cut it out."

Robert didn't move. He looked down at his Mistress, then gazed across the room with a smirking expression. "Hello, Alanna," he said. "Nice to see you. Very nice throw, too."

Shandal Karg sat up, stared in consternation at the hilt of the impaling weapon, then slowly with both hands began to extract it.

"No, Robert-*kaesha*," Alanna said in a deadly serious tone. "I missed. The blade was meant for you, my love. I won't let her use you like this."

Shandal Karg became furious. "My *love*?" She cried, mocking Alanna. "You stupid little bitch! You dare to use that ugly word in my presence. As if you could stop Me from using him in any manner I choose!"

"If I have to bring this keep down on all our heads," Alanna answered, clenching one fist, her whole body tense, ready to spring, "I'll stop you. You boast about your *children*. I have yet to introduce you to mine."

The Heart of Darkness gave a mad shriek. Gone were her taunts, her mocking laughter. Her eyes filled with an insane gleam as She touched her already healing wound and collected a smear of blood on her palm. The blood swelled up suddenly like a crimson soap bubble, rapidly growing. It drifted free of Shandal Karg's hand, continuing to increase in size.

"Run!" Eric shouted.

But the bubble was already upon Alanna, engulfing her, sealing her within. The wooden sheath of the *shinobe-zu* banged uselessly at the inside of the arcane trap as it lifted her from the floor and continued drifting straight toward the open wall and the balcony.

Just beyond the balustrade it stopped and floated in the air over the gaping abyss.

Inside the bubble Alanna grew still and locked her gaze on the Heart of Darkness, as if accepting what was to come. Even at a distance her eyes burned with hatred for Shandal Karg.

"Houseguests can be so rude," Robert remarked.

Shandal Karg shouted, her voice carrying to the balcony and far beyond. "The Heart of Darkness cannot be stilled," she raged. "I am immortal!"

Alanna answered with a sneer. "That's what you said about your *chimorgs*. But the dragons always knew better. Now we know better, too."

"Insolent whore!" Shandal Karg snapped her fingers, and the bubble burst. Alanna gave a short scream as she fell. "Take your knowledge with you to the bottom of the abyss."

Eric gave a cry and started toward the balcony, but Valis caught his arm in a firm grip.

"What about you, Priest," Shandal Karg said icily, wiping Alanna's bloody blade on the fabric of her sleeve before She cast it down. It clattered on the steps to lie at the foot of the dais. "I see you carry one of these, also. Do you intend to use it?"

"No," answered Valis as he removed the *shinobe-zu* from his belt and cast it down beside the other. "I came along for a different reason."

Shandal Karg eased herself onto her throne again. Eric watched Her, experiencing a moment of surprise as he realized her hand was trembling. A few beads of sweat gleamed visibly on her brow. Was it weakness he saw?

"Amuse me with your reason," She insisted.

Valis glanced around the chamber and toward the rafters in a nonchalant manner. "I've heard that Darkness has great power," he said, "knowledge of both Blood and Crystal magic that has been lost to the rest of us. I wanted to see the truth for myself."

Shandal Karg's mood seemed to change again. She allowed a tiny smile at this flattery.

Valis pressed his hands together as he glanced toward the empty balcony. "But I've also heard that, having no soul, Darkness is inherently stupid. I wanted to see if that was true, too, and it is. You have made such a grand mistake."

Shandal Karg leaned forward and stamped her foot, causing cracks to radiate outward to the very edges of the dais and down the steps. "Attacked and insulted in my own home!" She said angrily to Valis. "You have no purpose here, Priest, and no value to me." She crooked a finger to Robert. "Kill him, my pet."

Robert descended the three steps with deliberation, his gaze locking on Valis. The torchlight gleamed on the studded leather and on his bare shoulders and arms, in the wispy strands of blond hair that hung about his face. "Don't resist," he said to the big *sek-ournen*. "Because we were friends once, I'll make this quick."

Valis nodded his head. "Thank you, *Shae'aluth*."

Robert hesitated only a moment, then came ahead, unfazed. "Word games will not save you. But if we end it quickly, we can deprive Her of any pleasure She would take in our combat."

Eric stepped suddenly into the space between his brother and his friend. "That's an utterly ridiculous outfit," he said to Robert with a calm he did not feel.

Robert shrugged. "Don't blame me," he said with a tilt of his head toward the throne. "She picks out all my clothes."

He started forward again, intent on carrying out his instruction, but Eric stopped him by putting out a hand. "I don't blame you, Bobby," he said quietly, moving so that he blocked his brother's view with his larger frame. "I love you."

Robert's gaze shifted for a moment, and the light sparked in his green eyes as they focused on Eric. "I'm not worthy of love," he answered. "My deeds and thoughts and lusts have damned me, Eric. I belong to the Heart of Darkness now, body and soul."

Eric seized Robert's arms. "You're my brother!" he shouted.

Robert shifted his weight, executing a perfect *tai-otoshi* throw with lightning speed. Unprepared, Eric flew through the air and struck the floor with jarring force.

"I am her hound," Robert said without emotion as he turned again toward Valis.

Shrugging off the effect of his fall, Eric leaped up and put himself once more in Robert's path. "Don't make me fight you, Bobby," he pleaded. "I don't know what She's done to you, but resist Her!"

On her throne, the Heart of Darkness sighed. "This is delicious. Tell me, pet," She called, "who is this stranger before you?"

In a cold voice Robert answered, "I know him not."

Laughter flowed through the hall.

"Get out of here, Valis," Eric whispered over his shoulder, not daring to take his eyes from his brother.

Though Valis backed slowly toward the balcony, he shook his head. "I can't," he answered. "There's more here than meets the eye, and I'm bound by vows and duties to remain."

Eric had no chance to respond. As Valis moved, so did Robert, attempting to step around Eric in order to reach the retreating *sekournen*. This time Eric moved faster, catching his brother's wrist. Before he could follow through on a throw, however, Robert jerked free. Eric brought up his right leg and slammed a kick into Robert's ribs.

Robert danced back, avoiding most of the kick's force. Eyeing his brother through narrowed lids, he flowed into a classic crane stance. Then, in an astonishing display of agility, his raised leg came down, and he sprang, spinning in the air. His right heel lashed at Eric's head.

Eric sidestepped, dodging the kick and simultaneously throwing a knife-hand blow as his brother landed. Robert's own knife-hand blocked it; the impact shivered up Eric's forearm. Without an instant's pause Robert dropped to the floor and aimed another kick at Eric's knee, but Eric was no longer in the same place.

Rising, Robert turned toward his brother, face impassive, eyes cold, almost alien.

Backed against a column, Eric slipped quickly to a more open space. He couldn't allow himself to be forced into a corner. His brother was too fast, his technique too elusive. He doubted he could beat Robert, but he eased into a side stance and put one hand surreptitiously to the buckle of his belt.

Robert came at him like a human bolt, spinning, lashing out with a backfist, a cry exploding from his lips.

Eric dodged again, whipping off his belt. Seizing its ends in both hands, he caught his brother's leading fist in the strap, and whirled him off balance. Still, Robert managed to strike with his free fist. Eric's head snapped backward, but he held onto the belt, whirled again, and dropped suddenly to his knees.

Robert flew high over his head. Yet such was his brother's skill that he rolled on his shoulder and to his feet, unharmed. The belt lay on the floor between them.

A trickle of blood ran from the corner of Eric's lip. He dabbed at the cut, feeling the sting of the blow that had made it.

"Let me kiss it and make it better," Shandal Karg said laughing. Rising from her throne, She descended the three steps and placed her hand on Robert's shoulder in a sickening mockery of affection. "I have not made a *chimorg* in a thousand years, Eric Podlowsky," She said. "It will take many months and cause you much pain, but it will bring Me pleasure to transform you. Perhaps I will not kill the Priest after all, but transform him, as well. I may let the two of you mate, then, and breed me a whole new race of *chimorgs*."

She ran her fingers through Robert's blond locks, and he stood for it, tolerating her touch in a manner that filled Eric with revulsion. "Male and female have no meaning to my children." She leaned closer to Robert, whispering in his ear. "Hurt your brother for Me, pet. Hurt him very badly."

Without hesitating, Robert ran forward. Eric blocked a flurry of fists and elbows, but a snap kick caught him in the stomach, and a side kick smashed into his chest, sending him crashing against a column. He crumpled to the tiles, unable to draw a deep breath, unable to see through a red haze.

Still, he struggled to rise. A foot slammed into his ribs; a fist to his head drove him back to the floor. Eric turned on his side to find Robert kneeling over him. Another fist came toward his face. Somehow, he managed to intercept it, and he clung desperately to his brother's hand. "Bobby ..." he said through bleeding lips. "Don't ..."

The Heart of Darkness loomed behind Robert, her black sleeves sweeping around Her like the wings of a great bird of prey. "Save what little breath you have left, Son of Paradane," She sneered. "You came to save your brother. How noble. But Robert Polo is your brother no longer. I have remade him, molded him into the conscienceless creature you see before you. He would kill you without a thought if I told him to, just as in time he will kill the Son of the Morning for me. You have lost, Eric Podlowsky. You have lost everything."

"No ..." Eric muttered through waves of pain. He tightened his grip on Robert's arm, though he knew there was nothing more he could do. His strength was fading rapidly. "Not Bobby. You can't have my brother."

Shandal Karg threw back her head and laughed her most hateful laugh. "Mine," She said, resting a hand possessively on Robert's head. "Body and soul."

Suddenly, a new voice spoke from a darkened corner of the room. "If Polo belongs to anyone," the speaker said, "he belongs to me."

Eric looked up painfully as Shandal Karg whirled in surprise. On a far wall where the torchlight barely reached, cloaked in shadow, a huge golden door loomed. Near it, looking like a rabbit about to run, stood a tiny dwarf. But someone else stood there also, someone familiar, even in silhouetted form.

"You!" cried the Heart of Darkness.

Scott Silver walked out of the shadow and into the light. Once he might have been Robert's twin, but now his muscular body was rail thin as if from long hunger, and his blond hair hung past his shoulders. Still, an angry fire burned in the blue depths of his eyes.

Shandal Karg made a clawing motion in the air. "You're not strong enough to take him from me!"

"In this world blood is power," Scott Silver answered defiantly. "And it's my blood, not yours, that runs in his veins."

He held out his left hand, opening it slowly, revealing his palm and a long scar. His lips parted a sound issued forth, part rasping scream and part animalistic hiss, sharp as a razor. As if cut by that sound, the scar reopened and bright blood oozed forth.

"Before we came through the gate to your world," Scott cried, "we sliced our palms and pressed them together, wedding ourselves. No magic will ever break that bond!"

Robert reacted like a man entranced. Slowly, he extended his left hand. A similar scar on his palm was the mark of the blood bond he had made with Scott Silver one warm night on an isolated Chinese beach. His scar also opened, seeming to unzip itself, but instead of blood, red light poured from the wound, formed into a ball in the air between the two men, and faded away.

Robert looked at Scott for only a moment, then covered his face with both hands, weeping as he collapsed to the floor. Fighting off the pain of his injuries, Eric threw an arm protectively around his brother, for he saw the horrified look of shame that came over Bobby's face in the moment of his liberation.

Shandal Karg screamed in anger. At a gesture, Alanna's bare blade flew up from the floor and into her hand. She raised it over Robert. "He is mine," She shouted, "or he is dead!"

The blade came whistling down, but before it could strike, a new forced seized it, jerked it from her grip, and sent it whirling past the balcony and into the night.

Just inside the balcony Valis stood, his arms held high in welcome as thousands of vaguely perceived shapes surged around him and into the chamber. The air filled suddenly with the screaming of *banshees* and with the twinkling flames of *leikkios*, and though Eric could not see the *poltergeists*, he knew they were there, too, and that they had saved Robert from the sword.

At almost the same time another force struck Boraga, sending a tremor right down to the foundation stones. Dust showered from the rafters; a piece of marble cracked and fell off one of the pillars.

Shandal Karg stared in bewilderment as a second explosion, then a third, rocked her keep. Eric rose painfully to his feet. At the balcony Valis continued to wave his arms, but not to welcome more ghosts. The sky beyond shimmered with dragons, the hordes of dragons that had followed them all the way from the Domains, and the night sang with their trilling.

It was Eric's turn to laugh. Suddenly, he knew why Valis had reacted so calmly to Alanna's fall. What was a fall from a high place to a *sekournen*, except a game of catch played with one's dragon? Shandal Karg had made a grand mistake, all right.

Now, safe on Mirrormist, Alanna called to her army of *sekoye* and sent them in waves to smash the stones of Boraga.

Another impact, and a shower of black stone fell beyond the balcony as one of the five towers shattered.

Enraged, the Heart of Darkness clenched her fist. A bolt of bloodred lightning crackled around her fingers and lanced across the chamber, outward into the sky. It struck a dragon, whose wings burst into flame as it plummeted into the abyss.

Before She could throw another bolt, Scott Silver rushed to a position between Her and the balcony. Close to his mouth, he held a piece of quartz crystal, and as he let go a piercing screech, a brilliant light suddenly exploded from its facets, flooding the chamber, banishing all shadow and gloom.

Shandal Karg screamed and threw up an arm to shield her face with a voluminous sleeve. At the same time She let fly a weaker bolt. It struck Scott Silver in the chest, hurling him backward and causing the piece of quartz to tumble from his grasp, its light dying just as suddenly.

Robert stared at his fallen lover, and a shriek ripped from him. He sprang up, right in Shandal Karg's face as She lowered her arm. The stiffened, knife-edge of his hand rose and smashed downward with a powerful *ki* shout.

The *crack* was like the sound of thunder. The Heart of Darkness screamed again, not in anger, but in horror as She clutched the shattered stump on her brow where her proud, beautiful horn had been. The broken shaft spun through the air and clattered on the dais next to the throne.

"You damned fool!" She cried, reaching blindly for Robert, unable to see through the red ichor that flowed from the stump into her eyes. "I'll claw your heart from your body and crush it in my hand for this!"

Eric grabbed his brother's arm and pulled him back. Drawing strength from some deep reserve, he brought his right leg up and prepared to defend himself with a kick.

Another blast from outside rippled through the throne room. A pair of marble columns fell with a crash, and part of a ceiling beam split. Eric lost his balance and fell, dragging Robert with him. Shandal Karg staggered backward.

Invisible hands caught Her and swept Her up. The *banshees'* notes rose to a fever pitch of excitement. *Shades* and *apparitions* and all manner of ghosts swept into the air as the *poltergeists* juggled the Heart of Darkness as if She were a child's ball.

Scott Silver, a burn showing lividly on his bare chest, pulled Robert to his feet while Valis helped Eric up. "I think it's time to leave," Valis said with a nervous glance toward the ceiling, and Eric agreed. He reached for his brother's arm again.

But Robert pushed his hand away and stepped back from Scott Silver. He seemed frozen for a moment, unable to move. Then he reached up and unfastened the leather collar from around his throat and dropped it on the floor. Only then did he reach out and take Scott's hands and give them the slightest squeeze.

He had come to Palenoc to find Scott Silver, uncertain if Scott was alive or dead, and faced horrors one after another to achieve this reunion. But now, with Scott beside him at last, Robert seemed unable to look him in the eyes.

"I ran out on you," he said, staring past Scott toward the golden door at the side of the chamber.

Scott put a hand over Robert's mouth to silence him. Then he drew Robert close in a tight embrace.

"Let's get out of here," Eric said. "We've all got what we came for."

A deep red glow bathed the chamber before they could move. The *banshees'* shrieks became shrieks of terror, and the ghosts fled in all directions. Still in the *poltergeists'* power, Shandal Karg scratched her face and neck and arms and flung the droplets of blood from her nails. It seemed to burn the ghosts somehow, and finally even the *poltergeists* dropped Her and retreated.

Valis turned pale, and his lips parted in a silent, barely contained scream of his own.

Eric knew of his friend's strange bond with the spirits of the dead and of his vows to help ease the suffering of such unfortunate souls and set them on the bridge to Paradise. No doubt, the big *sekournen* had called these spirits here to join the fray, but now, through his bond, he shared their pain. "Shut yourself off from it," Eric urged, slipping an arm around Valis as his friend doubled up.

Valis shook his head, his face contorting in agony. "You don't understand!" he hissed. "You don't know what ... who ... they are!"

The Heart of Darkness picked Herself up from the

floor. Though her beauty yet remained, She seemed incredibly old, barely able to stand, and the air around Her wavered strangely. Her bloody scratches seemed to heal before their eyes. "I'm not through with you, yet," She said. With obvious effort She stretched out one quivering hand. "I have outlasted the stones of this world, and I will outlast you."

Her words came out in steaming clouds, and the temperature in the chamber plummeted. White rime formed on Eric's hand; his lips seemed to turn brittle with cold, and the next breath he drew stung like icy fire.

Shandal Karg began to laugh again, the insane laughter that was never far from her lips. Even as Alanna's dragon army struck the towers of Boraga, threatening to bring the keep down around her head, She laughed.

But from behind her throne a little man crept quietly on slippered feet and picked up the broken length of ebon-colored horn that lay forgotten on the dais. Clutching it in both hands, he stole to the very edge of the stairs.

"Most Blessed Queen of Night," he said calmly, dark eyes fastening on Shandal Karg.

His Mistress ceased her laughter. "Good, my fool," She said, turning toward him. "You've come to witness my victory."

The dwarf leaped at Her with a look of purest hatred. His hands came down forcefully as he plunged the horn through her breast and into her heart. "Queen of Nothing!" he cried as his weight and momentum sent them both toppling.

The Heart of Darkness sprawled on the marble tiles, eyes wide with disbelief, one hand wrapped around the spike that jutted from her body. The dwarf untan-

gled himself from the folds of her gown and straddled her.

Curses bubbled soundlessly on her lips, but all that
emerged was red spittle.

"Gaultnimble!" Scott Silver cried, starting toward
the little man.

Gaultnimble waved him back. "Leave here," he
snapped, his almond-shaped eyes burning with anger
and triumph. "I've kept my bargain with you, Silver
Man. Now keep yours. Leave Srimourna now and
leave Palenoc." He glared at Shandal Karg, helpless
between his legs, pinned like a huge, black butterfly,
and he spat on Her. "Most of all, leave me to what I
must finish."

The four of them stumbled toward the balcony, but
Eric glanced back to see the odd little man grab the
fabric of her gown and rip it open. Then he put both
hands on the blunt end of the horn and leaned all his
weight upon it, driving it in even deeper. A hissing
death sigh parted ruby lips.

Abruptly, Eric remembered his belt. It contained
his harmonica, which he would need to call Shadowfire. He ran back for it, drawing an evil glare from
the dwarf. No matter, he paused and stared before
snatching up his belt and extracting the Hohner from
its special pocket.

The Heart of Darkness lay still. With the spells that
preserved her illusory beauty shattered, She lay revealed truly. Small and large scars from old cuts and
old blood lettings covered every inch of her body.
Small prices paid out over centuries for her magics,
they had left Her an ugly thing.

Rejoining his friends on the balcony, he blew a riff
on his harmonica, summoning Shadowfire. The sky
blazed with the wings of dragons. On the far canyon

rim *sekoye* chased and slaughtered *chimorgs*. Above, safe on Mirrormist, Alanna directed scores of the great beasts in shattering attacks on Shandal Karg's keep, and two of Boraga's tallest towers were smashed to rubble. As Eric watched, an emerald-winged dragon slammed its bulk against another pinnacle, sending stone showering into the air and a tremor right down to Boraga's bowels.

"If you've called a taxi, I hope it gets here quick," Scott Silver said, watching the dragons. "This place is coming down around our ears."

Standing apart, Robert stared over the balustrade into the yawning darkness, still unwilling to meet anyone's gaze. Instead, he watched the dragons. "Shove it into the pit," he muttered, urging them on. "Shove every last stone into the pit."

Chapter Nineteen

THE twisted wreckage of the iron tripod that formerly crowned Sheren-Chad's rooftop had been cleared away, but no new tripod or globe of *sekoymelin* had yet been erected to take its place. Repairs to the soaring structure were already underway; the lower levels were noisy with artisans and workmen. The smell of brick and mortar filled the Sheren.

"This is beautiful," Scott Silver said to Eric as he leaned against the roof's rampart. The western view looked over the city and toward the Great Lake. Along the shore construction was underway and new wharves were rapidly going up. The wooden skeletons of two new ships, also under construction, rose up from the sands.

The sky was full of dragons wheeling and gliding above the city, some with riders and some without. Far out on the lake, a trio seemed engaged in a game of tag. They climbed and darted through the air, plunged low, cutting troughs in the lake's surface with the tips of their wings or tails, skimmed the white-capped waves like skipping stones, and climbed again.

Alanna emerged from the stairway and came to join them. Her raven hair, bound back by a golden cord, blew in the wind, and the loose folds and sleeves of a snow-white dress fluttered softly. Upon her breast her silver *sekournen*'s medallion gleamed on a new chain.

Eric held out his hands to her, and they embraced. "Congratulations," he said, beaming. "The Tarjeel made a wise choice. You'll make a great councilor."

To his surprise she blushed at his flattery. "I don't know if I have the patience for politics," she answered. "I'm more of a fighter."

"More *than* a fighter, you mean," Eric insisted. He led her by the hand to the rampart and gestured at the changes taking place in the city below. "Architect, master-planner, construction supervisor—you hid half your talents under those *sekournen* leathers."

"I have one more project you'll see shortly," she said with a mysterious smile. "Actually, *we* have one more project. Something we designed together," she added as she leaned past Eric and extended her palms to Scott Silver, who returned her greeting. "Good morning," she said.

"Your rebuilding is proceeding well," Scott Silver said. "I'm glad to see this side of Palenoc before I leave." Turning away from the view of the lake, he gazed eastward across the wide rooftop toward the distant Tahlequah Hills. "It's good to know there's more to it than darkness and evil."

Alanna stared toward the lake. "I wish you'd stay longer," she said. "Robert needs your support."

The wind blew through Scott Silver's newly cut hair. With his shorn locks, and dressed in bleached leathers, he looked even more like Robert Podlowsky. "After Polo escaped back through the doorway"—he paused and chewed his lower lip, obviously dealing with a difficult memory—"Shandal Karg sealed me in a coffin of ice. Time stood still in there, and I couldn't move. But my mind was completely awake. Just before She closed the lid, Gaultnimble managed to sneak a piece of quartz into my hand."

He reached inside his shirt and pulled out a small bit of crystal that hung on a leather thong. Though he'd dropped it during the fight in Shandal Karg's throne room, he'd made sure to recover it. "I could feel the stone in my hand," he continued, "but I didn't know what to do with it, or why Gaultnimble had pressed it on me with such an air of secrecy.

"I don't know how much time passed before Gaultnimble came back. He couldn't let me out, he said, but he began to whisper things to me. First, he told me Robert had returned to Palenoc. Then he told me about the Dream Stream and how to use the crystal to travel through it."

Eric nodded. "I saw you, or sensed you, before I knew about the Dream Stream," he said. "You warned me about—"

"Gaultnimble would learn her plans, then whisper them to me," Scott Silver said. "He taught me other things, too. From him I learned the power of crystals. But that wasn't enough to fight against the Heart of Darkness, he said, so he taught me about the power of blood. Then he told me to search the Dream Stream, and I would find others, like Phlogis, sorcerers Shandal Karg had slain. When I found them, they taught me still more, for they also wanted their vengeance." He swallowed as he put the crystal pendant back inside his shirt. "And that's why I have to leave."

Eric shook his head. "You're safe here. All that's behind you."

Scott's face clouded over with terrors Eric could only guess at. "No," he said firmly. "Do you know why the Domain leaders reject blood magic, Eric? It's like a drug that rots you from the inside out. It's seductive." A tiny smile lifted the corners of his lips, but the effect was chilling. "You don't know what I know or what I can do with this power." He turned and gazed straight into Eric's eyes. "On Earth, it won't matter. Magic doesn't work there. But here on Palenoc, I'm dangerous, Eric. Part of me *wants* to use this power. Over time it would destroy my soul."

Turning toward the lake again, Scott seemed to watch the dragons at play. "Gaultnimble knew that. He said I had a natural aptitude. He helped me to protect Polo and taught me how to fight Shandal Karg. But in exchange, he made me swear to leave Palenoc and never return. I'll keep that promise, Eric, because to break it would be just one more step on the road to corruption."

For long moments the gentle rush of the wind and the distant hammering of workmen were the only sounds. Then to Alanna, Scott said gravely, "You tell the Domain leaders to watch out for Gaultnimble."

"The dwarf?" Eric replied, raising a doubtful eyebrow.

Scott Silver stood stiff as stone. "He helped me escape, and then he hid me from Shandal Karg's detection. Can you be certain that the visions and dreams that lured you to Boraga were sent by Her? I tell you, there's more to Gaultnimble than meets the eye."

Eric looked at Scott Silver with new concern, unable to hide a frown. Maybe Scott wasn't as fully recovered from his ordeal as Eric had thought. In three weeks' time he had fleshed out again—the Sheren cooks had seen to that. But his face was haunted.

"There are things in the Dream Stream even older than the Heart of Darkness," came Scott's thin whisper. "Things and creatures willing to share their se-

crets for the right price. Gaultnimble paid that price.
I paid some of it."

He spun about suddenly, admiring a dragon that
swept close over the Sheren's roof. Its rider waved,
and Scott Silver waved back. "Enough of this," he
said. "The day's too bright, and this world is free, at
least for a while. How are your ribs?"

Eric touched his right side. Robert had broken three
of his ribs and bruised most of the others. "The bones
are strong again, thanks to Roderigo Diez's healing
crystals, but he insists on three more treatments.
Meanwhile, Maris has this wonderful herbal remedy."
He smiled. "I'm feeling no pain."

Scott Silver pointed over Eric's shoulder toward the
open door at the roof's center. "Speaking of Maris . . ."
he said.

Alanna's sister, and the head of Rasoul's governing
Tarjeel, rose up through the open door to the roof,
the folds of her white dress gathered in her hands
as she hurried up the steps. Concern and excitement
mingled on her face as she approached Eric.

"Come with me," Maris insisted, clutching Eric's
arm. Then she relented a bit, remembering his injuries.
"Something is happening in the chapel." The councilor hesitated, chewing her lip as she studied Eric's
face. Catching his hand a little more gently, she pulled
him toward the stairs. "All of you, come."

Down the stairs they went with Maris leading. Eric
followed, trying to avoid the hem of her dress as it
trailed on the steps. Scott Silver and Alanna came
after. Through the lavatorium they hurried, and down
past the level that once was Phlogis's sanctum. Down
the spiraling steps they proceeded at an urgent pace.
Maris refused all questions, just beckoning them to
follow as they descended deeper and deeper.

Past the ground floor and into the basements and subbasement the councilor led them. From a pocket of her dress she extracted a tiny, marble-sized globe of *sekoy-melin*. Though small, it exuded a potent amber light that cleaved the darkness and lit a path for them.

The air turned damp and cool. In the subterranean gloom scores of squat columns stood like silent sentinels as far back into the unbreached darkness as Eric could see. Among those columns rested mighty *pithos* jars, some as tall as a man, their contents a mystery.

The *melin* light fell upon a broad metal door. Maris seized the heavy ring with one hand and pulled. The door swung open on well-oiled hinges, squeaking faintly, and a bloody glow spilled over the threshold.

Within, a pair of low braziers poured smoke and heat into the air. The crimson glow came from a large red-stained glass globe filled with *melin*. The light fell principally upon a massive golden sculpture of Taedra, the Mother-dragon, and the vapor curled upward around it, causing the red light to shimmer on its back-swept wings as it set the diamonds in the statue's eyes to glittering.

Clad in a simple white robe, Valis knelt before the sculpture with his palms outward to it. His loose dark hair flowed over his shoulders and down his muscled back, which seemed to strain and heave as he sang soft words. Kneeling with him were two more robed figures, but hoods concealed their heads and faces.

One of those figures turned ever so slightly, and with slender fingers pushed back a fold of the hood to see the new arrivals.

From under the edge of that hood a lock of red hair flashed in the light. Familiar eyes met Eric's gaze.

"Katy?" The word caught in Eric's throat as he rushed forward. "Katy!"

Katherine Dowd sprang to her feet, flinging the hood away from her face, extending her arms as she ran into Eric's embrace. "You're alive!" she cried. "I prayed you were alive!"

For a moment the room and everyone else in it disappeared and all time seemed to stand still. He pressed her body to his, lifting her off the floor as joyful tears filled his eyes. She clung to him with the same fervent desperation, her own eyes flooding.

"She walked in less than an hour ago," Maris said soothingly from behind them, "with this man, Sulis Tel, and two others, insisting to see Valis immediately."

The second robed figure, a large black man, rose from the floor. Turning he spoke softly, but sternly. "I rejoice at your reunion, Katherine," he said, "but the priest must have quiet."

"What is it?" Alanna asked, eyeing Valis's suddenly still and silent form even as she caught one of Katherine's hands in a welcoming grip. "What's he trying to do?"

"We have a baby!" Katherine explained to Eric, her face clouding over.

"What?" Eric said, clutching her again.

Katherine eased his hands away and stepped back, returning to Sulis Tel's side near Valis. "Phlogis was with me when he was born," she continued with a hardening note in her voice. "He took my baby, I'm sure of it. All the way here, every step of the way, I tried to think what to do, and I remembered Valis had power to summon spirits."

And he has found me, Shayana.

The voice whistled eerily through the chamber. The

red-stained glass globe suddenly cracked open. The *melin* within boiled and steamed on contact with the air, and a glowing mist bubbled up through the fissure to swirl and writhe in midair. The chamber darkened. The light from the braziers, and even the light from Maris's tiny marble, seemed to spring away from their sources to join the *melin* glow.

The light continued to swirl, taking on the shape and form of one they all knew well.

"Phlogis!" Katherine screamed. "Where's my baby?"

Confused, Eric put his arm around Katherine's shoulders to restrain her. In her anger she seemed likely to attack the incorporeal creature that floated in the air before the sculpture of Taedra.

Sulis Tel, too, stepped protectively to Katherine's side as he glared at the ancient ghost.

Phlogis seemed to regard Valis affectionately before he answered Katherine's charge. *Rise, my faithful friend,* he said to the kneeling dragonrider. *Hearing your call, I came on my own. I will linger briefly.*

As if awakening from a trance, Valis shook himself and looked around. Seeing Phlogis, he rose uncertainly to his feet as he rubbed his eyes. Alanna, Maris, and Scott Silver all crept closer until the seven humans made a ring around the spectral visitant.

The Child *is safe with me,* Phlogis finally said, his gaze fastening on Katherine. *Thus it has been with every* Shae a'luth, *that the spirits of Palenoc take him in the night of his birth to teach him things he must know, and to train him in the understanding of his power. We will show him the secrets of Paradise and the mysteries of Or-dhamu. And in time, in his young manhood, he will return once more to live among you.*

"You monster!" Katherine raged, shaking her fists. "Give me back my son!"

Phlogis shook his head. *That cannot be, Katherine Dowd. I pray you will forgive me, but this is the way of our world.*

The fury seemed to leave Katherine, and she relaxed a little in the arms of the men who held her. "Is . . . is he all right?" she asked. "I didn't really even get to see him."

Phlogis nodded sympathetically. *You will see him again, Shayana,* he said. *I brought Kailuun with us, as well. The* chimorg *does not belong in the world, yet. But when the* Shae a'luth *returns, he will come riding Kailuun, and the two of them will bring a peace that Palenoc has never known before.*

Katherine turned into Eric's arms and laid her head on his chest. "What do we do, Eric?" she asked. "He's your son, too. What do we do?"

Eric's mouth felt dry. He tried to wet his lips, flicking a tongue over them before he spoke. He had a son, a son he had never seen, never held. His arms tightened around Katherine as he spoke to Phlogis. "You'll raise him well?" he said. "You'll keep my son safe?"

Phlogis nodded.

Eric pushed Katherine back to arms' length to study her tear-tracked face, seeking approval in her eyes as he continued. "Then we'll stay here, Katherine and I, and help rebuild Rasoul, and the Domains, and any part of Palenoc that needs rebuilding. We'll stay right here until you send our son back to us. Then we'll do whatever we can to help him spread this peace you talk about."

"What about love?" Katherine asked weakly. "Who'll give him love while he's growing up?"

You will, Katherine Hami Rana Sekoye, Phlogis answered. *He is forever a part of you, and he will feel the love you bear him in your heart every moment of his existence. No distance or time will ever weaken that bond or his awareness of it. And we, the spirits of Palenoc, will love him, also, just as you,* Shayana, *will always be beloved of us.*

"There's really nothing for me to go back to on Earth," Katherine whispered to Eric. "I'll stay ..."—she hesitated, swallowing as she drew herself erect and wiped away her tears—"and wait for my son."

From time to time I will send you a dream of him, Shayana. *May the peace of Or-dhamu be upon you all. I will not see some of you again.* The misty light of his form began to dissipate, but before he faded away, Phlogis stared curiously at Scott Silver. Then he was gone.

Sulis Tel returned again to Katherine's side and touched her arm. "She is weary," he said to Maris. "If you have a room for her, let me escort her there."

When Eric started to protest, Katherine stopped him. "It's all right, my love. Sulis has been my guardian for some time now. And I am so tired. ..."

She collapsed into Eric's arms with a quiet sigh. Sulis barely asked permission before he swept her up in his huge arms and cradled her like a precious child against his shoulder. Maris, her marble glowing brightly once more, led the way from the chapel. A room, she said, was all ready.

Eric lingered behind, watching the others depart. Scott Silver and Valis, however, remained at his side. Valis put a hand on Eric's shoulder. "A long journey on a hard trail sometimes forges powerful friendships and loyalties that can last forever," he said. "Don't worry about the Aegrenite. Katherine loves you."

"I'm not jealous," Eric answered. "A woman I thought was dead has returned to me, and I've just learned that I'm a father. It's a little overwhelming."

Scott Silver and Valis both chuckled.

They left the chapel, starting the long climb up the stairs to the higher levels of the Sheren. At Scott's suggestion, they returned to the rooftop, and to fresh air and sunshine. Moments after they arrived, Alanna joined them.

"Katherine is sleeping," she reported. "Roderigo Diez says he'll stay with her until she wakes." She reached into a pocket of her dress. "I brought you these," she said, extracting two of the *sekournen*'s silver medallions on chains. She gave one to Eric and the other to Scott. "With these you can locate and traverse the gates between Paradane and Palenoc," she told Scott. "I have others for Katherine and Robert."

Scott pressed his back into her hand. "It's better for Palenoc if I don't return," he said.

Alanna seemed almost to read his thoughts. "You'll be back," she said reassuringly. Leaning closer, she slipped the chain over his head and patted the gleaming cartouche. "But if you doubt, keep this as a souvenir." Unexpectedly, she winked at Scott Silver. "Now I have to see about a special project."

She left them, descending the stairs and beckoning Valis to accompany her. Eric and Scott leaned once more on the rampart and watched the dragons at play on the lake, the construction of the wharves, and the industrious passage of citizens in the streets far below. All around, the rebuilding of Rasoul went on.

Thoughts of Katherine filled Eric's mind. It was time to put aside his doubts and admit what was in his heart, to say to her the one thing he had never quite been able to say before. "Marry me," he muttered, trying the words out.

"I hardly know you," Scott Silver said, grinning as he gave Eric a sidelong glance. "Besides, there's another man in my life."

Embarrassed, Eric grew silent again, and Scott seemed to shift nervously. Finally, Eric swallowed and gathered his nerve. "You know more about what Bobby's been through than I do, Scott," he said. "Will he be all right?"

The blond-haired man who looked so identical to Robert sucked his lower lip and nodded thoughtfully. "She raped his mind," he said thickly. "He may never know which memories are real and which ones She constructed for him. Added to that, he feels guilty for not being able to resist her dominance. He thinks he failed everyone." He hesitated, closing his eyes, and when he looked up again, he held out his palm.

Just above the blood-bond scar, near the base of his thumb, was a small drop of red blood, drawn with one of his own fingernails. "I could make him forget it all," he continued. "I have the power. But I don't think that would be good for either of us." He wiped the spot of red on his trousers and peered over the side of the rampart.

Eric listened to the sounds of hammering drifting up through the stairway, trying not to think of Shandal Karg and her hideously scarred body hidden behind a veil of illusory beauty. All the time he studied Scott Silver out of the corner of his eye. "This isn't easy for me to talk about," he said slowly. "My family's pretty repressed and backward about such things. But if you really care for Bobby, I want you to know, it's not a problem for me."

Scott did not react at all for a moment, then he

laughed. It was a good, full sound. "I don't think I can get used to calling him Bobby," he admitted.

Eric felt like laughing, too. "Where is he, anyway?"

Scott's grin softened only a little. "Well, though he wouldn't admit it, he kind of envies you that dragon of yours. So Alanna and I conspired to give him a present. I knew the design, and she knew the craftsmen." He leaned over the rampart again, gazing outward and downward, searching. "Let's try the other side," he suggested. "I think she should have him aloft by now."

With Scott leading, they walked around the rampart. "There," he said, pointing.

Eric let go the laughter he'd been holding back, and for the second time that afternoon, his heart soared. "So that's the 'special project' Alanna mentioned," he said approvingly.

High above the inland side of the city, a blue-and-yellow hang glider drifted in the cloudless sky. Cradled beneath the bright construction, Robert flew serenely in gentle wide loops that took him to the far edge of Rasoul and close again to Sheren-Chad.

Shadowfire, Mirrormist, and Brightstar played close by Robert and his wonderful toy, flapping their wings, sailing beneath or beside him as needed to generate the fresh currents of wind that kept him aloft. Other dragons, too, seemed to glide at a safe distance, as if intrigued and amused by this newcomer to their domain.

In her saddle, dress flowing in the wind, Alanna kept careful watch over it all.

"He's going to be all right, Scott," Eric said, breathing easier as he watched his brother fly. "I know it now. It might take a little time, but we're all going to be just fine."

Epilogue

IN the ruins of Boraga's throne room, amidst broken rafters and crumbled columns and cracked stone, Shandal Karg's onyx throne sat tilted at a crazy angle, one rear leg disappearing into a fracture that ran the width of the dais. Nevertheless, Gaultnimble sprawled between the armrests and sipped from a cup in his hand as he petted Pusskins, who curled on his lap.

The keep, or what remained of it, was quiet but for the purring of the cat or the occasional fall of another loose stone. The ghosts were long gone. Gaultnimble raised his cup and drank a toast to them. The souls of the people of Tul Srimourna could finally rest. For nearly a millennium they had waited to win their revenge, and though their roles had been small, they had played their parts well.

He glanced toward the golden door in the farthest wall of the chamber and raised his cup again. A heavy, fallen beam lay against it, effectively bracing it shut.

Yet a third time he raised his cup and drank a toast to the brown, rotting corpse in the middle of the floor. The aroma of decay it gave off was perfume to Gaultnimble. On the horn that sprouted from the corpse's sunken chest, a fool's cap now hung.

Suddenly, Pusskins jumped off Gaultnimble's lap and trotted over to what remained of the Heart of

Darkness. The cat sniffed Shandal Karg's ear for a moment, then brushed its tail impudently over her face before it climbed upon a shoulder, walked between withered breasts, sat down on its haunches, and stared up at the cap. It seemed to look to Gaultnimble for approval before it raised one paw and took a swipe at the cap's tassel.

"Ahhhhh . . ." The sound creaked from the corpse's cracked lips. "Get thisss little beast off Meee."

Pusskins paid no attention. She swatted twice more at the tassel, then curled up on Shandal Karg's belly where she licked her whiskers and paws.

Gaultnimble swung one heel idly against the throne as he swirled the contents of his cup. "Your blood distilled into a very nice wine," he reported. He sipped again, cautiously, savoring the bouquet, feeling the heady, senses-reeling rush of power in the beverage.

Those unmoving lips emitted another sigh. "Youuuu foooool."

Gaultnimble allowed a faint smile as his gaze roamed the damaged throne room. "You're the one wearing the cap," he pointed out.

The barest quiver seemed to shake the corpse. "I cannot dieeeee!"

The dwarf leaned over the side of the throne and snatched up a fragment of rubble. With a casual toss he bounced it off her skull. Pusskins gave a yowl and sprang away. "Before I'm through with you, you'll wish a thousand times you could," he said. "Just lie there for a few more months, feeling your body rot. That'll give me time to dream up some real torments. Then, in ten or twenty years when I'm finally bored with you, I'll put you in the coffin you made for the Silver Man, and bury you and whatever is left of your awareness at the bottom of the abyss. That horn thrust through your heart ensures your helplessness forever."

"I'll get freeeeee!"

"Never," Gaultnimble answered, unconcerned. "If it's your empire You're worried about, I'll take good care of it for You. In ten or twenty years we might even challenge the Domains again. Just for fun, of course." He raised the cup again, feeling his power grow with every taste as the ruby wine flowed past his tongue.

Pusskins padded softly back to the corpse. The fabric of the tattered gown that still covered the corpse's legs rustled as the cat burrowed under the folds. For a few moments all was still. Then the tip of the cat's tail, all that showed under the edge of the bloodstained cloth, began to twitch.

A thin shriek rose from Shandal Karg's corpse. "It'sss chewing on Meeee!"

Gaultnimble tugged on the corner of his eyepatch, settled back on the throne for which he had schemed so carefully, and filled the ruins of Boraga with dark laughter.